THE FAILED AUDITION

CIRCUS IS FAMILY

KRISTA & BECCA RITCHIE

The Failed Audition Copyright © 2014 by K.B. Ritchie
Formerly titled Amour Amour
2021 Paperback Edition

Cover Photography by Regina Wamba
Cover Design by Twin Cove Designs

ISBN: 978-1-950165-29-2

also by
KRISTA & BECCA RITCHIE

ADDICTED SERIES

Addicted to You

Ricochet

Addicted for Now

Thrive

Addicted After All

CALLOWAY SISTERS SERIES

Kiss the Sky

Hothouse Flower

Fuel the Fire

Long Way Down

Some Kind of Perfect

BAD REPUTATION DUET

Whatever It Takes

Wherever You Are

LIKE US SERIES

Damaged Like Us

Lovers Like Us

Alphas Like Us

Tangled Like Us

Sinful Like Us

Headstrong Like Us

Charming Like Us

Wild Like Us

PROLOGUE

"You really want to do this?" Shay asks me for the tenth time. He plops roughly on the edge of my bed, wearing red, athletic Ohio State shorts and nothing more. Beside him, trade paperbacks thud onto the hardwood. My paranormal romances are so tattered and ragged, the ground won't hurt them.

I pluck more leotards off hangers in my dorm closet and chuck them into my rolling suitcase. Shay said he'd help me pack, but I rephrased that to: *watching me pack*. He's not the kind of friend that will neatly organize my toiletries into a shower caddy. I mean, when he saw a box of tampons on my dresser, he steered five-feet clear of it.

But he's not here for moral support either. "If I don't at least try, I'll regret it forever," I tell him.

"That's what you said the first time you had sex, Thora. And once you tried it, you *actually* regretted it."

I spin to him, and he raises his brows at me like *I'm right. You know I'm right.*

Okay. He may be right about that incident. My first time was in a hurry. At eighteen, I thought it was "time" and had a one-night stand with a guy from a no-themed dorm party. Cheap vodka may have been an advocate for the deflowering. It was sloppy and unmemorable. It also hurt, even with the boozy cocktail.

My second time was no better. Led to believe it wouldn't hurt as much, I slept with one of Shay's friends on our fourth date. It ended with a dissatisfied customer—me. It hurt again. A third time is probably needed. I won't judge sex yet. But so far, it's not that epic. Let's just say, I'm not eighteen, chasing after it anymore.

I'm twenty-one and chasing after things with higher payouts of happiness.

"I tried it the wrong way," I tell him, a white leotard heavy in my hands.

"Twice," he says, raising his fingers to demonstrate the exact number of regrets. I try not to dwell on them for long. There's no use.

"This isn't going to be like that," I say.

He's quiet for a moment. Shay does that a lot. It's not as though he's waiting for me to interject. It's like he's pooling all of his thoughts and emotions together. Ready to let me hear them in one fatal blow.

I prepare with a deep breath.

And he says, "You mean I'm not going to have to fly out to Vegas and pick up a sullen Thora James when all her hopes and dreams are crushed?"

I'm not angry at his proclamation; I just take it all in for what it is. But when I catch my expression in my floor-length mirror, a dark scowl tightens my facial muscles. It's my normal look, unfortunately. I have RBF (resting bitch face). It's one-hundred percent real.

When I first met Shay—thirteen, at a Cincinnati gymnastics gym—he pointed out my contorted, angered features. I was walking the balance beam with as much concentration as I could muster. Not annoyed. Just focused. And he sauntered over, resting his forearms at the end.

"Are you about to have a fight with the beam?" He smiled. "I bet I know who's going to win."

That day, Shay startled me so much that I slipped and fell on the mat. If I was fighting with the beam at all, I lost that battle right then. And I had no good retort back. I simply stood up, climbed on, and tried to walk it again.

In my dorm room, I open and close my jaw to relax my muscles. I look silly, but "content" isn't in my catalog of expressions. Unfortunate, again.

When I've successfully hidden RBF, I tell him, "I've wanted to be an aerialist since I was fourteen. This shouldn't be surprising, Shay."

He gestures to me, his six-pack and sculpted torso flexing. "I always thought you were joking around. Everyone says they want to do things that they never end up doing: acting, singing—wait." Shay pauses. Not one of those long ones. It's shorter. "Can you even *dance*, Thora?" His brown brows pinch like I'm insane for trying to join the circus.

It's not the traveling circus with fortunetellers and elephants. I'm not running off to escape something. Many gymnasts and other athletes, like Olympic divers, have joined Aerial Ethereal, in hopes of being an artist. A performer. An acrobat. Something more spectacular and extraordinary.

"I took three rhythmic gymnastic classes, remember?" I say, folding the white leotard while I watch his features.

His face scrunches in confusion and then he groans. "Thora, you were fifteen."

"And I was a fucking great fifteen-year-old rhythmic dancer." I really wasn't. I remember staying after to learn the choreography, determined to nail it. I never did. Not as well as the other girls. But I tried. I really tried.

After setting the leotard in my suitcase, I near him and gather the paperbacks on the floor. I plan to add them to my overflowing suitcase. I've never been much of a partier. I'll attend two a semester, my quota.

"Let me get this straight," Shay says, watching me collect my books. "There's one opening in a circus show—"

"Amour," I say, piling six books in my arms.

"Whatever," he continues, refusing to even acknowledge the name of my dream. "It's in Vegas, and you were called back because of a video that you sent in doing...what?"

"A double layout." *Plus some contortionist tricks.* I didn't have a partner, so I used the balance beam to do a handstand. Then I curved my legs over my shoulders, my toes meeting my fingers.

Shay gives me a look like I've officially lost my mind. "*I* can do a double layout in my sleep. That doesn't mean I'm qualified to join the circus."

Shay started gymnastics at five. I started late, at thirteen. Suffice it to say, his double layouts are more beautiful than mine. Like a fine wine to a Two Buck Chuck.

He's not the Clyde to my Bonnie or the Damon to my Elena. Shay is and will always be the Lucas to my Haley. A great, protective friend. Like that of *One Tree Hill.* Who will point out the storm ahead for me while I choose to relish in the sunshine.

"It's not just about technique," I explain. "I mean, that matters, but I've read on forum boards that they've turned down Olympic gymnasts for someone that looks the part. It's about luck too."

He skims my body in a slow wave: my dirty-blonde hair, my short five-foot-two frame, my wide hips, an hour-glass shape with muscular arms and shoulders. Add in longer legs and a shorter torso—I become a balancing hazard at first sight.

But I can balance fine. After years of practice, I'm much better than I used to be. But this dedication didn't stop my ass or boobs from growing. Both of which are larger than they probably should be for my sport.

I'm built like a normal girl, who picked up gymnastics later in life.

I'm average. And the longer Shay stares at me, I feel it. And I want to be more than that. Doesn't everyone?

"And what are they looking for exactly?" His eyes land on my C-cups. "Is there partial nudity or something?"

"Uh…no." I wish I had a better comeback.

"It's called *Amour*," he says, worry flashing in his light blue eyes. "Did you even think of that, Thora? What if they ask you to strip on stage?"

"It's not that kind of show." I turn my back on him, packing my books on top of my leotards.

"How do you know? It's one of the newer shows in Vegas," he retorts, shooting to his feet. "There aren't any videos online for it; I've looked."

I glance over my shoulder. "It's run out of Aerial Ethereal. In the entire troupe's collection of shows, there's not nudity in even one of them." I hold on to this fact, but I silently wonder if I'd be brave enough to join a more risqué show. To be in the circus, I think I'd do a lot more than Shay would want me to.

I hear him huff behind me. "So you're going to fly out on a whim. And what happens if you miraculously land the role?" He doesn't think I'll be offered the position. I'm not talented enough. My dad practically said that on the phone yesterday: *The other girls are in a different league, Thora. Don't get your hopes up.* I know. I'm not the best, but I want to believe that I have some sort of shot. Even if it's small.

"I'll stay in Vegas and perform for the year." A light energy bursts in my heart at that idea. It feels like happiness. A type of love that people search for all their lives.

"It's summer. Conditioning for the girl's gymnastics team starts in two weeks," he reminds me. "You'll lose your scholarship."

It's all a gamble, I realize. And I'm scared. I've never left Ohio for more than a week-long vacation, never by myself. But this is my *one shot.*

If I don't try now, I may never have another opportunity. And I'm tired of learning about finance and accounting as a back-up plan to the life that I want. The one that I can obtain right now.

So I'm going for it. Every part of my body says to jump and fly, no matter how hard voices like Shay and my parents try to ground me. I understand their realism, but I don't want to look back and regret not taking the plunge.

"It's a risk," I say softly, sitting on my suitcase as I zip it.

When he meets my eyes, he shakes his head at me. "You're one in a million, Thora. It's a pipe dream, you realize this?"

I nod. "Yeah, I know. But if I don't believe in myself, then who will?"

He lets out another heavy breath. "You know what this is like—watching my best friend enter a burning building, knowing it's going to collapse on her."

I must be scowling harder because he rolls his eyes at me.

"In short, I hate you right now," he says.

"Right back at you." That was a lame, kindergarten phrase. I sigh in frustration. I suck at bantering, even with someone I've known for years.

He laughs though, but it fades as soon as he watches me. Another long quiet moment passes between us. "Be safe, okay?"

I nod again. "Be happy, alright?"

"I am."

I smile, and my phone buzzes on the single bed. He's closest to it, and he grabs the cell. His eyes must graze the text on the screen. "Who's Camila?"

I left this part out to Shay. I thought he'd freak even more if he knew my plans. If our roles were reversed, I'd be a little worried for him too. But he's a guy, so the level of protection he needs on his own seems different, even if it shouldn't be.

"Camila is the girl that I'm staying with during my auditions," I say.

"She's another gymnast?" He passes me my phone.

"Not exactly…"

His lips part. Shay has this All-American look: a suitable body and face for Abercrombie. The short cut of his light-brown hair, the curve of his biceps. But I've only seen those lips part like that for me. In shock and worry. They part in lust for girls on the track team.

"Who is she then?" he asks.

"I found her on this couch-surfing website, and we exchanged numbers."

He rests his hands on his head in distress. "No."

"Yes," I say. "I'm going couch-surfing. It's supposed to be real and safe…I did some research."

"Have you seen her?" he asks valid questions.

"No, but she seems nice in texts." Off his growing wide-eyes, I add, "It's nearly free and way cheaper than a hotel. The plane tickets were expensive." Since my parents weren't one-hundred percent on board with my life choices, they said I should handle all the expenses. *I'm an adult now*, my dad said. He's right in a lot of ways.

Shay starts, "If I didn't have conditioning this week—"

"You'd fly out with me?"

His whole body goes rigid. "I was going to say that I'd drive to your parent's house and have them convince you to stay."

"They already know what's happening." I have a very hard time lying to my parents. I went to one party in high school and blabbed to my mom and dad the minute I snuck back inside. My mom made me ice cream, and I dished to her about the uneventful night.

"And they're okay with it?"

"They're a lot like you, actually," I say with a smile.

"It's not funny, Thora."

I think I'm smiling and scowling to hide my fear. It grows the longer he talks to me, and I'd rather stay confident.

"He could be a dude," Shay adds, pointing at my cellphone. "He could want to fuck you…or worse—*kill* you."

Chills run down my spine. "We're meeting at a nightclub where *she* works. It's a public place." *I'll know if she's a pervy dude or creep then.*

Shay is quiet for a second, and he stares hard at me, like he can break my optimism and my plans with a single, narrowed look.

He can't. I won't let him.

"You have one year left at college," he says, "and you're going to throw it all away?"

I shake my head. "It's the opposite," I tell him. "My life is just beginning."

ACT ONE

I roll my suitcase along the indoor cobblestone, a pathway leading towards The Red Death. It's the club where Camila works, inside The Masquerade Hotel & Casino. She told me the club's name was a play on Edgar Allen Poe's *Masque of the Red Death*, maybe to alleviate any worries that I'd be catfished and end this trip in a body bag.

I blow out my stress with a breath. "You can do this, Thora," I whisper to myself. The pep talk helps some.

I trek forward, struggling to avoid the pack of stiletto-heeled girls in glitzy dresses. They line up behind a velvet rope, fitting among the bright lights of Vegas like chameleons. Off to my left, casino machines glow and flash and ring while people bustle down the wide corridors with places to be, parties to attend, money to gamble.

I am the elephant, trudging around with my worn Adidas sneakers, spandex pants and oversized Ohio State shirt. Add in the frizzy hair from a four-hour flight and a bright red suitcase (almost pink from sun-fading) and I stand out. Badly.

The wheels of my suitcase clink against the cobblestone, drawing attention to myself. This breaks my usual straight-rigid posture. My shoulders begin to curve forward in ways I don't like. I take another breath and then slip out my phone and text Camila while I walk.

I'm here. The line is really long. Should I wait in it?

I press send.

I have no idea whether bartenders have the power to let their "couch-surfer" cut the line.

My phone pings.

I gave ur name to the bouncer. Go up to him and he'll let u in. – Camila

I continue striding forward then. Eyes zone in on me like lasers finding a target. The hot judgment sears my skin but I try to waft it off. Keeping my focus only on the bouncer—big, burly with tattoos that decorate his bulging muscles.

"Line starts at the back, sweetheart!" a guy yells near the front.

"Shut up, Trent. Maybe she's lost," a girl rebuts.

I clear my throat as the bouncer eyes my suitcase. "I'm Thora. Thora James. Camila's…" *Friend?* Couch-surfer makes more sense, but I don't know if he'll understand.

"ID," the bouncer says gruffly, a clipboard beneath his armpit.

I fish out my wallet from a pocket of my suitcase and pass him my license, hot sweat glistening my forehead. I wipe it with my forearm and peek at the door behind him, the unknown tossing my stomach.

The bouncer crosses my name off his list, and then pushes the large black door open.

Groans fill the air. "You've got to be shitting me," Trent complains. "I've been waiting for over an hour. You better be a fucking dancer or something!"

He has to shout that last bit because I'm already headed inside the hallway. The door closes behind me, plunging me into darkness. The faint sound of a thumping bass fills the otherwise silent room. I guess there are curtains somewhere for an entrance.

I take a few cautious steps forward and notice the outline of fabric, shielding my view of the club. The music grows as I walk closer, and when my hand brushes against the soft velvet curtain, pulling it aside, I finally see The Red Death in all its glory.

Flashing red lights illuminate the packed bar in the back left. Everything else is in near complete darkness. Except for the glow necklaces. Every person wears one, brightening their faces. Red. Blue. Green.

"Are you single?!"

I jump at the voice on my left. A young woman in a slim, tight-fitted purple dress mans a podium. She wears a green glow necklace, her arms layered with neon bracelets.

"Are you single?!" she screams at me again, trying to be heard over the electronic beats.

I can't make sense of this question. Is it a weird cover charge? Instead of cash, I have to tell her my relationship status? The longer I take to respond, the more her brows knot in aggravation.

"Yeah…" I say, not loud enough. Her eyes widen like *what was that?* "I'm single!" I scream it. And she passes me a blue glow necklace.

More people start to push through the curtains, easily snatching a necklace from the hostess. So I take mine without question and hightail it to the crowded bar. My heart drills into my ribcage. I hate looking lost, like a tourist—or worse, a goldfish slowly flapping and gasping for air outside of its bowl.

I don't want to be a water-starved goldfish.

So I stand taller, straighter. No more curved shoulders. And I roll my suitcase like I have important places to be. Like I'm an important person altogether. I march straight to the crowded bar. I've memorized Camila Ruiz's features on her Facebook profile: curly brown hair, golden-brown skin, and honey-colored eyes.

My suitcase bumps into a dancing couple. "Sorry," I tell them. Important people can still apologize.

The girl gives me a royal stink-eye. I wonder if my RBF is flaring up.

I scoot near the bar, unable to reach the stools just yet. I crane my neck and scope out the bartenders. Within a couple minutes, my anxiety pops. I spot her loose braid, her green glow necklace on her mane of pretty curls, like a crown. Her lips are bright yellow with pink eye shadow just as bold.

I haven't been catfished.

I take this moment to text Shay:

She's a girl. And pretty cool from what I can tell.

In seconds, he replies:

Still, keep your guards up. Stay safe. – Shay

I kind of wish he just said *I'm glad* and left it at that.

By the time I squeeze to the bar, she's pouring shots for a couple girls on the other end. I try and fail to scoot my suitcase closer to me. The hard frame hits a guy in the ass. He gives me a world-class glower for the accidental assault.

"Sorry," I say.

He makes a grunting noise and mutters under his breath.

I notice his blue necklace before I turn away. "Camila!" I shout over the music. She slides the shots to the girls and then grins widely as she sees me.

"Hey, Thora!" she yells back and starts pouring another shot. Then she slips closer to my end. She doesn't bat an eye at my wardrobe. She merely says, "We'll swap! Give me your suitcase and you can have this." She already passes me the shot of vodka.

I stare between my giant, hefty suitcase and the bottles of expensive liquor on the bar. I imagine tossing her the suitcase and knocking over all of them. This sounds like a strategy made from hell.

She reads my features and nods to the guy next to me, the one my suitcase most definitely struck. "Hey, John." She leans forward on her forearms. "If you can hand me my friend's suitcase without breaking any of *this*." She motions to the bottles of liquor. "I'll give you a free shot."

He wears an unamused smile. "Three shots."

She snorts. "This isn't a negotiation, cuz. If you don't like the price, I can find someone else who does." I try to find the family resemblance, but it's hard in the dark.

"You just gave her a free shot for showing up." He's already standing off the stool. "Pardon me for trying to barter a better deal." He grunts as he hoists the heavy suitcase. Much taller than me, he's able to pass it to Camila and avoid any collisions with breakables.

In her possession, she drops the suitcase on the ground, not able to hold it for long. I watch as she stores it underneath the bar.

John gives me a weird look. "You know, you could have just left that with concierge."

I shift my weight uneasily. "They do that here?" Now I feel strange. Like that dry goldfish. I need to put myself back in water. But honestly, I'm not sure how.

Camila mouths to him, *stop*. And then she says to me. "He shouldn't be bitching. He just got two free shots."

"Oh two free shots?" John wears mock enthusiasm. "My cousin, the real giver."

"I am a giver. What do you call this?" She waves towards me.

"Crazy," John says flatly. His honey-brown eyes meet mine again.

"Are you a lunatic or a sociopath?"

Uhh…

"Hey." Camila snaps her fingers at him.

"What?" He steals my free shot and sips it innocently. "Can I not be concerned for my little cousin? You're letting some stranger crash on your couch, who could very well murder you in your sleep." He makes a slashing motion across his neck.

Okay. At least the worry works both ways when it comes to couch-surfing.

Camila plants her hands on the bar. "Are you a sociopath, Thora?" Her lips twitch into a smile, finding it way more entertaining than John.

"No. I'm normal, I guess."

"See, she's normal," Camila says.

"She guesses," John retorts. He downs his shot and says to her, "The longevity of your life dwindles each day I talk to you, Camila."

"And your pessimism, cynicism and general attitude is going to turn you into a big dark raincloud that vacuums all your energy like a vortex." She inhales deeply like she's sucking out his soul.

He doesn't disagree. He just sits back on his stool and spins to me, outstretching his hand. "John Ruiz."

"Thora James." I shake his hand, his grip firm. Not surprising, since he was able to lift my fifty-pound suitcase with relative ease. Closer to him, I now notice his features: golden-brown skin, an unshaven jaw, and pieces of wavy dark brown hair hanging along his forehead.

He's about to say something to me when a huge commotion erupts from the center of the dance floor. Everyone breaks apart, forming a circle. People begin to cheer and whistle, hands clapping together at something beyond my view.

At first, I think it might be some sort of break dancing competition. But John starts cursing, "When the fuck is The Red Death going to ban these acts of juvenile delinquency?"

Camila passes me a new shot, and John steals that one too. "When

Aerial Ethereal doesn't provide for fifty percent of Saturday night sales," she tells him. "And stop taking Thora's shot."

He downs it in one gulp.

I fixate on the name of the circus troupe. My heart keeps skipping. "The performers from Aerial Ethereal come here?"

Camila opens her mouth, but it's John who replies.

"Every godforsaken Saturday," he snaps. "You'd think since they're athletes or acrobats or whatever—they'd choose somewhere that isn't a floor below where they work. It's lazy."

"It's convenient," Camila retorts.

Aerial Ethereal has three different shows running at The Masquerade Hotel & Casino, about fifty artists in each. But only locals probably know where they all blow off steam after a performance.

"You know," Camila begins with a grin, "Thora is here to audition for one of Aerial Ethereal's shows."

John gapes. "You're one of them?" he says it like I've suddenly turned into a cyborg.

"I still have to audition," I tell him the truth. I'm not an artist yet. I'm just a wannabe acrobat with large hopes. Which Shay says will be crushed soon.

More cheering erupts and splinters my thoughts. People clap and chant, so loud that I distinguish the words over the music: "TAT! TAT! TAT!"

"The God of Russia wins again," John says sourly, searching the counter for another free shot. It's empty. He suddenly stands. "Want to see what your kind is up to?"

"My kind?" My brows rise.

He latches onto my wrist. "Come on. The 'fun' is this way." He makes air quotes and the word *fun* sounds just the opposite. I glance over my shoulder, expecting Camila to interject, maybe even save me from the unknown. But she's a few feet down the bar, filling beers from the tap.

John maneuvers me around a couple who kiss aggressively, their hands lost in each other's hair. Both wear matching green glow necklaces.

"It's really not that interesting," he shouts back while he tows me along. "In fact, it's pretty stupid. But you should see the stupidity you're about to associate yourself with."

I stiffen, and my shoulder knocks into another girl's, so hard it makes a *pop* noise. I wince, "Sorry." I barely catch a glimpse of her pained features before I'm whisked further into hell's inner circle.

I don't want to believe John. About Aerial Ethereal being stupid. I always place my money and chips on me, even if it's the losing side. But I imagine AE's set decorations: the night sky of Viva, said to be painted so realistically that people believe they're watching from a forest. The intricate costumes: where every performer glows like lightning bugs and they move as swiftly too. I've seen pictures.

It looks majestic.

Not stupid.

"It can't be stupid," I suddenly tell him, aloud.

He gives me another weird look.

I clarify, "The circus is art." *Which is nothing short of precious.* I don't add this last bit, on account of his humored smile, more mocking than appreciative.

He actually laughs, and when I don't share it, his smile fades. "Good God, you're serious." He mutters something under his breath like, *Camila needs to stop bringing in strays.*

One minute later, he carts me to the front of the packed circle, whispering to some buzz-cut guy to scoot over. Strangely, they shake and bro-pat like they're friends or acquaintances. When he frees up the space, we gain a view of the clearing—basically what everyone is so excited about.

I slowly turn my head, not sure what to expect. Only one guy stands within the circle, an empty chair a few feet behind him. First impression: he's tall.

And very masculine. With needle-sharp focus, he inspects his surroundings. Us. The audience. My heart thumps as his gaze drifts closer. Why? I swallow hard, and I realize it's his daggered, concentrated expression. It's his muscular, I-catch-women-for-a-living body. And his powerful stance, exuding confidence like he's in charge, even if he's alone. Even if he's in the circle. The center of a show.

All eyes on him.

The red strobe lights comb over this area every five seconds, like clock-work. His features are bathed in the red hue, devilish and dangerous: black slacks, a white shirt, a few buttons popped open to reveal firmly cut muscles. His dark brown hair brushes the tops of his ears, the thick strands pushed out of his face.

With a strong, unshaven jaw, I predict he's in his late twenties. I check for a ring on his left hand. Just out of curiosity. I think. Or at least, I hope. And I notice that his fingers are free of any shiny jewelry.

He begins to walk forward, around the circle. Closer. *Thump.* His movement launches a series of hands in the air. Girls wave them like *pick me, pick me*, eagerly bouncing on their feet to be seen by this man. Like they're offering themselves up for sacrifice.

My arms stay awkwardly attached to my side, watching his gray irises graze the crowd with that *I know what I want* intensity. It lassoes everyone's attention. Weirdly enough, mine included. I find myself leaning forward, magnetized. The whole thing is bizarre—like being front-row to a show that I didn't buy a ticket to. And I'm not even sure what this show entails.

He steps closer. A natural reaction would be to flee. But curiosity cements me here. Maybe because he's in Aerial Ethereal. Maybe because he's roped me in like everyone else.

Closer. He searches the audience.

I stay still. Compelled to watch him.

Five seconds pass. And his eyes flit around my area. My heart aggressively pounds. I don't even know if I can handle direct eye contact with him. I silently pray it doesn't happen.

There's a good chance it won't, right—

His gaze suddenly lands on my…

Sneakers.

Pinning there for an extended moment. Confusion takes hold of me, my pulse speeding. His lip tics into what I think is an amused smile.

Then he beelines for me.

Just like that.

"Shit," John curses under his breath. "Don't look into his eyes." It's too late. My heart has abandoned me. I'm not just a voyeur anymore, a bystander, languidly observing…something. Dear God, my brain isn't even thinking intelligent things anymore. I can't even process what *something* is.

I'm dead.

Cardiac arrest. If I had a friend like Shay nearby, I'm sure they'd grab some paddles. But unfortunately, I'm friend-less. Internally flat-lining in sin city. The sin part—that's what I'm scared of most.

He stops maybe two feet from me before cocking his head. Waiting—it seems—for me to say something first.

I am frozen in a state of muddled shock. My joints are rusted together, and I think there's no hope to be oiled and set free. I breathe heavily through my nose, like I'm sprinting instead of standing in place.

Someone yells to him in Russian, and all I catch is *Nikolai* from the jargon. My brain works well enough to assume it's his name. Without breaking his gaze from mine, he replies back to the person in fluent Russian. Then he says to me, in the deepest, huskiest voice, "You're wearing running shoes."

I feel my facial muscles tighten. "And…?"

In my peripheral, John shakes his head from side to side like *no, no, do not engage.*

Too late again.

But John doesn't pull me out of this mess. He barely knows me. Maybe he wants to see how I'll react. What I'll do. *I have no clue. I am not prepared for this.*

"Very few people prepare for this," Nikolai says. If only he could read my mind. He studies my small frame like he's picking apart pieces of my life and filing the information.

What a useful tool. I need it.

Even standing like a confused statue, I still *can't* back away. Nikolai has a stronghold over my curiosity, concentration and poise—or whatever little poise I possess. A bit of jealousy flares in my belly. Yeah—I wish I had this type of power. To dominate a performance. To allure an audience. It's what separates an athlete from an artist.

He abruptly steps forward, into my space. I flinch back, a breath caged in my lungs, but he seizes my bicep to keep me stationary. What…is happening?

When I meet his pulsing gray eyes again, they only say, *don't be afraid. Trust me.*

I blow out a trained breath, my ribs expanding more.

He towers above me. Six-five maybe. I strain my neck just to fix my gaze on his. He stares down, lifting my arm like he's inspecting my muscles. He even brushes the sleeve of my Ohio State shirt. His large hand dwarfs my limb. I feel entirely little compared to him. In Shay's presence, I never felt like this.

He squeezes my shoulders. "You're an athlete," he declares, never asks. He even places a hand on my head, like he's examining my tiny height and my frame. He's having a bit of trouble determining what kind of athlete I am. "…a gymnast." Or I guess not that much trouble.

"Maybe…" Something about him makes me want to hold cards to my chest. I hear faint mutterings from the crowd, but the music drowns out most. I'm very much a part of the spectacle now. The entertainment for tonight.

Like a magician calling upon a volunteer from the audience.

Only I haven't really volunteered. Somehow, I think my sneakers did for me.

"Maybe?" he repeats, scanning me from head to toe again. He drops my arm. "No, you're definitely a gymnast. And I don't know you, which means you're not a part of the troupe." He tilts his head again, satisfied with his own conclusion.

I struggle for a good retort, open-mouthed and stupefied.

His lips tic, and this time they really curve upward. "You have some demonic-looking eyes, myshka." He stares right into them, and I barely graze over the foreign word *myshka.* "They're nearly black."

They are. Add that to RBF and I can't really denounce my demon-like qualities. My eyes flit to the red glow necklace that he wears. "If I'm a demon, then you must be the devil." It may be the corniest thing I've ever said.

"Maybe I am," he replies, very deeply. "And yet, here you are." His gaze remains on me and only me. "And myshka…" His voice turns to liquid sex. "You can't possess me, even if you tried."

"Ohhhh!" People laugh and hop up and down. But Nikolai never acknowledges them or feeds into the heckling. He just watches me.

"I'm not trying to," I tell him under my breath.

His charismatic smile wanes. And his eyes briefly flit to my chest.

Did he just stare at my boobs?

"Your tits are huge," he states it like a fact. *Thumpthumpthump.* I open my mouth to retort—but he continues, "Which means you hit puberty earlier than you should have. Most gymnasts end up stunting their growth."

He's right again. I started the sport later in life.

His eyes make a very slow travel from my mouth, to my chest, to my hips and legs and—he kneels. Right in front of me.

What…the…

With one hand on my thigh, to steady me, Nikolai knots the laces of my *untied* shoe. How he makes this seem sexual—I have no idea. And I think he knows the effect he carries, the charm and power. That devilish smile pulls at his lips again, before he even rises and acknowledges me.

"Guess what, myshka?" The glow necklace and strobe lights swath him in deep red.

"What…?" I hesitate.

He stands. Towers, really. And he tilts my chin up. With grays like gunmetal skies, bearing down from up above, he says, "I choose *you.*"

Not because I'm the prettiest girl here. I'm definitely not.

Not because I've caught his eye in a daring fashion. I didn't.

But because I'm wearing sneakers.

Shoes.

And I'm standing right in the middle of a mystery with them.

ACT TWO

Nikolai clasps my hand and draws me to the middle of the circle. I catch John pinching his eyes and muttering something like, *Camila is going to kill me.*

"You know what I think of gymnasts?" Nikolai says lowly.

I shake my head.

"Straight-laced..." His hand glides along my spine. My pulse kicks up an extra notch. "Back rigid, legs locked upon landing." His fingers brush the nape of my neck, and heat gathers across my skin. "Never split apart."

I keep breathing deeply from my nose. "I take risks," is all I say. I'm here. I'm in Vegas. That is a bigger risk than anything I've done before.

He digests this fact. Or maybe he considers it an opinion. "Tell me your name," he says. "And speak loudly and clearly so everyone can hear."

I lick my dry lips. "Thora," I say proudly.

"Thora," he repeats, that charming smile rising again. "You know the game." *I don't.* "But for everyone who's just arrived, I'll explain." He rests his hand on my shoulder, and he addresses the gathering crowd. "I bet Thora, this cute gymnast..." I space out at that.

Cute.

Shay called me that once, and he added with a laugh, "That's what you call an unsexy friend." I pushed his arm, and he nearly tripped into a campus bench. Shay's definition blinds me now.

An unsexy friend.

"...that she can't beat me in a handstand competition."

Wait.

I blink a couple times, retraining my mind on the important parts of Nikolai's statement. Backtracking: *I bet Thora that she can't beat me in a handstand competition.* A handstand competition? It nearly squashes my fears. I can do that. Easy.

"One-handed," Nikolai adds.

Okay...that increases the difficulty. And he's a guy, but I can beat him. Right? *Yes you can, Thora James.* Pom-poms are waving in my brain (Go, Thora, Go!) My own cheering squad. Confidence builds. Maybe misplaced confidence, but I try not to think about that.

The crowd breaks to let a server pass through. She enters the circle with a tray of shots.

Nikolai gestures to the shot glasses, a shiny silver watch attached to his wrist. "Three for her, three for me." His eyes drop to my feet. "The shoes won't really help you, myshka. But it was a cute gesture."

It clicks.

He thought I wore workout clothes for this specific reason—to participate in *this* bet. Wrong place. Wrong time.

"I didn't mean for it to be anything," I tell him.

He remains stoic, not really commenting on my comment. He just passes me a shot and takes one for himself. "I've been drinking since ten, so I don't have much of an advantage. This is as fair as it can be."

"Okay…"

"Tattoo or piercing?" he asks.

Inside, I startle like a frightened cat. Outside, I can barely move enough to shake my head. I'm about to say, *I have neither*, but he speaks before I can.

"If you lose," he clarifies, more to the crowd than to me again, "I tattoo or pierce you. I choose where. If I lose, though I never have before, you can tattoo me. Anything you like, any place on my body."

I restrain this fear that swarms my insides. So the terms of the bet are more than a little steep. They're *insane.* I glance around, and the spectators watch in crazed anticipation, beady-eyed and alert.

The stupid thing: I don't want to back out.

I want to obtain his power. I want his magic and his confidence. Maybe it's my competitive spirit or Vegas insanity, but I stay put. It's like watching a tornado through the window, the windstorm blowing the curtains and peeling off the roof. I don't disappear into the basement for safety. I watch in curiosity, to see how near it reaches. Leaving means never feeling the pull, never seeing the mighty force up close—never experiencing something that I'll always re-envision. I'll construct that tornado piece-by-piece, a replica of what it really was. A fragment of what I could've seen.

I no longer want to live in fantasy.

I want the images in my mind to be real.

It's why I'm in Vegas after all. Following my dreams.

I lick my chapped lips and straighten my back. "A piercing," I choose. It's more temporary than a tattoo.

He nods, like he thought I'd pick that option. Then he clinks his shot glass to mine. "Cheers, my demon." His eyes never leave mine as he throws back the tequila. He waits for me to do the same.

I hesitate for a few seconds.

He rubs his thumb over his lower lip, wiping off residual liquor. "This is your first time in Vegas," he says, figuring me out.

"Yeah."

"And you don't drink often."

He's peeling away my layers like he's stripping a bed. Quickly. Hurriedly. With little care of the mattress underneath. It makes me feel feeble. Nervous, even.

"One shot. You don't have to drink three." Okay, maybe he does care about the mattress more than he lets on.

"I can do three," I tell him, nodding a few times to myself in encouragement. I want to at least try. I put the rim to my lips and walk along a new path, one that's dark and full of potholes. *Please don't fall into one, Thora.* The sharp liquid slides down my throat. I withhold a grimace.

He passes me the second shot, and I realize that he's already consumed his three without falter. People chant, "Faster! Faster!"

I'm working my way up to it. Okay? Baby steps. The tortoise always beats the hare in the end.

"I can get you a Diet Fizz as a chaser," Nikolai says, "or a Fizz Life." He's about to order the server to fetch a soda, but I suddenly reach out and grasp his forearm. My hand very small around his muscles.

"No," I tell him. "*I can do it.*" I try to emphasize this phrase, and I wonder if I scowl too much.

If I do, he's not perturbed by it. He just nods and lets me continue.

Holding in a breath, I down the second shot. And I gag by the third one, still trying to forget the taste of the second. I wait for his laugh or peeking smile.

But when I raise my head, I see none. Just those gray gunmetal eyes. Lowering down on me. "Vegas is going to swallow you whole, myshka."

I don't want him to be right about this. I set the shot glass on the server's tray, and she departs to the bar, leaving me alone with Nikolai in the center circle.

He takes a couple steps back to prepare for this bet.

I instinctively tuck my baggy shirt into my spandex pants, thicker than leggings but just as tight. Then I tie my hair into a ragged, uneven pony. Tentatively, I glance back at Nikolai.

While scrutinizing my movements, he slowly unbuttons his white shirt. Some people whistle in the crowd. Others catcall him. "I love you!"

"Marry me!"

They have to be drunk. Or way bolder than me.

Nikolai's eye contact is killing my resolve. I swallow a bubble, and openly check out the definition in his muscles: an *eight*-pack, biceps that are only awarded to athletes that can carry and toss and cradle women. His body deserves the godly title that he's been given. All sharp cuts and brawn.

"On the count of three," he tells me as he tosses his shirt aside.

Okay.

"One," he starts.

I jump a few times, warming my blood.

"Two!" the entire crowd counts.

You can do this, Thora James.

My pep talks are the most cliché in the history of pep talks, but it always works well enough. I am my biggest cheerleader. Always have been. Probably always will be.

"THREE!"

I don't take a second glance at Nikolai or the stiletto-heeled girls surrounding us. I just rest a single palm on the cold concrete floor and hoist my legs in the air. Thighs pressed tightly together. My muscles stretch in this familiar position.

My shirt is secured in my workout pants, unable to fall to my neck and flash the audience. While upside-down, I catch a glimpse of Nikolai across from me—his strong build supported by a single hand. Unwavering. His thick hair spills over his eyelashes, and his flexed muscles carve in defined lines, running up his arms, veins protruding.

Still, it seems so easy for him.

He's like a rock that juts out of the ocean, the thing people cling to when they're caught in an undertow. No matter how powerful a wave crashes against him, he'll always just be.

Blood rushes to my head, the alcohol setting in minute by minute, flushing my skin in a hot, sticky sweat. More nauseous than dizzy.

The boisterous spectators overpower the electronic music with a new mantra: "God of Russia! God of Russia! God of Russia!" It has to take more than winning handstand competitions to achieve that title.

"God of Russia!" *Not helping.*

"Go, Thora!" a lone guy cheers for me, the underdog. It's not John—that I can tell. "Kick his ass!"

Nikolai lets out a short, irritated laugh and says something in Russian.

The guy responds with the same lilt. I take it, they know each other. When Nikolai speaks English, it's perfect. No accent really, and part of me wonders if he's Russian-American. Born here. Parents from there.

Concentrate, Thora. I inhale a breath, blinking as my stomach roils in violent protest of this position. And of what I ingested. My confident, focused glare morphs into unease. I glance at Nikolai again, and he switches hands on the concrete floor without even teetering.

Perfect balance.

My core tightens, and I sense my downfall before it even happens. Before he even gives me a look that says, *you're about to lose, myshka.* I know. I know.

Alcohol, handstands, and Thora James do not mix. Lesson learned.

It's not my arm that gives out.

It's my stomach.

An acidic liquid rises, and I impulsively drop to my ass, swallowing the vomit before it escapes. While the burn sets in, the cheers escalate, blistering my ears.

Nikolai effortlessly returns to his feet, and he takes the applause with less self-gratification than I thought he would. No blinding grin or smirk. It's not about the win, then. He likes this part, maybe. Where he pushes someone out of their comfort zone.

He squats right in front of me, almost eye-level. I watch him comb a hand through his dark brown hair, the strands out of his face, but pieces still brush his ears and neck. Then he says in that low, husky voice, "I won't lie to you. This is going to hurt."

My nose flares as I restrain more emotion. *I can do this.* "Okay."

He clasps my forearm and literally pulls me to my feet in one swift motion. The air plunges out of my lungs. His hand lingers on my hip. "Follow me," he says, heading to the empty chair.

I do. He leads me there, and someone hands him a piercing needle.

"Sit," he commands.

I cautiously lower my ass onto the seat, wondering which body part he'll puncture with the needle. *My ear*, I hope.

The silence between us pounds my heart. I'm left with those gray eyes, that strong jaw, and the red devilish hue that casts down on us. I'm breathing too heavily, and since he's so perceptive, he calls me out on it.

"Relax," he says, resting a hand on the frame of the chair.

How can I relax? He's a foot from my body, and he's holding a giant needle. I can't do anything other than pant like an out-of-shape linebacker.

"Breathe," he instructs, waiting for me to calm down. Though his eyes flit around me, trying to determine *what* to pierce.

"I am breathing."

He shoots me a look. "Breathe *normally*," he clarifies. He places a hand right below my collarbones. His palm feels heavy, weighted, but it carries an electric current that zips through my nerves. "Match me, myshka."

He takes my hand and places it on his bare chest, his muscles unintentionally flexing beneath, warm on my skin. My ribs want to padlock my lungs. I swear.

But I try to exhale and inhale, trained breaths this time. And his hand falls lower, towards my heart. His brows rise at me, and I realize he must feel my heart hammering, pulsing in a sporadic way.

I sink lower in the chair, and he lifts me up with his free hand, grabbing my waist. He says a couple words in Russian that I don't understand.

I shake my head at him.

"You're cute," he translates vaguely. *Unsexy friend.* "But you need to stay still."

I nod. "I can do that."

"Good." Then he uses his foot to push mine aside, abruptly breaking my legs apart. What… I open my mouth to ask what's happening, but he sits on the edge of the seat, facing me. He swiftly lifts me by the hips, setting me on his lap.

I'm straddling a Russian man. I can't tell if my eyes are about to pop out or if I'm scowling again. I'm rigid. Like he said I'd be. A straight-laced gymnast.

"Deep breaths," he coaches. A fraction of a smile peeks at his lips. He knows that he's driving me to an edge. A sexual, exhilarating one that I can't compute. My brain is frying too fast.

I don't know where to put my hands. "I don't…" I start. But I can't finish because he takes my hands in his and puts them on his shoulders. My arms must've been hesitating midair.

"Thora," he says, training my focus on his eyes. "You have a choice. I'm going to tell you what I'm piercing. If you want out, there's the exit." He motions to the literal club exit, a door in the far-right corner.

"What are you piercing?" I ask, not letting my mind mull over quitting. I've come this far. Right?

Without balking or breaking eye contact, he says, "Your nipple."

I gape. *What?* "What?" I think I've heard him wrong. My voice is lost in the shouts of glee from the guys around the club. Some even high-five and slosh their liquor.

"Thora," Nikolai says again. "Focus."

What? I pull my gaze off the surrounding people and back on him. "You said my nose," I say, wishful thinking, I guess.

He laughs. "No, myshka. I said your nipple." Again, he's unflinching. Like he's done this before.

"Have you done this before?" I question. "Pierced a nipple, I mean." I grimace at my own words. Why am I grimacing? He said nipple without flinching. I should be able to too. It's on *my* body.

"On men, yes. On women, no." He says, "You'll be my first." This lessens what little to no excitement I had. But he seems okay with the idea. "Most of my firsts are crossed off, so you're lucky."

Lucky. "I think…that's a strong word."

He rephrases, "I may remember you for a while, Thora." As though that's a prize people seek with him. Maybe they do. He's a performer—someone people observe from a distance. To be on his mind for even an ounce of time, that must be special to fans.

"Why my…nipple?" I ask, trying not to scowl or wince or cringe. None of the above.

"You tucked in your shirt before doing a handstand," he explains. "You didn't want to flash the crowds. I always choose the hardest consequences, the things people fear. You should know this."

Because I stalked him and wore sneakers, just so he'd choose me tonight? He's so off-base, but he never asks. He just assumes everything.

Waiting for my answer, guys start yelling at me to *not pussy out* and to *grow a pair of balls*. It makes me mad and angers me enough that my chest puffs out.

I nod to Nikolai, my mind spinning at this agreement. Standing up and leaving in front of this crowd would take more strength than I have right now. It may be the gutsier move than staying here, half-under peer pressure, half-under my own stubbornness.

"Sports bra," Nikolai guesses.

I inhale. "Maybe." *Yes.*

"I'm about to find out," he tells me, "so there won't be any maybes between us."

I'm keenly aware that his hand is on my thigh while the other holds the piercing needle. My legs hang loose around him.

"One piercing," he says deeply. "If you're frightened, leave now. I don't want you crying or suing me or the bar or Aerial Ethereal. We have a verbal contract that you're consenting to this, yes?" This sounds rehearsed, like he's said this plenty of times before to other girls and guys.

"Yes," I nod.

And then he removes his hand off my thigh, slipping it underneath the cotton of my tee. My breath hitches, his fingers skimming the smoothness of my bare skin, up to the line of my tight sports bra.

Without removing my shirt, he rolls up the bra to my collarbone. *Okay, I can do this.* He moves inconspicuously—thankfully. The sandalwood scent of his cologne dizzies my head.

He searches my eyes for reactions, reading me like an unraveling book. He hesitates for a prolonged second, and his eyes narrow at my blue glow necklace. "You're single."

It clicks. It should've clicked way before now, but I must've had sensory overload to compute the necklaces to relationship statuses.

Blue = single.

Green = ?

Red = ??

I glance at his red necklace, more curious. "Why do you ask?"

"I'm making sure you didn't lie," he tells me. "I don't want an angry boyfriend in my face tonight."

"I didn't lie," I breathe. "You know...you could've just asked me if I was single." *Instead of guessing based on my reaction to the statement.*

He doesn't say anything. His hand simply ascends to my left boob. Dear God. And he rubs my nipple between two of his fingers. My back arches in stiff awareness, the tequila from earlier doing nothing but covering me in a hot blanket.

"Your eyes are black again," he says casually, as though he's not massaging my boob right now. "Thinking of sucking out my soul?" He actually asks this. A real question. His gray eyes penetrate mine for an answer.

"No," I whisper. "You already said that you're the kind of guy who can't be possessed."

"But you seem like a girl who'd try, even if it's a losing battle." All because I accepted the handstand challenge—that's how he concluded this.

Even if I could respond, I wouldn't know what to say. He drops his gaze, and my nipple hardens for him. He slips his other hand beneath my shirt, piercing needle now closer to my boob. And it dawns on me.

"You're doing this blind."

He pauses off my fear. "Either that or I remove your shirt."

I shake my head repeatedly.

"I won't miss. Trust me."

"I don't even know you," I say softly, adrenaline pulsating through my veins. He has led me to the precipice of a cliff, pushed me off, and now he's clasping my wrist. He can let go at any moment, and I will fall.

"Every day," he says lowly, "I hold a person's life in my hands. The circus is based one-hundred percent off trust. I give it all to someone, and they give it all to me. I'm asking you, right now, to trust me."

His words seem genuine. His eyes seem confident. And somewhere, I begin to calm. Somewhere I reach into the furthest places of my mind and rewire the responses that say *stay cautious.* The ones Shay tightened before I left.

I nod for Nikolai to continue, my hands heavy on his muscular shoulders.

"Inhale," he orders. And I feel the cold metal of the needle. My ribs lift in a deep breath, and before I exhale, a sharp pain stabs my nipple. He's quick to secure the tiny silver balls to either end of the barbell. I stifle a wince, a foreign pressure lingering on the sensitive bud. Throbbing.

He wipes a trail of blood with a nearby towel, and then he retracts his hands from my shirt. I'm not sure if I should roll down my bra, but

I do anyway, ignoring the pain that wells. Nikolai lifts me from the chair and sets me on my feet as he stands.

The crowds cheer and drunken girls hop up and down, waving their hands sloppily to be picked next. My mind whirls in five different directions.

"Keep that clean," he tells me. His gaze already starts to break from mine, to focus on other girls, on more people.

But I hone in on his red glow necklace before we part from each other. I can't hold it in. I say, "Will your girlfriend be mad?" He just fondled my boob, and if the red glow necklaces mean *in a relationship*, then she might not be happy with him.

He cocks his head again, strands of hair falling over his forehead. He pushes them back. "Myshka," he says, "I don't have a girlfriend." He watches me inspect his red neon necklace for another second. "Green means taken."

"And red?" I ask.

"It's complicated." *It's complicated.* He takes a few steps away from me. "Enjoy your time in Vegas, Thora. I truly hope that you swallow it before it swallows you."

ACT THREE

Good luck, honey :) – Mom

I scroll through my texts after I fold up all the fleece blankets from Camila's couch, which was surprisingly comfortable last night. My left nipple is still sore, but the barbell piercing is perfectly even. Nikolai didn't miss. Thankfully.

Now I'm rested and ready to go. Auditions. Day one.

Don't forget to bring your pepper spray in the taxi. – Dad

I smile, glad that they're being supportive now that I'm here. I click into the last of my texts.

Don't fall. – Shay

I roll my eyes at that, but I feel my lips pull higher.

Kick ass, sis. –Tanner

My thirteen-year-old brother has been too excited about the prospect of his older sister working in this city. He's already planning trips here, as if he's legal to drink. I keep reminding him that he's eight years and fifty pounds away from enjoying the thrills of Vegas.

He flipped me off.

I'd like to say that I took the mature approach, but I returned the gesture.

I stuff my flannel pajamas into my suitcase and then zip it closed. Camila sluggishly emerges from her bedroom, rubbing her eyes with the heel of her palm. She yawns and her long kimono flutters as she walks to the refrigerator. "What time is it?" She squints at the microwave clock.

"Almost noon."

"Damn." She lets out a breath. "I could have stayed in bed an extra hour." She yawns again and begins to pour a glass of orange juice. Without the colorful makeup, she still looks beautiful, her bold features popping. "I gotta fix my bedroom clock." She nods to me. "When's your audition?"

"In about an hour. The taxi should be here soon." Her one bedroom apartment isn't far from the Vegas strip.

"How's the nipple?" Camila smiles into a sip of orange juice.

There was no way to conceal what happened. John told her the minute we returned to the bar. "Sore." I'm afraid to take the piercing out, but in my black leotard, it's barely noticeable. I mean, the barbell pokes at the material, but the dark fabric disguises it enough.

I just hope no one stares at my boobs.

"You chose right," she says. "Nikolai Kotova isn't kind when it comes to tattoos. Last week, he inked the words *suck it* on the inside of a girl's lip. And then drew a question mark on another's ass. If he did that to me, I would've decked him in his face."

Yeah, I'll take the piercing. I try not to think too hard about him groping a girl's ass either. I'm glad I didn't see that.

"Oh, and John can't shut up about you," Camila adds. "He says you're one of the stupidest people he's ever met. Which, from him, is a high compliment." She laughs and takes another sip of her juice.

I find myself smiling again.

And then a car honks outside.

I inhale deeply, like it may be the last one I take for a while.

This is it.

"Knock 'em dead," Camila tells me with the raise of her drink.

With the added boost of confidence, I feel better. More invincible. Shay would tell me that it's only going to make me fall harder. But I don't want to believe that today.

I'd rather soar.

THE GYM RESTS IN THE BACK OF THE MASQUERADE, behind the globe auditorium where performances for Amour happen twice a night, five days a week. A total of ten grueling shows. *It's a lot of work,* my dad said.

But it's all I want. So it'll be worth it. I hope.

It takes the taxi driver an extra ten minutes to find the *employees only* entrance, and when I arrive, a woman in a blue Aerial Ethereal polo introduces herself as Helen, one of the AE artistic directors for Amour.

She hands me a large sticker with the number three, and I press it to the collar of my black leotard.

Without speaking, Helen guides me to the main floor of the spacious gym, filled with different aerial apparatuses: teeterboards, bars, the Russian swing, red silk dangling from the eighty-foot ceiling and more. I'm out of my element, slightly overwhelmed, but one of the apparatuses is familiar to me. Aerial silk. I've practiced with it since I was fourteen.

"Here we are." Helen motions to six other young girls. They stretch on blue mats. "Wait right here and we'll give you further instructions in a few minutes."

I watch her depart briskly, aimed at the long table by the concrete wall. A few other AE directors already sit there, passing papers and tablets, as if reviewing our profiles before we begin.

I redirect my attention on the other hopefuls and notice that they all share a similar body type. Broad shoulders, short, no hips, no boobs. Perfect proportions for elite gymnasts. I spot a girl with white-blonde hair, a splattering of freckles along her cheeks.

She stretches her quads, earbuds in, her eyes narrowed with determination. She catches me staring and glowers. Intimidating is a weak word.

I feel new. Lesser, somehow.

"Elena seems to like you," a brunette tells me with a laugh. She sits beside me, her hair fastened in a tight bun like she's preparing for a ballet recital.

"Do you know her?" I ask.

"Elena Galkina? Yeah, sure." She nods. "Mostly from reputation. She made the Olympic team for Russia when she was sixteen, but she had to drop out due to an injury. Looks like she's fine now."

I steal another quick glance at her. Maybe she's only eighteen. I thought about auditioning for the circus as a teenager, but I chickened out. My father constantly hounded me about "going to college" and "getting a degree" that it seemed silly to do anything else.

I try not to regret my decision of sidelining my goals. I don't think I was emotionally prepared or ready to venture to Vegas alone right after high school anyway.

It really would have swallowed me whole.

I introduce myself to the brunette, and she says her name, Kaitlin Black, before Helen returns to the mats.

"Alright ladies, the audition process will be completed in two cuts. One each day." She glances at her clipboard. "First, I'd like to give a little background on the role."

My chest tightens, remembering Shay's concerns. *Is there partial nudity? What if they ask you to strip on stage?*

Helen's gaze redirects to the seven of us. "Amour is about six different types of love: obsessive, destructive, friendship, gentle, teasing, and passionate. Most of the acts are in pairs, but we have a few group acts as well." She taps her pen to the clipboard. "It's Aerial Etheral's most sensual and sultry show, and we've employed artists from eighteen to thirty-five."

Kids are in Viva and Seraphine, so it's rare to have an "above eighteen" stipulation. I know this at least.

"One of our artists sustained an injury, and you're all here to replace her. Well, one of you," Helen says. "You'll be auditioning for the passionate pairing. It's considered the female lead since the role includes two additional group acts. We need someone who can pick up multiple disciplines quickly and someone who has spark on stage. None of our substitutes did, so we're hoping that one of you will."

Elena pulls back her shoulders and raises her chin. And I thought I had pretty good self-confidence. I think she's in a league of her own.

Helen continues, "We've had to skip the aerial silk act due to Tatyana's injury, and it's sadly affected the quality of Amour. We want to find a replacement as soon as possible so we can put it back in the show." She checks her watch. "When I call your number, you'll be asked to come forward and dance. You've been chosen this far for your technique, but now it's about your stage presence."

I can't dance.

I shake the thought out of my head the minute it sprouts. I want to blame Shay for planting the seed, but it's not his fault entirely.

As Helen returns to the table, the gym door bursts open with raucous noise. "Perfect timing, Nik," Helen calls. "We were just about to start."

I turn to see who stole her attention. And I immediately recognize his face. Nik.

As in Nikolai Kotova.

My nose flares and my heart plummets ten-thousand feet below. I never even entertained the idea that Nikolai would be in Amour, let alone attached to this role. I couldn't…I couldn't have known. There are three shows in The Masquerade. That's one-hundred-and-fifty artists.

One out of one-fifty.

That's how unlucky I am.

The supremely tall Russian acrobat saunters forward with a yellow Gatorade in hand, a bagel in the other, his dark brown hair hangs over a red bandana like he just stepped out of a nineties movie.

Dressed in black gym shorts, shirtless, I accidentally hone in on his washboard abs. I force my gaze to his running shoes, to his unshaven face and his lips. He has that powerful stride, sexy and smooth like he knows each muscle intimately.

I hate that he has a great entrance to the *gym*. I just hope my future isn't bleaker by his arrival.

Nikolai gives Helen a charming smile, not even acknowledging the seven of us on blue mats yet. "I'm just happy we're finding a replacement." He stops by the table, pressing the rim of his Gatorade bottle to his lips.

And it's this moment that he chooses to turn and assess his prospective partners.

He coughs on his drink. Literally choking for a second, his stunning gray eyes fix right on me. My stomach twists, and my face contorts in that pained scowl. Any suppressed nausea starts to build tenfold.

"Is something wrong?" Helen asks, glancing between me and Nikolai and back again.

I open my eyes bigger at him like *please don't say anything about last night.*

But this only drops his concentrated gaze to my chest, staring like he can see through my black leotard, at the nipple he pinched between his fingers and stabbed.

I'm in trouble.

Last night, after he pierced me, he might as well have patted me on the shoulder and said *hope you have a good life.* There was *no* intention or expectation that he'd ever see me again. Ever. In my *entire* life. I wonder how many people traverse through his world. How many he eats up and discards like fodder for his performance.

He screws the cap on his Gatorade, collecting himself, but I can't tell if he's enraged by me or indifferent. I discount "happy" as a possibility. His stern, hard features are far, far away from any overjoyed sentiment.

"Nikolai?" Helen asks.

"It's nothing," he immediately says.

I inhale strongly, relief trying to surface. But for some reason, my muscles just constrict more. Nerves are trying to overtake me. With the brush of his hand, he wipes the sticky stream of Gatorade off his chest. And his eyes dance from Elena to Kaitlin and the other four girls, pretending like he wasn't completely caught off guard.

Helen follows his act to ignore the slipup. "Meet Nikolai Kotova," she says to us, rising from her seat. "He's the male lead in Amour and the second half of the passionate pairing. This show won't work if you don't have chemistry with Nik. Partnerships take years to cultivate, and we're asking you to grow comfortable within five months. It's a lot, we realize, but this has to work. Aerial Ethereal has millions of dollars in this show."

I mentally list off the perks. Land the job and I'll be awarded a one-year contract for Amour, complimentary room and board within The Masquerade, and if the show does well, Amour could be renewed for a twelve-year run. It's stability, something my parents want for me. Something I need.

But more than that, it's a dream.

It's a wonderful, faraway dream that I crave so desperately. I'm willing to work as hard as I can to live it.

Nikolai rotates abruptly, his back to us, and he starts speaking in hurried Russian to some of the art directors, choreographers, and whoever else is lined at the table. He grabs a few file folders and urgently flips through them. Only once does he glance over his muscular shoulder—and his eyes land on me again.

"Did you sleep with him?" Kaitlin asks me under her breath, anger wrinkling her forehead.

"What?" I frown deeply. "No. *No.*" This isn't like that…but maybe it is. I don't know. Is it that bad? Rare negative thoughts latch onto me. He's going to throw me out. Tell me to pack my bags. My one shot is gone before it's begun.

These jumbled fears jolt me to my feet, a string of excuses popping into my head. "I can explain," I start. The room tenses, the silence deadened, my voice echoing in the cavernous gym. Everything is heavy and uncomfortable.

Nikolai says something rapidly in Russian to the directors, and then he sets the folder on the table.

I continue, "I didn't know who—"

"Be quiet, Thora," he says, spinning around and walking straight towards me with a lengthy stride. His eyes narrow like *shut the fuck up.*

That look has permanently ripped out my vocal cords.

He steps onto the blue mats, only a couple feet from me. And then his voice lowers. "You're up first."

"What?" I gape in confusion.

He puts his fingers underneath my chin, physically pushing my jaw closed. My plump bottom lip meets my top. "You're up first in the audition."

A short, round man with glasses and peppered hair lingers off to the side, arms crossed, and he interjects with a flurry of Russian words.

Nikolai replies back easily, still staring down at me. Then he breaks into English. "Do you want to audition, Thora?"

I nod.

"Then bark like a dog."

What. The hell? I feel my eyes darken. "Is this a joke?" He's planning to humiliate me, for payback or something?

He wears a new expression, one full of severity. No curved lips. No theatrics. His tough exterior intensifies by ten-thousand degrees.

I can't shrivel. I'm solidified to stone by his change in demeanor.

"I take my job seriously," he says with force behind each word. "You want to be a performer? Then bark like a dog."

I hesitate, my gaze flickering to the table of directors. Some of them share furtive whispers, but for the most part, they watch us, poker-faced. They won't intervene then. He's taken over my audition and turned it into a crazy one.

I step forward once, closer to him, and say under my breath, "This isn't a game to me." This whole audition is so much more important than a bet.

His hand flies to my mouth, silencing me. His large palm practically fits across my entire face. "How badly do you want this?"

Badly.

What am I willing to do then? Barking like a dog isn't that horrible, in comparison to other things he could've said. Okay. *Okay, Thora.* When his hand falls, he waits for me to do something more. We're only a foot apart now, and I look up at him, silently hoping he'll give me a reprieve, an out at the last minute.

He doesn't.

I clear my throat. "*Woof woof*," I say, sounding as awkward as I feel.

Nikolai stares without a single ounce of humor. No one laughs. He just says, "A dog that has rabies."

I bite my tongue, hopefully suppressing a scowl. Then I think for a second. "*Grrr…arh arrhhhh…*" I find myself actually crinkling my nose too. I wonder if this is being videotaped. In the back of my head, I hear Shay laughing hysterically at me.

"Now," he says, not missing a beat, "crawl on the mat and pretend you're a cat in heat."

Kneejerk reaction, I shake my head.

"No?" he questions with a deadly stare. "You're going to quit." It's a statement. An assumption. I don't want him to be right.

I swallow a lump. "I meant yes."

"Get on your knees then," he commands.

The older man observing the audition suddenly points at me and speaks in rapid, hasty Russian. It flies in one ear and out the other.

Nikolai replies back gruffly, gesticulating with his hands as he talks.

The older man waves him off, his thick brows pulled together in a giant one. My stomach twists as I stare between them. The way the older man jabs his stubby finger in my direction—it makes me think he's not pleased by me. That he hasn't been on my side since the start.

To rectify this, I drop quickly to all fours, and their argument ceases like I chopped through it with my movement. I tilt my chin up. *A cat in heat.* I channel the most lustful look I can muster, my mouth partially open as a heady breath escapes. And I slowly crawl on my hands and knees, slinking around his shins.

I circle languidly, licking the side of my palm. And then I rub my hip against his calf, all the while a swelter boils in my body. But I do it again. And again, my arm brushing up against his skin.

His quads tighten in response. I tense just as much, and I catch a peek of his features, which haven't changed since the beginning.

"Purr," he tells me.

I freeze at the new command. Purr? How does one even *purr?* I'm going to try to attempt it. I have to. As soon as I open my mouth, the sound that leaves is nothing short of a moan, one that happens in private—not during an audition. *A job interview.* That's what this is. With directors in sight.

The other gymnasts are most likely crossing me off their lists. *One competitor down.*

Nikolai appraises me but makes no statement whether I'm succeeding or failing at being a horny cat. "Stop," he says.

A pit wedges in my ribcage, and I slowly stand to my feet, hot all over. I brush my hair into a tight ponytail. I can feel him scrutinizing my actions, and what's worse—he won't fill the empty air with talk. Not until I snap the band and plant my hands on my hips.

He has to stare down at me as he speaks. "I'm a marble statue," he declares. "You're obsessed with it. You dream about it, erotic fantasies that make you come at night. You see this statue, what do you do?"

Holy.

Shit.

He said all of that without balking.

I open my mouth, about to play into this pretend, weird scenario. The girl would probably grind against the statue. Right?

He cuts me off, "Show me."

I hesitate for one second.

And then the other man yells again in Russian, spitting as gruff words pour from his mouth. Nikolai shakes his head at him, and he shouts back, making another hostile hand gesture that I read as: *wait a minute.*

I inhale, about to go into girl-obsessed-with-statute mode, but the moment I near Nikolai, the Russian man charges onto the mat and physically separates us. He wedges his short, stalky body between me and him, and he spews Russian words straight to my face. Like I understand.

I don't.

Not one word.

"I don't know what you're saying," I tell him softly, my stomach practically convulsing with nausea. I have no idea what's going on. Maybe he's upset with Nikolai for putting me through a strange audition. By the snarl on his wrinkled face, he clearly hates me.

And if my hunch is correct, he's the choreographer for the aerial silk act.

He gestures to me and then to the mat with all the other girls. Nikolai tries to talk above him, but this only sparks another verbal shouting match.

Helen struts to the mats, approaching from a safe distance. "Thora, that's it for you," she says. "You can take a seat and wait for the other girls to audition. We're making the first round of cuts at the end of the day."

Her words knock me backwards a bit. She might as well have said: *you failed so much that we only gave you five minutes instead of fifteen.* My legs feel heavy as I trudge over to the girls. They shift nervously and none make snide comments or laugh and jeer about my cat-in-heat routine.

I plop down beside Kaitlin, who remains quiet. And I watch Nikolai and the choreographer come to a somewhat peace, their hands raised like *let's end this and move on.*

When they separate, Nikolai rubs his jaw and takes a few extra paces behind Helen. The older man stays on the sidelines of the blue mats. And it's Helen who calls the next girl forward.

"Number 1," she says.

Elena, the bleach-blonde, gracefully rises to her feet, nearly gliding to a halt in front of Helen. In her green leotard, her limbs seem thinner and her chest flatter.

I don't even want to watch, my insides stretching to their limits. I fiddle with my fingers, pushing down my cuticles while I cross my legs.

"You're a flower in a meadow," Helen says. *What?*

My heart stops.

"The winds are strong," Helen continues, and Elena begins to sway back and forth, like she's performing a lyrical dance.

This whole time, he wasn't messing with me? Nikolai observes Elena with a stiff, rigid posture. While the young gymnast pretends to be blown over, I try to make sense of my audition.

He was really trying to help me.

From the beginning, maybe.

Trust me.

He said that last night. Trust. I was supposed to do as he said, without question, because he's supposed to be my partner. *If* I get this role. It's looking grim now.

"Purr," Helen instructs. She might as well have kicked me in the gut.

And apparently humans *can* purr. The sound that Elena produces is like a vibration off her tongue.

Fuck my life.

I tuck my legs to my chest, and I plaster my gaze right on Nikolai, hoping he'll feel the heat off my stare. I'm not looking for reassurance. I think, mostly, I want to apologize. I should've stepped out of my box today. He was trying to pull me out of it, and I fought back. I resisted.

He concentrates solely on Elena.

"You're madly in love with the blue mat," Helen tells her.

And that's when Nikolai has enough of my penetrating gaze. He finally turns his head and gives me a look like *I'm working, Thora* before I can offer an apologetic one.

I mouth, *I'm sorry.*

I wish I could have a redo. I'm not sure I'd be a better horny cat or a more vicious dog, but I wouldn't have faltered so much.

I would've barreled forward, no matter how awkward I felt.

He shakes his head at me like *it's over now.* But his eyes seem to soften a fraction before he returns them to Elena.

I can't believe this is how it's all ending.

ACT FOUR

After each girl auditions, the directors go into deliberation and Helen says that we can look around the gym while we wait for first cuts.

I end up in the locker rooms, scanning the names on the blue metaled doors. I don't think I was the worst one at acting. One girl was asked to be fire and water, and she ended up doing the worm. But I definitely didn't possess Elena's grace or Kaitlin's head-first, no-holds-barred gusto.

Honestly, I think I faded into the background.

I skim my fingers over a worn name scribbled on the locker label: *Dimitri*

"Why didn't you tell me?"

I jump at the deep voice behind me. Nikolai leans his shoulder on a blue locker, arms crossed, his dark hair spilling over his red bandana. His intensity doesn't diminish.

"You never asked me anything," I whisper, even though it's already quiet here.

He blinks a few times and lets out an exasperated laugh before shaking his head like he can't believe this happened. I can't either. "At The Red Death," he begins, "did you even know what I was going to do?"

"I told you it was my first time in Vegas."

He rubs his lips, upset it seems. "I assumed you heard about what happens from a friend."

"No," I say. "I knew nothing."

His face turns grave, and he stares at the concrete floor, processing what this means.

"You never asked," I reiterate this.

"Because I thought you were no one!" he shouts at me, frustration lining his forehead. "I don't ask *anyone* at The Red Death *anything*, Thora. I don't want to hear about their lives while they're in Vegas for the weekend. There's no point. It's exhausting and I'd rather assume…" he trails off, realizing he assumed wrong this time.

"I should've said something then," I tell him. "You're right." I can't even recall why I stayed quiet. Maybe because I was ticked off by his lack of questions. Maybe because I was overwhelmed. Mentally, emotionally—last night is far off compared to today.

I find myself sitting on the wooden bench between the lockers. Silence stretches between us. I expect him to leave, but he stays in the same place.

"It doesn't matter anyway," I say softly, my eyes threatening to well with defeated tears. "You won't see me around anymore."

He lets out an exasperated noise and walks deeper into the locker room, nearing me. He stops a few feet away. "Look at me, myshka," he says lowly.

I lift my gaze to his.

"Don't count your losses before you see the scoreboard." While encouraging, he still looks agitated. "It'll plague you with insecurities that aren't worth your energy or emotions."

He just passed me an ounce of hope. Maybe out of pity. I'll take it though. "Thanks for helping me, before," I suddenly tell him. "I didn't realize what you were doing..."

"The choreographers usually judge easier on the first person who auditions. They know you're blindfolded for it unlike the others." He drops his gaze again, something he rarely does, I've noticed. "I'm not going to lie. I was angry when I first saw you, and I still am."

"Yeah, I can tell," I whisper.

He nods a couple times. "But I wanted to give you a better shot because I felt like I put you at a disadvantage, and that wasn't fair to you."

I frown. "What do you mean?"

His eyes rise to mine again. "Our relationship," he says, "is unprofessional."

I sway back a little. "I wasn't aware we had a relationship."

He still towers above me. "Whatever you want to call it—it's not right. I don't shit where I eat. I pierce and tattoo people looking to have fun in Vegas. I give them an experience. You were here for a job." He shakes his head. "I *regret* what I did. More than you can possibly know."

"Don't," I tell him. "It's just a piercing. And I said it was okay."

"We may work together," he says. "It's not just a piercing to me." He gestures to my small frame. "And how old are you?" He grimaces some. "Please tell me that you're not eighteen." Maybe because he supplied me shots all night. Or because he fondled my boob, and that'd mean we'd have a significant age gap than the one that already exists. I'm going with the latter.

"Twenty-one."

Relief floods his face, and he exhales deeply.

"What about you?" I ask.

"Twenty-six." He scans my body for a second, as though he's reading the language of my movements. "Despite the control I had at the auditions today, I have almost no weight in the final choice. They can pick any one of you, even if I say otherwise."

The tiny hope he'd given me might have been false after all. "The choreographer dislikes me," I recognize. He was introduced at the end of the auditions, so I'm certain he's the man who'll arrange the aerial silk routine.

Nikolai relaxes his shoulder on the locker again. "Ivan doesn't dislike you."

My chest inflates with more positivity.

"He actually hates you," he says flatly.

It pops just like that.

"Amour won't last the year if we don't find a replacement," he explains. "The Masquerade is threatening to shut down the show, and it needs the aerial silk act to complete the story. So Ivan is under a lot of pressure, as am I, and as will be my partner."

I want to believe that I can handle the pressure. I can say it every day, all day, but actions speak louder. I haven't ever been tested to this degree. Nothing this grand has weighed on my shoulders. I can barely even imagine what he's going through.

"And it doesn't help that you're not Russian." He checks the clock on the wall and heads to the exit.

I frown, his words ringing in my ears. "What does that mean exactly?"

He glances back. "It's aggravating when you can't communicate with someone. He tried to cut your audition short because of it." With this, he curves around the corner, disappearing out of sight. I hear the heavy door open and then click closed.

I stand up, more uneasy but a little more prepared than before. I pocket the false hope like a gem, refusing to believe it's fake for now. I need it. He gave it to me *because* I needed it. I won't let it go that easily.

ACT FIVE

I made the first cut.

I send the group text to my parents and my brother and then another text to Shay. I walk down the long carpeted corridor of the casino floor in sweat pants (over my leotard), still in a daze about the verdict. An hour ago, Helen called my audition number along with Elena, Kaitlin, and another girl's. I almost couldn't believe it.

Nikolai even made a point to nod at me when she announced that I made it through to day two of auditions. Maybe it was a pity nod, but it fuels me for the final round tomorrow.

At first, I planned to decompress in Camila's apartment, maybe finish *Bite in the Dark*, a vampire romance that I'm three-fourths through. But I think couch-surfer protocol forbids me from loitering. I sleep and go. And sleep again.

So I decided to take advantage of Vegas and soak up the atmosphere while I'm here. If I don't land the role, then I may never have the opportunity to return to this city again.

The slot machines ping and glow—a group of thirty-somethings clustered at a roulette table. They simultaneously cheer, raising their beers and cocktails. Everyone here seems to be on a high, skiing up it or sliding down.

The energy is new, and I feel a smile pull at my cheeks. Life is slow in Ohio. Not a bad slow. Just different. Vegas begins to take hold of my senses, drawing me deeper into the casino's sins.

Evening hasn't set in yet, so the crowds aren't as thick as they could be. I mosey around the tables and slots, watching people gamble from afar. I understand the enticement of throwing dice, playing cards, and pressing a button.

It's the dream, right?

To be granted money without any real work or effort. It doesn't matter who you are, what you look like, where you come from—we all have the same odds.

Vegas may be a genie, willing to grant wishes, but it's also a devil in disguise, here to slay our dreams just as quickly.

While I observe a really confusing game—craps, I think—my cell pings.

Duh, you made the first cut. Booking my plane ticket already. – Tanner

I smile and try not to think about my realistic parents, who've probably made plans to pick me up from the airport.

Before I pocket my phone, it pings again.

Natalie and Jordan miss you. They keep asking when you'll be back. – Shay

He's lying. For one, Natalie and Jordan didn't even notice when I had bronchitis our freshman year and missed three practices. If we didn't share a single commonality—the girl's gymnastics team—I doubt we'd even be Facebook friends.

I text quickly: I've been gone for a day and a half.

This is reason enough that no one probably misses me. I wouldn't even miss myself for that long.

I think I'd need a solid month. Then I'd start missing myself. Maybe.

He replies back with a devil emoji. I send him an angel one.

Right as I return to the craps game, I spot someone familiar dealing cards at a blackjack table. My feet lead me there before my head does.

"Oh no," John says as I approach. "This table is reserved for non-AE artists."

"I'm not an artist yet," I tell him, resting my hand on an open stool. "I'm just a gymnast." If I'm really unwanted, I can go wander aimlessly somewhere else. Maybe I'll find a good reading bench.

John looks surly, so I begin to back away.

"Wait, wait," he says slowly and motions for me to return. "It's been a quiet afternoon, and I'm predicting an onslaught of loud, obnoxious fraternity guys. It always happens. It's an easy day and then fucking tobacco-chewing, sunglass-wearing douche bags roll in, pretending they're professional poker players, leaving two-dollar tips and bottles of brown spit." He shuffles his cards. "But if you sit here, you'll most likely detract them from my table. You'll be my asshole repellent."

I hesitate to ask. "Why will I repel them?" I settle into the open seat, taking the invitation regardless. I mean, I don't have many options. Or friends here. So yeah, I'm left with moody John Ruiz. It's not bad, all things considered.

His eyes flicker to my black leotard and loose pony, flyaway pieces of dirty-blonde hair around my oval face. "They go for the empty tables or the ones with models. You're neither invisible nor a model. No offense."

"None taken." I'm glad he doesn't ask about my auditions. Not dwelling has alleviated some stress. I watch him shuffle another deck. John wears a tux with a gold bowtie, the dealer's uniform, and he scowls so much that his forehead wrinkles.

"You have RBF?" I blurt out. I internally grimace. Why did I ask that? Maybe I can relate to someone else who suffers from Resting Bitch Face.

I've bonded with a girl on the gymnastics team that way. We unite together. But it's not like that term is common or even a "thing" with lots of people.

His face scrunches more and he gives me a weird look. Then he says, "No, I'm just a bitch." He smiles dryly.

I can't help but smile back. And the corner of his mouth even rises in a more genuine one.

"What's your bet?" he asks me.

"Can I just watch?" I didn't bring any money to the casino, and this is a pretty expensive table.

"Elbows off the table," he suddenly tells me.

Okay, that must be a rule. I don't even know proper poker etiquette. I quickly take them off. And then he passes me a glass bowl of Chex mix. "I'm usually not this nice. But you look like you need a friend, and I'm *never* that friend. Never." He shakes his head like this is cemented in truth. "This is only because you're working for me today. Incentive to stay when I become surly at two-thirty. Happens every afternoon. Prepare yourself for it."

"Surlier than now?" I ask with the raise of my brows.

"You're meeting the most cheerful me there is. I can't help it if the world is fucking lousy. There's not much to take pleasure in. And the only reason more people aren't like me is because they're living in a fantasy world of cupcakes and daffodils and—"

"Glitter," a guy suddenly interjects, sliding onto a stool, two separating us. "Can't forget the glitter, old man."

John solidifies, and he shoots the new guy a glare as dark as thunderstorms and lightning. It's a look only reserved for people you know.

I whip my head from one to the other. It's like they're silently having a conversation through their eyes. I scan the young guy's features: dark brown hair, long in the front so the tips brush his eyelashes. Pale skin. Thin, almost gangly build underneath a leather jacket. Topping off his look with high-cut jean shorts and boots.

By the shorts alone, he seems a bit brazen. And not one of the tobacco-chewing, sunglass-wearing assholes that I'm supposed to repel.

John breaks the death-stare first. "There are ten other blackjack tables, Timo. Go find another one."

Unperturbed, Timo places a tall stack of chips on the green felt. "I would, definitely, go find another one. You are my least favorite dealer in all of The Masquerade. Congratulations on that, by the way. And yet, I have this *feeling*—" he touches his chest dramatically "—that today you're going to bring me some luck, old man."

"Stop calling me *old man*," John retorts, his mood darkening as the seconds pass by. "I'm twenty-fucking-five. Don't make me bring over security again."

Timo shrugs. "Do it," he eggs on and then nods to me. "Sorry about this. John doesn't understand that I'm *twenty-one*, and he can't throw me off his table."

John lets out a short, humorless laugh. "He's *eighteen*. And he has a fake ID that everyone in this place overlooks because his last name is Kotova."

What? My eyes threaten to pop out of my face, and my mouth falls. I focus on Timo again. His hair is the same dark shade as Nikolai's and his eyes are the same light gray. But his body is built differently, less muscle mass than Nik. My mind reroutes to John's statement—about how The Masquerade provides special privileges to Kotovas.

That seems highly unlikely. Right?

"I'm sure he's twenty-one," I say. "A casino can't let someone underage gamble just because of his last name." Don't they have undercover cops to crack down on that law?

Timo grins, his smile magnetic. "I like you," he announces and leans forward, holding out his hand. "Timofei Kotova. Born in Munich. Raised in New York, mostly. You are?"

I shake his hand. "Thora James. Born and raised in Cincinnati."

John gives me a supreme withering glare, as if I just made a blood pact with the enemy.

"Cincinnati," Timo muses, his eyes shimmering. "I've been to Cleveland once. I was four, I think."

"Riveting," John says, surly.

"We're not all John Ruiz. Born in Las Vegas. Raised in Las Vegas." Timo's eyes fill with mock enthusiasm. "You are stupendous, my friend."

"We're not friends," John retorts. "And my family is from *Colombia*."

Timo raises his brows like *so what?* "And my family is from Russia, old man. Want to battle?"

John pinches the bridge of his nose, his sour expression overtaking his features. He lets out a heavy sigh.

I tentatively slip back into the conversation. "I still don't understand why the Kotovas get a reprieve."

"Because we're awesome," Timo tells me, eating some of the Chex mix.

John steals the bowl back, setting it away from us. "Let me break it down for you, Thora. There are *three* different Aerial Ethereal shows just at The Masquerade." He counts on his fingers. "Viva, Infini, and Amour. The Kotovas make up over one-third of the cast for *each* show."

Timo raises his fist in the air.

John's expression says: *I so want to smack the back of your head.* He huffs and continues, "Some Kotovas are even the directors and coaches. The Masquerade acts like they're demi-gods, so yes, they let the underage kids pass through security as long as they look twenty-one-*ish*." His stormy gaze returns to Timo. "And *by the way*, you can't pass as twenty-one. You look like a child."

"So wait," I cut in before Timo can reply. I extend my arms, my head spinning from the info. "Is your beef with Aerial Ethereal performers or the Kotovas?"

Timo's eyes brighten. "Great question."

"*Both*," John growls.

"Alright then," Timo says, "seeing as how I'm doubly hated by the dealer, beating you will be doubly rewarding." He pushes his chips across the green felt and nods to me again. "You playing?"

"Just watching," I tell him.

John grumbles something under his breath as he reluctantly shuffles the cards, clearly surrendering despite his speech. This must happen a lot.

He deals the cards quickly: a king and seven for Timo and a queen for himself. John flips the edge of the face-down card to peek beneath it.

Timo raises his brows. "Anything interesting?"

John stays silent and maintains his *I loathe the world, my job, and everyone in the universe* face.

"That bad, huh?" Timo grins, unzipping his leather jacket.

"Just play," John says roughly. When his gaze falls to Timo's torso, he rolls his eyes. "Why the fuck aren't you wearing a shirt? Seriously? Seriously." He looks to me. "Do you see this?"

Oh yeah.

Timo is bare-chested beneath the leather. I try desperately to restrain a smile at John's distress. There's something about it that's more comical than anything.

"Is there a shirt policy?" I ask, biting my gums.

"Yes, there's *a* shirt policy. *Everywhere* there's a shirt policy. People don't just gamble without clothes."

"He's wearing a jacket," I say. I can't be a fashion police. Sweats. Leotard. Sneakers. My regular ensemble.

"I *am* wearing a jacket," Timo says to John. "She makes a perfect point." He has that same intense eye contact that Nikolai does, the one that sucks someone into his vortex. John has great, moody defenses, but clearly he's fallen into Timo's trap more than a few times. Or else Timo would've been kicked off the stool from the get-go.

"Are you staying or not," John snaps, referring to the card game.

Timo waves his hand like he's slicing air. I've seen the movie *21*, so I know that he's staying this round. John flips his card: a five.

He turns another: a ten. John busts.

Timo's face breaks in pure elation, and his excitement bubbles into me.

"Congrats," I say with a brighter smile. John hands him a couple of red chips, and Timo gives me a thumbs up before he places another bet.

"You shouldn't be congratulating him," John tells me as he deals the cards again. "Not after what his brother did to you last night."

I go cold, like the air conditioning wafted a chilly gust on me. Did he really have to bring that up? I've been doing an okay job of forgetting The Red Death and that piercing. My hand almost flies to my boob, as if protecting it on impulse.

"Which brother would that be?" Timo's brows furrow slightly as he skims his cards. A five and a seven against John's eight.

"Oh you know, the one who gets off on tattooing question marks and arrows on girls' asses."

I internally cringe.

Timo taps the table, and John deals him a ten. I add the numbers in my head quickly. Nikolai's little brother busts at twenty-two.

"Fuck," Timo curses, setting his hands on his head. Then he glances at me. "Nikolai tattooed your ass last night? That was you?" He appraises me swiftly like he's trying to fit an image to the memory.

He was there? I wonder if I saw him… "No…" I trail off, half in thought as I scrutinize his features a little more. "He pierced me."

Timo's face breaks into a giant grin. "That's right. You're the titty piercing. I thought I recognized you."

Titty piercing. My eyes bulge. *That's what I'm being referred to as?*

Timo snaps his fingers in remembrance. "I even cheered for Nikolai to lose that round."

So he was the lone guy, rooting for me. Wait—I hone in on the way he phrased that. He just wanted his brother to fail that time, not necessarily hoping I'd win for any other reason. *Way to go, Thora.*

His gaze flits down my body for a quick second. "You look different in the day, you know…maybe it's because I'm sober right now." He stretches his arms over his head and turns back to the table like *let's do this thing.*

Just like that, the ordeal rolls off his back, like it was a small moment, insignificant and ordinary. It encourages me to do the same, even if Nikolai believes it was monumental.

"The world has laws for a reason," John tells him as he deals the cards. "You should abide by them. It's called being an adult."

"Really?" Timo asks. "I think it's called being a stiff."

I ask John, "Are you one of those people who never cross the street on a red signal?"

"Yeah, because I want to fucking live. I like my life."

"Really?" Timo says again, actual surprise coating his face. "You should be an actor, man, because you have the whole 'I hate everything' vibe pretty down pat."

John's gloomy face actually darkens, and Timo connects with it, locking eyes, never shying away. His pink lips slowly curve upward the longer John glowers.

Then Timo puckers his lips, kissing the air and winks at him.

"God," John groans and looks to the ceiling like *why me?* I've had those moments with God myself. Usually I feel like I'm complaining to the ceiling tiles though.

Timo waves his hand to stay over his cards, and he wins the next round. John shakes his head, aggravated the longer he has to endure Timo. After a few more hands, a server swings by and asks for drink orders. I pass since I may head to the gym later, for more practice.

"Can't," Timo tells the server. "I have a show tonight."

His easy brush-off of the liquor surprises me. Maybe because he seems more irresponsible than I thought. But being in John's presence doesn't help. He makes everyone under seventy-five look like a rebellious teen.

Timo wins another round and throws his hands in the air. He laughs into a grin as he looks to me, and he points. "Why didn't you tell me you're lucky, Thora James?"

I think back to the piercing. "I'm usually not."

"You are for me," he says. "Stay comfortable. We're in this for the long haul."

John grumbles under his breath like Timo just speared him in the chest. And he starts dealing again. Timo leans forward, and when he glances my way, with sparkling, dazzled eyes—full of youthful energy—he ropes me in. Lassoing me with charm. Just like his older brother.

Nikolai possesses a darker version of it, but it's a talent that I find myself envying again. It's something that separates an ordinary person into something captivating. Spellbinding and extraordinary.

I can't take my eyes off Timo, and he's not even on stage.

I wonder if this is a gift you're born with. If it's something that I'll never be able to learn. Part of me, the more cynical side that I try to stomp away, believes so.

But the brightest side says—*maybe.* Maybe I can be something more than I am. If I can learn at all, the best place is here. Vegas. Where the Kotovas reside.

ACT SIX

I lie wide awake, not because I'm tormented by tomorrow's final cut or the discomfort of Camila's couch.

My mind snaps alert because of the sounds that emanate from Camila's bedroom. Her breathy moans puncture the air, mixing with her boyfriend's heavy groans. The squeak of the mattress springs is even audible through the thin walls. I've only ever heard noises like this from HBO's *True Blood.*

And as soon as the sounds of ecstasy in the apartment end, a new type of sound begins. Screaming. Yelling. Not-so-pleasurable noises that vibrate the air. My imaginative mind starts to create visions of Camila having rough, angry sex with a vampire. Only this vampire is a giant asshole who ends sex by arguing about stupid things.

Needless to say, my imagination is wrong.

Vampires don't exist.

And just as Camila's non-vampire boyfriend stops screaming, the pleasurable moaning begins again. It's a cycle that has kept me awake all night.

In college, I chose to live in a single dorm after my freshman year fiasco. My roommate brought her boyfriend over almost every night, and I slept on Shay's futon more than I did my own bed. I managed to avoid other people's sex noises for that long.

My clean record is now broken.

Camila's boyfriend must be stellar because the bedposts thump against the walls. I smash my pillow over my face and exposed ears. I just don't want to be half-asleep tomorrow. Zombies can't act like felines in heat.

Sleep, I command myself.

Camila cries out in pleasure.

Sleep, Thora.

Please.

MY EYES ARE HEAVY-LIDDED, AND THE GYM'S fluorescent lights sear my pupils. I yawn into my jacket sleeve as Kaitlin slumps down on the blue mat beside me.

"Late night?" she asks with a mild look of disdain. I catch the very, very hidden meaning.

"Not with anyone," I tell her. *Definitely not Nikolai.* "I was by myself." That sounds like a lie for some reason. "I just had bad sleep."

She nods, her guards dropping. "Me too."

Not only did Camila go at it on the bed last night, but she switched to the shower. To top it off, when I finally caught some shuteye, I had a nightmare.

And I fell off the couch, face-planting, hard. Which triggered a bloody nose. Now I have a bruise on the bridge and another bruise on my cheekbone to show for it. Concealer covered some of the purplish tint but not all.

"You nervous?" Kaitlin asks. Her brunette bun is so tight that the follicles along her hairline look ready to snap.

"Kind of," I say honestly with another yawn in my arm. "Are you?"

She nods and leans in close to me to whisper, "Elena has been chatting with Ivan in *Russian* all morning."

Her gaze drifts to the aerial silk, where Ivan and Elena stand. As though about to instruct her. Like she's already been awarded the role.

Kaitlin reaches for her toes, stretching. "I swear these things are made for people who can talk their way into them."

I'm not a fan of that reality—the one that says the hardest-working individual will always lose out to the most sociable. And I don't want to live in that world. Shay would tell me that I have no choice, that this isn't fiction. I have no say in which world I live in.

As I spread my legs open into a split, I reach as far as I can, my muscles extending with the position. The back doors suddenly burst open, and the directors march into the gym, carrying folders, tablets and clipboards. They exude an air of superiority, vacuuming all oxygen.

Nikolai is among them.

He chats with Helen as they near the long table. Dressed in his usual gym attire (shorts, red bandana, shirtless), I wait for him to turn his head and acknowledge the four of us left to audition. But he's in a heated discussion with Helen, and I catch him gesturing to Ivan by the aerial silk more than once.

Helen raises her hands in defense, and Nikolai's lips snap shut, his nose flaring. She speaks calmly, it seems. And then her eyes plant on me.

I freeze, wondering if I was just caught eavesdropping. Everyone was doing it though—I assume. I'm about to look to Kaitlin for verification when Helen calls my name, "Thora."

I instinctively jump to my feet. Glancing briefly at Nikolai, I can't read him beyond his six-foot-five, masculine dominance. He's an intimidating fortress in a gym full of straw huts.

"You're first today," Helen tells me. "We'd like to see some basic acro dance lifts. We want to know how well you work with Nik. He'll lead you through them."

I try to bottle some of my nerves, slowly approaching the center of the mat. In the corner of my eye, I spot Elena twisting the red silk in her fist, clearly being instructed by the choreographer to practice. My stomach twists and backbends and somersaults—in the worst ways.

"Thora," Nikolai breathes, very close. He grips my attention, his concentrated gaze on me. "Don't watch them. Right now, this is about you and me. Do your personal best, so that whatever happens, you have no regrets."

I inhale a deeper breath, flooded with more confidence. I nod and retrain my mind, blocking out my competition.

He steps even closer, and I sense my ribcage jutting out in a heavy rhythm. He notices, concern knotting his brows. Which only causes me to breathe harder. Fantastic.

His intense steel gaze searches my features with headiness, care and lust. Intimate. A combination for long-time lovers, for something greater than a friend. Than anything we are. His acting is up to par. That's for sure.

His large hand cups my oval face, his thumb brushing my cheekbone. His frown darkens, and heat builds across my skin at one thought: *what if he's not acting?*

"Did someone hit you?" he asks lowly. His jaw muscles tic.

The bruise. "No, I, um." I roll my eyes at myself. "I fell."

Doubt crosses his features.

I realize *falling* is a cliché excuse used to cover worse things. But it's sadly the truth here.

He says slowly, "You fell. On your face?"

I sound like a royal klutz. Someone you would definitely *not* want as an acrobatic partner. "I had a nightmare," I explain, my throat closing. I'm a ball of hot lava right now, the swelter spreading and it's not just from embarrassment. It's just—he's so close. *Of course he is, Thora.*

"Must have been some nightmare."

I was being drained of blood by vampires. I purposefully leave this part out. "Yeah…it was really gruesome."

"Let's hope you don't land on your face again, myshka." His finger lightly brushes along the ridge of my nose, like a feather tickling my skin. If I blinked, I would've missed it. "What's your favorite lift?" he asks before I can process anything else.

I go cold, despite his hand that falls to the base of my neck. "I…" *have never done an acro lift.* Or worked with a partner on aerial silk. I've been solo since no one would practice with me.

His eyes dance around my face, reading me quickly. "Do you have any formal circus training? Even a summer camp?"

"Not formal." I watch him glance cautiously over his shoulder at Helen and then focus on me again. His closeness and deep, hollow voice cement my joints to stiff, unbendable shapes. When I should be just the opposite.

Flexible and lithe.

"You'll follow my lead then," he says. "I'm assuming you can do that unless you tell me otherwise."

"I can," I nod, more eagerly than usual. I want to learn. As much as possible.

He stares down at me again, his gaze raking my small frame in a long wave. "This isn't about executing the best pitch tuck or vault somersault. There's no score at the end of a show. People attend the circus to see the impossible become possible, and it's up to *us* to create that illusion." His hand descends to my hip, his grip firm. "And we do that using our bodies."

I'm wide awake, all yawns vanishing. His touch leaves hot imprints across me.

"We'll try something simple first..." He clasps my hips and swiftly lifts me to his waist, and I instinctively wrap my legs around him. *Thump. Thump.* I can feel my heart slam into my ribs.

One of his hands rises to my hair, clutching the back of my head. And his unwavering bedroom eyes try to melt parts of me. On purpose. This is purposeful lust that I cannot defend myself against. It's too strong. *He's* too strong.

"Whatever passion you've ever encountered in your life, you use it now, Thora," he tells me, reminding me that this is more than gymnastics. This is a performance.

Passion.

I wrack my brain. And I see a sloppy drunken night. And I see an awkward, short-lived one. Passion has never been in the cards for me, but that doesn't mean I can't fake it. That's what acting is, right?

We're all putting on a show here.

I take another strong breath, fixating on his lips in hopes that I look sultry enough. I'm tiny in his arms, little and breakable but still strong. *Not as strong as him*, my conscience retorts. *I'll get there*, I snap back, attempting to snuff out any self-doubt.

"We'll try a handstand on my shoulders," he instructs. "I'll be able to tell if you're struggling, so don't worry about falling." He searches my eyes for affirmation that I understand. But his hand caresses my cheek, my whole body warming and my mind jumbling. "Thora?"

"Yeah?"

"Relax. Breathe *normally*," he tells me with a smile beginning to lift his lips.

"I can do that," I say positively.

"Good." His hand drifts to my spine, pressing my body closer. My thin leotard is all that separates my skin from his. I feel his chest rise and fall a bit heavier than before. And then his unshaven jaw skims my cheek; his lips to my ear, he says, "I'll swing you, and with that momentum, you'll reach my shoulders. Don't be afraid."

I wonder if I'm expelling fear. I don't mean to be. "I'm not afraid," I whisper.

"Then show me."

With this, I unlock my legs and he grasps my forearms, lowering me. Not to the ground. He swings my body out, and when I careen back into him, I spread my legs so I don't whack into his knees. We repeat the movement only twice before I'm high enough to grip his broad shoulders.

The adrenaline flows through my veins like an electric shock. My fingers whiten as I clench his shoulders as hard as possible, forcing my body to this position. Upside-down, my head rushes with blood. He stays perfectly rigid, and I press my legs together, mimicking his pose so we're in a straight, tall line.

Then he places one hand firmly on my ass, the other remaining on my forearm. As though he doesn't trust *me* enough to release his hold. I point my toes and whisper, "Let go."

His eyes flicker up to me once before he *very slowly* drops his hands.

"Step forward," Helen suddenly says, challenging us.

Nikolai's muscles flex and emerge as he carries my weight. Without shifting his posture, he takes an extra step. My body teeters a little from the movement, and I struggle to remain fixed in place.

His hand instinctively returns to my ass, then to my hip. Trust definitely goes two ways in a partnership.

"Can you contort your body?" Nikolai asks me.

I think I understand where he's headed with this. I spread my legs into a split and then I slowly curve my torso, so my feet end up on either side of my arms, like a contortionist. I flipped myself around, so I'm able to sit on his shoulders, my legs dangling on his chest.

Helen nods a couple times and murmurs to the other directors at the table.

Nikolai briskly grabs me around the waist, spinning me. My chest melds against his, his eyes pierced through me, and my breathing heavies again, panting like my endurance has depleted with one swift move. We don't break eye contact. It's more intrusive than anything I've ever felt before. Like someone tugging at things deep, deep inside your soul, stripping that bed again. This time, it's like he's trying to cut open the mattress.

It's a look that defeats all other looks.

And I'm not sure what I express back either, other than breathiness, just dazed. I slide down his muscular build, the tension pricking every nerve.

Then he clutches both of my legs, parting them around his torso. He releases my hands from his biceps. "Use your core," he instructs, his palm on my abdomen to illustrate. I swallow hard.

And I fall backwards, my head dipped towards the mat, but instead of descending like a limp noodle—I tighten my abs. And I become a flat board, hanging off him in a neat horizontal line. I extend my arms above my head to lengthen the shape.

My thigh muscles burn, especially as he retracts his hands, letting me show off my strength. I blow out breaths from my nose. And then his palm slides from my lower abdomen up to my chest. The black fabric of my leotard has never felt thinner—and I swear, his thumb glides over my barbell piercing.

I skip a breath.

His hand reaches my neck, and I find myself shutting my eyes, losing myself for a moment to his touch. His fingers sensually disappear into my hair, massaging the tense muscles. I force my eyelids open, and he languidly kneels, causing my shoulders to gently hit the mat. Like he's resting me on a bed.

This is a position that leads straight to sex, my legs still broken apart around him. He leans over me, our lips in kissing distance. *We're working*, as he once said. That's why he carries such severity in his movements.

Authoritative, in control. But as the silence pools between us, I only become aware of the person above me.

He is power. Man. And strength. He is charm and desire and indestructible things.

I want to emit an equivalent passion. I want to be strength and desire. But I'm not sure how to match him and still move. It's easy to be confident in the face of average-standing competition. It's hard to pretend you're something greater in the face of someone who's already beyond great.

He combs pieces of my flyaway fluffy hairs from my forehead. "I'm going to swing you on my shoulders again." He stays in character, his words dripping with sex. His eyes flit along me like he's not even giving chaste instructions. "Stand on them. Then step onto my palm. I'll hold you upright." He pauses. "And Thora?"

I let out a breath, one of his hands traveling to the outside of my thigh. "Yes?"

He looks right into me. "You're doing well."

I cling to that honesty. Just as he makes a move to sit up, gruff Russian words chill my bones.

That's Ivan. I crane my neck and see him charging the blue mats from the table with Helen. I'm not even sure when he ditched teaching Elena. I was focused on the lifts with Nikolai, as he said to do.

Nikolai sits up and replies to Ivan with as much aggravation. He holds up a finger like *one more.* One more lift maybe?

One more minute?

One more shot.

My stomach clenches at Ivan's reaction. He storms closer, and from this vantage, it almost looks like he's going to kick me. A bout of panic surges through me, my heart lodging. Before I can react, Nikolai swiftly picks me up, spins me around—his back now facing Ivan. He stands between me and the choreographer, setting me safely on my feet.

And his unusually softened and apologetic eyes speak before he does. "I'm sorry."

It takes a moment for those words to sink in. And I can feel the color drain from my face. This is the end of my audition.

I can barely breathe "normally" as I restrain these sentiments that crash and attempt to pull me under. *Maybe it's still uncertain.* I grapple with false hope. I can fool myself until every girl tries out. I can stay positive. I can do something… "It's not over," I whisper to him.

His features twist before they harden, his jaw tightening. And he shakes his head once. "Maybe another year."

It's not over yet, I pretend still.

"You should go," Nikolai says deeply. I know he means *to the mat* and not home. But his voice basically tells me: *move on and forget this. You tried your best.*

I don't want Shay and my parents to be right. I wanted, so desperately, to prove them wrong. That I'm worth success. That I can do more than they think I'm capable of.

I don't wait for Nikolai to guide me or push me away. I unglue my feet and dazedly wander to the other girls while another is called to audition.

It's not over yet. Something hot and wet rolls down my cheek.

I wipe the one tear and take a seat.

ACT SEVEN

I haven't been able to tell anyone back home the news. It's been three hours since reality decided to sucker punch me. In retrospect, I should've seen the failure coming like everyone else did. But I didn't want to. So maybe I deserve the onslaught of tears in The Masquerade's public bathroom, cramped in a tiny stall.

Elena landed the role. Predictable.

I couldn't even stomach watching the other girls audition. I fiddled with my fingers and acted so interested in my cuticles. I feel more like a loser and a coward right now than in my entire gymnastics career. And it's this moment—tear-streaked with a toilet paper dispenser digging into my hip—that I wonder if I'm one of those foolish dreamers.

The kind that believes they can sing when they're so clearly out of pitch.

The kind that believes they can dance when they have nothing more than two left feet.

I shut my eyes, more hot water cascading and searing. What is life if it's not in pursuit of the things we love? People search a lifetime to find one soul-bearing desire, and now I'm going to have to find two. Because I'm not good enough at the first.

It's devastating.

I'm clawing at something that doesn't want me. And to say goodbye is like severing a part of me that I can't easily replace. I'm lost.

I'm going to be so lost.

The minute I return to college. I won't know which direction to go.

It's terrifying.

It's everything I never wanted, and I can't bear the thought of my parents saying *I told you so.* To see their disappointment reflect back at me.

Because it's admitting cold defeat. That *nothing* I do, no amount of hours I practice, no matter how hard I try, I cannot succeed.

One in a million, Thora James.

I'm not that one. I know.

I know.

"IF YOU GO HOME, WILL YOU EVER RETURN TO Vegas and try again?" Camila asks curiously. She has her feet up on the barstool, overtaking all three as she lounges and eats her slice of pizza. The sleeves of her kimono almost knock over her Diet Fizz.

"Probably not," I say softly, sitting at the kitchen table with John. I use Camila's laptop to check plane and bus tickets, deciding which will be cheaper for my return trip to Ohio. My appetite has been lost since this morning. I barely even nibble on pepperoni.

I blink constantly, my eyes dry and scratchy from crying more than

I ever have. I ended my pity-party about a couple hours ago at The Masquerade and took the fifty-minute walk to Camila's apartment.

My phone buzzes, and I catch a glimpse of the text.

How did it go? Is it over? – Mom

I ignore it for now. John watches my rejection of the text as he sips a Lightning Bolt! energy drink. Preparing for a snide remark, I shut my eyes—but it never comes. He stays quiet, for once.

"You know," Camila continues, licking the pizza sauce off her finger. "Vegas clubs are always looking for female acrobats doing their thing on trapezes and hoops. Why don't you just try out for other jobs around town?"

My brows pinch. I never even thought of that avenue. My parents wouldn't approve. They'd think it was no more than being a waitress in Los Angeles, hoping to become an actress one day. They'd say that a tiny fraction succeeds, and it's fruitless to waste my time and try.

Off my silence, she adds, "It's definitely not as prestigious as AE. I was thinking more short-term. It pays the bills, and in the meantime, you may run into someone who has connections to Aerial Ethereal."

Connections. My lungs expand. That's what it's all about. I won't run into anyone important or useful in Ohio. Not when the industry is here.

I realize I'm clinging to any hope. No matter how small. There is a part of me that wants this trip to mean something. If I go home, everyone will tell me that I wasted hundreds of dollars on a flight to Vegas. That I made a mistake.

My cell vibrates again.

Call us when you can. It'll be okay. We can help you out for your return flight. – Dad

He already thinks I lost. *You did, Thora.*

My stomach churns from the lack of food, and I bite into a piece of pizza. It hurts to swallow. My parents will be distressed if they hear that I gave up my scholarship on a whim, to stay here and work at a club.

They're the ties that bind me to Ohio, the strings that root me to safety and security. I fear cutting them. It's like saying goodbye to the little girl who turned to my mother for advice. Who glowed when my father's pride for me shined bright at gymnastics meets.

There is no pride from this decision.

There is just more disappointment.

"Don't put ideas into her head, Camila," John chimes in. "Let her leave Vegas while she can." He nods to me. "You're one of the lucky ones who still has the chance to get out."

My face twists, unsure of what I feel anymore.

Camila leans forward and narrows her eyes at her cousin. "You *love it* here, John. More than any of us."

"I would *never* say that," John grumbles. He sips his energy drink while Camila huffs.

"If you hate it here," she says, "then why haven't you left?"

"Because I'm clearly insane like the rest of you." He raises his Lightning Bolt! in cheers.

I return to the computer, the flight arrival times blurring together. In my heart, I know that I want to stay—no matter how frightening that idea seems. No matter how much I'm risking. The *what if* will haunt me for the rest of my life. I wonder if I'll be fifty-years-old, looking back at today and wishing I had the courage to take the path less traveled. The one without security and family.

I lick my dry lips and clear my throat. "How much easier will it even be to get a job in a club?" I ask Camila. Those have to be hard to come by too.

Camila perks up now that I'm entertaining her idea. She points at John and waves her finger like *ohh ohhh*. "John, you must know someone who's hiring."

"No more than you." He slouches further and spins a peppershaker.

"Hey." She snaps her fingers. "Thora needs help, and you know everyone at The Masquerade, Bellagio, and Cosmopolitan."

My eyes grow big. "Really?" I figured out that John likes to listen to himself talk. But I didn't realize that he was Mr. Popular. At the blackjack table, those frat types never showed up, but a group of elderly women did, and they bantered back and forth with him for a solid two hours. Even sullen and surly, he's somehow incredibly endearing.

"No," John snaps, like his cousin is lying. "That's a complete gross exaggeration, Camila."

She gives him a look and shifts her gaze to me. "He's a social butterfly and refuses to acknowledge it."

"I'm not a fucking butterfly," he says under his breath. Louder, he snaps, "I hate *everyone.* Sure, I have people's numbers, but only because they hang around and talk and talk and won't shut up. I'm not a cardboard cutout that says: *please dump your life story on me.* But people fucking do it anyway."

"Now *you're* exaggerating," Camila retorts. "Your pessimistic, cynical-self talks more than everyone else. And you like when people listen to you complain." She points at him again. "The point is that you must know someone looking to hire a female acrobat."

He shakes his head vehemently for maybe a full minute before he says, "Yeah, probably."

Camila throws her hands in the air like she just ran through the finish line of a 5k. "So you'll help, Thora?"

I realize now that my stomach has been coiling. *If he's willing to help me, I'll stay.* The thought hits me at once. It's another bout of hope, something that makes this decision a bit easier. Not by much. But I'll take anything.

The table vibrates.

Any news? – Shay

I ignore that text too.

When I look up, John is scrutinizing me and the phone. He takes pity on me, sighing into a full-on groan. "Fine," he says, "I'll make a couple calls."

My body swells, and my eyes burn with tears. "Really?"

"Please don't cry," he grimaces.

I smile instead. "Thank you…so much."

"You can stay here until you find a place," Camila tells me with a wink.

Maybe I am lucky after all.

I pick up my phone as it buzzes once more.

Sis, did you make it? – Tanner

I can't fathom opening these floodgates of disapproval. If I tell Tanner, he'll tell my parents. Lying to them hurts less. I've never done it before, but I just want to be the kind of daughter they're proud of. Not the one they cringe about when someone brings me up. *Is your daughter in college?*

No, she dropped out.

I don't want to saddle them with judgment from their peers.

"Are you sure you want to do this?" John asks me seriously. He must see me hesitating, staring at the phone like it holds my future. "Once I make the call and get you in, I don't want you to flake. Last thing I need is to owe some asshole club manager a favor."

I let my heart guide me.

"I'm sure," I tell him.

I'm all in.

I text my brother:

Yeah. I landed the role.

ACT EIGHT

Only a week into my job and the manager of Phantom has already badgered me *twice* about amplifying my sex appeal on the aerial hoop, dangling from the ceiling.

My act, apparently, is too tame for the Vegas nightclub. But if I shake my ass anymore, I might as well walk down the strip to a triple X joint. Honestly, they probably pay better.

I knot the straps around my long knee-length coat, hiding my costume: a black corset, matching underwear, and fishnet stockings. I wobble in my five-inch silver stilettos as I depart from the club. I try to comb my fingers through my tangled dirty-blonde hair that poofs around my oval face.

Last time I tried to hang from the hoop, my hair in a bun, the manager cursed me out and called me Virgin Mary. Unfortunately the nickname has stuck around the workplace. But I'd rather not be fired in my first week, especially since John stuck his neck out to help me.

The upside: I'm in the air ninety-nine percent of the time at Phantom. And one of the girls gave me the address of a gym with circus apparatuses. I've signed up for a couple classes. Maybe I can strengthen my skills while I'm here.

And a plus has been the location. Right in the heart of The Masquerade. I only have an elevator ride down to The Red Death, where I plan to meet up with Camila and drink to surviving my very first week in Vegas.

Just as I exit the elevator, my phone rings. I read the caller ID: SHAY.

I've been screening his calls more than usual this week. I shelter my anxiety and slip into the nearest hallway bathroom, pressing the phone to my ear. "What's up?" My eyes flit to a couple girls who fix their makeup by the mirror.

"You've been ignoring me," he says. "I get why you're lying to your parents because they'd flip their shit. But you've already told me the truth, so what the hell, Thora?" I hear the sound of a bouncy ball being tossed at a wall.

I picture him lying on the floor, against his bed. Throwing and catching the blue rubber toy. The Cincinnati gym, where we practiced together as teens, had a bouncy ball dispenser in the front, and we both spent way too many quarters for handfuls of them.

I say under my breath, "I'm just scared you're going to tell me that I'm making a mistake."

He's silent. Biting his tongue, maybe. "You're going to miss conditioning tomorrow."

"I know."

"Have you called the coach?"

"I sent him an email." I swallow a lump.

He exhales heavily. "So how has it been? They don't make you wear heels, do they?"

I glance down at the uncomfortable silver stilettos that neither fit my personality nor really my body, my toes aching. "They're not that bad," I say optimistically. "I'll wear them in."

He laughs. "Yeah right."

I realize how this conversation—and most of them lately—have been circumnavigating around me. Friendships go two ways. "What about you?" I ask.

"I'm not wearing heels any time soon."

I smile. "No, I mean, how are you? Is conditioning going well? Are the freshman looking good?"

"They're okay. It's same-old-same-old, you know—well, I guess you don't know." The bouncy ball sounds like it pops hard against the wall.

"Shay," I whisper, resting my hip on the sink counter. "Do you ever dream that you're meant to do something…more?"

"I like my life here," is all he says. "It was going fine until…" He sighs in frustration. "I'm just used to you being around." I hear the ball bounce on a floorboard. "I have other friends, but you're the one who annoys me the least."

I smile wider. "It's because I'm your only friend that's a girl." And probably because we *are* best friends in most ways.

I can feel his smile too. "Be safe, okay?"

"I will. Be happy, alright?"

"I am," he assures me.

"Okay." Someone else begins to call me. I check the ID. "My mom is on the other line."

"Don't hang up on her," Shay tells me quickly. "Your parents have been pestering my parents who've been pestering me about you. They just want to know how you're doing."

"What do I say?"

He sighs again. "Tell her that everything is going great. Your dreams are coming true. Zip-a-dee-doo-dah."

I roll my eyes. "Helpful."

"You asked," he reminds me. "Good luck."

"Thanks." I switch calls before I lose her. "Hey, Mom." The girls in the bathroom readjust their purses and strut out the doors, inadvertently giving me more privacy.

"Hi, honey. I just wanted to call and see how practice has been."

I check my watch. It's late, especially in Ohio. "Shouldn't you be in bed?" I ask, confused and concerned.

"I've been up," she admits, her tone gleeful. "So...has it been everything you hoped it would be?" Her excitement rings over the line. She's happy for me. For my non-existent success.

The lie festers in my stomach. *You can do this, Thora James.* "It's been...amazing." My voice turns wistful almost. "I can't believe I'll be a part of Amour in five months."

Five months. That's how long they're giving Elena to train for the show. That's how long I have to land a role before my parents fly out to Vegas to "see" me perform.

"We're so proud of you, Thora," she says. "Your father has been telling everyone at work." I sense her face stretching into a blinding smile. My parents are both chemical engineers—so I'm guessing I was the talk of the lab.

My daughter is in the circus. That big one in Vegas. It's highly competitive, you know.

I close my eyes before they well. "Thanks, Mom. I love you both."

She repeats the sentiment before we agree to talk more often. Then we hang up.

I feel *awful.* Like I need to absolve my sins in a confessional and do charitable deeds. I'll make things right with them. I just need some time. I do my best to shed my guilt and leave the bathroom.

ACT NINE

1:18 a.m.

After I make it to The Red Death, I check my phone for the time, the number illuminating my screen. Back at Ohio State, one in the morning was followed by sleep. Here in Vegas, it almost feels like the beginning of the night.

Just like last time, the female hostess mans the podium. "Are you single?!" she asks over the loud bass, glow stick necklaces stacked beside her in boxes.

"Yeah, I'm single!" I shout back, and she hands me a blue one. I fasten it around my neck and skirt past the drunken Vegas nightlife, shrouded mostly in darkness. A few elbows and hips bump into me as they dance, intoxicated on something stronger than alcohol.

By the time I arrive at the lit-up bar, a bachelorette party swarms the other end, swamping Camila's attention. Flagging down the second bartender also proves near impossible. I wait patiently while those around me grow more and more frustrated and just wander off.

"Oh man, not another bachelorette party," a guy says as he sidles to the open space beside my stool. He wears black leather pants and nothing else. Lanky with defined, cut muscles. "Hey!" He leans forward and taps the bar. In the red overhead lights, I suddenly make out his face.

"Timo?" I ask.

His head whips to me, his dark brown hair falling in his lashes, the sides shorter. His dangling cross earring sways with the abrupt movement. "Thora James," he says my name into a wide grin. His gray eyes brighten, his smooth face illuminated red, green and blue by three stacked neon necklaces. "I didn't know you live here."

At the blackjack table, I never confessed about my job situation to Timo. Nothing about the audition ever came up, so I'm sure he assumed that I was a girl moseying in and out of Vegas.

"I do now," I tell him.

"I'd toast to it, but you know…" Timo rests his forearms on the bar and leans over. "Bachelorette prejudice!"

Camila flips him off from the other side, her cheeks flushed from being hurried.

Timo shakes his head. "Next time, I'm wearing a *bride-to-be* sash if that's all it takes to get service."

"TAT! TAT! TAT!"

My pulse pitches. I crane my neck over my shoulder and notice the cluster of people, huddling together in the center of the room. Nikolai bets people every Saturday night then. Maybe because Amour isn't scheduled for Sundays, so he won't have to wake early for work. Wild and responsible.

It's crazy to think that just behind the wall of people, he stands there, poised and confident—ready to provide an "experience" for some other girl.

Timo lets out a long groan. "I'm missing it." He hunches over, keeping his forearms on the sticky bar, and he turns his head to me. "So what do you do in Vegas?"

"I just started working at Phantom."

His brows jump in surprise. "*Phantom.*" He inspects my long coat and stilettos. "Are you one of the jello shot girls? Not that I'm judging."

"No jello shots." I highly doubt the manager would allow the Virgin Mary to lie on the bar and let men and women suck shots off my bare stomach, covered in pungent alcohol and wet dollar bills. "I do an aerial hoop act for a few hours and then they swap me out with another girl."

His dazzling smile extends even wider. "A club acrobat. I always wanted to try it out, but my parents would never allow it. Too much entertainment, not enough art."

I can't see his parents stopping him from doing anything. He's underage in a Vegas club, drinking. They seem really relaxed to me, but then again, I don't really know him or the Kotovas. "You're eighteen," I remind him. "You can do what you want, can't you?" It's a stupid question. I understand, so well, the pressure to please a parent.

"I'm *twenty-one*, Thora James." He gives me a look, and his lips twitch up in a smirk. "And it's not just my parents. Nikolai would have me by the balls."

"Timo!"

I freeze at the sound of *his* deep voice.

"Speak of the devil!" Timo yells, whipping around and setting his elbows on the bar. "Please tell me you know some trick into breaking the bachelorette hypnosis on all the bartenders."

My joints stiffen as Nikolai scoots closer, not noticing my lingering presence. I keep my eyes planted on the racks of liquor instead of confronting him. But I sense his towering frame behind me.

I thought there was a *slim* possibility that he'd be here tonight. The scariest part: I think I hoped for it. My belly flutters with nerves. I don't want him to think I stuck around Vegas *for him.* That'd be weird. And beyond awkward.

Nikolai slides even closer to the bar, and his arm actually grazes my shoulder. He's not fazed by the touch, nor does he acknowledge the brief contact.

I'm frozen solid to this place.

Nikolai raises his hand and flags down a female bartender. She immediately zips over to him.

"What the fuck?" Timo curses, annoyed and amazed at how easily his brother could summon the girl.

"I'll take a Jack and Fizz." Nikolai turns to his brother, his back facing me. His height is not only impressive and intimidating but it shrinks me to a little tiny thing. I might as well disappear from sight. "What do you want?"

"A Manhattan." Just as the bartender goes to leave, Timo adds, "Wait!" He leans over the bar to look down towards me. "Thora, what do you want?"

Boom.

My cover is blown.

While Nikolai's sweltering gaze bears down on me, full of what-the-fuck confusion, I peek at the drink specials. "Tequila sunrise," I manage to say clearly.

The bartender swivels to her liquor bottles and juices, concocting our drinks. Every tendon snaps as I slowly turn to meet Nikolai's piercing grays, steel that drills right through me. His glow necklace turns his white button-down into a deadly red hue.

I open my mouth to say something, but I'm not sure *what* to say. I end up swallowing air.

"You stayed," he speaks first, his voice lower than before. He seems more than just indifferent, but I can't place his sentiments. Good or bad. He inspects my outfit with a once-over, his eyes descending in a hot wave. "What for?"

He asked me a question for once. A *personal* question. I wonder if I've just become worthy of a backstory.

"I stayed for job opportunities." I notice his jaw muscles tensing, and my frown deepens, maybe even into a scowl.

Timo slings his arm around my shoulder. "Thora, here, works at Phantom."

Nikolai is incredibly rigid, and his eyes flash hot. "Doing what?"

"I'm a club acrobat," I say. "I need money for an apartment, and I'm...taking some classes at a gym. So..."

"Formal training," he says, understanding what I mean. "It'll take much more than that to land a job in this industry, Thora. It may be months before there's even another opening. I hope that I didn't give you the inclination that a few classes is all you need."

I shake my head, about to tell him no, but Timo holds up his hands in shock. "Wait—you two know each other *beyond* a nipple piercing?"

My neck heats, but I stand tall, not shrinking.

Nikolai shoots his little brother a disapproving glare and growls out a few words in Russian.

Timo gapes and touches his bare chest "I have tact."

I help clarify, "I was auditioning for a role in Amour."

"Oh," Timo says with a nod, his smile returning. "Small world."

This trains Nikolai's attention back on his brother, the origin of why he even sauntered over here. He starts speaking in Russian, and I can't piece apart anything except the aggravated tone. Timo's lively features morph into mild irritation.

His reply comes out even more hostile.

The bartender appears and slides our drinks over. I collect the one with orange juice, fishing out a few bills. The other two drinks, a cocktail with dark liquid (plus a cherry) and a glass with soda and whiskey, go unnoticed by the Kotovas.

When Nikolai steps closer to Timo, his finger pointed at the exit, I pick up a new name: *Katya.*

A girl's name, clearly. I wonder if she's his friends-with-benefits. A chill creeps up my spine, and I tell myself that it's simply the guilt of eavesdropping.

Timo glowers, his chest falling in a heavy, annoyed breath. Clearly upset, he spouts off a string of Russian words while he walks backwards. Then he flips Nikolai off. With two hands. And he storms away without his drink or another glance.

Nikolai rakes his fingers through his hair. He roughly snatches his Jack and Fizz, chugging half of it in one gulp. He must feel my loitering gaze because he says, "I told him to go home." He grips the edge of the bar. "What did you leave behind, Thora?"

"What do you mean?" I take a very small sip of my drink that's more tequila than orange juice. It burns my throat.

His eyes are suddenly dead-set on me again. "What are you giving up by being here?"

I chose not to look at it that way. It's easier seeing the things I gain than the things I lose. Cold washes over me again. "Parents, my little brother," I start listing things off, "my friends and…" I pause, knowing this last one will not be waiting for me when I return like the others. "…a gymnastics scholarship."

He downs the rest of his drink and motions to the bartender for another. "And why the circus?" He no longer faces me. No longer peels back my layers with his intrusive gaze. He's glaring from the gathering dancers to the racks of liquor bottles. A look that I'm glad I don't meet head-on.

Why the circus? I've never had to share this story with anyone other than my bedroom mirror. "When I was fourteen, my mom took me to the circus…I fell in love with it." I pause to form a better explanation, of how I sat in that velvet-lined seat and longed to share the performer's experience. To be the girl flying in the air, to captivate an audience and enchant them. To be superhumanly strong.

To be something more. Awe. And power. And grace.

The words stick to the back of my throat.

"What show?" he asks.

"Aerial Ethereal's Nova Vega." It was one of the most popular touring circus shows, going on a twenty-year run, and now it's found a permanent home in Montreal. As Nikolai stays silent, I wonder… "Were you…in it?"

The bartender passes him another drink, and he nods to her in thanks. To me, he says, "When I was twelve, I assisted the Russian swing in Nova Vega for a year."

So I didn't watch him perform exactly, but still…small world, as Timo said. I guess the industry is tiny.

He swishes his drink, in contemplation maybe. "You're one of many, myshka. I hear that same story countless times. Girls say how they wanted to be ballerinas after seeing Swan Lake in Moscow, boys dying to win gold medals in hockey after watching a game up close."

One in a million. I know I'm part of the many. It's a thought I've been given by too many people. "Are your reasons for being an acrobat unique?" I ask.

Surprisingly, he shakes his head. "No."

"No?"

He spins to me now, his features harsh, his glare still daggering his eyes. It would be harder to meet if I wasn't so curious. "I was born into this," he explains. "I'm a fourth generation acrobat. It's more common than you might think."

I believe him.

Then he briefly drops his gaze, trying to hide his incensed emotions maybe, or at least trying not to direct his aggravation my way. He rests his elbow on the bar, fixating on the crowd, his fingers tightened around his glass.

I hesitate. "You're angry." He doesn't answer. So I add, "You think I'm stupid for being here." To try again so soon.

He takes a sip. His Adam's apple bobs as he swallows. "I think you're brave," he tells me. "But there's a greater chance this city will strip whatever innocence you have left before you succeed, Thora." He tilts his head at me. "And there's a good chance you'll fail. I have trouble imagining a girl like you on the brink of misery in a city that doesn't want her. So yes, I'm *angry*. But not at you."

My stomach roils. These truths are hard to hear, I'll admit that. *But I can't leave.* I lick my lips, tasting the tequila. "I can't leave," I say aloud, resolute on this decision. "I'm not turning back now. I'll spend years regretting it." I'll go home empty-handed. With nothing but a big mistake on my chest, worn like a badge of shame.

He finishes off his second drink and slides it on the bar. "I used to be like you."

"Brave?" I wonder.

"Idealistic."

"What happened?" I ask, my drink cold in my hand.

"I grew up," he tells me, a swift kick. "I have more responsibilities. There are people I can't afford to leave behind."

"Hey, Thora!" Camila calls out, stealing my attention. She slips to my side of the bar, but her presence only builds a strain between Nikolai and me. Like last week, her green glow necklace rests on her brown curls. Her gaze floats to the Russian guy. "Hey, sexy, don't you have a bet to get to?"

"I'm taking a break." And then he rests his palm on the small of my back. I cage a breath the longer he touches me out of the blue. "Thora has been telling me about her new job." Each word sounds like liquid sex all of a sudden. He can layer on the smooth charm too well.

Camila's lips rise, coated in purple lipstick. "Oh yeah, she's a vixen at Phantom now." The bride-to-be waves Camila down at the other side of the bar. She sighs heavily and focuses on me. "I need to talk to you about something important. So don't move." Her voice pitches a bit, and worry infiltrates my frozen state of being.

"I thought we were just celebrating my first week here."

"That too," she calls out as she darts away.

Nikolai studies her, way more attentive than me. His hand ascends to my shoulder, and he squeezes once, almost in comfort. "How long have you known her for?"

I shrug. "Just the week."

"I don't think she invited you here to celebrate."

She does seem nervous.

So Camila might've asked me here for another reason. That doesn't mean it has to be a bad reason, right? I find myself chugging my drink distractedly, and I cough into my hand at the sharpness. As I go to take another sip to clear my throat, a very senseless act, Nikolai covers my glass with his hand.

Then he flags down a bartender as easily as he did the first two times. "I need a water."

She's quick to fill another glass, even plopping in a lemon. When she disappears, he passes it to me. I gratefully switch drinks, opting for the nonalcoholic one.

To lessen the tension, I change to a lighter topic. "Tattoo anyone special?"

"Everyone is special," he says. I try to catch his sarcasm, but it's hidden in his deep voice. I wonder if he's still imagining me being sucked in Vegas' black hole of sins and broken dreams.

"Anyone memorable then?" I wonder.

"There was the forehead tattoo..."

My jaw unhinges.

His brows shoot up. "Joking." And a smile pulls at his lips, a charismatic one.

I must be scowling because he gives me this usual stare like *you seem mad.* I've been asked "what's wrong?" for merely walking along campus with headphones in. I thought I looked fine, but my face sucks at conveying my emotions properly.

He tilts my chin up with two fingers, his eyes doing most of the smiling now, searching me. "What black eyes you have…"

"All the better to devour you with." That wasn't me. I'm not that witty. Camila is back with a bigger, wider grin than she's worn all night. "Are you two friends?" She radiates at that possibility. And I swear she glances at my nipple, recalling that *he* was the one who pierced me.

Neither of us answers. We're not exactly friends, but we're not strangers anymore either. The music switches to a louder dance beat by Jennifer Lopez.

"This is so perfect!" Camila shouts over the song. She stretches over the bar to talk to us. "I've been stressing out all day, trying to find you a place to crash."

The bottom of my stomach collapses.

What?

I struggle to ask at first, but I find my voice. "What happened to your couch?" My throat throbs. I told her that I'd be out of her place in a week and a half, the day I receive my first paycheck. She said that was fine.

"My extended family is here, and they want to stay closer to the strip. So they're going to use my place. They surprised me with the news this morning. I'm really sorry." Her green-shadowed eyes apologize enough. "John's brothers are crashing at his place, so he has a full house too. I've called a few girlfriends, but no one is answering tonight."

I'm essentially on my own.

"It's okay," I tell her, wracking my brain for the cost of a room at The Masquerade. I can tap into my savings until my paycheck comes in, I think. But what if my parents snoop into my account and see what I've spent my money on? They believe I'm receiving free room and board, so they'd question the charge. It's my only choice though. "I can figure it out. A few nights here won't be that much."

"No, *no*," she forces with giant eyes. "I would feel terrible if you had to spend your money because of this." She reaches out and latches onto Nikolai's wrist. "You're friends with Thora, right?"

"Best friends," he says deeply. And he curves his strong arm around the slant of my hips. He tugs me to his side. *Thump. Thump. Thump.*

Cardiac arrest is in sight again.

I feel winded. I look up at him for answers, but he pins his focus on Camila. Not me.

"So you won't mind?"

"Not at all," he says. *Wait…what is happening here?* "I have a spare couch."

Is he offering—

"Thank you *so* much." Camila releases her grip on him, and she falls to the flats of her feet. She nods to me. "I'm so busy tonight, but I'll see you later this week, right?"

I nod, realizing she's telling me goodbye. She waves before she darts over to someone in a suit-and-tie, decked out in blue glow sticks.

Nikolai's hand rises to the back of my neck, a place he's fond of touching, I've concluded. "You're glaring at me," he states.

"This is my confused look." I scrunch my face to relax the muscles. Frustrated, I give up the lame attempt.

He's trying hard not to smile. "Let's go, my demon," he says, tossing cash on the bar counter.

"Go where?"

He pockets his wallet. "My place. You can sleep on my couch for a few days, whatever you need."

I shake my head on instinct, my heart and stomach performing intricate choreography. "Why are you helping me?"

The muscles in his arms flex: stiff, unbending posture. "I feel responsible for your wellbeing," he says. "And don't ask me why. Because I don't have an answer." I watch his gray irises peruse my features in a languid stroke, like he's caressing my cheek.

Even outside the gym, he has serious bedroom eyes.

It's almost too much to handle. I exhale a shallow breath. "Just tonight," I tell him.

"Whatever you need," he repeats. I wish I could tap into his mind, even for a moment. To see how he sees me. For as much as Nikolai conveys, he's still a mystery.

And I'm the curious girl who'll step into it. Time and time again.

ACT TEN

1:52 a.m.

I've ultimately decided that with good luck comes bad luck.

There isn't plain good fortune, at least not for me. On our way to the lobby elevators, I stopped by the bathroom and discovered that I started my period. Worst timing, considering my suitcase is at Camila's place and I only have one emergency tampon in my clutch purse.

My thoughts are tumbling on all the comfortable things I'm abandoning in her apartment. Maybe one of the hotel's stores will have a survival kit. Including tampons. Please.

"Where's home for you?" he asks, punching the number 42. The elevator groans before rising. He already swiped his hotel keycard into a slit above the buttons, reserved for AE artists. Luxury suites, a perk that not many hotels offer performers.

It takes me a minute to process this question and reject my worries. "Cincinnati." I don't mention Ohio State in Columbus. I wore a collegiate shirt that first night at The Red Death, and he's observant enough to put two-and-two together. "What about you?"

He pockets his keycard. "My home is the circus."

"Timo said he was born in Munich," I remember.

Nikolai stiffens at the mention of his brother. I forgot that they had a small fight tonight. I internally grimace. *Way to go.*

But he alleviates any awkwardness by saying, "My mother traveled with the circus, even pregnant. Where it went, she went. Moving around is all I really know." He rests his shoulders against the elevator wall. "Of all my siblings, Timo was the only one born outside the United States. And he likes to tote that fact around like a prize."

I try to absorb these facts and let them distract me from my swirling thoughts. Tampons. It's truly sad, but I can't stop wishing I had a beautiful pink box of them. Actually, any color box. I'm not picky. I'd even take the giant, uncomfortable cardboard applicator kind.

"You're nervous," he points out. I really wish he wasn't so good at reading body language. I must be standing with my arms glued to my sides.

"I'm not," I refute, trying to loosen my limbs. I end up cracking my knuckles which sounds violent.

He snaps off his red glow necklace. "And you're a bad liar."

"I just…I don't have my bag." There. I let it out. Now I feel…not any better. Fantastic.

"I probably have everything you need."

I snort, on accident. I cover my face with my hand. A serious face-palm. I'm feeling a lot lamer than usual. I mean, I know I'm half-lame most of the time, with flat comebacks and unintentional demonic glares. But I'm reaching new levels.

"A toothbrush," he guesses, playing into it like a game. I peek at him through my fingers and realize he's smiling. "I have an extra one, never used."

"That's…convenient."

"One of my brothers is a kleptomaniac and likes to steal pointless things from the gift store." He adds quickly, "Don't tell anyone I said that."

"Timo?" I wonder.

"Luka. He's nineteen and another pain in my ass." Even as he says it, there's an incredible amount of love in his voice.

The elevator makes a stop on the twentieth floor. I expect more people to gather on, but it's empty, just delaying our ride.

"Pajamas," he guesses.

I didn't even think about that. My suitcase will never know how much I miss it. "I'm going to sleep in what I have on." I immobilize for the thousandth time as he inspects my long coat and stilettos again. Probably imagining what little there is underneath. The corset wire is definitely poking into my boob.

"You can sleep in one of my shirts," he offers, not as a sexual advance or anything. I think it's a friendly gesture. But then those gray irises inadvertently tear through my defenses and practically shed my clothes—I can't tell anymore. That's not a look you give to a friend.

"Thanks," I manage to say, zeroing in on the fact that I've only worn one guy's shirt before: Shay's.

"But that's not what you're stressing over," he realizes, sweeping my features once more. He turns his body more towards me, genuinely intrigued. "It's something that you don't think I have."

"Correct assumption," I nod tensely. Part of me doesn't even want him to guess it—

"Tampons," he says, right then. Yeah, I don't feel any better by that either.

The color drains from my face.

"I'm right." He tilts his head at me like *aren't I?* He doesn't balk. Or flinch or cringe.

"Maybe…"

He gives me one of the nicest smiles. "I live with a girl, myshka, so I have some. Don't worry."

I stay ashen, and the bottom of my stomach plummets to the carpet. What's worse: I sense him studying my reaction, and his lips lower, smile entirely gone.

"That's…cool," I reply back, unsure of what else to add. The elevator doors spring open, on his floor.

I'm about to step into Nikolai Kotova's world.

I just wonder who else is in it.

BY THE TIME WE REACH HIS DOOR, MY NERVES have been shot to hell. It doesn't help that music blares through the walls and into the hotel hallway. The loud pop beats are emanating from *his* room—no one else's.

Nikolai's demeanor has changed, doing a one-eighty. His eyes tighten and no longer fix on me but whatever's happening inside.

I picture drugs. Lots of drugs. Alcohol. Maybe even dry humping. An orgy of epic Vegas proportions.

"Is…this normal?" I ask. "The music, I mean."

"It's not uncommon, unfortunately," he says lowly. He swipes his card, and when the light flashes green, he pushes through with an authoritative stride.

But I freeze right in the doorway. Surprise widens my eyes.

It's empty.

No grinding bodies. No spilt liquor. No rolled dollar bills and cocaine.

I tentatively walk inside, his suite a lot fancier than I anticipated. The back wall is all window with a skyline view of the city. The furniture is modern and sleek with black and white décor. I can't help but notice the strain in Nikolai's posture as he walks further inside, and I don't think it's about me staying at his place. Or else he would've been like this on the elevator.

Suede decorative pillows litter the ground, and the television blares, playing reruns of a popular reality show. Nikolai finds the stereo remote on the glass coffee table, powering that off first.

My ears almost stop ringing, but the television speakers are louder without the interference. On the TV, four guys stand in the cold, surrounded by snow. One sneers, "You must be a real f**king idiot if you think we'd be okay with someone our age sleeping with our girlfriends' seventeen-year-old *little* sister."

"She's a model, man. We've spent nights at our friends' flat—" The television blinks to black. Nikolai sets down the remote.

"I hate that guy," he says under his breath, referring to Julian, the show's villain.

My brows rise. "You watch *Princesses of Philly*?" It's a guilty pleasure, only one season to keep rewatching.

"Katya is obsessed with it," he says. I guess he watches it with *her*. Whoever her is. Maybe he has a Shay. A girl Shay, I mean.

A Haley to his Lucas.

For some reason, this thought only downturns my lips. I trek forward while he bends down and picks up a pair of black heels and checks his watch again. I try not to notice the silver purse and studded clutch lying around too.

My collarbones protrude as I hold in a breath. "I didn't think Aerial Ethereal rooms would be this nice," I say, making small talk. I pass the kitchen and enter the carpeted living room where he stands.

Nikolai glances back at me. "I wish they weren't. AE uses it as an excuse to keep our salaries lower than they should be. I would give up the view for another grand a month."

I probably would too.

Unconsciously, I assemble more evidence of Katya living with him: a scarf on the leather barstool, lip gloss and mascara beside the coffee pot, and necklaces dangling on a key hook.

His attention is latched on the spiral staircase that leads to one bedroom up above, like a loft. I wonder if that's her room.

I re-knot the straps of my coat. "Is your girlfriend going to be upset by me staying here…?"

I trail off as his masculine gaze pins on me. "I don't have a girlfriend."

"Girl that's a friend," I throw it out there.

"My little sister lives with me," he clarifies for the first time.

I feel like an idiot. "You have a sister?" I think I'm wincing at myself.

"And four brothers," he says. "But Katya is the only one who stays with me."

I relax at the notion that I won't be causing drama tonight. At least, that's what I'm telling myself. It's for no other reason. "Does she care that I'm crashing here?"

"I haven't told her yet."

My breathing is strained, and I know I wear another pained expression. His sister will hate me on our very first encounter, the rude interloper who's occupying her couch and disturbing her marathons of PoPhilly. "Did you text her earlier or drop any hints?"

Please say yes.

"She didn't answer me. I'm going to tell her right now, and likely, she won't mind. So breathe, Thora." His eyes graze my collarbones.

I exhale deeply, taking his word for it.

He climbs the metal stairs, and then his knuckles rap the upstairs door. "*Katya*," he says her name with a Russian lilt. "*Katya*." Then he adds something in Russian. He stops himself short in what appears to be mid-sentence with a frustrated noise, and then switches to English. "Open the door. I need to talk to you."

No reply. He twists the knob and disappears inside the room. Only a second later, he rushes out, skipping two or three stairs on his way down.

My pulse jackhammers. "What's wrong?" I ask.

"She's not in her room."

I check the time on my phone. "It's only two in the morning. It's Vegas, right? She could just be out with her friends."

He bypasses me and grabs the keycard off the kitchen counter. "She's only sixteen," he says, setting those pulsing grays on me. "She has a curfew."

I'd be panicking if Tanner was wandering around Vegas too, so I immediately understand his concern.

I hang back, uncertain on my place in this situation.

But he stops by the door, a hand on the frame and motions to me. "Come on."

"I can stay here," I tell him. "In case she returns."

"I have cousins for that."

Maybe he's afraid I'll steal something if he leaves me alone. I can understand that too. I'm a stranger, really. I use this fact to head over to him.

"We need to be quick," he says as I pass his body. "I want to find her before three a.m."

"What happens after three?" I ask.

"I don't know." His voice is deep and hollow. "I've always found her before then."

ACT ELEVEN

2:27 a.m.

My ankles and toes are blistered, the summer heat building beneath my coat. We walk briskly on the crowded strip, and I try to keep up with his lengthy stride to my short one.

The seventh drunk guy whistles at me from afar. I spot him waving his wallet. Nikolai has his hand firmly on the small of my back while he speaks quickly into his phone. If I was venturing alone, I think I'd be a little frightened. I'd need one wingman or wingwoman with me. Like a Camila.

But I can't deny—a six-foot-five Russian athlete has been the best defense. No one has approached us or even really considered the feat.

I listen to Nikolai's deep voice, picking up Katya's name through the jargon. He's called all of his brothers and now he's onto a list of his cousins. Apparently she didn't mention her nightly plans to anyone.

He suddenly pockets his phone. "This way." His hand tightens on my waist, and he redirects me to a crosswalk, a hoard of people gathered underneath the red-hand symbol.

"You found her?" I ask.

"One of my cousin's friends saw her at Fellini's. It's a restaurant on the strip." So we're close. Even so, he never relaxes. His eyes flit to my stilettos. "If your feet start to bleed, tell me."

I think they're probably close. I suck up the pain and just nod. His sister is missing, and the last thing he really needs is a five-minute break to inspect a couple blisters.

Cars screech to a halt, and everyone begins to cross. I dodge an incoming girl in a huge feather headdress, like her burlesque show just ended. Nikolai isn't fazed by the Vegas nightlife, standing erect and steadfast. But all of it distracts me.

The fancy dresses, the limos, the commotion—a city that never sleeps. He nearly braces me to his side, probably so I don't face-plant in my heels.

"Does your sister break curfew a lot?" I ask.

"Only recently." He pauses. "She doesn't want to live in Vegas anymore. She's been begging me to let her audition for Noctis, and I keep telling her no."

"Noctis," I recall the name. "That's one of the traveling shows."

He nods. "It's the show my parents are in. She just wants to be closer to them."

It clicks. His parents aren't even *in* Vegas, so that's why she lives with Nikolai. And why Timo runs around The Masquerade so freely. In the short silence, Nikolai is lost in thought and I try to pay attention to the divots in the cement sidewalk.

He hugs me closer as a group of rowdy guys pass us, and then he instinctively wraps his arm around my shoulders, as though claiming me as more than a friend. Just to ward them away, I know. If I wasn't wearing a "what's underneath the long coat?" getup, it'd be a different story. I think. Maybe.

Maybe not.

He's the most touchy-feely guy I've ever encountered. I'm not surprised either, considering he's in tune with his body and spent years lifting and catching women for a living.

Thankfully, no one accidentally shoves into my arm. And I'm left in a warm cocoon, made by Russia. Believe me, I'm not complaining.

Even after they've gone, Nikolai keeps this embrace.

"Why not let your sister audition?" I ask him.

"Because she wouldn't pass the first round. She's not good enough for Noctis."

I wince. "She could get better—"

"She could," he says, "but she doesn't try. Katya is average in her discipline. It's just a fact."

I frown. "What's her discipline?"

"Russian bar." He tucks me close to his side again as a giant bachelor party passes us. "She's in Viva at The Masquerade, but all shows have different levels of difficulty. The Russian bar routine in Noctis is too complicated." He adds, "And she'd be angry that our parents wouldn't pull strings for her, just so she can be in it. I'd rather Katya hate me than hate them."

That's more than just kind. It's selfless and something I'd never expect of him the first time we met at The Red Death.

It hits me right now. He's a full-fledged adult, a man, with more responsibilities and maturity than I probably contain in my pinky finger. And it's…scarily attractive. When it should be just the opposite. I should draw towards career-driven, young guys who just graduated from college. Who don't have their shit together. Just like me.

But I guess when my world is in flux, I naturally gravitate towards someone who's more stable.

And he's that fortress again. Standing tall in a land of straw huts.

"This is it," he tells me, stopping abruptly in front of Fellini's. He pushes inside the upscale Italian restaurant that's at least a mile from The Masquerade. People cram around the door, waiting to be seated. The dim lighting is going to make it hard to spot his sister.

His hand falls to my lower back again. "This way," he says, guiding me past the hostess podium.

"What does she look like?" I ask him, inspecting the cloth tables and leather booths from afar, walking deeper into Fellini's. Everyone wears formal outfits: suits and ties, cocktail dresses. Nikolai fits in with his black slacks and white button-down.

"Brunette, young..." he trails off. "There she is." Relief fills his voice, and he zeroes in on a girl in a corner booth, a purple feather boa around her neck. Her straight brown hair is parted in the center, draping along her thin shoulders.

Glitter is splashed across her pale skin and chest, wearing a low-cut top.

She looks her age.

The extra mascara and red lipstick, applied with a heavy hand, makes it seem like she's trying too hard to be older, like costume makeup. Pain twists my stomach.

Nikolai storms forward, his angry stride way too lengthy for my leg-span. I lose his pace the minute he detaches from me.

As soon as Katya notices her brother's giant, consuming presence, her large, orb-like eyes widen even more. "Oh crap," she says.

It's like slow motion. I watch her turn, as if to shield her face with her wall of hair, and her elbow catches the half-filled martini glass. It splashes on the tablecloth and just barely misses the candle.

One of the three other girls giggles and rights the glass. "Party foul."

Katya slumps further in the leather cushion, refusing to meet Nikolai's eyes as he halts right beside her—with me in company. He doesn't give the other girls a single glance. But I do.

They appear even older than me, maybe early thirties or late twenties. With curled hair and bandaged dresses. Katya, slender, lanky and flat-chested, is just a girl in comparison. I try to think positively. She probably knows the women from the circus. It could be worse, right? At least forty-year-old men didn't accompany her to a late-night dinner.

Nikolai speaks in Russian, his tone rough and biting. I waver beside him, unsure of my place again. I'm certain it's probably back in Cincinnati.

Silence lags in Nikolai's speech.

"I'm not talking," she hiccups, "…to you." She hiccups again. "Unless you speak in…" She sips her water. "English." Her eyelids droop, and she slips on some of her words. I wonder if "no Russian talk" is a tactic that Katya employs out of anger towards him. If so, it works. He's most definitely frustrated by it, his nose flaring and forehead wrinkled.

"Stand up, Katya. We're going home."

"To…Russia," she hiccups, her lids still heavy.

"You've never been to Russia, so no," he says lowly. "Stand *up*."

The blonde says, "Don't be a mood killer. Stay and have a drink with us."

"Yeah," another pipes in. "We have plenty of room for you and your friend." They scoot closer together, smashed in the middle.

I'm no longer invisible. Katya finally looks over at me, as if I appeared out of thin air. Surprise breaches her face for a second, especially as she stares between me and her brother.

She suddenly rises from the table, too quickly, and falls back into the seat.

"Party foul," the blonde laughs again.

I actually put my demonic-looking eyes to good use. Unfortunately, she never meets my glare.

Katya tries to stand again, and Nikolai reaches out and grabs underneath her arm, steadying her. "This is what happens," Nikolai says, "when you decide to go on a Vegas adventure without one of us. At least *text me*, Katya. Stop screening my calls."

She presses a hand to her ear. "You don't…have to…scream." Her hiccups infiltrated that statement, big time.

"I'm not even raising my voice. You're drunk, Kat." He shakes his head repeatedly, and I see the guilt and concern brim.

She stumbles on her own feet, and he wraps a strong arm around her shoulders. "My purse," she says quietly.

I collect her bright pink clutch and pass it to her. She meets my eyes, and I notice that hers glass with something much different than Timo's youthful light and Nikolai's unyielding darkness. Hers are full of sadness and nothing more.

"Katya," her friend eagerly calls.

She fixes her purple boa, avoiding the girl.

"What about those tickets to Amour?" the girl asks. "You can still hook us up, right?"

"We only have two more nights here," the other adds. "We need them soon."

My mouth slowly drops. They aren't part of the circus…or even Katya's friends. They're just random people, using her.

"Buy the tickets yourself," Nikolai sneers. "Don't solicit a sixteen-year-old girl for them."

All three women recoil.

Good.

I don't know why, but I feel insanely protective of Katya. Just by looking at her. She's like broken glass in a world of steel and iron. I sense Nikolai studying me for a second, and when I turn to him, I know my thoughts are written on my face.

If I'm protective—then his concern is on another wavelength. A scale reserved for parents to their children. And I don't mean to point out that he's not doing a good job parenting…but his locked jaw, his coiled muscles, they all say that he feels it.

That he's failed his little sister somehow.

But he found her. That's the important part.

"HOW CAN YOU BE HIS FRIEND?" KATYA ASKS ME in the taxi. She hugs the door while I'm wedged between her and Nikolai, how she wanted to be seated. "He's so mean."

Nikolai stares hard out the window, his jaw muscles tensing. Katya's glazed eyes almost well with tears.

This is a bad night.

I'm stuck in the middle of Kotova family issues, and honestly, my heart aches more than it ever has. I never thought staying in Vegas meant diving deeper into their lives. And so far, I don't think I would take it back.

I'm not sure I can be any kind of helpful presence, but I can try. My perseverance is all I have. "He's been really nice to me, so far," I mention.

"You're the only one then," she mutters.

Nikolai rotates to Katya. "Thora is spending the night. If you have a problem with it, tell me now."

Her chin trembles a little, and her big orb-like eyes flit to me. "You know, he's never…ever brought a girl over for the night before."

I frown at Nikolai. "I…didn't know."

He whispers under his breath to me, "Not that she knows of." Right. He'll sneak late-night hookups in and out, maybe. He watches his sister for a second as she rests her temple to the window. "Don't wear Timo's glitter anymore, at least not on your chest, Katya."

I don't think that's the problem. It's just how much she applied. I wonder if her mom ever had the chance to teach her about makeup before she left for Noctis. Maybe all she's had are her brothers and performers, who apply costume makeup.

"I heard…you the first time," she say slowly, trying not to slur her words.

"I thought you said that you're ignoring everything I say in Russian."

"I am. I was…" She winces and touches her head like a migraine is setting in. "Do you mind…not talking to me right now?"

"Yes, I mind."

Her chin quakes again. "He's my least favorite brother."

"And you're my least favorite sister," he retorts.

Under her breath, she whispers, "I'm your only sister." Her voice is so solemn. I offer a side-hug, and she wipes beneath her eyes, smudging her mascara. I use the sleeve of my coat to rub off the black streak.

"Thanks," she sniffs, her skin pale. I can tell she's nauseous by the way she hunches forward.

"If you puke in the taxi, you're paying for the extra fee, Katya," Nikolai tells her.

Way to kick a girl while she's down. He's kind of tough on her, but I guess, maybe he should be. She did break her curfew. She did drink underage.

Katya puts her hand to her mouth and stifles a gag.

"We're almost there," I tell her. I'm actually not sure how far we are. "You've got this," I encourage. If I'm good at anything, it's motivational boosts.

She shuts her eyes and concentrates on her breathing while I rub her back. Her head rests on my shoulder. I think she may pass out soon.

A phone rings, the normal default tone. Mine is wind chimes, so I don't even open my purse. Nikolai tenses as he digs into his pocket and puts the cell to his ear.

He says one foreign word, like a greeting, so I figure it's a relative on the other end.

Maybe two seconds pass before his nose flares and he rubs his face roughly. When he begins *yelling* in Russian, I know the night isn't over just yet.

I sense that it's one of those never-ending ones. Where the early morning seems to extend for infinite amounts of time, until so much happens that you question why a week hasn't passed yet.

I wonder how many of these nights Nikolai experiences. In my life, I've had maybe one: a drunken New Year's Eve party that went from a 24-hour diner, to a friend-of-a-friend's house, to the roof of a hotel, ending in the backseat of Shay's Jeep.

I can't imagine this being the norm. Not for anyone.

ACT TWELVE

2:53 a.m.

By the time the taxi screeches to a halt in front of The Masquerade, Katya has passed out on my shoulder, just as I predicted. Her mouth is open as she lets out short breaths.

I carefully reach over her to open the door, but Nikolai has already walked around to my side of the cab.

"I have her," he tells me, slipping his phone in his pocket.

He lifts his sister in his arms, cradling her, and I climb out and shut the door. I saw him pay the driver, so I don't ask about it. "What's going on?" I'm the seventh wheel to imaginary people. I can't make sense of his cousins or brothers because they're just deep voices on a phone line.

"You'll find out soon," he says lowly, his brows hardened like his voice.

I don't prod. I follow him through the revolving glass doors and into the hotel lobby that pairs with one of the casino floors. We stay off the carpet that contains the slots and tables, just walking on the cobblestone.

My feet scream with each step. The straps pinch my pinky toes and scrape against my ankle. I'm seconds from unbuckling my heels, right here. Just as I consider the plan, a boisterous crowd tears my mind in a new direction.

By the map kiosk, young guys, twenties most likely, all talk over each other, gesticulating with their hands. It's not like they're fighting. They're just having too many conversations at once.

One stands out with a gold carnival mask and staff that he twirls with precision, his cross earring swaying as he whips his head.

Timo.

It's not hard to discern their features from here: dark brown hair, extreme height, broad shoulders and gray eyes. Kotovas. A mixture of cousins and brothers, maybe.

I feel like I'm descending deeper and deeper into Nikolai's life with each passing minute. I'm the last audience member at his performance, the ringleader drawing me slowly behind the curtains. His world is just so different from mine that it's hard to turn away.

Nikolai speaks under his breath to me, "I'm going to have a fight with Timo. Just to warn you."

"Okay," I say softly, not sure what else to add.

He gives me a look that I regard as *thanks*, one that encompasses more than just this moment, I think. I've been tagging along all night, and I haven't done much. But I haven't made his life harder, so there's that. And I thought his biggest stress was Amour—carrying the weight of an entire show on his shoulders.

"Luka," Nikolai shouts as we approach all of them, still chatting like nothing has changed. An athletic guy, dressed in a plain gray shirt and jeans, squeezes through the pack before standing beside his brother.

I thought I was invisible with my five-foot-two height, but somehow Luka trains on me first.

"Hey…I recognize you," he says. I feel my facial muscles tense. "You're the titty pierc—"

Nikolai smacks the back of his head, skillfully holding Katya with one arm.

Titty Piercing. I'll take the Virgin Mary nickname over that, any day.

Luka gapes at his older brother. "What?" He touches his head.

"I'm *holding* our passed-out sister, and that's the first thing you have to say?" he nearly growls out the words. His eyes slice through Luka. And I thought I enraged him during the first auditions—this is a new spectrum of pissed off.

"Dimitri would've made the same comment!" Luka rebuts.

"Dimitri?" Nikolai lets out an aggravated sound. "If you're modeling yourself after someone who's been to jail three times, then I've severely miscalculated how smart you are, Luka."

"Pissing on the street shouldn't even be a crime," Luka retorts, still gawking. He outstretches his arms like *come on.*

Nikolai just glares. Right at him.

And Luka shrinks back, his shoulders lowering in regret. He just now registers his little sister in Nikolai's arms, and guilt spreads across his face. It's clear to me that Nikolai has a lot of influence over them—that his words matter to his siblings.

"I'll take Kat back to her room," Luka offers, glancing once over his shoulder. Timo staggers as he laughs, full-bellied ones that brighten his face beneath the gold carnival mask. He rests his hip on the map kiosk while his humor overtakes him. "He wants to go to Hex down the street."

Nikolai rubs his jaw. "The bar that closes at five?"

"Yeah." Luka scoops his little sister, cradling her body with ease. "You can't tell him no. He's eighteen."

"Just let me handle it," he says. "Keep your phone on. Don't steal anything. And thank you for calling me about him."

Luka nods, mutters a few things in Russian, and breaks from the pack, aiming for the elevators. This shift in the group alerts Timo, and it takes him about one-point-two seconds to finally zone in on us.

He points his gold staff at me with a dazzling wide grin and says, "Thora James." Then he bows. I can't smile this time, partially because I feel Nikolai boiling beside me.

It's like when I'm in the air, about to land a double layout, and I know I've overcorrected. I know that I'm going to stumble when I hit the mat.

It's just like that.

I see the bad thing before it happens. It's rare that I fixate on the incoming storm, but I'm starting to, I realize.

Timo notices Nikolai beside me, and his sparkling grin slowly fades.

Nikolai steps forward, and the entire group silences. More out of respect than fear, I believe. The power he possesses, over a bunch of rowdy, drunken guys, takes me aback. "You didn't check on Katya like I asked," he says lowly.

Timo leans his bodyweight on the staff. "I called her. Chill out, Nikolai. Or better yet, go to bed." He laughs, expecting everyone to join in with him. No one does. The rest of the guys mutter quietly and shake their heads. Everyone is on the God of Russia's side. No one cheers against him.

Except maybe Timo.

Nikolai speaks again, his voice harsh and words coarse. Someone wins a jackpot, the casino floor blaring the electric slide song. Nikolai never trips up, and Timo's knuckles whiten on his staff. They shout back and forth—for what feels like five minutes, until we're ushered outside by hotel management.

On the other side of the glass doors, no cool breeze lessens the sticky heat beneath my coat. I linger, unsure of where my place is again. Then Timo pushes his mask up to his forehead, their argument switching to English for the first time.

"I'm not twelve anymore!" Timo screams, pain leeching his voice. His face reddens with the words. "I want to *live* my life, and you can either follow me or *leave me alone*." He hails a cab, shutting his brother out.

Nikolai breathes deeply, like he's run a full marathon. He rubs his lips and then turns his head, searching almost. I'm surprised when his gray irises land on me, about ten feet away. He gestures to me with two fingers like *come here.*

I approach, wobbling in my heels. His eyes flit to them once.

For some reason, I decide to speak first, "Do you need…a hug?" I internally cringe at how lame that probably seemed.

The corner of his lip tics upward, barely. "No, but I have to make one more pit stop. I'm not leaving him with my cousins."

I swallow my uncertainty. "I can wait here if you want."

"I don't want that," he tells me. "I'd rather you join me. Don't ask me why." He shakes his head a couple times. "Because I still don't have an answer."

Part of me questions whether he sees me as a sibling. Like another Timo and Katya and Luka to fret over. It worries me. Because in no way do I want to saddle this guy with more stress. That's not my intention by staying in Vegas. If that's the case, I can step out of his world.

"Your eyes are black," he notes, his lips downturned. "If you want to stay—"

"Do you think of me as a sister?" I suddenly ask. "Is that why I'm here? I mean, here, as in crashing at your place. And…" I look around at the outside of The Masquerade, taxi cabs dropping off drunken girls and more casino high-rises lit-up and twinkling in the distance. It's one of those moments that I just wonder—how did I end up *right here* in my life? In Vegas. With a fourth generation artist. It's one of those surreal moments that I don't want to take back, even if it's confusing and muddled and gray.

I feel his fingers beneath my chin. He tilts my head, so that I irrefutably meet his powerful gaze. I see the answer in them. Before he even says it.

"No, Thora." His hand slides to the back of my neck, each fingertip hot. His grasp protective. He steps nearer, his legs knocking against mine, tension winding my muscles. His other hand cups my jaw, most of me in his possession. Right now.

It's definitely not a familial gesture. It's not even a friendly one. Shay would *never* touch me like this. He would never let his body do the talking like Nikolai. He'd tell me straight up: "I think you're cute, but not like *that,* Thora. Come on, we're friends."

Nikolai's thumb skims my cheek, like I'm worthy of more affection. His gaze dances again. Along my lips. *He's going to kiss me.* I read his movements, as he always reads mine. And I keep concluding, *he's going to kiss me.* He draws me even closer to his body.

He lowers his head towards mine, and just when he's so incredibly close, he changes course to my ear. Huskily, he whispers, "Come with me."

It sounds sexual off his tongue. Especially now that he's touching me this way outside of the gym. He's not acting or putting on a show. This is him. Entirely.

I open my mouth to form a semi-coherent response.

"Nikolai!" a guy shouts. Nikolai raises his head, away from me. His cousin has a hand on the frame of the cab and waves him to join.

Nikolai glances back at me, the pull not lost. He lets go and I unconsciously sway forward.

"Your choice," he breathes, his gray eyes raking my small frame before he heads to the cab.

I'm not usually this impulsive.

On a normal day, I list pros and cons. And I listen to the pros (rightfully so) and then go from there. So it takes me a second longer to gather my bearings and decide on my next action.

I don't want this never-ending night to end. Not like this. Not in this way. I'd be imagining what he's doing while I sulk alone. I'd construct a hazy picture of Hex and the events that lead thereafter. And I'd wonder what would've happen between me and him had I attended.

But the mystery of the night is not always kind. It can end in regret.

I watch him climb into the cab.

And I listen to my gut that says *you got this, Thora James.*

Don't be afraid.

Whatever regrets I do have—it won't be staying back, wondering and imagining. I want to live to the fullest degree. So I sprint to the cab, and slide in before he has the chance to shut the door.

I don't look at Nikolai yet, but I sense his surprise.

I just stare straight ahead, feeling way cooler than I know I am. "To Hex," I tell the taxi driver, like in the movies. How the badass girl just controls her own fate.

And then Nikolai says, "I already gave him the address." There's a smile in his voice.

Nice one, Thora. "I'm a work in progress," I say softly, more to myself.

He wraps his muscular arm around my shoulders. "We all probably are."

ACT THIRTEEN

4:01 a.m.

Bubble machines blow out shiny orbs, multi-colored lights casting pink, blue, and yellow shades all around us. Timo dances in the center of Hex like nothing can ground him. Full of energy. Of life. Most of the Kotovas are at Sublime down the street, but we've stuck around this bar.

"You're trying to get me drunk," Nikolai says after I push a fifth vodka shot towards him. I lower my butt on the stool next to his, empty glasses scattered in front of us. I've been nursing another tequila sunrise and supplying him shots for the past thirty minutes.

"I'm not trying to take advantage of you," I say, no filter.

He grins with raised brows like *you're serious?* When he realizes I am, a full, gorgeous smile overpowers his features. And then he tilts his head at me. "That's highly unlikely. First, I'm six-five—"

"I guessed right," I say to myself, resting an elbow on the cold bar in delight.

He says something deeply in Russian.

"What was that?" I ask, not as scowly I hope.

"I said, *you're cute.*" He throws back the shot, not even a little tipsy yet.

"Like an unsexy friend?" I blame the tequila for that. Never would have I said it sober. I think.

He licks his lips and leans closer than before, his mouth next to my ear as he breathes, "Why do you think you're unsexy?"

Because that was sexier than anything I've ever said or done before. I heat all over. "...that's what cute means. Or so I've been told."

"Your friend is an asshole," he suddenly says, "whichever one told you that." His gaze darkens.

"He's my best friend."

"It's a guy?" His brows shoot up. "Even worse."

I shake my head. "He was just making a point," I defend.

"That you're unsexy and only his friend?" He cocks his head. "That point could've been made a better way." He downs another shot. "And secondly," he returns to the main topic, why I can't take advantage of him, "I'm Russian. We drink until the bottle is empty." Meaning he can hold his liquor.

Still, I have my motives. When we first arrived at Hex, he acted like Timo's chaperone, hawkeyed and on alert, prepared to spring from the stool and break up an impending fight. There is no storm, I've decided. And it's pointless to stare at the sky, waiting for one.

"The shots are a distraction," he says, gripping my attention again. "I know."

"Is it working?" I ask.

We face each other. His back isn't to the dance floor. He still has a good view of his brother out of his peripheral.

"Not completely, but it's cute of you to try. And by cute I mean the opposite of your *best friend's* definition." He says "best friend" very bitterly, like I need to find a new one.

I take the plunge. "Do you want to be my…" *new best friend.* I chicken out. That's the right hook or line or whatever to sound smooth and cool—something Camila would've said in response. And I effed it up.

He drums his fingers on the bar as he studies me, knowingly. "Do I want to be your best friend?"

I open my mouth to say *yeah*, but I lose the words by his amusement. "…maybe."

"Maybe?" He gives me a look. "No, that's definitely what you were going to say."

"You can't know that."

"Tell me I'm wrong then," he challenges.

I surrender. I'm weak in the face of lies. "Okay, you were right. Do you? Want to be my new best friend, I mean?" I wait for his answer, wishing I would've just had the bravado to unleash that from the beginning.

He takes his time, *sipping* a shot, very slowly. He's doing this on purpose.

"Are you going to answer my question?"

When he finishes it, he licks his wet lips and sets down the glass. Then his eyes unhurriedly meet mine. "No."

I frown. "No…about the question or being my best friend?"

He simply stares at me, knowing very well that he holds all of the cards. I'd rather not be at the mercy of this question and his vague answer. So I speak up again.

"I change my mind," I say. "I don't want to have the devil as a best friend."

"So says my demon." His finger runs along the rim of his shot glass, absentmindedly. I wonder if by slipping into the cab, I agreed to sleep with him. More than just on the couch. Sex. With a twenty-six-year-old Russian athlete.

I'm on my period, my inside voice shrieks in horror. Maybe I shouldn't have asked if he saw me as a sibling. The answer has altered my perception of little things—like how he watches me intently. How his gaze dips to my coat, the straps beginning to unknot and reveal my risqué costume.

I'm seventy-five percent sure that he might be thinking about sex. About the devil screwing all of his demons. On red sheets.

Okay, I'm one-hundred percent thinking about sex. Not the act of doing it. But all the baggage that is attached to it. And *I'm on my period.* And he knows it. Which is so much worse.

Now I'm thinking about him thinking about my period.

This is too much.

I chug my tequila sunrise. It burns. I set it down roughly, about a quarter left. And I gasp for breath like I downed lighter fluid. Slowly, I look at Nikolai.

I shouldn't have. His brows just rise, his lips slightly upturned. I'm overly aware of how much older he is than me. And of his *it's complicated* status.

I think I need to change mine.

This is so complicated my head hurts.

...maybe that's just the tequila.

He reaches down and seizes my ankle, lifting my leg onto his lap. I watch him unbuckle my stiletto heel, revealing a battered foot with three blistered toes, nearly bloody. But they're free, the air stinging the sores. He gives me a disapproving look—since I didn't tell him how badly they'd been hurting.

Then he removes the second stiletto and keeps my legs draped across his lap. "Better," he knows, sipping his next shot. He soaks in my long legs and then says, "When you perform, you have beautiful lines." He pauses. "It's what every director said after you auditioned. It's why you were brought here."

I stiffen. I've shut out the audition, filed it away in that dusty folder.

Now that he's retrieved it, a nauseous pit wedges between my ribs. Sex is a better agonizing thought, I realize.

But I take the opportunity to ask him, "What do I need to work on then?"

"They said that you were just background. Others onstage would outshine you. You don't have the passion."

My throat feels dry. *I don't have the passion.* I've flown across the country to be here. I've risked everything. What is that if not passion? I know it's not sexual or sensual, the passion they mean, but it's *something.* There's something in me.

I just have to translate it to everyone else.

"Okay. I'll work on it." *Somehow.*

"Do you ever quit?" he asks me, his tone serious.

Softly, I say, "I can't."

"Why? Even if everyone tells you that you don't possess the right amount of talent, you'd keep trying?"

"Because I love it," I say like there is no other option. In my bones, there isn't. I feel like I'm fighting for my happiness. And no one else can sense it or see it but me.

"You're cursed then," he tells me. "There are people with far greater talent, who don't love it the way that you do."

The weight of his statement sinks in.

That's just life, my dad would say.

People will always be better than you. Whether they enjoy it or not isn't a factor. It's superfluous.

"Do you love it?" I ask him.

His eyes fall as he contemplates this. "Not as much as I used to. But the circus is my only love."

"What about your family?" I think of Katya and Luka and Timo. I can tell—just by the way he protects them—that there's a tremendous amount of love there.

He smiles. "Circus is family."

The sentiment washes over me, a second wave of chills. Not even a second later, the bartender pushes more vodka shots towards us. Timo knows him, so he's been supplying us free drinks all night. I pick up a shot since my sunrise is almost empty.

"To finding your sister," I tell Nikolai.

He raises his shot. "No," he says, "to your first week in Vegas."

My heart clenches. He remembered why I stopped by The Red Death to see Camila. I sway a bit, and the overflowing shot spills on my fingers. Fantastic. I try to peel the soggy napkin from the bar.

Then Nikolai smoothly takes my hand. And he sucks the vodka off my fingers.

I freeze as his eyes flit up to mine, while his lips warm my skin. Sex pops back in my brain. Especially as his tongue works with skill.

When he finishes, he even sips a little from the rim of my glass, so I won't spill more on myself.

This happens in maybe less than fifteen seconds. It felt like eternity. He clinks his glass back to mine. I haven't unfrozen yet. *He wants to have sex.* No, he doesn't. He downs the shot, and his eyes flit to my boobs. *Yes he does.*

"What are your plans?" he asks, out of the blue. Or maybe it's been on his mind instead of sex. I can't tell anymore.

"To practice every day before work at Phantom, audition for any openings that come up," I say with a satisfied nod. I like this plan. It seems solid.

He tenses more. If the alcohol is doing anything, it's making him even *more* touchy-feely than he already is. His large hand stays firm on my legs. But he's still rigid, commanding. All masculine and man. What anyone would expect of a lead male in a show about love.

He checks on his brother with a quick glance before focusing one-hundred percent on me. "It's unlikely that Amour will ever have another opening. What happened with my old partner…it's rare." He hasn't ever mentioned Tatyana before now. I can tell it's a sore subject, so I won't surface it any more than he has.

"There are other shows besides Amour," I say. "There's Infini and Viva. Seraphine is traveling, but they'll be in Los Angeles around May. Plus there are other troupes if Aerial Ethereal isn't hiring."

The charm drains from his features, leaving gunmetal eyes with no shine. "High Flyers Company isn't safe, Thora. They hire riggers as contract employees, pay them close to nothing, and give them *days* to learn how to harness artists before beginning shows."

"I think I'll be alright in my discipline." Riggers sometimes have an artist's life in their hands since they fasten harnesses and work the wires.

"Aerial silk," he guesses my discipline right. "But if you're in group acts with intricate choreography and a new apparatus that *needs* a harness, you'll be asked to wear one. You're risking your life with High Flyers, so please be smart and don't even entertain them."

"Emblem & Fitz Circus," I say, one that's based in London. High Flyers is AE's direct competition, since Emblem is known for their carnival shows. Elephants. A ring leader.

"That can't be the circus you've fallen in love with if you're here," he says. "It's apples and oranges."

"So what do you suggest I do?" I ask, about to retract my legs from his lap, but he holds tighter.

"I'll train you."

My lips part. "What?"

"I want to train you."

"You're drunk," I breathe, half hoping he's not.

"I'm nearly sober." He adds, "Every January, AE has auditions to find new talent, regardless if a show is new or not. Most contracts are renewed and cancelled every new year, so you have a better shot to fill a role then."

January.

That's seven months away from now. He's willing to train me for *seven months.* "You don't have time," I say. "You have a new partner—"

"If I don't train you," he says each word like it's uniquely important, "you will fail, Thora. You're *not* good enough. I can't put it more plainly than that. I'm sorry."

I want to be the better person and not accept it—knowing how much he has on his plate. But this is a dream offer. He has so much experience, the kind that I need to survive in this industry. "Why help me?" I ask softly. I expect him to say, *I don't have an answer.*

"I admire your courage. I know what you've given up to be here. I know the kind of artist it takes to land a role. I know that you won't receive one on your own. And I imagine you, myshka, two years from now, working at Phantom with the same aspirations, the same dreams, in the same place where you are now. It's wasted courage. And wasted love. You shouldn't have to waste those things."

I'm speechless.

And overwhelmed. When someone reaches out and gives you a hand—for no other reason than to see your success—it's powerful. And rare.

He wipes beneath my eye with his thumb. "I'd rather feed your hunger than watch you starve, and you're foolish if you say no."

I shake my head, another tear slipping. "I wasn't going to."

He cups my jaw, tilting my head up so I stare right into him. "Good."

4:54 A.M.

My head spins. Buzzed. No wait—I teeter, sans heels, on my bare soles. The sidewalk hot, even in the summer night. Definitely beyond buzzed. I drank past my limit. They just kept comin' and I kept grabbin'. I think I was dazed and confused by Nikolai's offer.

"It was a real offer?" I ask him, his hands firmly on the crook of my hips beside me. I think I slurred a bit of that. But he smiles in my foggy vision and mutters out a response. I only caught: …*again*… I've asked it multiple times?

I'm the sloppy drunk.

And judging by his roaming hands, he's the flirty one.

It's everything I imagined in life.

At least my sarcasm is internally on point right now. My mind is amused. I think we're waiting for a cab, his cousins—lots of cousins—and Timo surrounding us.

We're back in a group.

It's hot.

I shed my coat and sling it over my forearm. It whips out of my possession and into Nikolai's. He blazes me with his intensity, searing trails down my corseted waist, pushed-up cleavage and my thighs in black fish-net. He's thinking about sex. I'm thinking about sex.

We're all thinking about sex here.

"Those eyes…" I point a finger at him, my breath shallow. "…are bad."

His lips rise. And all I hear from his response is *myshka*. My nickname, whatever that nickname means, has never sounded more sexual off his lips. And then his hands fall low to my hipbones, too close to more sensitive places.

He knows this.

Right?

I rest my palms on his sculpted abs. "You're touching me."

"I've touched you before," he says huskily.

Truths.

Lots of truths tonight. Barefooted, my head reaches his chest. Literally. His bedroom eyes are things made from sin. "The devil is… very, very…hot." I wonder if that went smoothly or not.

Probably not.

I feel his lips brush my ear with the heat of his breath. Then he lifts me, so effortlessly that we may as well have been on stage.

I'm closer to his jaw, his mouth…

One of his hands clutches my ass, and my legs hook around his waist. "What am…I doing here?" I say aloud. Did I say that out loud?

"You're in my arms." He holds the back of my neck, his thumb putting the right pressure on the right tender muscles. A pleasured sound tickles my throat. I'm not even sure if I contained it.

His cousins begin to shout. I think. I hear a couple car horns and laughter.

"Why am I in your arms?" my drunken, sloppy-self asks.

He tries to hide his smile, but I see it peek from the corners of his lips. "Because you're little. And I'm not." He combs my flyaway hairs, and he rests his palm on my cheek, sliding it to the back of my neck again.

His touch electrifies my skin. I shiver. Or shudder. Maybe both.

Timo speaks, somewhere close to us. "You're a Grade-A flirty drunk..."

Nikolai replies in Russian, and my thoughts fly with the scene. I become fragmented. Like snapshots of a whole night, and I vividly recall only certain moments.

I straddle Nikolai's lap, my head on his chest while I listen to his heartbeat. His voice vibrates against my ear while a taxi bumps along a road. It takes a lot of energy to look up at him, but I do, tilting my head. He stares down at me, his hand stroking my tangled dirty-blonde hair, no longer in a pony.

"I can walk," I whisper. Why am I whispering?

"Prove it," he says deeply.

I place my palms on his chest again and try to lift myself off him, and I recognize that we're in a taxi again. Where I cannot walk. Even if I tried.

He laughs.

I scowl.

His hand travels up my corset, to my chest, and his humor fades, replaced by a more desirous, *hungry* look.

Shockwaves course through my body, and a noise, like a high-pitched moan, rumbles inside of me. I can't discern whether he hears the needy plea—one that I've never made before.

Not with anyone.

Not even drunk.

He pulls me even closer to his body, and I'm welded against him. In his care, and his lips close over my jaw. I swear they do.

I'm on a bed.

I'm *on a bed.* In my corset and stockings. Metallic-colored sheets and comforter beneath me. The corset wire pokes into my skin, and the weight of someone else undulates the mattress, rocking my body. I prop myself on my elbows.

Nikolai is shirtless.

He is very, very shirtless.

Even in the darkness, moonlight creeping through the white curtains, I notice the ridges and lines in his muscles, his perfect set of abs. A body that belongs to an athlete or vampires and werewolves, the supernatural in general.

He hovers over me, his fingers untying the front of my corset where it all binds together. *We're going to have sex.* It's a lingering thought.

We're both drunk.

That is true too.

My mind soars to new heights. "I'm floating," I whisper. *Or spinning.*

"Close your eyes, myshka," he breathes in a soothing, deep tone. I don't close them though. His forearm rests beside my head, his body less than an inch from descending into me.

"What does that mean?" I ask softly. "Myshka?"

His eyes search mine, hypnotic, soulful. Ones that tether me here, to him. And his lips close over my cheek before drifting to my ear. "Little mouse."

Little mouse.

I spin.

And the blackness of the night takes me completely.

ACT FOURTEEN

My head pounds viciously.

I roll over, whirling. A soft, metallic comforter molds my body, like a fluffy pillow. I freeze. This is not my bed in Ohio.

I'm in Vegas.

And this is *not* Camila's couch.

My blurry eyes begin to grow and clear. The never-ending night suddenly floods me in choppy, disjointed waves. What. Did I do? *I'm on my period.* It's the first terrified thought I have.

Did I have sex?

Those two—sex and menstruation—they don't mix. I'm going to look down and see a horrific bloody mess, something from a scary movie. Like *Saw.* The eighth sequel took place in Nikolai's bed.

Before I agonize any longer, I take a peek. No blood.

No mess.

I pat my body for my phone, and it dawns on me. I'm wearing a men's black button-down. Bra-less. Or rather, corset-less. No stockings. No—wait, I still have my black underwear on, the bottoms that matched the top.

I find my phone sitting on a pillow beside me. No other body is here.

He kissed me?

Maybe. Did he?

Did we have sex?

I want to turn off my frantic brain. Please. I stare at the ceiling, expecting to have a one-on-one talk with God, but this isn't the time. And I don't think He wants to hear me groan about my drunken black-out night.

I just hope it's not one full of regret.

I check the time on my cell. 9:32 a.m.

Why am I up so early after going to bed so late? What's wrong with my body? Doesn't it understand that it needs sleep? I'm about to fall back into the pillow and force my eyes shut.

But a fist raps the door frame.

Nikolai stands with a glass of green slush, wearing black workout shorts and a gray shirt. Strands of his hair fall over his rolled, red bandana. Like usual, it's distracting and more attractive than he probably realizes.

"How is your body functioning?" is the first thing I say, of all things needing to be said.

"I can handle my liquor," he reminds me. "I'm assuming you feel like shit."

I sit up, suddenly aware of last night again, the important parts. I anxiously pull at the hem of his shirt so it covers my thighs. I swallow, my throat dry. "Right assumption."

His brows pinch as he studies me for a second. Then he approaches with the green mystery concoction. "Drink this." He passes it to me.

I cup the cold glass with one hand, keeping my thighs covered with the other. He watches me attentively, and I try to speak my questions through my eyes: *did we have sex?* I don't think I can say the words aloud.

He has to be reading me right. "You blacked out," he finally concludes. "At what point?"

"I remember bits and pieces after we left Hex."

His jaw hardens. "Drink," he tells me. "You'll feel better."

Wait? He's not going to tell me if we had sex or not? This is killing me. "Did we have sex?!" I accidentally shout it.

Fuck my life.

"No," he tells me without a smile. Without humor. His seriousness pounds my heart.

"Did we kiss?" I ask softly.

"No, not really." He picks up a blue plastic AE water bottle off his dresser. "I helped you change into that shirt after you said a wire was hurting you, but I knew you were more intoxicated than me. I wouldn't take advantage of you, Thora."

I finally let out a breath.

He gestures to the green slush. "Hurry up and drink that. We're leaving in ten minutes."

My eyes grow. "What? Where?"

"The gym. Your training starts today."

"Today?" My head throbs still, a splitting migraine that jackhammers my temple. I shouldn't be anywhere near an apparatus.

He sits on the edge of the bed, really close to me. "I have rules."

Of course he has rules. I lean my shoulders against the black headboard.

"No complaining."

"I wasn't complaining," I mutter, sipping the green drink. It's vile. I gag at first, but his look of *suck it up, little mouse* forces me to drink more of it without flinching. I remember the nickname, and I can only guess he gave it to me for my height compared to his. I also remember his strict anger at the auditions, and I wouldn't expect anything less from him now. Clearly, he takes work seriously.

"If I call you with a free hour, you'll stop whatever you're doing and train. Except if you're working at Phantom."

"Okay." *I can do that.*

"No drugs," he says.

"That won't be a problem," I mumble into my next sip. I've never even smoked pot. The call of narcotics isn't strong for me.

He adds, "Don't show up to training drunk."

I hesitate mid-gulp and then wipe my mouth slowly with the back of my hand. "Problem…I'm slightly drunk right now."

His facial muscles never even flinch from their no-nonsense, stern position. "Don't arrive late to training. You waste my time, we're done."

"Fair enough," I say softly. He's doing this out of kindness, no other reason.

"No boyfriends."

My lips part, and my heart jumps. "What?"

"It's a distraction," he explains, "and if you're not one-hundred percent committed to becoming an artist, then you're wasting my time again." His eyes smolder hot. "And if you do end up with a boyfriend, I don't want to know about it. I don't want to hear it. That stays out of the gym. Understand?"

I digest all of his words with a heavy frown. I don't think I misinterpreted the attraction between us last night—but maybe that's all it was, a drunken night. And I hate myself for fixating on *him* like *that* when he's giving me a handout that I've desperately needed.

"You're glaring," he says. "I didn't realize your love life was more important to you than your career—"

"It's not," I retort; my pulse speeds the longer we discuss this. I feel like puking.

He lifts my chin with two fingers, his hard gaze pushing through me. That stare—it's so intrusive. So intimate. That it might as well be a form of sex. Eye sex. Eye *fucking*. I understand it now. And he says lowly, "Then no boyfriends."

"I wasn't planning on it," I breathe.

A knock sounds on the main door, the noise dull in this room but audible. Between his siblings and cousins at The Masquerade, I'm surprised there aren't more knocks.

"Is that all the rules?" I ask as he stands.

"Unless I think of more later," he tells me, basically declaring that he can amend the rules at any time. He holds all the power—as he should. *He's doing you a giant favor, Thora.* I'm so grateful that I can't complain, even if it wasn't on his list of rules.

"I left Advil on the bathroom counter for you," he tells me on his way to the door, the knocking louder. When he leaves to answer it, I scan the room for my bag. A couple seconds pass before I remember that my suitcase is at Camila's—along with a change of clothes, underwear and my shoes.

I exhale, my stomach still queasy. I'm not sure the green juice is helping any. Camila is most likely busy dealing with her extended family, and I don't want to complicate her day with my baggage—literally. I smile weakly at the pun, and then quickly frown when I realize it has not solved my problems.

Nikolai left the door ajar, and I hear voices escalate in the living room, enough that curiosity propels me there. I edge near the wooden frame.

"It's not that I don't trust you," the familiar male voice says. "It's just that I don't trust you." I imagine John Ruiz's surly, unapologetic face.

"That makes perfect sense," Nikolai replies. "What am I going to do with Thora's clothes? Steal them? Wear them for myself?"

My clothes. I'm opening the door in a flash, too pleased with the slant of the universe, dipping on my side. My solution just walked into Nikolai's suite with my suitcase. I creep into the living room, my toes throbbing from the torture I put them through last night.

It isn't until John sees me that I notice my mistake. His eyes travel down the length of my body, clad in a black button-down. Nikolai's shirt. And nothing else.

The universe giveth and taketh away.

"I can explain," I say quickly. "We didn't..." I motion between Nikolai and me. He stays quiet, domineering, not helping at all. "Do anything—we didn't do anything. I just didn't have a change of clothes." It's the best excuse there is. Maybe because it's true.

"It's not my business," he says, my hefty suitcase by his side. "But either way you're still certifiably insane." He lets out a dry laugh. "You really would rather stay with *him* than go to a hotel or a hostel. Honestly, Thora, I pegged you as a degree above stupid."

A degree above stupid must be a fairly good compliment from John.

Nikolai's biceps flex, a sign that he's ticked off. "And what'd I do to you?"

John never backs down. Not even shrinking in place. Even if Nikolai is taller, broader, and a year older—John is angrier, moodier, and tapping into the *I hate this fucking world* vibe with expertise.

"For starters," John begins, "you turn a perfectly good club into an idiot fest every Saturday night. And the rest of you Kotovas are all the same. Thinking you're above the rules. Your little brother practically pisses everywhere he goes—"

"You can leave," Nikolai interrupts, his jaw hardened severely. His muscles coiled, on offense.

They have some sort of staring match that I can't make sense of. John unflinchingly stays his course, as though he expected that type of reaction from Nikolai. He breaks the eye contact first, not in defeat really. He just hands my suitcase off to me, and I grab the handle.

"Camila told me to tell you not to ditch her just because you're not crashing at her place anymore," he says. "She doesn't have many friends who stick around here."

I nod, my heart swelling that she'd even want to stay in touch. "I'll text her. Thanks for this."

He shrugs. "Camila made me do it. Don't think I'm a nice guy."

"That'd be impossible," Nikolai says, his voice deep and threatening.

John rolls his eyes dramatically before giving me a half-wave and exiting out the main door. When he shuts it behind him, Nikolai spins back to me. As if nothing happened, he says, "Get dressed. We have practice."

Right.

Practice with the God of Russia.

I wonder if I'm about to see why he's called that.

ACT FIFTEEN

Aerial Ethereal's gym within the hotel & casino seems different now that I'm no longer auditioning. I still feel like an interloper, but not quite as much as before. Sunday morning, only a few coaches and choreographers linger by the glass office doors. Barely any artists practice now, and I have a feeling their main source of training comes from ten live shows a week.

Nikolai has spent the past fifteen minutes giving me a tutorial on circus equipment, probably waiting for my hangover to subside. I stumbled into his body *three* times, still slightly intoxicated. I've never been that black-out drunk before, so this is all new to me.

I'm just proud of myself for not vomiting.

He places his hands on my shoulders, rotating me towards the apparatus. I've been staring at the wall for two minutes. Dear God. He gestures to the red aerial silk that's rigged on the eighty-foot ceiling.

"I know this one," I tell him. "I had a makeshift silk in my garage." My dad helped me rig it when I was fourteen. At the time, I think he believed it'd stay a hobby. If he thought it'd turn into a career aspiration, I wonder if he'd still lend a hand or allow it.

Nikolai pinches my chin and turns my head to face him. "That's dangerous, Thora."

"It was secure," I defend as he releases his grip, my attention now his. It's harder to capture when I'm hungover, and I can tell it's frustrating him. "I never got hurt."

"You could have," he refutes. "You'll work on this equipment. Don't go to a different gym or build your own apparatuses." I catch the concern in his voice, and I guess his paranoia comes somewhere fresh. Tatyana, his old partner, was injured for reasons unsaid.

Honestly, I'm too nervous to ask why. He's been more than generous, and I'd rather not scare him off with my insensitive curiosity.

"This way." He rests a hand on the small of my back, guiding me across the gym to a new apparatus, the aerial silk already out of view. We barely spent any time there, but maybe it's awkward. It's the discipline I lost out to Elena. It's the one they're using together, not me.

After showing me around the Russian swing, a large apparatus that oscillates front to back, allowing the flyer greater height, he brings me to a new kind of structure. Something built specifically for a show. It looks like a metal jungle gym, or metal cubes stacked together, bars and bars. And a teeterboard lies underneath.

"*That's* dangerous," I point out. I imagine someone jumping on the end of the teeterboard, catapulting an artist at the other end, like a springy seesaw. If they're off, even a degree, they could smack into a metal bar. Hit their head. Land wrong on one—this is a death trap.

"It appears that way," he says, "but there's enough room for a triple layout. Every movement has to be precise and calculated, but that's with anything here." He takes a few steps to the side and watches me. "When you stare at this, what do you see?"

I take a deep breath and inspect the bars from afar. "A jungle gym?" I'm not sure if this is the right answer.

"What do you feel?" he asks.

I open my mouth, unsure of what I'll even say. But I hesitate as he sits on the blue mats, his forearms resting on his knees. "Show me," he says, about ten feet from the apparatus.

I look at him uncertainly and he nods in encouragement. Okay. I try to smother drunken, hungover Thora James as I approach the metal structure. Up close, it dwarfs me, looming like the bare bones of a futuristic house. I rub some chalk on my palms and grip one of the cold bars, a vertical beam.

Nikolai says a few Russian words to someone by the glass office, and they slip back inside. Melodic, sweet sounds fill the cavernous gym, the main speakers playing a familiar song that simultaneously soothes and quickens my pulse. I recognize it as "One Day I'll Fly Away" from Moulin Rouge.

What do I feel?

I exhale another breath and use my upper-body strength to lift my torso horizontal. I concentrate on the angle and then reach out for another beam, this one like monkey bars. I jump onto it and then swing my body out, gaining more momentum.

There's another bar in sight.

I think I can reach that and do a handstand or a double (unlikely).

"Drop down," Nikolai suddenly says, the music cutting off. I obey his command instantly, my feet hitting the mat.

He's beside me in seconds, his hand on the bar above my head. "That's what you feel?" He says it like I might as well have been a soulless ghost.

"I've never been on this apparatus before…" I throw out an excuse.

He shouts a few Russian words at the lady near the office again. The song replays, and I watch him closely. He breathes as though he's inhaling intangible things. Love. Magic and beauty. And then he climbs up one of the vertical beams with ease, standing on the top of the structure.

He saunters across it like a tightrope, and his gaze—it never leaves my body. As though he's performing for me. As though the music is mine.

And then he drops straight down, my stomach plummets like he just fell from a forty-foot-height, but he catches one of the bars, channeling the power to do a double between the rungs. It's effortless, like he's slicing through air. He comes to an abrupt stop on top of a bar, squatting.

He slowly stands, power radiating in this one action, and his stormy eyes bear down. He walks closer on the bar. So swiftly, he drops again. He clasps another beam, and I soak in his dominant, precise movements—that fill with life and…something greater.

When he finally lands on his feet, beside me, the song is near its end. He's trounced my mind with carnal, euphoric things. He pulls me strongly to his chest. Like whiplash, my head floats off my body. My lips part, and his hands cup the back of my head, his muscular body welding against my small frame.

I melt in ways I never have before. Beneath that look.

Beneath his passion.

"That," he says lowly, his eyes dancing across me, "is what *I* feel." As soon as the music shuts off, he drops his hands from me, steps back. Demonstration over. He just balled my emotions and fucked them, hard.

I can't even speak. I just shake my head like *I'm not sure I can ever be like that.* And I wonder if he's able to do this with any girl. Every girl. Not just me. I don't want to picture it.

"You have to leave your heart and soul here," he tells me. "Every night. Every time. It's your job to make the audience *feel* something."

I definitely felt something. Mission accomplished—for him at least. "How?" I ask. I'm used to being instructed on my technicality, not the sentiments behind my movements.

He rests an elbow on a metal rung, and his deep gray eyes penetrate me, a mystery behind them. The kind that leaves me unprepared for what's to come. "The easiest way is to draw upon personal experiences," he says. "Think about the times you were in love."

I sway uneasily and unglue my eyes from his. I wait for it…

"You've never been in love," he states. *There it is.*

"I'm only twenty-one," I defend. "I still have plenty of time to fall in love after I pursue my career."

He nears me, only a couple steps closer, but his body heat radiates and warms my skin. "Then evoke the same passion you feel when you have sex."

I internally cringe.

As if the times I had sex were filled with wild, hot fervor. "I'll try," I say under my breath. That's all I can do.

Awkward silence gathers between us, and I sense him reading my features. I just wonder how outwardly I'm cringing. I attempt to relax my facial muscles, but it's too late.

"You've never had sex," he deduces.

"No," I say with the shake of my head. "No, I've had sex. Twice, actually."

"Twice?" His brows rise like *that's it?*

Why did I give him a number? I would face-palm myself if I wasn't frozen solid. "They weren't memorable." Just lame stabs at crossing off "to-do" lists. It took me some time to realize the list shouldn't have existed in the first place.

He remains quiet, mulling this over, maybe. His lips in a thin line, his eyes more narrowed.

It dawns on me. "You've never had terrible sex, have you?" My heart pounds, and a light bulb triggers. "Is that why they call you the God of Russia?"

His expression morphs into an unamused, *don't be ridiculous* one. "If your past relationships aren't enough to help you, then you'll need to find something that will. An image that's moved you, a book, a song—anything that you can focus on while you perform. If you're too concentrated on your actions, on the next move, that's all the audience will see."

I have passion for the circus. It's my greatest, life-long love. Even if it's a figment, a dream—more than reality. I still feel from it.

I'm just not sure how to show what's in my heart.

And I can't take forever to learn this skill. I have a deadline.

"We'll work on it," he tells me.

My pulse jumpstarts, and I watch him watching me. "You…want to help me feel passion?"

"I want to help you express passion. I'm sure you feel it. You're here, aren't you?" It's strange how one person can see the hidden parts of you in a short amount of time that others don't even understand in years.

He rests his warm hand on the back of my neck. "This way, myshka." As he says it, he's looking straight through me. *This way.* To him.

His hand slides to my spine, and he redirects me to a new apparatus, as though nothing really transpired. But my body is tight. My muscles bound together.

Be professional, Thora, I tell myself.

I think back to our first few encounters. When he said, "Our relationship is unprofessional." Even though he's training me, I have a feeling that still stands. There is a line that cannot be uncrossed. We've leapt over it from day one, and now I just have to bury this tension.

Or draw upon it.

ACT SIXTEEN

Tuesday night and I'm in the air.

Lights flicker around me as I twirl upside-down, my body supported by the aerial hoop. I tuck my legs around the steel and continue to spin and spin and spin, all the while maneuvering my torso, contorting into long lines and elongated shapes.

When the music hits a faster tempo, I grip the top of the ring, stretching out as the hoop rotates in quick circles. Being high, in the air, frees me completely. The slight prick of fear heightens my adrenaline, setting a fire beneath me.

Who can explain the drum of their heart or the burst of their lungs? Give me that person. I need them because words fail my senses.

A second passes before whistling breaches my serenity. It pricks my ears and pulls me out of the moment.

"Show us your splits, baby!"

"Yeah, spread your legs!"

Phantom isn't a strip club, but some of the drunker patrons act like it is. I ignore their catcalls and do the opposite of the splits in spite, tightening my legs together. I drop to the bottom of the hoop, hooking my arms around the frame. And I twirl faster and faster, speeding my momentum with my strength.

Proud clapping fills my head, not the room. I don't much care if I've imagined applause for myself. I'm still my biggest cheerleader and possibly even my biggest fan.

When I slow, my mind dizzying, the lights blanket me in a dark purple hue, my one minute cue. I gather up the last of my momentum to hoist my legs outward, as though I'm sitting down in the air. I release one hand and support my entire weight with my right bicep.

I let out a breath from my nose, keeping the line straight and steady and symmetrical.

The purple light blinks to white and the aerial hoop begins to descend. Faint, almost bored applause trickles in the room. What can I really expect from this crowd?

My heels hit the stage, and I take a quick bow, trying my best to cold-shoulder the two men in the front who howled for splits.

"You didn't even show us your pus—" *Ignore.* I tune him out and hightail it behind the stage, slipping through a black door. Some of the waitresses, in lingerie costumes, decompress with cocktails while others reapply makeup at vanities.

I'm about to head to my wooden locker when I run straight into the manager, his mop of red hair and sinewy arms. Fantastic.

Roger's green eyes become lasers, burning holes in my forehead. "Virgin Mary," he calls out and gestures me over with a plump finger.

As much as I dislike Roger, if I have any chance to move to an apartment and support myself, I need this job. I'm sure people can smell my desperation a mile away.

I approach him at a safe distance. My corset lifts my boobs, nearly spilling out. It's not a look you'd talk to your boss in, but he has no problem loitering back here while girls change.

Roger's eyes flit from my breasts to my face. "Look," he snaps, his throat scratchy like he smokes a pack a day or yells far too often. "I know you're fucking flexible. I see it out there. And that's exactly what I want. Men *love* flexibility."

I can feel myself scowling. I don't want to listen to Roger generalize the entire male population, picking out their likes and dislikes.

"It's what they rub one out to," he continues. "Girls doing the splits *on* their faces and all of that." He lets out a heady breath, like the image turns him on. Okay, I did not sign up to hear Roger's personal fantasies.

I internally cringe. "I'll keep that in mind," I say, hoping to end this here.

He points that plump finger again. "You need to stop trying to make it so artsy. Make it more sexual, Mary. This is fucking Vegas, not Kansas."

"I'm from Ohio," I mutter. I'm also pretty positive he no longer remembers my real name.

"Same thing." He waves me off, and he hones in on my breasts. "And I'm tired of seeing this same costume. Go buy more. I want a different one every night. Change it the fuck up." He glances at his phone, the screen glowing from an incoming call. "Also, try a red lip next time. The pink is too virginal." He walks off at that, leaving me to calculate the price of seven more costumes in my head.

My teeth ache from clenching them.

At least…he didn't say that I completely sucked. There were some positives there, right? Layered beneath disgusting comments, sure.

I exhale slowly.

Temporary. I have to repeat it over and over in order to retain my sanity.

This is temporary.

I SWIPE THE KEYCARD INTO THE SLOT ABOVE THE door, entering Nikolai's hotel suite. Yes, I have a key to his place. Yes, it feels weird. But after our marathon night—chasing Katya and chaperoning Timo—Nikolai feels less like a stranger and even less like an acquaintance.

Still "friends" may be a strong word. Maybe he's more like my trainer. *A trainer that's hot enough to bang.*

"Unprofessional, Thora James," I mumble under my breath. I walk further into his place, setting my purse on the barstool and slipping into his bedroom. Then the bathroom.

I'm also using his shower.

"And as far as unprofessional goes," I say to myself, releasing my boobs from the corset, "this has to be high up there." I try not to waver or second-guess my actions.

I'm here, right now, and I need a shower, no matter if I'm naked in my somewhat-friend's or trainer's bathroom. So what. Right? "He already pinched your nipple," I mutter. This is a good fact to keep me moving.

I swing open the glass shower door and turn on the hot water. I step in, the hot liquid raining on me. In a couple minutes, the steam mists the mirror.

Soothing. Until I catch sight of the male body products—the men's shampoo and soap. If I wasn't being doused with hot water, I might've frozen again.

"Thora."

I jump.

And knock over the shampoo bottle and a washcloth. I carefully set them back in their proper places. My heart performs a death-defying acrobatic routine without my permission.

"Thora," Nikolai calls again, muffled behind the door. The shower is loud enough to drown out most noise, including him returning from Amour tonight.

"Yeah?!" I call back.

"I have to wash my face," he tells me, his deep voice hard to hear. "I left my remover…" He's drowned out by the splash of water on tiles.

I whip my head to the rack of gray towels nearby. I can snatch one and spread it across the fogged glass, but it's misted enough that he'd only see my body shape, nothing more. I think.

The brazen side of me, the one that I've been tapping into, says *what if?* What if I stay put? Just like this. I've been satisfied being the unsexy friend in Shay's eyes, but my stomach drops at the thought of Nikolai ever awarding me that title.

I channel my confidence and run my fingers through my wet hair, able to see a blurry outline of the door as it opens. Nikolai slips inside, shirtless, I can tell. After shutting the door behind him, he takes a few lengthy strides to the sink.

"Sorry," he apologizes in that low tone. He wipes fog off the mirror with the side of his fist. "I would've washed my face backstage, but I needed eye drops…*fuck*."

I instinctively wipe the glass like he did—a clear streak by my face so I can see him better. His eyes are tightened shut like makeup got in them. He fumbles around for his eye drops and remover, searching through the cabinet and cupboards for the bottles. Frustration lines his forehead and binds his shoulders.

I'm about to step into the most fearless part of myself. Without hesitation, I shut off the shower, secure a towel around my body and go to his aid.

He knocked over his eye drops in the sink, and I find his remover in the lower cupboard. I quickly gather them. When I rise fully, he squints in my direction, his eyes incredibly bloodshot. Dark purple shadow is smudged beneath both lids and black liner swept above. He has dots of silver paint by his hairline and brows.

I'd think he wore it well if he wasn't in pain. "You must be allergic to something," I say softly.

He gestures to the purple shadow. "I bought a new brand…" His face contorts. I wonder if his eyes burn. Before he rubs them, he turns away from me and rinses his face with sink water, gripping the counter with white knuckles.

I soak a cloth with the remover, and after he dries his face, the makeup horribly smeared across his eyes and forehead, he rotates back to me.

"I can help you…if you kneel," I tell him, a lump rising to my throat.

His brows knot while he contemplates my offer. He scans my body, covered in only a soft gray towel that stops at my thighs. Beads of water roll down my neck to the tops of my breasts. I breathe heavily, as though his gaze depletes my energy.

I didn't have time to dry off. My sopping dirty-blonde hair is splayed over one shoulder, and a pool of water collects at my cold feet.

The tense quiet grows, and I'm about to open my mouth and retract the offer. But he slowly drops to his knees, his face much closer to mine, his reddened eyes never deterring from me.

The washcloth feels heavy in my hand. "Stay still," I tell him.

The corner of his lip nearly lifts. "That's my line."

I recall the bet at The Red Death, when he pierced me. "Okay, then close your eyes," I say. "That's not yours, is it?"

He smiles now, even as his lids shut. "I've used it before, but it's cuter coming from you."

I absorb this compliment right before I press the washcloth beneath his eye, gently rubbing the makeup off. His hands ascend to my hips, holding onto me. I hone in on the pressure of each fingertip, only a towel away from my skin. I wonder if I can even concentrate enough to remove the purple shadow.

Focus, Thora.

I'm trying. But there is a six-foot-five Russian athlete kneeling at my feet, clutching onto me, shirtless—while I wear *only* a towel. My body responds with rhythmic pulses between my legs. And I do everything I can to shut out these feelings.

Small talk.

I'll make small talk. "Thanks for letting me stay here," I say first, applying more remover onto the cloth before I dab at his forehead.

"It's no problem," he says. "If you need to stay longer, the couch is free."

His hands practically burn through the towel.

"I'll be out by the end of the week," I tell him assuredly. I thought about returning to Camila's, but she hasn't mentioned anything about it. I don't want to overstay my welcome, especially when I was supposed to be out of there soon, regardless of her family. "My paycheck comes in then, and I've already narrowed down a couple studio apartments." I don't mention any logistics, like having to dip into my savings for the deposit. But it'll be worth it in the long run. I hate mooching off him, and it's been weighing on me.

He says nothing, but his jaw muscles tense, as though he's clenching his teeth. The silence creates a chasm, and so I fill the air once again.

"I thought the colors for Amour are red and pink."

He opens his eyes, most of the purple makeup gone. But he has a bit of black liner left and silver dots on his forehead that I'm wiping away.

I focus on my hand, the one that holds his unshaven jaw, my fingers and palm small compared to him.

"You've never seen the show." It's not a question, but I hear his surprise.

"I've seen a show," I say in a whisper.

"But not Amour."

I'm about to reply, but my phone vibrates loudly on the sink counter. I retrieve it and click into the text message.

> I told coach to keep your spot open for another few days. Hopefully you'll realize how crazy you're being before then.
> – Shay

While I skim the words, I feel Nikolai stand. He comes up next to me and reaches for the eye drops.

His gaze briefly travels to my cell. "Let me guess, your best friend." I hear a hint of bitterness.

"He just thinks there's more to offer me in Ohio."

Nikolai towers above me, squeezing drops into his eyes. "Like what?" he asks. "Him?"

"No...he just cares about me enough to want me to succeed, and he doesn't think I will here." I lean my back against the sink. After he sets down his drops, he steps closer, standing in front of my half-naked body. Another step forward and his legs knock into mine.

I hold my towel securely, and my lungs eject. As soon as he places his hands on either side of the counter, cocooning me here, I scale my attraction to him.

It's catastrophically off the charts.

He stares down at me, his intensity present, bringing me to a boil. "When he throws you a lifeline, Thora," he says, "don't grab it."

"Why?" I expect him to mention the pull that is occurring right now, the kind that has his reddened eyes drawing lines along my neck and collarbones.

"The more crutches he gives you, the more you'll contemplate quitting. It's the easy way out, and you've done this much already."

He's right, in a way. When Shay gives me an alternative route, it's easier to pack up my bags and go home. I don't think I will though, and knowing he's there—it's comforting. "If I fall, he's my safety net," I explain to Nikolai. Shay will be the one to pick up the pieces. That's why he wants me to come home now.

He cups my face, his hand coarse, masculine. And strong. "Thora, he doesn't even want to give you the chance to fall. That's not a safety net, it's a harness."

I go cold. "And what are you?" I ask. "My safety net?"

He takes a step back. And another. I guess I said the wrong thing. Or maybe the right one—I have no clue anymore.

"I'm just here to help you succeed," he says. "I don't know what that's called."

"Me either…"

He combs a hand through his hair. "I'll give you some privacy so you can change. Katya wanted Thai, so there's more in the kitchen if you'd like to eat."

"Thanks…" *for everything*. I think my eyes express it enough because he nods a couple times. I read into our conversation, and I wonder if he's telling me to be strong enough to cut all ties—that the only way I can do my best is to be all in. No matter what.

I've slowly been snipping lifelines since I've been here, but some of them are harder to cut than others.

Some of them hurt more. There's no other truth but that.

ACT SEVENTEEN

"Everyone always makes college sound epic," Katya tells me, eyeing my Ohio State shirt that I changed into, plus a pair of collegiate sweats. I twisted my wet hair in a low pony, and it soaks the red fabric of my tee.

On the couch, the sixteen-year-old girl kicks her feet on the glass coffee table, a fresh plate of chicken and vegetables teetering on her leg. I'm not sure what kind of Thai this is, but it's like the athlete version, almost no sauce. I'm sitting beside her with a half-filled plate in my hands.

"It's not like you see on TV," I explain. Then I frown, recalling a couple drunken parties with an inflatable theme—guys carting around blow-up dolls and girls dressed in balloons. "I mean, some of it is, but they don't show the studying and cramming."

Katya sips a blue sports drink, contemplating this. Sober Katya is a much different Katya. More tomboy than the girl I met with caked-on makeup and a martini. She wears jeans and a white tank top, no costume jewelry or feather boas.

Surprisingly, she's taken my invasion of her couch really well, all things considered.

"Sometimes I feel like I'm going to miss out on something," she says softly. I'm about to give her some encouragement when the pipes in the wall groan, Nikolai's shower shutting off.

I tense, and a piece of chicken lodges on its way down.

Katya stabs at her broccoli. "But it can't be that great if you left it, right?" Her orb-like eyes seem to grow. In the daylight she appears more wistful and otherworldly: pale skin, big lips, eyes and ears on a thin, willowy figure.

"It's not that it wasn't great," I say, carefully choosing my words. "I just wanted something else."

She chews in thought, nodding her head like she understands. Her brown hair is parted in the middle, still wet from her earlier shower. Viva ends earlier than Amour, but she had tutoring right after. Like home school, she said.

I can't imagine never attending an actual school, one with hallways and bells that chime every hour. But from what she's told me, tutoring in between practices and shows is the norm. All her brothers did it, including Nikolai.

"Do you know any costume shops around here?" I ask. "Or I guess lingerie ones? I have to buy some corsets and things for my act at Phantom. I need them relatively cheap though."

Her gray eyes brighten, and she drops her feet from the coffee table, leaning closer. "I know the best place," she says excitedly. "Are you free tomorrow afternoon?"

"No." That wasn't me. It was the six-foot-five Russian-American man entering the room.

Katya pouts. "I wasn't talking to you."

I turn my head to Nikolai and choke on a vegetable. He stands by the kitchen bar, a towel slung low on his waist. So close to naked: sculpted biceps, shoulders and abs that draw attention. I accidentally glance at his crotch, hidden behind the fabric. His nearly-naked-self is not distracting to anyone but me. I quickly sip my water, knowing he caught my initial reaction.

"Thora is training with me tomorrow," Nikolai says. *Unless I have a heart attack before then.*

Katya lets out a frustrated breath and sets her plate down. "I finally have a friend who isn't related to me and you have to steal her?"

My spirits rise. Katya likes me enough to call me a friend? Secondly, I've made another one since being in Vegas. I think I'm headed in a good direction.

Nikolai rests his arm on the bar counter. "She's not here to be your friend, *Katya.* She's here to train." He pauses. "And she was my friend first."

I try to hide a smile. "I can be everyone's friend," I mention softly.

Nikolai wears a stern expression, facing me. "Do you want to train or not?"

"I do, you know I do." I talk to Katya before she explodes on her brother. She's about there, sitting on her knees and gripping the couch, like she could jump to her feet and charge. "We can go another day. I still need you to show me the store."

"What store?" Nikolai interjects, slipping into the kitchen that's in view of the living room, no wall or divider separating them.

"Coco Roma," Katya tells him, plopping down on her butt.

He was midway in opening the fridge, now he shuts it without grabbing anything. Whatever he says next is foreign to me. His gruff Russian fluently leaves his lips.

Katya stares at him blankly, and I'm thankful for her rebellious rule—the one where she'll only converse with him in English.

He sighs, more agitated, and switches languages. "Were you planning on going to that part of town with just Thora?"

"No," Katya snaps back. "I would've brought Timo."

Nikolai glares. "Take someone as big as me or bigger or you're not going."

I scan the length of him as he crosses his arms. He's the definition of intimidating—tall, muscular, all brawn and man. And I'm sure there's plenty more beneath his towel. "There are people bigger than you?" I say—aloud. I cringe. I don't even pretend to hide it.

I swear his lips tic upwards, humor lighting his stormy eyes.

Katya is the one who answers. "You should see Dimitri. He's like a tank."

I watch Nikolai's features harden, and he returns to the fridge, his back to me.

Katya adds, "But he's also obnoxious." She picks up my tattered paperback from the couch cushion. I lent her my favorite paranormal romance after she asked what I was reading. "You have my number, right?" she questions for the third time, as though I deleted it.

I nod. "Yep. Katya Kotova, permanently saved in my contacts."

She smiles when I mention *permanently*. She stands and rotates to her brother, but he's busy pouring a glass of water at the sink. "I'll weigh my options about who we'll bring and get back to you."

"I'm assuming I'm not an option."

Katya crinkles her nose. "Maybe if you were more fun."

He sips his water with the most authoritative, stern look in the history of looks. He's not even trying to convince her otherwise, and I think he prefers it this way. I remember Hex, his flirty, roaming hands, and The Red Death, his dazzling, high-octane bet.

He can be fun, but he switches that off in front of his siblings. Katya rolls her eyes and waves him off as she departs to her bedroom in the upstairs loft.

Nikolai sets down the water and walks to a high cupboard, retrieving a bottle of red wine and *two* glasses. Nervous flutters invade my stomach. I wonder if I should reject the wine. Then I remember my long night that contains catcalls and Roger's complaints about my wardrobe. A glass of wine sounds relaxing, and it's not like we're back at Hex, slamming down shots.

I won't have a painful hangover in the morning, unable to adequately train.

Even so, I find myself hesitating. "Maybe I shouldn't," I say as he goes to pour the second glass. He pauses with the bottle above it, ready to stop. His actions—that he'd be willing to listen to my wishes—ease every part of me. "Maybe I should though?"

"Your choice, myshka."

"Okay." I nod him on.

He fills the wine glass only a quarter of the way. When he enters the living room area, he hands it to me. "I didn't want to take out the bottle until Katya left," he says as he sinks in the white chair across from the couch. "She would've asked for some."

"And you would've said no?" I guess.

He nods, more morose and pensive as he stares at the carpet. "It's one thing to say *no* when only I'm here, and it's another to do it in front of someone else."

I think I can understand that. She would've wanted to be treated like me, not like a kid since she's sixteen, a teenager. Hardly a child.

I try not to stare too hard at him while we talk. But he's still in a towel. It's very hard not to notice it. I set my half-eaten plate down, appetite gone thanks to the nervous flutters. I'll stick with the wine. "So you have four brothers," I throw it out there.

"I do," he says without elaborating. He smiles into his next sip of wine, knowing I'll have to ask further.

I'm glad my horrible small talk efforts can entertain him. "I've met Timo and Luka, but where are the other two?"

"Madrid, until the end of the month, then they'll be in…" His brows furrow, and he rubs his eyes, less reddened than before. "Valencia or Sevilla, I can't remember."

"They're touring?" I guess.

"Noctis," he says with a weak smile. "They're on the European tour for another year and a half; then the show will go to Japan for a full twelve months."

"Wow…" That's a lot of traveling and separation from the rest of his family. I can see why Katya wants to join it—if that's the only way she can see her mom and dad. I don't want to pry, but so many questions sprout. I must wear them on my face since he speaks first.

"I haven't seen Peter and Sergei in six years." He pushes back the longer strands of his hair, still damp from his shower. Rarely does his gaze drift from mine, but in recollection of the past, he has a thousand-yard stare. "We talk on the phone, but it's not the same as being here."

"Are they young…like Katya?"

He shakes his head. "No. Peter is twenty-four, two years younger than me, and Sergei will be twenty-eight in July, two years older."

I want to ask what happened—how they ended up split apart—but I'm not sure he'll tell me. I'm not even sure it's something he shares often. Just by his dark, faraway expression, I can tell it brings him to a place he's not fond of going.

I sip my wine with rusted joints. Since I unearthed a sore subject, I decide to lighten the mood. I take the plunge. "Don't tell me you sleep in the nude." I nod to his towel, my lame attempt at a joke. I put the rim of the glass to my lips, gulping a sizable amount.

His eyes smile. "It's much more comfortable."

What? I choke on the liquid, coughing hoarsely.

He rises from his chair, as if ready to give me mouth-to-mouth. I hold up a hand, and he pauses in the middle of the floor.

"Thora?"

After another couple of dry coughs and a sip, I find my voice. "It went down the wrong…pipe or whatever it's called." I wince. I will never be a good smooth talker. It's hard to even look at his face right now. He admitted to sleeping naked, even in jest. And he's in a towel. Towering again. We're also drinking wine.

Like old friends.

Nikolai returns to his seat, his eyes twinkling in amusement when I meet them.

"It's not funny," I say.

"It depends which part you're referring to." He rests his arm on the back of the chair, stretching, lounging. It's a nice view.

I decide to jump topics again. New one. "How was the show tonight?"

"Fair," he says. "But that's how it'll be until the aerial silk act returns." He watches me take another gulp. "Careful, my demon."

Do not choke. His comment almost made me, but I channel whatever poise I have and swallow the wine without falter. My entire body heats, not just from the alcohol.

Nikolai leans back into the chair, and the towel shifts, exposing more thigh, closer to something else. What if he's called the God of Russia because of the size of his cock? The curious parts of me want to know. The sensible parts do not.

"How was your work?" he asks. A normal question, but the hairs on my arms rise.

"Fair," I say, not mentioning the drunken guys, urging me to split my legs apart.

His gunmetal eyes seem to darken, and he rubs his strong jaw. He has to be imagining what "fair" entails at Phantom. Neither of us surfaces the unspoken words. It strains the air.

"Are you normally so bold?" he asks.

I try my shot at sarcasm. "You mean bold enough to sit in a living room in nothing but a towel?" I continue without thinking about my words. "It's natural, yeah. I do it all the time." I'm so lame.

He breaks into a fraction of a smile. "I mean you coming to Vegas on your own. Auditioning, staying even though you didn't make it." He knows I would've stayed whether or not he offered to train me. Maybe that's the bold part—striving for something without a break, familiar face, or any help.

Back in Ohio, I would've never thought to crash at a Russian acrobat's hotel suite—someone with a reputation for being a god and a devil alike. This is all new. One part exhilarating and three parts terrifying.

"I think there's something in the Vegas water," I end up saying. It's triggered the bold in me.

He shakes his head just twice before boisterous voices fill outside—in the hallway. I can't make sense of the jumbled noises, like people talking over each other. All at once. My stomach drops at the familiarity. During the never-ending night, I heard these sounds.

From a hoard of Kotovas in the casino's lobby.

I look up at Nikolai, and I realize that he's been studying my reaction, not at all surprised about what lies outside his door.

ACT EIGHTEEN

"Dude, my keycard isn't working!" someone shouts outside the door. I think it was Luka, but I can't be sure. A slew of Russian jargon overtakes his voice, and it sounds like shoulders and bodies slam into the wood as they fight to open the door.

Nikolai rolls his eyes and sets down his wine before he approaches.

"Let me try," Timo says. (I think it's Timo.)

I crane my neck over the couch for a better view. Nikolai turns the handle and swings the door wide open. Timo nearly falls forward with Luka by his side. I mentally count about six or seven heads…no wait, eight. Eight Russian guys are outside.

I'm not ready for this—

"Hey, Nikky's in a towel," someone else says, and in two-point-two seconds, a pair of hands whips the fabric off Nikolai and snaps it against his thigh.

My jaw unhinges. His ass. His toned, bare ass. I'm staring at it. Dear God—what is going on? Nikolai doesn't flinch or even balk. He says a few words, lightheartedly, in Russian and proceeds to return to the kitchen like he's fully dressed.

What do I do?

Do I look?

I cover my face with my palm, clearly peeking through my spread fingers. I want to see. *No you don't.* Yes, I really do.

My frozen body makes the decision for me. While the rest of his relatives filter into the suite, Nikolai passes the living room buck naked, heading for his bedroom. His cock is in view. I see—so much. There is *so much* to be seen. As he nears, I force my gaze upwards. But he's already looking at me, his brows lifting. He caught me gawking at his package.

I don't watch him walk past, I slump down and press my fingers together in a real face palm.

"Thora James." Timo plops roughly next to me, slinging his arm around my shoulder. "Did you just stare at my brother's dick?"

Fuck my life.

"She's probably already seen it," Luka chimes in, hopping over the couch and sliding down on my other side. He combs his dark brown hair before readjusting his worn, blue baseball cap, wearing sweats and a plain gray tee.

Timo is the brazen one. In high-cut jean shorts and a leather jacket. Nothing else.

A couple larger, older guys say something in Russian as they enter the living room, one fisting the bottle of red wine. They look vaguely familiar, with short cut hair and hard features. Maybe from the never-ending night or in passing at the gym.

There is a lot of testosterone in this room, and they're all eyeing me like I'm a new species. "I…don't speak Russian," I put it out there, just like that.

Timo tilts his head. "No shit, Thora James. I thought you understood me all this time." His smile brightens his whole face, a youthful glow about him. I also feel less socially inept.

One of the burlier guys sits on the couch's armrest and flips through television channels with the remote, the stereo speakers adding to the general cacophony.

"We haven't met," someone says behind me.

I crane my neck over my shoulder and stare upside-down at a very tall guy, around Nikolai's age, with short brown hair and ocean blue eyes, his jaw also unshaven. His shoulders also muscular and broad, but with a longer face, he seems pretty compared to Nikolai—not as hard, rugged or devilish. If I met him first, I wonder what my initial reaction would be.

"I'm Thora," I tell him.

"Dimitri Kotova." *The tank,* as Katya called him.

"He's our cousin," Luka says as he digs into his pocket. He pulls out a handful of plastic-wrapped mints.

"The rest of us are," Dimitri says, gesturing to the other five guys. He saunters deeper into the room and snatches the wine bottle from another guy, pressing it to his lips. He makes a show of taking a large swig in front of me.

"Go back to Animal Planet," Timo says, pointing at the television. "That giraffe was about to give birth."

"I don't want to see that shit," the guy with the remote refutes.

"It's the miracle of life," Timo gapes. "What's better than that?"

"Texas Hold 'em."

"Fuck giraffes." Timo folds instantly, and when the channel turns to a professional poker tournament, he leans forward, hypnotized.

"Want one?" Luka asks me, my mind whirling in a dozen directions. He holds out a mint and I accept it with a smile—at least I think I smiled. Everything is moving really fast.

"Those better not be stolen." Nikolai's stern voice pricks my neck. He walks behind the couch, now dressed in black sweats. I train my eyes on his face, not on his dick. But he briefly looks to me like he knows that I'm thinking about it. Of course I am. I'm sure if the carpet had eyes, it'd be fixated on his cock too.

"They're *free* mints," Luka gawks. "I can't steal things that're set out for everyone to take."

"You're supposed to take *one*, not the whole fucking bowl," Nikolai shoots back.

"What do you do, Thora?" Dimitri suddenly asks, rerouting my attention. He sits on the coffee table, facing me, still clutching that wine bottle. His tribal tattoo peeks from the sleeve of his white tee, the inked design spindling up his neck. It makes me more aware of Nikolai's tattoo, one I hardly ever notice since it's on the inside of his bicep: a collection of fir trees with long lines as trunks, ending at the crease of his elbow.

I focus on the question at hand. *What do I do?* I guess I could answer this numerous ways. I choose the most honest one. "I work at Phantom."

Dimitri smirks, and his crude gaze lingers on my boobs. "I heard they tip well if you have a cunt." He chugs the wine.

My lips part, my insides turned to stone. I don't even know how to respond.

"Stay! Stay!" Timo shouts at the television. He rests his hands on his head and groans. "What a moron."

"Want another mint?" Luka asks, passing me a second one. I haven't even unwrapped the first. Then Nikolai appears beside his nineteen-year-old brother, gesturing him to stand. Luka rises, and his collection of mints litters the carpet. Nikolai brushes a few off the cushion before sitting next to me, his arm wrapped protectively on the couch behind my head.

Dimitri and Nikolai seem to be having a testosterone-fueled staring contest that I don't understand fully. This is the first impromptu gathering of relatives in Nikolai's suite since I've been here, but something tells me that they happen often.

I decide to text Katya: I don't know how you handle all these guys like this.

She's my hero.

"Fold! Fold! Come on!" Timo springs from his seat, arms extended at the television.

Dimitri fills the newly free spot on my left, and I go entirely rigid, a wine glass in one hand and my cell in the other. I try not to make eye contact, but I feel his arm ascending. About to swoop around my shoulders.

Nikolai beats him to it, tugging me closer to his body and away from Dimitri, more territorial than anything I've ever been caught in between.

Dimitri lets out a short laugh and says something to Nikolai in Russian. Frustration binds my muscles, mildly irritated that I can't understand them. It's like being a part of the wrong foreign feature film.

I muster the courage to say, "You can talk in English."

Dimitri smirks again. "How old are you?" The way he asks—it's like he's gauging whether or not I'm legal to screw.

Nikolai dips his head down, his lips brushing my ear, "I promise you're safe, myshka. Don't read into him." He knows I am. Because he's reading into me.

"Twenty-one," I answer softly.

My phone buzzes.

Headphones help – Katya

And then another text drops beneath that one.

It's still impossible to block out the annoying parts of them. You should come upstairs. My cousins aren't allowed in my room. My rules. – Katya

Before Dimitri asks another question, I spring to my feet, Nikolai's arm falling off me. "I'm going to go…" I point at the twisty iron staircase. "…talk to Katya."

Both guys say nothing. No facial expression beyond their intimidating builds and strong jaws. No smiles. Okay…*you have this, Thora.*

Confidence still intact, I spin on my heels and head to the staircase. About three guys watching the television start to shout over each other. It strengthens my determination, somehow, and I climb the stairs to Katya's room.

I'm about to knock, but she shouts, "You can come in, Thora!"

I open the door and shut it behind me, the hollering faint now. Her room is tiny, like the size of my dorm. On her dark purple comforter, Katya leans against a headboard, paperback in hand.

I scan her space: clothes strewn over a desk chair, textbooks stacked on a window. It looks less like a hotel and more like a teenager's bedroom, with posters from different circus shows taped unevenly on the cream walls.

Nova Vega

Celeste

Somnio

Infini

Seraphine

Viva

Amour

The largest poster hangs above her bed: Noctis, orange words scrawled over a moon. It's clear which Aerial Ethereal show she favors.

"Did Dimitri hit on you?" she asks, plucking earbuds out and closing the paranormal book.

"Does he have a reputation for hitting on anything with two legs?" I ask, sitting at the end of her bed, tucking my ankles underneath my thighs, crisscrossed.

She nods, her hair dried straight around her thin face. "Unless you share the same DNA. Which, you don't. And he's..." She crinkles her nose.

"What?" I frown.

"He's really competitive with Nik," she says. I wait for her to elaborate, but she doesn't. I'm left to assume that Dimitri wants what Nikolai has—that's most likely why he found me interesting at all.

I gesture to the paperback. "How's the book?" I've loaned out books before, but rarely are they ever read. So it's kind of special to see someone actually dive into the story.

"I think I like the werewolves more than the vampires," she says.

I've always been the opposite. "How come?"

She shrugs. "They seem to care about each other more." She squints at the cover in thought. "Like why did Rafael leave his brother alone, knowing predators were surrounding the castle?"

"He was bloodthirsty, and he thought his brother could protect himself."

Katya frowns deeper. "...but he didn't even bring extra blood back."

I never looked at it that way. "His brother survived," I tell her. "Oh wait, did you get to that part yet?" I can tell she didn't. I raise my hands. "Okay, I'm stopping myself before I spoil anything else."

She smiles, not upset.

The door suddenly swings open without a knock. Luka slips in and shuts it. "Hey, Kat." He reaches into his pocket and reveals three packs of Skittles. *His pockets must be huge*, is my first random, unhelpful thought. He tosses her the candy, and she gleefully gathers them in a pile.

"Don't tell Nik," he says. I wonder if he stole them. "And don't get another cavity. He'll blame me."

She gives him a look. "Like I can help that."

"Chew slower," he refutes.

I try not to laugh. There's no way the pace you eat stops a cavity from forming, but it's kind of cute that he'd suggest it to his little sister. And by cute, I do mean the "unsexy friend" type.

"I'll share with Thora." Katya nudges my hip with her foot and throws me a packet.

Luka leans his shoulders against the blue Celeste poster, scrutinizing me more closely, like a cop would a suspect. I guess it's only fair. I'm stepping into his world without his permission.

"Are you going to rat me out?" He glares. And a Kotova glare is harsher than most, I've found.

"For Skittles?" I say like it's a silly notion. Though it's more than that—he's gauging how loyal I am to Nikolai. And maybe reading into that too, for a relationship status. Or maybe I'm going crazy, assuming things that shouldn't be assumed. Like Nikolai does. Okay, I may need to reevaluate my thought process soon.

"Yeah," he says tensely, "for Skittles." It's like Skittles has become a code word. I'd be funnier if he wasn't so serious right now.

"I won't rat you out for Skittles," I assure him.

After a long cagey moment, he finally nods, accepting my answer. Then the door cracks open again, this time Timo slides in, strands of brown hair touching his eyelashes. "Anyone have a hundred I can borrow?"

I frown and accidentally blurt out, "A hundred bucks?"

His lips rise, stuffing his hands into his leather jacket. "If I could gamble with a hundred hugs, you know I would, Thora James." Yeah—I imagine John not liking that turn of events very much.

Luka stays quiet, but Katya reaches for her silver-studded clutch on the nearby dresser.

"Or a fifty." Timo checks the Marilyn Monroe desk clock, antsy.

"You should really save up for Saint Petersburg," Katya tells him, unzipping her wallet.

"I've already been to Saint Petersburg."

"As a baby. It doesn't count." Katya leisurely inspects each credit card slot, avoiding the cash one. I think she's purposefully prolonging this conversation, to have extra company, even for a moment's time. "Nikolai let Luka visit when he was eighteen, and he said in two years, he'd let me go with you—"

"I'm not going to Russia," he cuts her off. "I like it here, Kat. We *all* like it here. Right, Thora?"

I raise my hands, pleading the fifth. "I just got here." I uneasily stand from Katya's bed, afraid to be caught within the crossfire of a sibling fight. Since Tanner is so much younger than me, my relationship with my little brother is distanced at best. Sure, I love him, but we never hung out as friends. I've never been a part of close, in-your-face annoyances that brothers and sisters stir up.

I'm wading in new territory. Which has been my Vegas experience since day one. At least it's not that unexpected anymore, some positives there.

Without peeking into the cash slot, Katya slowly zips her wallet and even buttons the flap, as though sealing Timo's fate. "I have no money."

This isn't going to end well.

Timo's face falls. "Come on, *please*. Don't do this."

She sticks her earbuds in, ignoring him.

"*Katya*," he pleads. "You don't want to go to Saint Petersburg. What's there?"

Her cheeks flush red, able to hear him. "Family."

Timo shakes his head wildly, his earring swaying. "Your family is here. Have you even talked to Luka about his trip?"

Luka shifts his weight apprehensively. "Stop, Timo."

But Katya takes the bait, pulling out her earbuds. Her orb-like eyes tentatively flicker to me, for reassurance, I think. As though I can tell her the right path. I can't. That's for her to decide. I'm honestly just a bystander, a voyeur in the Kotova backstage experience. This time, I think I did purchase a ticket to it.

"What happened?" Katya asks her older brother.

"Nothing," Luka says. "Nothing happened."

Timo points at Luka, about to share details that aren't his. My interest has peaked. Curiosity—it's a naughty, wicked thing.

"You said you felt lost. Don't lie," Timo retorts.

Luka removes his baseball cap, combing his fingers through his short hair. "Look," he says to both his siblings. Then he struggles for the next words.

Like Katya, he turns to me for that same support. I almost wonder if Nikolai fills this role in their lives. I just nod to him in encouragement, internally saying *you can do this,* whatever this is.

His chest inflates, his shoulders rising. "…I thought I'd feel…home when I got there, but I didn't. A lot was foreign to me. *I* felt foreign. Growing up here with part of the culture is different. We're different, and we don't fit in there…Kat."

Tears well in her eyes, and her chin trembles. "But we don't fit in here."

Timo chimes in, "Yeah we do. Maybe what you're feeling is *internal,* so don't take it out on us." He's still trying to get her cash.

Katya flips him off.

I smile.

Timo groans. "Come on, Kat—" She dives underneath her comforter, physically icing him out. He sighs in frustration and turns to Luka.

"No."

Timo focuses on me and presses his palms together, in prayer formation. "Please, please, Thora James. I'll even take a twenty and pay you back fifty after I win big. You know I can."

When I sat with him at John's table, he won forty extra dollars, but he only left because he had to go prep for Amour. I tell him the truth, "I don't carry cash on me."

The door whips open for the third time, and I realize that the television is shut off, no interfering noise below. Everyone must've left. Nikolai stands strict in the door frame, and Timo and Luka go suspiciously quiet.

We can all hear Katya crying softly beneath her purple comforter.

"What'd you do?" He looks between both his brothers.

Timo rolls his eyes, but I see the remorse flood his features, his bright gray irises beginning to cloud. "I told her that I'm not going to Saint Petersburg."

Nikolai glowers like *why would you ever fucking tell her that?* He pinches the bridge of his nose.

"Everyone knew I was never going to go," Timo refutes.

Luka whispers back, "You could've let her believe what she wanted, at least for two more years."

Timo touches his chest. "I'm being criticized for telling the truth. Does anyone see how wrong this is?" He looks to me. "Thora?"

"Don't bring her into your shit," Nikolai cuts in. He gestures to me with two fingers, and when I approach him, he slips his hand in mine. I relax almost instantly, muscles loosening that I didn't even realize were strained.

"She was my friend first," Timo snaps. "Just think about that when you're fu—"

Nikolai interjects with a bunch of Russian words. My eyes nearly pop out. *He was going to say when you're fucking.* We're not doing that. No. My neck heats.

No.

Timo huffs, more angrily, and then waves Nikolai off. If we're being technical, I met Nikolai before any of them. I can't say we were ever friends though.

Maybe a minute later, Nikolai disengages from his siblings, and I descend the staircase with him while they remain upstairs for a moment or two longer.

I can see the apologies in his eyes before he speaks. "I like your sister," I tell him first. "She's sweet."

He's taken aback, like no one has ever called Katya sweet before. "She's still figuring things out," he says.

"I get it," I breathe. She's trying to find herself. Some days I still wonder if I've found me. Maybe we never stop searching. Maybe we evolve the way seasons change, seamlessly without really knowing, not until all the leaves have fallen.

This is who I am today.

Tomorrow I may be the same.

But in years, I'll be someone else. Someone I may like more. Someone I may like less. And that's okay. Because I'm still living.

"What are you thinking?" Nikolai asks, lifting my chin as he stares down.

I just give him a weak smile. "What time should I wake up for training?"

"Early," he says, dropping his hand. "I have a show at two tomorrow."

I nod, knowing his schedule well enough. I'm about to go to the couch and plop down for the night when he catches my arm.

"About Dimitri." He pauses. "I've known him since I was a little kid, and he's always been this way. I just take him for what he is. I promise he won't affect your training."

I feel like we're skirting around something deeper. It can't be all about training. So I throw it out there, "No boyfriends, right?"

His features harden. "Don't sleep with him."

My eyes widen. "I wouldn't...date your cousin."

"I didn't say date."

"Nikolai—"

He turns his head from me, his jaw muscles contracting. "Never mind. I shouldn't...I have no say in who you have sex with. You can do what you—"

"I'm *not* going to sleep with him," I say assuredly. "Even if he wasn't your cousin, I'm not remotely attracted to Dimitri." I'm just saying whatever feels right, and surprisingly going with the moment helps.

Nikolai's tense shoulders lower some, and he faces me. Saying nothing else. He seems conflicted, confused, knee-deep in a gray area that I've grown accustomed to.

I clear my throat to break the silence. "Yeah…so there's that."

"You have better judgment than most then." He searches my eyes for clarity. I have no more answers than him. When he realizes this, he adds, "I'll see you in the morning, Thora."

Then he hesitates for a moment, and I wonder if he's going to kiss me. Even my cheek or forehead. Something. He leans closer like he may.

At last second, he simply releases my arm, and he leaves my side. My life has never felt more complicated, but this is a complication that I'd rather exist than not have at all.

ACT NINETEEN

I am sweating.

Not the sexy sweat that glistens with a thin beautiful sheen—if that's even real. I'm starting to question television and movies and humanity. My red Ohio State shirt is *soaked.*

In two hours—I've done pull-ups, sprints, kettle balls, curls, a plethora of weight lifts, dead lunges, jump rope, and now I'm staring at a vertical beam that resembles a stripper pole, but it's ten times higher and covered in rubber. I already know I'm going to have to *climb* the pole, my muscles shrieking at me to stop now.

Nikolai breathes heavily like me, hands on his sides, his bare chest *glistening* with sweat. He joined me on the torture-filled workout. It's a hellish version of what I would've done this summer for gymnastics conditioning.

He really is the devil.

But he claims this is his normal routine, only modified for my height and size and discipline.

"When do...we practice..." I pant and gesture to the aerial silk light-years away from me. "...on that?"

His rolled red bandana collects his sweat, damp strands of hair hanging over it. "When you're strong enough."

I'll be soaring forty-feet in the air without a harness, so I understand his concern. But... "You forget that I do an aerial hoop act every night, and I'm strong enough for that."

He takes two lengthy strides near me and seizes my bicep. He lifts up my arm and points at the reddish burns that mar my skin, from armpit to elbow. "If you were strong enough, you'd be able to support your entire body weight to avoid this."

"Hoop burns are normal." *I think*. The friction of the metal and my skin is like a version of a rope burn—not the most pleasant sensation. "The other girls at Phantom have them."

"The other girls at Phantom aren't trying to join Aerial Ethereal."

He makes a lot of sense.

"No complaining," he adds, dropping my bicep. "Rule number one."

"I was just kindly *mentioning*...something." My mind travels away from me, especially as he rests a firm hand on my shoulder. My chest falls more deeply than before—and he seems to notice, eyeing my ribcage. Yet, he keeps that hand in place.

"Use your core." He rests his other palm on my abdomen. "And climb halfway up. If you can support your entire body weight with just your hand, extending your body away from the pole, we'll move onto aerial silk."

I blow out a breath. *I can do it.* Even though I've never done that before—*I can still do it.* My cheerleader sounds less assured than usual.

When his hands fall, I near the pole, clasping it firmly. One more breath and I make the ascent, using the tips of my toes but mostly my arms, my muscles pulling tight.

Up.

And up.

You can do this, Thora. It's the lamest mantra in the history of mantras. I know this. But it's the best one I have. It's the one I always use, clearly. And still, the overuse doesn't diminish its effect.

I keep my swift pace, the ceiling closer.

And closer.

Then halfway up, my quads spasm.

No. I try to block it out.

Don't think about it.

I climb a bit higher, and the spasm clenches my entire muscle, spindling towards my ankles.

A cramp.

Two cramps. They're not the little ones that I can shake off. It's the crippling kind—from too much strain and maybe not enough hydration.

"Thora!" Nikolai calls.

I'm hugging onto the pole, my legs wrapped around it. "Just give… me a second!" I shout back, a wince contorting my face. *You can do this, Thora James. Climb this fucking pole.*

I use my hands to pull my body higher, my legs worthless beneath me. One handhold extra and I stop. There's no way I can support my weight with one hand. My body is out of commission. At least until the cramping ends.

"Climb down!" Nikolai shouts, his voice pitching in worry, but the severity—the strictness, chills my bones.

I inhale. "One more—"

"*Now*," he forces. "I'm not playing the fuck around, Thora."

When I glance at him below, he braces a hand to the pole, standing right underneath it like he's prepared to catch me if I let go and accidentally drop. His whole no-nonsense demeanor sways me. And I slide down the pole like a fireman or little kid in an indoor playground.

My feet hit the mat, and my knees instantly buckle beneath me. I thud on my ass, and while I stifle the heat of failure, Nikolai towers above my small frame.

"Do you want to be an AE artist?" he asks in a growl.

"You know I do…"

"Then *listen* to me," he seethes. "If I tell you to jump, you jump. If I tell you to get *the fuck* down, you get the fuck down. Without question."

I nod tensely, my calf cramping so cruelly that I can't do much else but cringe and wish for it to stop. I imagine my muscles constricting to the point of snapping, band by band. It's illogical, but it's the feeling, most definitely. Pulling and snapping.

With a heavy breath, Nikolai sits and splays my leg across his lap. My quads visibly spasm, and he applies pressure to my thigh muscle, massaging the area. He watches my reaction and my muscles like he's accustomed to cramps of this nature. I've had them, *maybe* once. When I forgot to stretch. But not this extreme.

He digs his fingers a little deeper in my thigh. I wince and instinctively reach behind me, gripping the pole. I rest my spine and head against it.

"Relax," Nikolai says huskily.

It's hard. For multiple reasons. My whole body wants to lock by his closeness, my nerves flapping. "I'm trying," I whisper.

His brows knot as he concentrates on my legs. My hamstrings suddenly tighten, and a literal cry breaches my lips.

His eyes flicker up to me, just once. And I see something different in those grays—something that causes his Adam's apple to bob. Without much falter, he massages underneath my thigh, and I reach out and hold onto his forearm.

"Wait," I say, unsure of whether he's making it worse or better.

"Breathe normally," he instructs. "It'll help."

I blow out like I'm in a Lamaze class.

With my hand still clasped to him, he kneads my muscles. They slowly begin to uncoil, the pain lessening with his rhythmic movements. My next breath is almost a relieved sigh. "Thanks," I manage to say.

"You need to drink more water," he tells me. "And how much are you eating?" His eyes find me again, and they carry this real concern. It's a new look from him.

"I was on a twenty-five-hundred calorie diet in college," I say softly, watching his hand move back up my thigh. The gymnastics team had a nutritionist that gave us tips about healthy eating.

"You used the past tense."

"Well…since I've been here, I haven't been able to really eat…as much." My voice trails off at his glare.

"When you work with me, you're on a three-thousand calorie diet," he demands. "No exceptions. And I'll start you on a few supplements, the ones that the female artists take in AE." He pauses before he adds, "I'll get a copy of their nutrition plan for you."

Three-thousand calories. I try to add up the cost of eating *that* much a day.

Plus the cost of new costumes.

Plus rent.

And the down payment.

I already feel sick.

But I have to make it work, somehow.

"I'll help you stretch and then we'll call it a day. I don't want you to pull a muscle." His hands no longer apply pressure, but they remain on my bare skin, on my thigh. His intense gray eyes graze the length of my legs.

My lungs collapse as silence stretches for an extra moment or two. "…sounds good," I say to break the quiet.

He turns his head some, like he's lost in thought.

I lick my chapped lips. "I'm sorry, for before. I should've listened to you and come down."

"It's not all you. I have a lot I'm dealing with, and I'm just trying to be more cautious."

I wonder if he's referring to his old partner or his new one. I haven't asked about his training with Elena because it's never surfaced until now. Curiosity overpowers me. "How's Elena?" I put it out there.

His hands run down to my knee, resting there. "She's decent." He chooses his words carefully. "A fast enough learner, but she's young and not as emotive as…" He stops himself, shutting down some, like he's drawing up the bridge of his fortress.

"Tatyana?" I wonder.

He nods. "It's not fair to compare anyone to Tatyana. She was a third generation acrobat and one of the best in her discipline." He shrugs, unbendingly. It's probably still raw—her injury and dismissal from Amour. "I shouldn't tell you this. It's not important to your training."

"But it's important to you," I say under my breath.

He flashes a weak smile. "Which has no business in the gym."

Right. "You forget," I point out, "that we're already unprofessional."

He smiles, a real one this time. "I never forget, myshka." He rises and holds out his hand for me. Without hesitation, I take it, and Nikolai helps me to my feet.

ACT TWENTY

By the end of the week, my body has gone through a brutal beating. The tiniest muscles ache, even the ones in my pinky finger. I can't support my weight with only my hand yet, not while extending my legs outward in a horizontal, straight line. So we haven't moved onto aerial silk. I just keep envisioning my final goal: a contract with Aerial Ethereal. *Any* contract, honestly. I'd even take Magus which is still in the early planning stages.

I try not to focus on the five-month deadline where Elena will grace the globe auditorium in Amour, and my parents will believe that I'm supposed to be there. I'm still trying to formulate another lie to keep them in Cincinnati before that happens.

Tonight, I practice the art of relaxation.

The Red Death is at maximum capacity, a long line spindling outside the door. Like every Saturday night. A perk to knowing Camila:

I just slipped right on by again. Currently pop remixes blare through speakers and create a unity of grinding bodies.

I rotate my blue glow choker, the connector resting against the back of my neck. Admittedly, I hesitated on whether to take an "it's complicated" necklace—but it's not really that complicated, I guess. Nikolai is training me. That's it.

I grab a shot of tequila from Camila while she mans the bar, green glow ring atop her curls. She has more colorful makeup on, pink sparkles beneath her eyes and cheeks, gold glitter on her neck and collarbones.

"I can't believe you haven't fucked him yet!" She shouts to me over the music. Then she leans closer, forearms on the bar. First thing she asked was my relationship status.

I can't be the only girl who'd choose this path. "We're just friends," I assure her.

Camila looks disappointed, like she was ready to pass me extra celebratory shots.

"Why the hell are you pouting?" John asks his cousin. He sits on the stool next to me, fisting a beer. "And please don't tell me you're living vicariously through Thora's sex life. That's just sad. Especially since you have a boyfriend—no, not a boyfriend actually. More like a fuck face, piece of shit." He raises his beer to her in cheers.

My eyes grow big. I met Craig at Camila's apartment during my couch-surfing days. He seemed normal. Nice, even. He brought Camila a bouquet of roses, just because.

Though I can't deny their intense verbal sparring matches that shook the walls at night. Maybe John knows about those.

Camila stands straighter. "It's called *empathy*," she says, sidestepping the boyfriend insult. "Something that was removed from you at birth."

"I can empathize with people. But I choose not to because I'm the only sane person in this godforsaken country. Seriously, why should I feel bad that Thora didn't get laid? She probably saved herself from an STD and a broken heart." Dear God—I didn't even think about STDs. I cringe.

"*John*," Camila snaps.

He lets out a breath and rolls his eyes. "I'm just making conversation."

"Nikolai doesn't seem like he sleeps around a lot," I mention. Though I'm not certain about this. Katya never talks about his previous relationships. He's a full-on mystery there, and I feel like it's stepping out of bounds if I even ask.

"See," Camila says, pointing a finger at John.

"Whatever," he mumbles. "I need another drink." He slides his cousin the empty beer bottle, and she retrieves him a new one.

"Thora James!"

I whip my head and notice Timo approaching, his face bathed in green, red and blue from three stacked necklaces. He's added silver glitter on his bare chest and cheeks to his usual attire: no shirt, leather jacket, and dangling cross earring. He looks like part of the club folk.

John curses under his breath the minute Timo nears. He can't keep his mouth shut though. "The under-twenty-one club is down the street," he tells him. "It has a big giraffe and R-Us at the end." He gives Timo a dry look before taking a swig of beer.

Timo only smiles more. "The over-ninety club is also down the street. It's where all these headstones are, old man. Can't miss it." Then he rotates to me, and he lets out a long whistle, scrutinizing me from head to toe. "Thora James, turning it on tonight."

I'm actually dressed up this time—not in sneakers or my Phantom costume. Camila lent me a tight black dress that zips in the back and lifts up my boobs. I keep tugging the hem since it rides up as I sit on the barstool, appearing shorter.

"Better than the sweats?!" I have to shout over the loud bass.

"Most definitely!" he yells back. "My brother is going to love it!"

My stomach clenches. "That's…" *not what I planned.* My voice drowns in the music. *Okay, don't fool yourself, Thora.* If I can't be honest with myself, then I am fucked.

I knew Nikolai would be here tonight, as he is every Saturday.

And yeah, I wanted to look my best. I wanted to draw a reaction from him—the kind that electrocutes my nerves and tingles my skin.

Tingles.

I'm talking about tingles in association with a *guy*. I internally groan. Shay would call me ridiculous. But I don't even want to take the wish back. I'm only human.

John slices through what would've been an awkward moment from my open-mouthed, stupefied-self. He zeroes in on Timo again. "This area…" He motions around us. "…is for people who can *legally* order at the bar." He shoos him away with the swat of his hand.

Timo's blinding, magnetic smile never fades. "In another life, you were a fat old police officer addicted to donuts."

Camila spits out her water from behind me, and the spray dampens my neck. "I'm sorry!" she says between fits of laughter. "That's just…"

My laugh begins at the sight of hers, and she shakes her head, her stomach heaving with humor. She has to hold herself upright.

"I can't…" She flashes her palm like she has to step away, heading to another couple who wave her down.

I reach over the bar for a little square napkin and pat my neck, my hair in an edgy French braid. (Camila did it for me.)

"Your cousin likes me." Timo cocks his head at John.

"She likes everyone. This comes from a place of love when I say that she has the *worst* sense of judgment. For everything, really. Including people."

"Hey," I say. "She likes me."

"And you're sharing a bedroom with a Kotova," he rebuts. "That kind of puts your quality at the bottom of the barrel."

"I'm sleeping on the *couch*," I emphasize.

"Wait," Timo cuts in with a confused look. "You don't sleep in Nik's bed?"

What is with everyone and this? I'm not abnormal. "I…" I trail off as his frown deepens.

"Do you not like him or something?" He scratches the back of his head, more downtrodden than usual. He didn't phrase the question as: does Nikolai not like you or something? As if it was all my choice to sleep on the couch.

"I mean, he's just training me." Those are Nikolai's words too. He's said them to me before.

Timo looks just as perplexed as I feel. "I thought he liked you."

I rock back, my heart convulsing. It's like someone fisted my internal organs. "What gave you that idea?" I think I want it to be true.

I shouldn't.

He's just training you, Thora. Stay concentrated.

Goals. I have goals.

John stares at the ceiling like this conversation is killing him.

"You're living with him," Timo says. "Duh, Thora James."

I don't feel like I'm so oblivious. I just think we're all more confused than they'd have us believe.

John suddenly stands and nears Timo, only an inch taller than him. "What is this?" Clutching his beer, he gestures to the three glow necklaces.

"I'm single, complicated and taken," Timo replies with a burgeoning smile.

John looks to me. "He's a liar." Then to Timo. "Seriously, you're a liar."

"Or I'm just a mystery, old man."

John swiftly snaps off the red and green glow necklaces, leaving Timo with only blue. "Look at that, I solved your pathetic mystery."

Timo licks his bottom lip and laughs. "You want me to be single, John?" This took a turn. I stare between them, my eyes pinging back and forth with intrigue.

John puts the beer to his lips. "I'm out of your league, Timo."

"If you say so."

"TAT! TAT! TAT!" The room yells over the pumping music, and my heart double skips. John groans at the commotion, but his feet carry him closer to the spectacle.

Timo clasps my hand, tugging me along. I've somehow slid deeper into the Kotova circle. He slings his arm around my shoulder and follows John Ruiz. "He's a walking contradiction," Timo says, amused. His eyes lower to John's ass, squeezed in a pair of dark-colored jeans.

I just ogled John's butt. I scrunch my face. That was not on my to-do list tonight.

I don't have to ask Timo to clarify his statement. John is cynical, pessimistic, claiming to be drama-free, but he seeks it out and thrives on watching it. He's also popular enough that three people scoot over, awarding us the closest view.

Timo wedges between John and me, his other arm swooping around John's shoulders. I'm shocked when John doesn't push him off.

My gaze casually drifts to the open circle, where the crowds have parted for Nikolai. And the minute I see another girl in it, my whole face tightens. Nikolai leads the twenty-something brunette to the lone chair, his hand on the small of her back.

His hand on the small of her back.

This shouldn't marbleize me, but I'm cold and unmoving.

"Fifty bucks she picks a tattoo," Timo says.

"Don't you do enough betting on the fucking floor?" John snaps.

"I'll take that as a *no.*" Timo nods to me. "Thora?"

I can't answer. My muscles coil, taut and inflexible. Nikolai sits on the chair first, his intense gaze never deterring from the girl's. Her blue glow necklace contrasts her red mini-dress, one with sparkly stiletto heels. He says directions to her, not audible from where I stand.

Then she lies *over* his lap, hiking up the bottom of her dress to reveal her ass.

My stomach compresses without my permission—my heart on a strange, foreign descent. A burly man with a thick neck passes Nikolai a tattoo gun.

"I would've won," Timo announces, disappointment lacing his voice. Though he squeezes my shoulder like *cheer up, Thora James. It's okay.*

I must look as horrible as I feel.

"Everyone wins eventually," John says, his tone less hostile than usual. "It doesn't mean you can't lose."

Nikolai places his hand on the girl's ass, concentrating on the needle as it digs into her flesh. He tells her something, his lips rising in a charismatic smile that lights his gray eyes. And she laughs. I want to look away. I don't want to watch this—because it hurts.

It shouldn't hurt this much.

And yet, I can't. Move. I can't lift my foot or spin around. I torture myself by staying here.

The red glow of his necklace swathes his face, his features as devilish and masculine as that first night we met. Only I'm not the subject of his intensity. *You know this happens every Saturday, Thora.* I know. It's nothing, really. It all means nothing—in every direction.

A couple brutal minutes pass and he's finished, inking a well-drawn heart on her left butt cheek. Carefully, he places a bandage on the tattoo and tugs her dress down, covering her thong. She wobbles as she stands, and he rights her with a protective hand to her waist.

"Thora," I hear Timo say in concern.

I open my mouth, but no words come.

In a millisecond, the girl goes from clutching his biceps. To leaning in.

Her lips are on his.

And he grips the back of her head, reciprocating the single kiss. My breath is padlocked in my lungs. Even after they disconnect. Nikolai kisses her cheek and gestures to a group of girls who cheer and shout things like *get it, Rachel!* They must be her friends.

The girl returns to them with the smuggest, happiest grin. She kissed the God of Russia and can now recount the tale. He's already scanning the room with a charming smile, searching for his next volunteer. Hands shoot all around me.

Timo squeezes my shoulder again and then he shouts something in Russian. His voice overpowers the music and causes Nikolai to rotate towards us.

His eyes stop dead on me.

And that smile fades in an instant.

I can't pick apart my feelings. Or his. But if I could assume anything at all—it'd be on the precipice of pain and distress. I'm rethinking my choice in glowstick. This is utterly complicated.

"Let's go dance," John tells me, reaching for my arm past Timo.

"Yeah, I could dance," Timo nods.

"Not you—ugh, whatever, come on, Thora." John guides me through the masses and closer to the mosh pit dance floor, people jumping or grinding, depending on their level of intoxication.

I'm surprised my feet moved at all.

John tips a waitress an extra twenty to steal the drinks off her tray, and he passes me the shot and keeps the other two for himself.

"You seriously aren't going to share?" Timo asks with the tilt of his head. He rests his forearm on John's shoulder.

"I'm seriously not sharing," John replies, and to further his point, he throws back the first shot and then the second.

Timo isn't discouraged in the least. He dances with better rhythm than most everyone here. The three of us group off in a cluster, blocking out the surrounding people. I'm less overwhelmed, and the shot will help too. Normally I'd take an economic sip, but I mimic John and toss mine back.

It burns my throat, and I cough into my fist.

"Easy, Thora James!" Timo shouts over the music. When I look at him, his eyes beam like he's having the time of his life. In the prime of his youth. And it lightens my weighted body, immeasurably.

It's ordinary when you're simply happy.

It's remarkable when you can make others feel what you do.

"Don't stare into his eyes!" John shouts to me. "Little parts of you will die inside!"

He almost lifts my spirits.

A smile stretches Timo's beautiful features. "So you're admitting to feeling something from me, John?!"

John glares. "*Death*. I feel death!"

Timo whistles, but I can't hear the sound from the pop song. "That's a strong feeling."

John looks like he wants to drown his irritations in an eighty-foot pool, though he's still here. So there's that. He snatches more shots off a tray, and this time, the server lets him take them. He knows her, I guess. And he passes me two shots and keeps one for himself.

I down both, the burn not as terrible. I actually like it. Then I sway to the music, and I notice older guys near a high-top table eyeing our three-person group. Only their attention is plastered to Timo—with lustful, *I want to fuck you* looks.

I realize that Timo has been scoping out the club, and he grazes that area a bit, knowing how many men are watching him. A weird pressure sits on my chest, and it takes me a second to discern the sentiment.

Protective—I feel strangely protective over him.

He's eighteen, I remember. But he carries himself like the world is a playground for his appetite. *Vegas is his home.* He's not a fish-out-of-water like I was—still am sometimes. He's okay.

John follows my gaze to the other guys. He rolls his eyes and quite literally blocks them out with his back.

Hands touch my waist, and I jump and slide to the left to see Nikolai. I freeze cold. He stares down, his gaze deepening into mine, carrying a storm past comprehension. I don't know what to make of it.

"Hi." His husky voice solidifies my bones. Just one word. That's all I get.

"...hey," I manage with a nod. The liquor starts to churn my insides like molten lava, no longer warm and comforting.

Nikolai keeps his hand on my hip, filling the almost non-existent gap between me and Timo. I hone in on his hand, on each finger that slips further around me. I can't—I step out of his grasp, and his arm falls. I stare at the red strobe lights on the ceiling as though God will impart me with some much-needed wisdom.

"Don't you have an ass to tattoo?!" John yells, his surly tone sounding a hint more malicious.

It shouldn't matter, Thora.

I know. I know.

I'm trying to make it not matter. How do I do that? My mind and my body are not on the same wavelength, clearly, and I'm having a difficult time reuniting them.

He grabbed a girl's ass and sucked on her face.

Stop. Stop.

"I'm done for the night!" Nikolai shouts over the bass. "Are you two…" His voice dies in the music. I look up and see his grays darting between John and me. The look he wears—it matches the one I had earlier, when I saw him lip-locked with that girl.

His facial muscles tightening, his shoulders strict.

John seems highly unamused. "She's not my type! While her ambitions are slightly endearing, they're *mostly* delusional! But that's not even the problem." I did catch that compliment in there. I mean, this could be worse. Right?

"What's the problem?" Nikolai asks, opening the floodgates.

"She has a vagina!" The music switched songs right when he screamed that. It came out so much louder than it should have.

I shut my eyes with a wince. Yeah, he just mentioned my vagina. To Nikolai. To make a point that he's gay, and it's just—a lot to take in. I just really, really hope I'm the only one picturing my vagina right now. *Please let this be true.*

I tentatively open my eyes by the silence. Timo is smiling like he's already known this fact about John. And I can feel Nikolai's hot gaze penetrating me.

Don't engage—John basically said as much the first time I met Nikolai. Maybe I should've listened to him back then. I can still try now.

At least when we're not at the gym.

Right?

I'm confused. I'm confusing myself.

"I'm going to get something to drink." Timo speaks first. He begins walking towards the high-top table of men.

John curses under his breath before shouting, "The bar is the other way!" He shakes his head a few times.

Timo glances over his shoulder and grins, descending further into the throngs of dancers.

John sighs heavily and stares between me and Nikolai. *Stay here. Do not leave me.* I hope I'm expressing all of these things in my eyes. I wouldn't be surprised if I just scowl harder though.

"Well this is unfortunate," John says, and his gaze falls to me. "I just want you to know that I'm leaving for the alcohol and to avoid being a third wheel to whatever *this* is."

It's starting to set in: I'm going to have to confront my feelings. Head on soon.

John pats my shoulder and weaves between the bodies, picking up his pace to reach Timo.

Now I'm alone with Nikolai. Well…not *alone* alone. Technically there are bodies around us, some even pressing close to invade Nik's space. I even spot girls gawking at him from the packed bar, whispering like they're concocting plans to approach the God of Russia.

Good, I think.

My heart plummets.

Body and brain, still not aligned.

Nikolai leans down, his unshaven jaw rough against my cheek, and I smell the tequila from his breath, reminding me of his bet. *Tattoo or piercing.*

"Can I talk to you?" he asks lowly, his deep voice melting my defenses.

"Don't you have to watch your brother?" I instantly regret adding more stress on him. Because whatever *this* is (as John called it) already weighs down his shoulders.

"It won't take long." His words send a shudder of alarm through me. *He's going to stop training me.*

I nod and start mentally preparing ways out of this: *I won't see you outside of the gym*, for starters. *Or hang out at your suite anymore*, also goes with number one.

Or pretend that I have feelings for you.

My eyes are burning. *Stop burning.*

Nikolai glances at the VIP area of the club, but it's packed with bodies, allowing for no privacy. He spins to the other direction, near the bathroom. And he guides me with his hand on my hip, dropping to the small of my back.

I wish he wouldn't touch me at all. It'd make this clearer. Easier.

I side-step out of his grasp again, and when I catch a glimpse of him, his face is contorted like my action impaled him through the chest. We don't say anything. But it's hardly quiet.

The music never masks this vast, unyielding tension that tugs my senses. The line to the bathroom snakes along the wall, but he walks past it, aiming for a new door. One that says: *employees only*.

He turns the handle and slips inside, me right after. When he shuts out the cacophony behind him, I realize that we're in a very cramped storeroom with extra bundles of napkins, stir-sticks, and racks of cleaning supplies.

With barely any space to move, my legs hit his, my head reaching the height of his shoulders. I'm tiny. In a tiny room. With a six-foot-five Russian man. And an even bigger elephant. His emotions, my emotions. There are many, many emotions here.

I tug at the hem of my dress that exposes my bare flesh. "What do you want to say?" I ask softly, avoiding his gaze. I fixate on the saltshakers that line the shelf in a neat row.

"Your eyes are black."

My blood simmers, and I gape. "You brought me in here to tell me that my eyes are—"

His lips suddenly meet mine with force and urgency, his hands wrapping around my small frame like he's wanted to hold me all night. My heart explodes. *I* explode, his tongue parting my lips in the fieriest kiss, one that grips my core. One that knocks my back into the shelves.

I struggle for breath—high on his touch, the way he lifts me around his waist, breaking open my legs. He deepens an already sweltering kiss, his hot hand protective on my neck, his thumb caringly brushing my skin while the rest of him—masculine, powerful—rushes through me.

I brace myself by clutching his arms; my body has won out to my mind. I've been overtaken, overpowered, overpleasured.

My lips sting as he slows down an already strong kiss, his chest rock hard against me. I feel unwound, flyaway strands of hair sticking up—like he electrocuted me.

He kind of did.

My spine digs into the metal shelf, and Nikolai kisses my cheek, my forehead, as though I'm precious enough for more than just the thrill. He gives me the unhurried, measured moments, the kisses that seem to ache more.

A noise trembles my throat, a breathless cry.

He lets out a deeper sound against my neck. And his red glow necklace stares back at me, a blinding reminder of all that I don't understand.

What are we doing? What is this? My mind has revived and come to haunt me.

"I…don't understand," I whisper.

He only draws back to cup my face. His lips are a stinging distance away. I can still feel the force of them, the heat of them, on me. His mouth curves upward some, as though he finds my confusion funny.

"It's not funny," I whisper.

"You're cute," he tells me. "I thought my actions said enough."

He likes me. "There is…something between us then?" I wonder. I haven't been fantasizing about the tension. It hasn't been one-sided. It's just been ignored.

He stares so deeply into me. "There is definitely something, my demon." His lips rise more.

I can hear my heart beating. The bass from the club vibrates the shelf behind me, adding to my elevated senses. "What now?" I ask. I shift my hands from his biceps to his shoulders, skimming the red glow necklace. It's where most of my uncertainty lies.

He kisses me again, slowly, his fingers along my neck. It's languid and relaxed, like we've done this all our lives together. When he parts, he whispers, "I've been hesitating because I don't want to step in the way of your dreams."

I try not to fear that. I understand my goals. But—I don't like looking at the bad things before they happen. It's not worth it. "You won't."

He gives me a look like *wake up, myshka.* "I don't want my attraction for you to ruin all that you've sacrificed," he rephrases.

It doesn't deter me. "Is it impossible to love two things equally? I mean, not that I love you…I just…" I blow out a breath. I'm screwing this up. I fail at words sometimes. We're just at a crossroads of *are we pursuing this or leaving it behind?*

He tilts my chin so I meet his eyes again. "I understand what you mean."

"I just—I don't want to believe that a love for one thing will overtake the love for another." It's a cynical view, isn't it? Or maybe mine is just a hopelessly optimistic one.

"Today, if I gave you the option between the circus and a man, you would choose the circus. But later—"

"I'll choose the circus," I say.

He gives me that same look. *I don't want to wake up yet.* "I can't be a reason you give up on your dreams."

"I *won't.*"

The way he's staring at me. It hits me. His rules. No boyfriends. *Not even him.* I feel like he's about to crush something that hasn't even started yet. "Nikolai—"

"But I realized something tonight." His eyes hold so many painful, conflicting truths. Realities that I need to meet. "I realized that it's too late. I distract you—you distract me. And since I don't want to distance myself from you, there's only one option."

His gaze flits to my lips, and he kisses me tenderly, my body winding tight.

I inhale strongly as he presses even further up against me. Clutching me. He's saying that he wants me. I can see it. I can feel it. My eyes burn at the unspoken proclamation.

In a whisper, he says, "And I'll still train you."

The next kiss is so soulful that I feel the promise within it: to never stand in the way of my dreams.

I breathe heavily as he draws back again. His chest rises and falls deeply, waiting for me to speak, giving me a choice to accept or deny this new turn.

Nikolai may assume a lot of things, but when it comes to my own life—he steps back and lets me pick left or right.

"You're complicated?" I ask, eyeing the red glow necklace.

He stiffens. "My past relationship is. I haven't been looking for anything recently, and I didn't even look for you." He pauses. "This was unintentional."

It became something more without noticing. Without realizing. "Am I a mistake—"

"No, myshka. You're just the unexpected, beautiful thing in my life."

My heart is full tonight. I can hardly breathe as it swells. I've never felt this way. "As long as she's not still in the picture..." That scenario is too devastating to jump into.

"She's not," he forces like he's promising me. "You can trust me."

I nod. It's not as blind as the first time we met. I trust him a lot more now—because he's been here for me. And I believe that he wouldn't hurt me. Not intentionally, at least.

"Okay," I breathe, placing my hand on his, the one that warms my cheek.

He kisses me, powerfully, sensually, and his other hand finds my zipper by my shoulder blades. He slowly unzips my tight black dress, stopping at the small of my back. His lips drift to my neck, sucking on the most sensitive spots. His body thrums against mine.

"Nik…" I shudder and remember something—something more important now than it was before. "I'm moving out tonight."

His hands fall underneath my ass, supporting me around his waist. And he looks at me with a frown. "You decided this now." He states it.

"No…" I shake my head. "No, I meant to tell you tonight…I signed a lease for a studio apartment. And maybe it's…better that we don't live together, I mean. It'll make things slower." I hesitate to add the rest. *I want slow. I'm not used to fast.* But he already knows I've only had sex twice. That's the exact *number* of times. It's not even just two different people.

Before he responds, the storeroom door swings open. Camila startles back the minute she sees us: my legs around his waist, my dress partially unzipped. His hands on me.

I cover my face with my palm, my fingers splayed so I can most definitely still see her reaction morph from surprised to something happier.

"Oh my God! I'm sorry." She's smiling. "Continue on." She even flashes me a wider, excited grin. When she shuts the door, I actually go to zip up my own dress.

Nikolai sets me on my feet. "Come here." He tugs me closer and his fingers brush my bare skin as he zips me up. Just as slow as he unzipped me. His eyes dance around my features. "I'll help you move in to your place tonight."

"Actually, I think I should do that on my own." I worry he'll see the shoddy apartment and convince me to stay with him.

He hesitates, his gaze darkening. I think he must read my intentions. "It's in a bad area."

"No," I refute. "It's a good area." *Sort of.* It's not the worst area, so I'm not lying exactly.

"If it was, you'd let me see it." He combs some of the flyaway hairs out of my face. "Okay." It takes me aback but he adds, "I trust you. And I can understand wanting your own space."

"Thank you," I whisper. "Are…you also okay with slow?"

His lips rise like it's funny.

"It's not—"

"It's cute," he says again, this time laughing. "Slow is cute, and I'd go slow for you." He kisses my temple. "Ready?" He nods to the door.

I never thought there would be more paths to choose. I came here thinking I'd already picked my course. The dark, mysterious one—filled with potholes and faraway dreams.

I've found that life is a series of crossroads, dead-ends and U-turns. There is no real destination. There is no goal to end all goals. As long as we're living, we'll always keep driving.

I'm more satisfied with this than I would've been before Vegas.

So as I head out the door, into The Red Death, I know I've switched lanes. I'm headed in the same direction, but my route is slightly different.

The landscape has changed.

ACT TWENTY-ONE

My studio apartment has a single bedroom-kitchen-living area and a confined bathroom. One where I can sit on the toilet, use the sink or reach in the shower at the same time. The kitchen is also miniscule with portable counters, a hotplate, a microwave and a mini-fridge. Actually, miniscule is probably a forgiving word to describe the place.

But I don't care much.

I lie on my mattress, an old one that Camila helped me pick out at a thrift store. Gross, yes, but I put new and clean sheets on top of it. No springboards. It rests on the scratched hardwood floors as is. I stare up at the ceiling tiles, yellowed and maybe moldy.

My lips tug up.

I can't help it.

I'm here.

In Vegas.

I've made enough to have my own apartment.

Independence has never felt so satisfying. I'm grateful for every second of it. And I don't ever want to forget this feeling, right now. I did something—I accomplished *something*. I won't let anyone's realism take that from me.

This is the first strong foothold of my new life. The beginning of my dream and career.

I wipe the wetness beneath my eyes. "Well done, Thora James," I whisper.

My phone buzzes on the floorboards, and I roll onto my stomach and grab my cell. I notice the name on the screen before I press the speaker button. SHAY.

"Hey," I say, my face all smiles.

I can hear the sound of weights hitting benches and muffled chatter in the background. It's safe to assume he's at the gym. "Hey," he replies. "So from your text earlier, I take it you're not coming back." His dejection sinks my stomach, my smile vanishing.

This morning I texted him a picture of my new view: the side of another stucco apartment complex. I thought it'd be funny. Especially since I told him I was apartment hunting last week. But maybe I should've known he'd be sullen. Friday he sent me a link to off-campus apartments in Columbus, Ohio.

I guess it's just wishful thinking on my part—that he'd see the positives of why I'm here.

"I told you I wasn't going back home," I mutter, picking at the sheet on the mattress, dazed.

My parents called for my new address so they could mail me some boxes of things: clothes, dishes, and stuff I took to college. When I gave them the address, I mentioned how it'd be easier to ship boxes to my "friend's" place than have to pay The Masquerade the fee to receive large packages.

They bought the lie. They had no reason not to. I've always been truthful with them. Maybe that's why it hurts to even think about.

"At least tell me you didn't sign a year lease, Thora," he says.

"I'm going month-to-month."

"First smart decision."

Ouch. I stay quiet, squinting at the ceiling. I know he's just trying to leave a door open for me, so I can return to Ohio. But I need to be all in here. *When he throws you a lifeline, don't grab it.* Even if it's hard.

Shay sighs in frustration. "I didn't mean it like that."

"It's okay," I breathe. "How's conditioning?" Partly wanting to divert the discussion and partly wanting to hear more about him.

"Alright. Coach wants me to up the difficulty on my pommel horse routine."

"You should," I tell him. "You're good enough to do it."

"Thanks." Voices escalate, and he muffles the phone as he talks to someone else. When he returns, he says, "I have to go. Some of the guys want to grab subs for lunch. Talk to you later?"

"Yeah." We say our goodbyes, and I sit up, already wearing workout clothes.

Before I click off my phone, I notice the time.

Almost three.

My eyes grow and I spring to my feet, already late. I'm supposed to train with Nikolai today. I mentally calculate the bike ride to The Masquerade. If I don't pedal fast, I'm going to be later than late.

I check my texts that I must not have heard.

Where are you? – Nikolai

Call me. – Nikolai

You're breaking a fucking rule. – Nikolai

I text back: On my way. So sorry!

Last night, I grabbed my suitcase from his place, and he walked with me outside The Masquerade. I didn't have to wait long for a cab, and he kissed me before I climbed in and left. I have trouble containing this smile in remembrance. I even subconsciously touch my lips.

I'm falling for him.

But I haven't seen Nikolai since then. He had to practice with Elena this morning, so he scheduled a later time to train me.

I don't know how things are going to be. I guess I'm about to find out. I just need to get there first.

BY THE TIME I ARRIVE AT THE GYM, MY FOREHEAD is dripping with sweat, my cotton pants sticking to my legs, butt and thighs. I rode my bike (another thrift store find) as fast as I could without breaking the rusty, old thing.

Halfway there, I feared the chain would fly off. My one thought was: *don't fall off.* Not *don't be late.* My mental energy can't turn back time. I'm just happy that I'm here, in one piece, with a bike also in one piece.

I spot Nikolai sitting on a large blue yoga ball, his eyes flitting to the clock with agitation and maybe some concern. He clutches his cell tightly.

When I approach with hurried feet, his head swings my way, pieces of his hair falling over his red bandana. I throw up my hands. "I'm so... sorry..." I lose my initial thoughts at the relief in his eyes. "You didn't think..." *something bad happened.*

He stands. "I have no idea where you live, Thora," he reminds me. "Just don't be late again." He gives me a harder, stricter look, delivering the lines with finality. Then he takes a few steps closer, with a much more intense gaze.

Butterflies swarm my insides. *Stop smiling like a fool, Thora.*

I bite my gums so hard. And I nod. "I will…I mean, I won't." Why? Why am I screwing this up right now? "You know what I mean…" *hopefully.*

He crosses his arms over his bare chest, his brows raised. "Think you can hold your weight today?" He's all no-nonsense, seriousness—business.

Right.

He's determined not to step in the way of my goal, and that means keeping things as professional as we can in the gym. *Good*, I think.

"I've been practicing on the aerial hoop," I tell him, "so I hope so."

"We'll see then." He leads me to the pole.

I stare up at the thirty-foot vertical structure that stands between me and the aerial silk. *You can do this, Thora.* I exhale a tight breath and step out of my cotton pants.

"Use your core," he reminds me. "Don't put all of your weight in your arm."

I grip the pole. *You can do this.*

There is so much that says I can't. But I'm going to try—with everything I have. I begin the climb in thin acro-shoes, using the tips of my toes and hands as I quickly make the ascent.

"Stop at ten feet," he calls to me.

I gauge that height and halt not even halfway up. I exhale through my nose and tighten my clutch. Then I begin to extend my legs out, toes pointed. The muscles in my forearm burn and my body shakes.

"Use your core, Thora," he says again.

It's natural to want to use my arms as the force behind my power. I shut my eyes, exhale again, and try to focus on my abdomen, flexing and extending my body outward. In a curved line. *You need to be horizontal*, I tell myself.

I have to lift more of my weight. And I need to release one of my hands.

It seems impossible.

Try.

I will.

Two more breaths. My muscles constrict as I raise my body another degree. Every tendon burns. Sweat beads off my forehead.

No longer vibrating, I dig deeper and channel strength in my quads, in my core.

I am horizontal. Then I slowly release one hand. And I immediately grab the pole again. My legs drop like someone poked a balloon, busting whatever helium kept me afloat.

I feel heavier. Sagging in defeat, I slide down the pole, careful the friction doesn't burn my bare thighs. I touch the blue mat and finally meet Nikolai's narrowed gaze.

"You look upset," he says.

"I just thought today I'd be stronger." *I feel like I'm wasting your time when I fail.* It's not a good feeling.

His eyes smile. "Today you were much stronger than yesterday. And tomorrow you'll be even stronger. That's the great thing about practice, myshka, you can only go up."

I'm weightless again. It's rare that someone else boosts me more than I do myself. "Thanks. I'll try again tomorrow then." I figure he'll want to do some sort of workout: dead lunges, crunches, sit-ups, pull-ups—

"No." He fractures my thoughts.

"No?"

"We're moving on." He nods to the aerial silk.

My shoulders rise, and I've already begun to smile. "But I didn't—"

"You held your weight with one hand. Even for a millisecond, it was a millisecond more than most can do." He studies me for a second, and I realize that I'm rocking on the balls of my feet, too excited to stay completely still. "You know the basics?" he asks.

I nod rapidly. "Yeah. I can do a Half-Moon and Back Walk-Over and other…stuff." He's trying to contain a smile of his own. "What?"

"Nothing." He places a hand on my shoulder, but his fingers caress my neck, so subtly that chills prick my arms. "This way."

My heart beats quicker, curious about what he'll have me do. We reach the red silk, rigged to the high ceiling. But we don't immediately start. He makes me stretch my arms first.

After that, I slip off my acro-shoes and Nikolai leaves my side. He pulls the fabric apart, displaying two silks. "I need to see your skill level. Show me the splits, a Back Walk-Over, and a simple single-foot-tie-in."

Before he passes me the nylon material, he grabs a bottle of resin nearby and approaches, the aerial silk skimming my cheek as a foot of space separates us. The fabric opens up, and we're almost cocooned within the crimson, wispy material.

His intimate gaze cuts through me for a second. He pauses and soaks in my features.

My breath shallows.

"Hold out your palms," he whispers lowly, the words sounding like sex.

I flip my hands over, and he sprays resin on them, which'll help my grip on the silk. When he sprays some on his palms, I realize that he may demonstrate later on.

He passes me the silk. "Show me."

The material is more elastic than what I used in my garage, a higher difficulty, but I'm determined to perform these few tricks and poses. I climb up the silk with my hands, my muscles burning from the earlier routine. I wrap one foot, recalling the technique.

"Where'd you learn this?" he asks, watching me closely.

"Am I doing it wrong?" I wonder, my eyes popping out. I look at my foot, secured in the fabric, to the point where I can stand up with ease. My heel and toes aren't covered with the red material.

"No, it's right. I'm just curious."

"Don't laugh when I tell you." I remember when Shay went through my DVDs in my dorm room and snickered like *you can't be serious?* Then he actually said, "At least it's not pole dancing." I didn't have the heart to admit to studying YouTube clips of pole dancers and being envious of their tricks.

Nikolai's brows pinch in more confusion. "I wouldn't, Thora."

"I learned from videos. There were more when I got older though, when YouTube existed." While he digests this, I grip the top of the silk and extend my body, my spine curving inward and creating a shape like I'm flying. Instead of just dangling my other leg, I bend my knee and point my toe.

"You're self-taught," he says. "That's not something anyone should laugh at you for."

My cheeks heat. And I climb higher on the silk. Then I break it apart and wrap my foot in each. I let go, dropping upside-down. The blood runs to my head, and I easily do the splits by stretching out my legs. Climbs. Wraps. Drops. It's the bread and butter of this apparatus. That, I do know.

Nikolai is silent for the rest, and after a few more minutes, I finish and drop down. I can't read his expression well enough to figure out if I'm better than average. So I just ask. "How'd I do?"

"I thought you'd be worse."

I nod with my hands on my hips, breathing a bit heavier. "That's good. I'll take that."

He rubs his lips and breaks my gaze.

"What?" I frown.

His hand goes to his eyes—he's rubbing his eyes *in distress.*

No. *What did you do, Thora?*

He says, "I want to kiss you—even more than that. It's distracting me." He pinches his eyes. "I shouldn't have said anything."

My belly flips and somersaults and refuses to stay stationary. "Really…?" I pause, wondering if that sounded rude. "I mean, you really want to kiss me? I wasn't responding to your second…" *statement.*

He grimaces as he shuts his eyes tightly, as though I'm making it worse.

I'm gaping, very breathy. I manage to close my mouth, but I imagine my lips on his. His body against mine. Tangled together. I try to wipe away the visuals, but they keep coming.

After Nikolai exhales a deep breath, he tries to mask his feelings. He's more severe again. "You need to work on your presentation." *Back to business.*

"What do you mean?"

"You're performing for an audience, not for yourself. You're not trying to master the hardest trick, you're trying to create the illusion that you're dancing in the air." He clasps my hand. "Be graceful. Be lithe and elegant with every move you make. Everything about aerial silk should look seamless."

He combines the silk with one hand and takes a short running start. His feet lift off the ground. He flies like he lives up high. Like he's never been grounded before. My ribcage juts in and out, watching as he effortlessly circles around me, as he supports his body with one fist wrapped around the silk. He extends his arm out to me.

Grab his hand.

The next time he nears, I do. I clasp his palm, my soles leaving the safety of the blue mat. My heart has never beat this hard. Or this fast.

"Climb up," he commands.

I scale his rock hard body, as though he's the pole I've been practicing on, and when I reach his chest, I grasp his shoulders.

"Breathe," he whispers.

I let one out, his eyes boring through me. We start to slow, the momentum depleting. He wraps the second silk around my hand. We're going to detach. I strangely, *strangely* would love to stay right here. Pressed against him.

His eyes flit to my lips.

Business only, I try to read his mind. I think I guess right because he forces those gray gunmetal skies on my almost-black irises.

"Inhale," he instructs.

I'm forgetting to breathe. How am I forgetting to breathe?

I inhale. Exhale. In. And out. Then he pushes me off his body, with so much power that I go flying. I try not to smile too much. *Graceful.* With this speed, I can spin. So I do. I twirl with pointed toes, using the power he's given me to go even faster.

When I near him in my full rotation, I reach my hand out, and he seizes it, slinging my body into his chest, not too hard, but enough that a jolt of energy courses through me. Adrenaline. An intoxicating rush.

He hugs me close, one of his hands rising to my face.

Again—I'd love to do this again and again. With him. Only with him. I can't say I'm entirely graceful and completely lithe. But I feel weightless once more.

It takes me a moment to realize that we've decelerated entirely. We've come to a stop. He unwinds my hand as though he's gently removing lingerie, with the most sensual, slow-burning movement. He keeps me clutched to his chest as he descends, his feet hitting the mat before he sets me down.

It feels like we had aerial sex.

Aerial sex. Now I'm thinking about that—the *real* act of it. Dear God in heaven. Is that even a thing? Do people do that?

He tosses me my towel, waking me up from my dirty stupor. "You still need lots of work."

"But I'm not hopeless." I smile.

"Like you said," he nods to me, "you're a *work in progress*. But landing a contract, there's luck involved. You need some of that too."

"I know," I breathe. He's not trying to elevate my hopes too much.

"That's it for today. Make sure you wash the resin off your hands and use lotion every night. It'll dry out your skin if you don't."

I dab my sweaty hairline with my towel and just now notice how rigid he is, his shoulders unbending. I slip on my cotton pants and acro-shoes while he puts our water bottles in his gym bag, not saying another word. It spindles more tension in my joints and muscles.

"I'll walk you out," he suddenly adds.

He's never walked me out of the gym before.

The nervous flutters return. I wonder when we leave the gym if business will end. And something else will begin. I'm not sure what happens after we exit the double doors. This is all really new.

Since it's Sunday and not the morning, there are more than a few people practicing today. We pass a couple doing hand-to-hand tricks, her palm flat on his forehead as she lifts her legs vertically. A handstand. On his head.

Insane.

Nikolai lets out a growl of annoyance. Not at the acrobatic couple. He clasps my hand, tugging me in a new direction before I can even follow his gaze.

Katya lies on top of a giant rolled mat, earbuds in and reading *One Last Kiss, Please*. The paranormal romance I loaned her. Nikolai drops my hand and yanks out the cord to her iPod.

She gawks at him and sits up. "Hey." When she notices me, her eyes seem to light up. "Hi, Thora. I just got to the *best* part—"

"You're supposed to be practicing," he cuts her off, and a wave of guilt washes over me. My book has inadvertently become a distraction, but in my defense, that is one *hell* of a good werewolf-vampire novel.

"I am," she says. "In my mind." She's about to put her earbuds back in and lie down again.

He steals her iPod and the book out of her hands.

"Nik—"

"You almost didn't land a tucked back somersault on Friday."

I remember Nikolai mentioning that she works with the Russian bar, as the flyer apparently. It's dangerous, an elevated balance beam held by two people at each end. She springs into the air and has to land straight back down. But I guess, what isn't dangerous here.

Her mouth falls. "Luka told you that?"

"He's one of your *porters*, Katya. If you fall and break your leg, he's going to blame himself." Her older brother must help support the bar, I deduce.

"I wasn't going to fall," she mutters, the remorse pulling her lips down.

"If you want to try out for Noctis, you need a full-in, full-out or a triple sault, and you're not going to get there by sitting on your ass, reading..." He scrutinizes the paperback's title and cover (legs intertwined on a blue silk sheet) with confusion and then gives me a weird look.

"It's a good book," I assure him. Though I start to wonder whether it's age appropriate. I mean, I was reading explicit adult books at twelve—but I didn't really understand some of the graphic sex scenes. Sixteen can't be that bad.

"I love it," Katya adds, reaching out to snatch it back.

He stuffs it in his black gym bag with her iPod. "It's mine until your practice is over."

"You're so mean," she says, sliding off the rolled mat and thudding to her feet. "It's not like I'm *ever* going to land a full-in, full-out."

It dawns on me. That's why she doesn't even want to try. "Who says you can't do it?" I ask.

"The universe," she tells me dramatically. "I was born a girl."

I don't understand. "So?"

"So my brothers are always better than me. I do everything slower than them, so there's no point." To live in the shadow of the male Kotovas, of every sibling and cousin—it must be hard.

"Don't you want to at least try to show them up?"

"I have tried," she refutes. "It's impossible."

Nikolai cocks his head. "You've never even stayed late after practice."

She crosses her arms over her white tank top. "It's not that easy."

I don't want to gang up on her. So I say, "I know the feeling. I spent most of my days in gymnastics, trying to be better than my best friend.

And I never was. Not once. He always won. But every time I tried to beat him, I actually ended up improving anyway. So there were some positives in there." I realize I might be rambling, so I add quickly, "I just like to look on the bright side of things, I guess."

She's quiet for a moment, mulling over her thoughts. Then she turns to her brother. "You better give that book back to me. I'm at the part where Rafael fights Derek."

That's the climax. "It's a good part," I tell Nikolai.

His lips almost tic into a smile. Then he nods to his sister, agreeing to return the book later. "You're going to practice." It's an assumption.

"Yeah."

It's a *right* assumption.

She leaves with a wave, and Nikolai guides me back towards the double doors. He doesn't speak. The conversation with Katya seems to flit away, left behind us.

His arm brushes my shoulders and my pulse kicks up, even more so when he rests it there, drawing me closer to his side. The no talking has my mind on a freefall, unable to pick apart what'll happen soon. I just descend.

Quick. Fast.

ACT TWENTY-TWO

Maybe it's only a minute before we reach the exit, but the trek is the longest of my life, with my stomach tossing, my muscles constricting, my heart speeding—there is no reprieve when you're falling for a guy. It's the worst and best carnival ride.

After he pushes through the door, we enter the narrow hallway, walls lined with framed Aerial Ethereal posters. The elevators are in sight which'll bring us to the lobby of The Masquerade. *Make it to the elevator without stumbling, Thora.*

I can do this. Share the company with a six-foot-five Russian-American man. Muscular, brawn—all power. Five years older, who's a perfect flirt and an even better kisser. I imagine all of him possessing me, controlling most movements, leading the charge—pushing *into* me.

Thora.

I can almost hear my own breath. *Stop panting.*

Five steps into the carpeted hallway, I'm about to try my hand at small talk again, just to break the quiet. He drops his gym bag though. And he clasps my hips, his gaze peeling off every thin article of clothing, stroking my skin.

I keep him at a foot's distance, even though I can tell he wants me closer. "I'm…sweaty," I throw it out there.

He tilts my chin. "So am I, myshka."

I let him tug me to his chest, one of his hands warming the back of my neck. The longer he just stares through me, the heavier my breathing becomes. He's eye fucking me. My legs tremble, the spot between my thighs pulsing for a harder pressure. For *him.* I've never ached for that this much.

I lick my lips. "Why do you call me myshka?" I've known, but I want to hear him say it.

"Because to me, you're little." His hand drifts from my hip to my lower back, pushing me right up along his body. No room between us. He's not even hard and the bulge in his shorts presses against my abdomen. He looks at me knowingly—knowing that I can feel him, knowing that he's outsized me, knowing that his dominance is beginning to melt my bones.

With his height and size, compared to mine, I can't even begin to fantasize how big he is fully erect. How small I'll be.

He lowers his head to kiss me, pausing a breath away. I unconsciously buck against him, and his chest collapses in arousal. When his lips touch mine, the intensity bursts, and he grips me hard, pressure building everywhere as his tongue dances. As his hands roam. His thumb skims my nipple, the leotard thin, and he continues the back and forth rhythm over the barbell piercing.

My nerves prick, and I stand on the tips of my toes, aching to be even closer.

He hears my silent plea, lifting me up around his waist, my legs split. He's right. Every part of me is little to him. My limbs, my size, my lips, my eyes—and every part of him is large to me. His arms, his shoulders, his jaw, his thighs.

I feel myself become wet.

My lips swell behind the force of his aggressive, non-stop kiss, the kind that blinds me. I want his hands everywhere. All at once. He explores the bareness of my arms, of my neck. My mind is combusting into a million thousand shards. I can't…I break the kiss and rest my forehead on his shoulder, panting for breath.

"I just…" I try to collect myself.

He holds the back of my head protectively, caringly. His breathing is as heavy and staggered as mine. I feel him studying my movements, fluent in body language. I'm still a novice, but if anyone is going to teach me, I'd want it to be him.

I can't stop thinking about our size difference. "We're not going to fit together," I say *aloud.*

He cups my face to look at me. By his strong, unshaven jaw, I'm deeply aware of his age again. "Physically or metaphorically?" he asks with raised brows.

My lips part, slightly wishing I kept my thoughts to myself.

"Physically," he answers off my expression. "I'll be able to fit deep inside you. And when I do, you're going to be entirely full of me." Sex. His voice is sex. Everything is liquid sex. He kisses my forehead, my body shuddering one last time before he gently sets me on my feet.

I'm rethinking my "slow" proclamation, but I remember the last time I had sex. After the fourth date. It was lackluster, and while I doubt that word belongs to the attraction I have for Nikolai, I want to solidify something more permanent before we take that step. I want this to be different. Better than that.

He leads me to the elevators, arm around my shoulders. "Can you be back here around seven?" he asks me.

"Yeah. Are we practicing again?" I frown as he pushes the button on the wall. It lights up while we wait.

"No," he says. "I'm taking you out."

My body responds with those anxious flutters and tightened muscles again. *A date*, I realize. I'm going on a date with the devil.

ACT TWENTY-THREE

"Sorry about that," Nikolai states. He pockets his cell, one that has been buzzing since we sat down. We're on the balcony patio of Rush, metal torches flaming along the railing. It adds to the heat of the summer, my hair down, the pieces curling by my face, the rest probably frizzing.

Despite the view of Vegas being gorgeous tonight, I feel dazed by my surroundings and my own body. Camila helped me pick out a teal empire dress with a silver Aztec necklace, and so that's what I'm wearing.

"It's okay," I say. "My phone isn't behaving any better." Just as I say it, another text pings. This one from my Mom.

Tanner placed first in science wars! Be sure to text him. – Mom

I already did with about fifteen emojis. My brother called me lame. But my parents have been proudly group texting photos of his project all night. And the buzzing won't end. I thought about turning off the notifications but stopped after the guilt set in.

After I pocket my phone, I stir my straw in my tequila sunrise, a drink I've grown accustomed to, no more choking on the liquor.

"Everything okay?" He nods to my phone and then leans back in his wooden chair, red wine his choice of beverage.

I meet his gray eyes that seem to say *you can tell me anything*. He looks supremely handsome tonight: black slacks, black button-down, his hair pushed out of his face, the longer strands a bit higher than the base of his neck.

One of his arms stays on the table, his hand near me. Like if I reach up, he'll thread his fingers with mine. It's tempting to test the waters.

But I stay still, legs crossed and hands in my lap, more rigid than him. "My brother won a science contest. It's a big deal for my family…" I trail off when his phone buzzes on the table, lighting up. "What about you?"

I stare at him for a long second, and he keeps my gaze. I can tell his interruptions don't derive from good news. He lets me see that in his stormy grays.

"Timo," he finally says, pocketing his cell. "My cousins are texting me about him. He's…stuck on some three-card poker table. Down a couple hundred and won't get off. I'd like to say this isn't the usual. But it is."

My heart sinks. I think I've known this all along about Timo. I just hoped it wasn't true.

He reaches for his wine. "I'd take him out of Vegas if I thought it'd help, but he was this way in New York." He takes a larger swig of his drink.

No holding back, I reach out and place my hand on his, beside my knife and fork.

He doesn't seem too surprised, and I wonder if he was waiting for me to do it. He traces the lines in my palm, his eyes flitting to mine, a smile behind them. It warms my soul.

He says a few words in deep Russian, and he even kisses my fingers.

"What'd you say?" I ask with a growing smile, one I can't suppress now. The pull between us is mellow, but hot, like magma that slowly rolls down volcanic rock.

"I said, *you're very beautiful.*"

He could have his pick of any girl in Vegas. It's hard to believe he'd fall for me. "What do you see when you look at me?" I ask in a whisper.

He's quiet for a moment, soaking in my features.

And his expression only floods with more and more intensity, the kind that says *I am attracted to you on many, many levels.* It shallows my breath.

"I can't describe my demon," he tells me with rising lips. "I just feel her."

I scowl. "And I'd say you avoided the question, but I think I can read you now."

"You can?" His brows rise in surprise. "What am I thinking then?"

His penetrating eyes descend to my lips, to my collarbones, to my breasts, creating a sweltering trail. All the way until the table blocks the rest of my frame.

My eyes widen. *You want to fuck me.*

It's clearly the answer, but I struggle to say it out loud. I open my mouth, close it, open it, close it.

He smiles into his sip of wine, knowing the effect he has on me and possibly every girl he's ever encountered.

"And now?" he asks, setting down his drink and looking at me with the most sincerity, the most genuine sentiments, traversing into me, like a gunshot that propels clean through.

I can't put words to that expression. "I don't know," I say softly.

"I admire you."

"That's funny," I say, "because I admire you."

He tries to hide a smile. "Why is that?"

"You raised your siblings. You realize that, right?"

He lets out a short laugh. "Not well enough."

I frown and shake my head. The waiter comes around and takes our orders. A salmon dish for me, and chicken for him.

"You're wrong," I tell him, the flames creating shadows over his strong features in the dark. He looks like a devil dressed in black at first sight, but coming to know him, he's the god that everyone describes. "Katya is sweet and friendly." I think about his brother, the one who offered me mints and stole Skittles for his little sister. "Luka is generous and kind." And Timo—magnetic. There are no just words to define him. I smile, staring off. "And Timo is…captivating, more full of life than anyone I've ever met."

When I look up at Nikolai, his brows are furrowed, overwhelmed. He combs his fingers through his hair, turning his head as he processes my words.

He lets out another short laugh, this time in disbelief. "When people first meet my siblings, they see the worst in them." Lines crease his forehead. "Katya is too naïve. Luka is too irresponsible. And Timo is…" He shakes his head. "Timo is chaos."

"That's rude," I state.

He laughs into a bigger smile. "Where did you come from?"

"I think the same thing about you, you know." He's given me so much in a short amount of time. Determination, motivation. I am overflowing with better, brighter sentiments.

"According to you, I came from hell." There is light behind his gunmetal eyes.

Technically that was John, but that thought has definitely impacted me. I struggle for a response. He's distracting. Everything about him—his unshaven jaw, his soul-bearing gaze, his masculinity. I can't concentrate, even if I was good at bantering.

I mutter, "Demons are from hell." It sounds lame.

"Thank God for that."

Maybe I'm not so bad at this. I stir my straw, the ice cubes melting. There are so many mysteries to him still. Stones left unturned. "Can I ask you something personal?" I wonder.

He stays relaxed. "Sure."

"What happened with your family?" I pause to clarify. "I mean, your parents and other brothers are at Noctis, but it's a new show. You said you haven't seen them for six years, so…"

He lets go of my hand on the table, and I almost regret bringing it up. He sighs heavily like the past bears down on him, a weighted pressure that I can't even begin to understand.

"I'm sorry, you don't have to—"

"No, I can," he interjects. He rubs his jaw in thought, of how to start. He must not explain this often. "When I grew up, we were traveling with Nova Vega and then Celeste mostly in North America. All together. It'd been that way until my parents were recruited for Somnio, to oversee the Russian swing. It would go on a five-year tour, through Asia, Europe and South America."

He stops for a second, staring faraway at the memory. It's not often that he wears this look. It strangely pulls at my lungs.

"My closest aunt and uncle, Dimitri's parents, were recruited for Infini, which would go to New York for three years and then move to Vegas. So my extended family would be split for the first time. We all couldn't be in the same show, the same place, and unfortunately, Katya, Timo, and Luka had no choice where they ended up."

"What…?" I breathe.

His jaw locks for a second, and he breathes through his nose. "My parents," he starts. "They wanted stability for the younger kids. They were ten, twelve and thirteen at the time." He looks up, at the night sky, blanketed with stars. "It left Peter, me, and Sergei with a choice. Somnio would pay better. Somnio was more elite. And it'd award us more freedom." When he takes another long pause, sipping his wine, I digest every syllable, every word.

"You were the only one who chose to be with them," I realize. At twenty, he decided to take on his parent's responsibility instead of living his own life. It's not only admirable—*that* is courageous. There are tears in my eyes that he can't see. He's staring out at the city.

"Peter was eighteen, he wanted to travel," he says. "Sergei was twenty-two, he had no desire to stay with our younger siblings. I wasn't going to leave them and hope that our aunt and uncle would pay attention. They have five kids of their own."

"So when Somnio ended…"

"Noctis began," he says. "So did Amour and Viva."

It cemented the fact that they'd be apart much longer than they might've intended.

Maybe that's why Kayta is so upset. She could've been counting down to Somnio's closing night, in hopes that her parents would return then.

"Do you miss them?" I ask as he turns back to me.

"Some days," he says quietly. He finishes off his wine, and a phone rings (not just a text), the default tone. He digs into his pocket and answers the cell in Russian. His face morphs into that familiar anger, his eyes narrow and muscles tensing.

He shouts something and growls in irritation. He repeats a couple of the same words, over and over, and then he shuts off the phone and rises quickly, pulling out his wallet. My pulse throbs in worry. Our food hasn't even arrived, the date ending early.

"What'd you say about Luka—being generous?" He shakes his head, tossing a few bills and then extending his hand for me. "He's *generously* wearing on me."

"He stole something," I assume, as I rise and take his hand.

He leads me out of the restaurant, in such a hurry that I have trouble keeping up with his lengthy stride. "He's sitting in jail," he says, so lowly that I wonder if I heard wrong.

"What?" My eyes bug.

He hails down a cab. "He's in jail."

Okay, I heard right. My pulse kicks up—and I wonder what he could've stolen. Or if it was something worse. We slip into the taxi together, and Nikolai leans close and suddenly kisses me.

It's a new kind of kiss.

Soft, gentle but more full. His hand is lost beneath my hair, clutching me, and I inhale with him, my arms on his. His lips brush my cheek, then my ear, to whisper, "In case I forget, know that I loved tonight, with you. No matter what happens from here."

He's about to turn on his protective setting, the one where he's all severe. The warm sentiments buried low beneath.

I touch his rough jaw, my hand small. "What happens from here?" I ask softly, my words sounding more sexual than I ever believed they could.

He tucks my frizzy strands of hair behind my ear. "I'll tell you a truth myshka," he whispers, his lips closing over my cheek before touching mine. And very lowly, he breathes, "It's all a mystery to me."

I STAND WITH LUKA BY THE JAIL'S TINTED GLASS, double doors. He hardly says a word, his gaze literally planted on the ugly brown carpet. We wait for Nikolai, who fills out paperwork at the front desk, out of earshot. Apparently Luka tried to shoplift a four-hundred dollar snow globe.

"Who sells snow globes in July?" I ask aloud.

Luka finally smiles, albeit a weak one. "It was a collector's item or something." He's not even sure what he stole? He inspects my outfit for the first time: the teal dress, the glitzy necklace and my mascara and pink lipstick. His face contorts with remorse, especially as he looks to his brother. "You were on a date?"

"Sort of," I say, trying not to make him feel worse.

He buries his face in his hands. "Shit…I'm sorry."

"It's okay." He's really lucky that he only has to pay a fine this time. "Why the snow globe?"

"Huh?" he frowns in confusion.

This can't be an odd question. Right? I mean, everyone would ask this. "Out of everything you could steal, why that?"

"Oh…" He sighs and shrugs, his shoulders tense. "It just seemed harder to steal than the deck of cards."

I guess he takes things for the thrill and excitement, the adrenaline rush maybe. Which is strange, considering he's surrounded by death-defying apparatuses. "A television would've been hard to pocket," I ponder. "Way more useful than a snow globe."

"Hey," he says with a growing smile. "That snow globe is *four-hundred* dollars."

"Totally overpriced."

He laughs, for real, and Nikolai glances back with a withering glare like he should in-no-way be cracking jokes. This is probably true, but my strong suits aren't giving punishments. If Tanner was ever in trouble growing up, I baked him cookies.

"You're a porter for Russian bar, right?" I ask, remembering that he's in Viva with his sister. I wonder if it's not all that exciting for him.

"Yeah." His smile fades. "I was supposed to be in Amour, you know. But they found out that Timo was turning eighteen around the show's premiere, so they switched us." He stays quiet for a second.

"Why would they do that?"

"Have you seen Timo?" He raises his brows at me, stuffing his hands in his jeans. "He's so good at what he does. And he picks up new disciplines in half the time as everyone else." He shrugs again. "Look, I'm not jealous or anything. He deserves that act in Amour. I'm just, honestly, bored."

"Do you like any of the other apparatuses?"

He shakes his head. "It takes so fucking long to learn a new one. It sucks."

I mentally scroll through all the disciplines while we wait. "I wish they brought back the Wheel of Death." I've seen YouTube clips, and it looked like the most terrifying metal structure that only crazies would jump on. But I heard they retired the act from Infini.

"Timo used to do that."

"Really?" My eyes widen.

"He said it was easy."

Damn. "He must be really good."

"No kidding."

I sigh. "Well, whatever you end up doing, it has to have a hell of a lot better view than this."

He scans the holding room, where a few guys sit in plastic chairs, handcuffed and waiting to be booked. It also smells like stale cheese in here.

Luka's gaze lands on Nikolai, and that regret floods his features again. "Don't break up with him because of me, okay?"

The panic in his tone actually freezes my muscles. I swallow a rock. "I won't," I assure him.

He nods a couple times, trying to believe me.

ACT TWENTY-FOUR

I have extra practice tonight, so I can't go :(BUT I'VE SENT THE BEST REPLACEMENT!!!! – Katya

I click into the text as soon as I arrive at our meeting spot in The Masquerade, beside the enormous fountain of Dionysus: god of wine, and loosely, carnivals. I planned to head over to Coco Roma to buy lingerie. Roger keeps pointing out my "excessively over-worn" costume, and spit flew when he yelled this time.

Since the wires have poked out of all three corsets I own (and tried to impale my boobs), I knew it was time anyway. I just haven't mentally prepared for a new shopping companion.

Please not Dimitri, I keep chanting the phrase, hopping up and down some as I wait. I'd rather spend an hour with Dionysus, the *fountain*, than share Dimitri's company. I try to extinguish the nervous jitters, but they flap around incessantly.

"You ready?" That voice emanates from behind me. I spin on my heels, already recognizing the deep tone.

Nikolai has on nice slacks and a gray V-neck that matches his eyes. The nervous flapping never dies.

He's going lingerie shopping *with me.*

Nikolai.

I've been on a few dates with him by now. Slow. We've been going very slow at my request. And the gym has been a pool of tension, both of us probably needing a release. This seems like a bad idea.

You're going lingerie shopping with Nikolai Kotova.

"No," I accidentally say.

His brows rise, knowingly. "You'll be fine."

I'm so not ready for this.

I SIFT THROUGH THE CORSETS ON A CIRCULAR rack of mostly burlesque items: feather boas, umbrellas and *tons* of lingerie. But I'm so distracted. Nikolai towers behind me and massages my constricted shoulders. Honestly, he can't be real. Although, he did point out my nervousness, so his kindness also came with unleashing my anxieties.

I have no idea why I'm internally running in circles and shrieking in alarm. Maybe because Phantom is a temporary part of my life that I'd like to close off from him.

And because it reminds me of the never-ending night. The one where he untied my corset and my drunken-self slept in his bed. "I don't even know what I'm looking for," I say softly.

"What'd he say you needed?"

"Something sexier, I guess." Now he's thinking about me, wearing close to nothing for an audience. I'm thinking about it too. *Everyone* is thinking about it.

I am a frozen waterfall. With no hope to unthaw.

He easily reaches over me and pulls out two hangers, my heart thumping too hard. "Try these."

Try these. What are these…oh. Wow. The first is a white one-piece, that laces in the front, no wires, stretchy enough to move in. It's not overtly sexual, but the low cut will be more than enough. The second is a rouge lace panty-set, also no wires. It's pretty, actually.

I slowly turn around to face him, clutching the lingerie pieces to my chest. Should I try them on *for* him? Or invite him in the dressing room? Or just…I lose my thought as his gaze strokes me in one wave.

"When you're at Phantom," he says, "you need to be careful."

"I'm always safe on the hoop—"

"I'm not talking about the hoop. I don't trust some of the people there, and I honestly hate that you work when I work." His whole body is a rigid, stiff fortress. If I was tall enough, I would even contemplate giving *him* the massage, but in my Toms, my head reaches his shoulders.

Little mouse.

Yeah, it fits alright.

"I'll be fine," I tell him.

His intensity barrels through me. I love it more than he knows and more than I ever realized, his concern only flushing me more.

I add, "Don't worry about me." My sweltering body disagrees.

He gives me a look like that's just not possible. "I've worried about you since you first showed up in Vegas and could barely drink a shot." At The Red Death, when he said the city would swallow me whole.

"Really?" *That long?* He's naturally protective, but still, I smile.

He lifts my chin. "I don't lie."

"That's good to know." My face tightens, realizing that response sounded flat on my account. "So…"

He kisses me, and I almost drop the hangers in a daze. If his eyes are hell, his tongue is heaven, and I would gladly return. I walk backwards with him, my lips stinging and my body aching. His hand falls to my hip, and it crosses my mind—he's guiding me.

Leading me.

Somewhere.

My legs move of their own will, my brain no longer attached. I hold onto his waist, succumbing to wherever he's taking me. The backs of my knees hit a bench. And he breaks apart to shut the dressing room door behind him. It's tiny with a mirror, a wooden bench against the wall and a hook.

"Did anyone…see us?" I pant.

"It doesn't matter," he says lowly, his eyes devouring me. He steals the lingerie and hangs it on the hook. I look up. He stares down. A foot of space separating us.

I remain stationary, allowing him to dictate what happens next. The mystery pumps blood through my veins.

Nikolai fingers the hem of my green tank top, and he lifts it over my head, my dirty-blonde hair draping over my bare shoulders, only in jean shorts and a simple blue bra.

My breasts rise and fall with my heavy breath, especially the longer he studies my motions. I remember back to the first night at The Red Death, when he could tell so much about me from so little.

He kisses me again, my lips swollen with the pressure, and his hand slips to my shorts. He skillfully unbuttons them, lowers them, and I step out of the fabric. Now in a bra and white cotton panties. Had I known he would be coming here with me, I wonder if I would've chosen a less innocent color.

When he studies me again, I'm careful about appearing relaxed, my arms at my sides, not covering my chest. I want him to touch the barest parts of me and my nerves shall not stop him. I won't let them.

"Breathe," he instructs as he steps near again, his hands on my hips. His tough skin along my soft.

I blow out my usual trained breath. His eyes only say *I want you closer to me.* In one swift motion, he lifts me up to his abs, my legs split apart around him. I'm too short to even cross my ankles. He kneels on the wooden bench and pushes my back up against the wall.

This is…happening.

I'm uncertain what *this* is but I'm not opposed to finding out.

He gauges my reaction. "Breathe, myshka."

"I am," I whisper. Am I?

He kisses me, and he forces oxygen into my lungs, one of the most intimate moments of my life. Right now. Then his fingers brush along the clasp of my bra. When he breaks the kiss, I pant, "I can't…believe you've already seen them." I pause. "I mean, my boobs." I would face-palm myself if I wasn't clutching his arms.

His lips curve, so close to mine. "You've already seen my cock." He kisses me again, a slow, unhurried one.

In between, I whisper, "That is true."

He unclasps my bra, the straps sliding down my arms until its all the way off. The cold air bites me and almost instantly hardens my nipples. I can see myself in the adjacent mirror, of how heavy I breathe, of how small I am in his arms. More than half-naked.

It's one of the most visually stimulating things I've ever laid eyes on—and it involves *me*. The unsexy friend. The girl who doesn't know passion.

He follows my gaze, and the desire in his movements amplifies. Times a million. He lifts me higher on his body, my breasts lined with his mouth. He tongue flicks over the barbell piercing, sensations bursting in lower places.

"Nik…" I gasp, and as my clutch tightens, so does his. Each finger scalding against my skin. *You're in public, Thora.* Dear God.

I rest my forehead on his broad, muscular shoulder, biting my gums to keep these pleasured noises at bay. The spot between my legs *throbs* now. He drops me some, my forehead now to his chest. He places a hand on the back of my neck and the other rubs the inside of my thigh, teasing.

I rock into him, subconsciously craving a hardness that he can give me.

His teasing hand shifts my panties, and the moment he rubs my clit, my body shudders. His hand tightens on my neck, holding me in place, warming me, protecting me. My lips part, a noise stuck in my throat, as the sensitivity escalates.

I need something hard—

His finger slips inside of me while his thumb creates circular, rhythmic motions over my clit. I shut my eyes, blinded by a new fullness. A sheen of sweat builds across my skin.

He presses his body harder, pinning me more to the wall. I reach down to feel his hand between my legs, and he kisses me again, my head floating away.

He pulses his finger inside of me, and he pauses for a brief second to fit another. I lean my head back. "I don't…" *know. If this will hurt.*

He kisses me like *trust me.* "You're wet enough," he says lowly, his arousal clipping his deep words.

I inhale and lean back towards him, resting my cheek on his chest. I wrap my arms around his ribs, as far as they'll go (which is not far at all). And he slips another finger in me, tight but not painful.

His pace begins again, deeper.

I'm going to come soon. I climb up the tallest pole, towards the peak. I tremble, my mouth open against his flesh. I cry into his chest, the noise muffled there. And then I feel myself clench around his fingers, my eyes almost rolling back.

While I ride the descent, he holds me still, his thumb caressing the skin on my neck. In my ear, he whispers, "Get used to this. It's going to happen more often."

I don't see how I can *ever* get used to that. It'll always be a rush. But I'm not complaining at all. I'm definitely an advocate of experiencing *this* again.

I pull back some, registering where we are. In the middle of the day. A dressing room. "I think…I'm going to just buy those…" I say with a nod at the lingerie hangers.

His intense eyes are fixed on me. "Good idea." He licks his lips. "Exhale for me."

I do. And he slowly retracts his fingers, a slight pinch of pain down below. I stifle a wince and inhale sharply. "We're not going to fit together."

"We are," he says lowly. "In all ways."

I hope he's right. Because I don't want this to end here.

ACT TWENTY-FIVE

Three and a half months in Vegas and summer is gone, but today is still the hottest day of the year, which is cause for celebration in this city. The Masquerade's Wet & Wild Bash is one of the biggest pool parties I've ever been to, and I'd revel in the DJ, masses of bikini-clad girls, six-pack guys, open bar (for Masquerade employees only) and decently cold water if I didn't feel like a semi-truck rolled over me this morning.

Bruises mar my arms, thighs, ankles—war wounds from apparatuses and training seven days a week. Now in a salmon-pink bathing suit, the bruises are visible, including a nasty green and brown welt on my upper-thigh.

I try to hide the pain in my muscles and joints while I stand beside a high-top table near the cabanas, overflowing with people. I can't even see the lounge cushions beneath the bodies—same almost applies for the pool.

I rub my swollen knuckles, waiting for Nikolai to return with drinks. Amour isn't playing tonight. Management scattered Infini in their timeslots, and Nik didn't seem pleased by it. Maybe it's a sign the show isn't performing well.

Elena could change that though. In six weeks she'll take the stage in the aerial silk act, opposite Nikolai. I try to be happy for him, that he can finally perform his act again, but it's hard to think of her and not see what I lost.

The high-top table vibrates from the DJ's blasting speakers, and I rest my hands on the surface to steady it. A passing couple gives me the stink-eye for commandeering a table all to myself. *Sorry. I'm waiting for someone.* I doubt that I channel the apology through my face. Scowling. I've been scowling this whole time.

Resting Bitch Face fail.

My spirits lift slightly when I see a person behind them, a real grimace on his face every time someone bumps his arm. John looks ready to douse his beer on their heads. By the time he makes it to my table, he sighs heavily, like he just walked through the Sahara and barely came out alive.

"They're all going to need a tetanus shot after this." He gestures to the pool. "Idiots."

I smile. "Nice to see you too, John." In swim shorts, he's way more toned than I thought he'd be, more definition in his abs.

He raises his drink at me in hello and scans the congested area, searching for someone. Then he turns to me. "So..." His dark brows tic up.

I frown. "So...?" I repeat.

"How do you two even work?" His face is still in that grimace. "Are you always on top?"

"*John*," I say, wide-eyed. How Nikolai and I fuck is honestly—it's something *I'm* still trying to picture. I don't even want to be on top that much, which is the worrisome part.

Near us, a romantically-entwined couple starts making out with *major* tongue, and John's lip curls at the affection. "Get a fucking room," he says, loud enough that the guy shoots him a glare. "I'm not the one sucking face." The guy flips him off but actually leaves our area. "Asshole." John turns to me, my heart pounding. "You can't be that surprised. When people see a giant fucking Russian man with a five-foot-something tiny blonde, it's the first thing we all think."

"No…" People aren't that curious. But then I envision myself in their shoes. I internally groan—*how do they have sex* would be in my top five thoughts, for sure.

"You know what they say," John grins into a grimace, "you fuck a Kotova and you go directly to hell. No passing Go."

My hand is half-covering my face. "I think you just say that." I inhale, mustering some confidence and drop my arm. "And to clear things up, Nik and I haven't actually…had sex yet." *But we've done other things.*

John chokes on his beer. His brows jump. "It's that difficult?"

Dear God. "No…it's not because of our height and size difference." I'm trying not to be insecure about how we don't exactly "fit" together. But it's hard when I have people like John reminding me.

"You're a virgin." The look on his face—you'd think this was the best piece of gossip John's heard all year.

"No," I say slowly, dragging out the word. "It's possible for two people to go at a slow pace." *It's not weird.* Right? Every relationship has a different timeline.

"You've been in Vegas for almost four months, and you see the guy every single day."

"Those are some facts, yep," I nod.

He gives me a weird look. "It's decided. You're my strangest friend."

I burst into a smile. "You called me your friend."

He rolls his eyes. "A figure of speech. I have *no* friends."

"Camila is definitely your friend," I note.

"Camila is my cousin. We're forced to be *somewhat* cordial."

"Right," I laugh. If I had to label their relationship, it'd be *best friends*.

He points at me with his beer bottle. "You know, she's the one who told me to pry into your sex life. I'm supposed to get free shots out of it."

"Well, you can tell Camila that you've successfully earned your shots."

His face contorts into a sour expression. "I don't know. It feels cheap to earn shots off something so sad."

I think I'm scowling harder. But he doesn't shrink back. I'm sure staring in the mirror has made him accustomed to all types of glowers. "Shouldn't you be congratulating me for *not* succumbing to a Kotova's charm? I'm not going to hell." I shake my fists in mock maracas, my sore muscles screaming and my swollen knuckles crying. It's a distressing faux celebration.

"You're dating him, so there's still time for stupidity to seep in. I'm not discounting it." He pauses to add, "I've also heard rumors about the size of his dick."

"What?" My eyes threaten to pop out again. I can tell he's been itching to switch to this topic, leaning forward a bit more.

"Can you confirm or have you not hit that base yet?"

He loves to pry. If I had any inclination about his own love life, I'd put him in the hot seat. But he's really private on that front. "What are the rumors?" I ask, my curiosity peaking. I've definitely been through enough bases to have seen his cock, but I didn't have a ruler or anything. All I know is that he's much bigger than the blurry, drunken guy I slept with that one time in college. Or at least, my foggy memory says so.

John makes a measurement with this hands. I'm not sure how many inches he's alluding to, but it seems huge.

"That has to be a lie."

"So you've never seen his dick," John deduces, putting his beer bottle to his lips.

I open my mouth to explain.

"Who's dick?" Nikolai's deep voice pricks my arms.

Worst timing.

He sidles next to me, passing me a plastic cup with tequila and orange juice. He sets down his beer and then takes my hand, pressing a cold baggy of ice to my throbbing knuckles.

That feels so good. I find myself relaxing my hip against his body: shirtless, in just gray swim trunks. It's a god-like view.

I didn't even have to ask for this gesture—he must've seen how puffy my knuckles were this morning. It happens if I'm not careful with the aerial silk, bearing down on the tops of my hands.

I actually forget about Nik's question for a second. That is, until John speaks.

"Yours," he says, unabashed. "We were talking about the rumors."

"Rumors about my cock," he says flatly. It's not a question.

"Don't act surprised, this entire fucking establishment—" John gestures to the Masquerade and enormous pool "—is obsessed with your kind."

Nikolai's no-nonsense, intimidating glare starts to harden his face. I shift my weight uneasily. He says, "You seem really concerned with *my kind*."

"Because you're everywhere," John retorts. "I can't walk into the bathroom without running into one of you. It's like you were bred in a factory."

"Okay, John," I cut in, afraid he's offended Nikolai. "You've had your fun—"

"I would hardly call it fun." His eyes narrow back at Nikolai, and they engage in a glaring contest that I can't fully understand. Seconds tick by, straining the air. There seems to be something deeper here—

"Don't fuck with my brother," Nikolai forces. There it is.

John lets out a humorless laugh. "Oh God, you have *no idea*." He shakes his head repeatedly. "Timo chases after me—because I am the only man on the strip that says *no* to him. Think about that for a second. Are you letting it process? Because there are some *gross* fucking tobacco-spitting, fifty-year-old men here."

He really hates tobacco. It's the only thought that stops my stomach from roiling.

Nikolai is unmoving, still glaring. A pit wedges in my ribcage.

"WET T-SHIRT CONTEST!" the DJ announces in the mic.

"Fucking cliché," John says under his breath, but raises his beer to me in goodbye now and steps away from our table, predictably heading to the stage.

Nikolai focuses back to me, switching the ice bag to my other hand.

"I'm sorry John insulted your family," I say in a cringe.

"He's not the first Masquerade employee to hate us. But most of them have better sense than to insult me to my face." The ill-will must derive from the "special treatment" they think the Kotovas receive. Both Timo and Luka are allowed in clubs and on the casino floor.

I wonder though if they're just highly persuasive.

"Thora!"

My name and that voice reroutes my attention. And Nikolai's. Our heads turn at the same time. A few feet from my table, I see the very familiar gymnast, and my heart explodes with emotion.

Shay.

Just like that, my old life slams into me at a hundred miles per hour.

ACT TWENTY-SIX

Too excited to stay put, I run up to him, his smile growing brighter as I near. I stand on my toes to hug Shay around his broad shoulders, reaching his five-foot-seven self.

"Miss me?" he whispers in my ear, reciprocating the hug with a tighter one around my waist. Almost four months without any familiarity, after spending nearly eight years being surrounded by Shay and gymnastics and my parents—his sudden presence, it overwhelms me. He knows my answer by the escaped tears that land on his shoulder.

I squeeze him, just to ensure he's not a mirage. "You're really here."

I can't believe he's here.

"Only for a few hours."

"What?" I thud to my feet, disappointment flooding me. I try to stay positive. Three hours is better than nothing. Most definitely.

He holds my face and wipes the wetness beneath my eye. "I know. It fucking sucks. But the only way I could get my parents to pay for the ticket was for the 'benefit of my career'." He uses air-quotes. "I'm on my way to L.A. for an interview with USC. They have a job opening up in January since some athletic trainer is leaving. I made sure there was a layover so I could see you."

I can't contain my smile, and we both start inspecting each other, as though to spot the differences. "Your hair…" I touch the much shorter light brown strands.

"Just cut it." He squeezes my bicep. "Damn, Thora." My arms are much more defined and muscular than before. The mention of me, of my change, pulls my mind in focus. And my stomach drops. I've been completely oblivious of the person I ran *away* from.

I turn my head to the table, and Nikolai's strong jaw tics, his stormy grays puncturing me with skepticism and hurt.

Shay is just my friend.

But I imagine the situation reversed, and I can feel my insides heaving in distraught—at the idea of Nikolai running up to another girl. Her arms flinging around him.

I'll make it right.

But what's worse: Nikolai isn't alone right now. Timo stands next to him, clutching an orange mixed drink and throwing daggers into me. From someone usually so happy—it stings cold.

"There's someone I want you to meet," I tell Shay as I rotate back to him.

His gaze darts between me and the Kotovas, piecing together what this is about before I can even introduce him. "No," he groans. "Thora, you didn't."

My heart lurches. "Didn't what?" *Please don't look at me like that.*

His face is bent in disappointment, as though I took a wrong path. *You didn't. You're where you're supposed to be, Thora James.* My cheerleader is waving her pompoms in my face.

"Please tell me you're not *with* him." I follow his accusatory finger to…Timo.

"No…I'm not with him…" My smile has vanished, replaced by fear. I take a couple steps from Shay, and my gaze connects with Nikolai again. He can read me past recognition, approaching my side quickly and without falter.

I know how this looks to Shay, someone thousands of miles across the country.

Girl moves to Vegas to follow her dreams.

Girl gets trained by Guy.

Girl falls for Guy.

Girl forgets about her dreams in favor of love.

But I moved to Vegas to join Aerial Ethereal. Nikolai is helping me do just that, and he'd rather me succeed than start a relationship. *Circus or a man.* I'm choosing the circus. Now. And forever.

And if I forget, Nikolai promised he'd remind me.

Shay's face hardens as soon as he notices Nikolai. Next to me. Since the wet T-shirt contest is on the other side of the pool, there are slightly less bodies and general commotion. But eyes flicker this way, and I have the sense that people are watching us from cabanas and the water.

I swallow a lump and step forward to introduce them. "Shay," I start, "this is—"

"Don't say it," Shay tells me, shaking his head with a twisted face. He's already come to the right conclusion. That I'm with Nikolai. So his reaction—it's a valid one. "Dammit, Thora. You're better than this!"

His voice slices my gut.

"You must be the best friend," Nikolai says with a great deal of disdain. If looks could kill, Shay would be dead five times over.

Shay layers on a murderous glare of his own. "And she's never said *one thing* about you." *Because I knew you'd react this way.*

I raise my hands between them, standing directly in the middle of two different worlds. I wonder if they will ever bridge, if they ever can.

"Please, let me explain." More and more people filter over here, with drinks in hand, to watch this "fight" that's become a bigger spectacle than a wet T-shirt contest.

"Sure," Shay says, his voice caged with hurt. "Explain to me how the Thora James I've known for eight fucking years could throw away a college scholarship for a guy. One year, Thora, you had *one year* left."

"He's training me." Tears sting my eyes. "Okay, he's *helping* me." I am pleading with him to understand, to picture what I do. But my viewpoint is a solitary one.

"Bullshit." He points at Nikolai now. "I *see* the way he's looking at you."

"I didn't leave everything for a guy!" I shout back.

"Then tell me I'm wrong! Tell me that you're *not* with him."

I struggle for breath, swallowing air before I say, "I can't…"

He rests his hands on his head like I sucker-punched him. "Goddammit, Thora. *Goddammit.*"

"I'm the same person." I haven't changed in the way he believes. My dreams are all the same.

He drops his arms. "Wake up. You're never going to be an aerialist in a world-renowned troupe. Do you hear how crazy that is?" I'm shaking, fighting back tears. "He's giving you false hope so he can keep you around, probably to *fuck you—*"

"You're a coward." Nikolai's hollow voice nearly silences the muttering crowds. He's by my side, and then he protectively passes me, brushing my hand like saying *I'm here for you* before he takes a few steps ahead and faces Shay. "If you're going to slander me, speak directly *to me*, not to her."

Shay's doubt leeches my brain. His belief isn't true. It's not true. Nikolai's intentions are as pure as mine. I know they are, in my heart. I know it.

"Yeah, I have something to say to you," Shay grits.

"Ooooh," people in the pool echo, hands cupped over their mouths to create the noise. I realize I've shuffled to the side, in order to see both Shay and Nikolai from a spectator position, but I'm still closer to them than anyone else at the pool party.

"Leave Thora alone," Shay sneers. "If you like her at all, you'll stop feeding her bullshit—"

"It's not bullshit." Nikolai glares. "She has the ability to be better."

"With your help, right?" Shay nods like he sees right through him. My stomach clenches. *It's not true.*

"Yes," Nikolai says lowly. "With my help. I've spent twenty years training on the apparatus she loves. I've spent my entire life in the circus. I have knowledge and experience that she needs. There is *nothing* for her in Ohio." Anger protrudes the veins in his arms and neck, his muscles flexing.

My throat swells. Behind Nikolai, I now notice all who gathers. Not just Timo. There's Luka. And Dimitri—there are dozens…no, *several* dozen athletes, all broad-shouldered, strong and hard-jawed. Gray eyes.

Most of them have those gray eyes. Kotovas. Cousins. Brothers. His family.

They stand as though they're ready to back him. For anything. For everything.

"Her whole life is in Ohio," Shay retorts. "She doesn't belong here."

Shay is *my* family. He is the one familiarity I have.

"Fight! Fight! Fight!" people begin to chant, not only in the pool but around us.

I shake my head. No. *No one* is fighting.

The Kotovas start speaking in Russian, shouting over each other and the hostile encouragements. Nikolai rotates a fraction and yells a few foreign words back to them.

I meet Shay's concerned gaze that fixes on me. His eyes soften so much. *You know him. For years. You know him.* His voice is drowned by the crowd, but I read his lips: *Come home.* He's telling me to come home. With him.

My eyes burn, restraining combative emotions.

"Thora," I hear Nikolai's loud voice in the mass.

I turn my head.

His sincerity, his intensity, it rips right through me. "Don't leave. *Please.*"

I inhale a pained breath. I'm warring with my dreams and with reality. Is it courageous to stay here or is it just a fool's chase? I'm not sure…

"*Thora,*" Nikolai forces, my attention his once more, "you can succeed."

Shay's hands ball into fists. "Says the guy who's been sleeping with her."

"Fight! Fight! Fight!"

My stomach knots and unknots at Shay's disillusion and the real fact. I haven't slept with Nikolai. That's not what this is about. In the pit of my ear, I hear his words spoken from months ago.

It's wasted courage. And wasted love. You shouldn't have to waste those things.

I can do this.

You can do this, Thora. It's not over. It doesn't have to be.

Not yet.

Nikolai takes a few commanding strides towards Shay, who stands his ground. My heart thrashes. They won't fight. "*What* does it matter to you if I have?" He's subtly implying: *do you have feelings for her?*

No. Not like that.

"She's my best friend. If I see a guy using her, I'm going to step in the fucking way."

"FIGHT! FIGHT! FIGHT!"

I keep shaking my head.

"This is the life she wants. Let her live it."

Shay lets out an aggravated laugh and shouts over the chanting, "You think she wants to live this life?! The minute she doesn't land a contract, she's going to be back in Ohio. And you're going to lose your fuck buddy—"

Nik decks him, his knuckles slamming into Shay's jaw. My hands fly to my mouth. Shay rights himself quickly and throws his fist into Nikolai's ribs.

In my peripheral, I see movement from the Kotova men, and I sprint so fast, imagining the fight turning into a brawl all against Shay. I extend my arms and all of them rock back at my appearance. "Stop."

I can't step between the flying fists behind me, but I can thwart a bigger fight. Out of everyone, Dimitri tries to challenge me, nearing my small frame.

I point a warning finger at him. "*No.*"

Dimitri seizes my wrist, tugging me to him. His glower says more than enough but he speaks, "I'm not letting Nikolai be punched by *your* friend." What did Nikolai say about him: *I've known Dimitri since I was a little kid.*

I think I've underestimated the strength and loyalty beneath a childhood friendship.

I'm just trying to protect Shay. "I won't let you gang up on him," I force. Nikolai has dozens of people to back him. Shay only has me.

His fingers dig hard into my skin, my bones screaming.

Timo yells in Russian at Dimitri, his face reddening as he tries to get his point across. I see Nikolai land a right hook at the same time that Shay knees Nik in the ribs. Both blows pack a powerful punch, so much that they stagger back for a second.

"Stop!" I yell at them. My voice reaches their ears, their heads whipping to me in unison. They zero in on Dimitri's clutch, and it diffuses their fight, redirecting their rage.

He releases his hold on me, and I walk quickly to the two guys as hotel management approaches in black suits, physically standing between them.

"Booo!" the crowd roars.

The DJ speaks into the mic, "She must have some pretty titties." Ew. I cringe. They were not fighting over me like that. And even if they were, that's—no. I cringe more.

I pass Nikolai, who speaks to one of the black-suits. And I make sure to brush his hand a little, just to show that I'm not choosing reality.

Not today.

I still want to dream. But my reality is also precious to me.

So I walk right up to Shay, my heart flip-flopping at his face, much more beaten than Nik's. I'm not surprised. Even though he's incredibly fit from gymnastics, he's not even close to Nik's size. I touch Shay's cheek, the skin split open from a punch.

He winces and clasps my hand. "It's fine…" He spits a wad of blood on the cement.

"I'll help you clean up in the bathroom."

He nods, accepting my offer. And I lead him out of the pool area, a series of *boos* following us all the way inside.

ACT TWENTY-SEVEN

Shay is leaving in ten minutes. After washing his face, we sit on the edge of the Dionysus fountain, staring at the revolving doors that lead out of The Masquerade.

Our friendship has never been this strained. Miles and miles apart and my aspirations have begun to destroy it. "I'm sorry," I whisper.

He lets out a heavy sigh. "Thora..." He looks to me, his eyes reddened. "I don't want you to make this mistake."

"I know." *I know.* My chin almost trembles, and I bite down. "But you have to let me make it." *I really, really hope it's not one.*

He rubs his eyes and then stares at the ceiling. For answers.

His jaw is already tinted red. "Your interview..." I trail off, imagining him shaking hands with the boss: split-knuckles, bruised cheek and swollen eye. His chances of landing the job are now slim.

"I wasn't excited about it anyway," he says under his breath. "I hate the idea of being an athletic trainer, watching other guys compete in the sport that I still want to be in—it's depressing."

I don't ask why he's taken the classes to pursue this career. His parents pushed the plan as a back-up when gymnastics ended. Shay qualified for the Olympics one year, but he never made the national team. It's not a pursuit he's ever tried again. He said the training was too rigorous, and he knew he wouldn't make it a second time around.

"What are you going to do then?" I ask, my voice soft.

He shrugs and shakes his head a few times. "I have no fucking clue." He turns and smiles weakly at me. "What a life, right—or I guess you wouldn't know...You've had this crazy circus idea in your head since you were fourteen."

"You remember how old I was this time?"

His gaze falls to his hands, his bloodied knuckles ten times worse off than my swollen ones. "I remembered before. I just hoped you'd reconsider this." He checks his watch. "I have to go."

We both stand and I almost start to cry—scared of him leaving again. It was easier the first time. When I still kept strings attached to him and me. When I knew I'd see him another day. This feels like the end of a novel together, not a chapter.

I hug him.

He hugs me tighter. "Be safe, okay?" he whispers, choking on the last word.

I squeeze him. "Be happy, alright?"

I wait for Shay to say: *I am.*

But he stays quiet. Then he lets go, picks up his duffel that he left with the concierge, and exits through the revolving glass doors.

ACT TWENTY-EIGHT

"I'm not a fortuneteller. Those who award themselves the title either have a penchant for trite metaphors or are liars. If I'm going to lie about something, it's not going to be about projecting an inconceivable future. To be honest, that's too stupid for people like me." On the television screen, Connor Cobalt presses his fingers to his jaw in conceited contemplation, his Rolex watch glitzy on his wrist.

"Damn," I say, sharing a pint of Cherry Garcia with Katya as we watch an old episode of *Princesses of Philly.* She texted me about five minutes after Shay left, asking for details about the fight since no one was sharing them with her. And I came up to Nikolai's suite to explain.

The reality show takes my dazed mind off the turn of events, never *ever* believing Shay would show up here. Or that Nikolai would hit him. I wear an eternal pained grimace when I even think about it.

Apparently Nikolai and everyone else are still outside, speaking to management. I haven't even figured out what to say to him yet, so decompressing with Katya is the perfect medicine to a hectic afternoon.

"Nikolai used to be Team Scott," Katya tells me, pushing more of the fleece blanket on my side. She must see the goose bumps on my arms. I wish I'd brought a cover-up or worn jean shorts over my bikini, at least. But like Connor just said, I couldn't have predicted the future.

"I liked him at the beginning too, with Rose, but it almost seemed forced at times. I mean, they *rarely* stood even two feet near each other."

"I know, it was weird. I always thought she had more chemistry with Connor."

"Who's your favorite?" I ask her as the show switches to a series of commercials. "Of all the Calloway sisters and their men?" I expect her to say Ryke Meadows or Loren Hale—the two most popular guys of the bunch. One is overly protective, the other in complete I-would-die-for-you love with his childhood friend.

"Easy." She eats a scoop of ice cream before saying, "Rose Calloway."

I flinch in surprise. "Rose?" I think I prefer Lily Calloway, the one who's a bit shy, but in the face of so much publicity, so many warring voices, she's stood strong in the end. It's bravery that I think I need.

"Rose is always so well-dressed and put-together. And she's smart." Katya shrugs. "When she speaks, everyone listens. You know, when the show first aired, I'd often think What Would Rose Calloway Do?" She smiles with the spoon in her mouth.

I contemplate this. "What would Rose do in my situation?"

Katya's smile fades. And I think we're both mulling over the same answer: *she'd choose to be on her own.* Be independent. And try, stubbornly, to succeed without help. Without handouts. But she'd have an advantage in the end. She's rich.

Her family owns Fizzle—one of the largest soda companies. My parents are like gold fish on the career pyramid. I'm more alone in that sense. Less lifelines and opportunities to phone a friend.

"Rose doesn't always do the right thing," Katya points out. "She makes mistakes too."

I think about how the one-and-only season of *Princesses of Philly* ended, my eyes growing big. "This is true."

The door suddenly opens. Only Nikolai enters, tensely. I can't read him well enough to see if his strict demeanor derives from guilt. His quiet rage could just sprout from Shay and the fight.

I quickly peruse his body, a slightly reddish tint to the side of his ribs. That's it. Clearly he outmatched Shay. He knows he's bigger than him. And he still hit him. My blood runs cold and not even the fleece blanket stops me from shivering.

"Thora, can I talk to you alone?" He nods to his bedroom, and his chest rises and falls in a heavier breath, maybe preparing for me to say no.

But I want to hear what he has to tell me. I stand, setting the blanket down, and I head to his bedroom in my bikini, Nikolai trailing me. The temperature drops below zero when he shuts the door behind him.

My body shakes, the hairs on my arms rising. To distract myself from the cold, I sit on the edge of his metallic comforter, his bed made, his room minimal and modern. Spotless, the perks of hotel maids, I guess. *Why are you thinking about hotel maids, Thora?*

Because I feel him towering. I feel him studying me. He slips into the closet for a second, and I tighten my legs together for heat, my shoulders locked and curved forward. When he returns, he carries a black Aerial Ethereal sweatshirt and he holds it out to me.

I'm not too prideful to reject it. I pull the sweatshirt over my head, the soft fabric dwarfing my build, the hem at my knees. The longer we share company in silence, the longer my chest constricts. I strain my neck to look up at Nikolai. He nears me, and very slowly, he kneels, his hand on my thigh, now more eye-level than before.

I remain fixed and unmoving. My face tight. I just wait for him to fill the cavernous quiet.

The first thing he says is, "Are you okay?"

"Can't you read me?" My voice is stilted and as cold as I feel.

His eyes finished their dance across my features long ago. "You're angry and confused, and you wish I hadn't hit your friend. You're also upset that he left early, but you won't admit that to me. And you're freezing right now."

My nose flares at his on-point assumptions.

"I'm sorry," he says. "But I'm not the kind of man who'd stand by while someone berates you. Even if he's your friend."

"You're twice his size," I refute.

"It's not like he was defenseless, Thora. He's an *athlete*."

And he assumed right. Again. Probably based on Shay's height, frame, build—like he did me that first night in Vegas. "Can you at least pretend to be full of remorse and regret?" *This would be so much easier.*

"No. A devil protects his demon."

I scowl.

His gaze flits all over me, branding me like the tip of a fire-poker. His sandalwood scent dizzies my head, and I try to stay resilient under his masculinity, the dominance that is nearly begging him to stand up, lay me back against his mattress and take control of me.

I can tell that he struggles to keep still on his knees. "Have you slept with him before?" There's something in Nik's eyes, something kept secret from me. I wonder if it's jealousy. Or fear.

"No," I say. "Shay set me up on a date with his teammate. He has no interest in me like that." A chill runs up my spine, and a shiver snakes back down.

Nikolai rubs his hands along the tops of my thighs, the friction immediately warming the coldest parts of me.

I shut my eyes for a second, thinking. Trying to place why I feel so strange. And the thought clicks. I have to release this off my chest.

When I open my eyes, his gray irises pierce me in questioning, a raging powerful storm.

With a sharp inhale, I'm swept in it.

"I didn't choose you," I tell him. The pain of the statement is a hot, metal knife, wedged between my ribs. "I chose the circus." It barely alleviates the sting. *Why does that hurt?* If it was the truth, it shouldn't hurt this badly. Right? It can't be a lie. Because then Shay is right. Everything he said—

"I'm glad," Nikolai says each word like they're weighted with cement. His eyes redden the longer he holds my gaze, suppressing more emotion.

My chin quakes. *He's glad.* I nod a couple times, letting this sink in.

And then he lifts me in his arms and tucks me to his chest, warmth blanketing me. We're on his bed, beneath his comforter in seconds, and he just holds me, strong, muscular arms wrapped around my frame.

I press my forehead to his collar, trying not to shiver so much. He kisses my cheek and whispers soft Russian words that bathe my skin in heat. I turn them over in my mind, clinging onto what sounds like: *Vot moe serce.* And then others…that I can't uncover.

I tilt my chin up, silently asking.

He repeats the Russian words, so deeply, but refuses to translate this time. It's enough as it is. Whatever the meaning, it leaves me sweltering.

ACT TWENTY-NINE

"Are you still complicated, Thora?!" the hostess of The Red Death yells at me for the countless time. I now know her as Erin, twenty-four, aspiring model, friend of Camila's.

I've been snatching the red "it's complicated" necklace since Nikolai and I started dating, and likewise, I've never seen him without the red glowstick. So my choice is an easy one.

"Yeah!" I shout.

She passes me the red necklace, and I snap it on as I slip past the black curtain. I inhale hot, sticky air. The club is suffocating, the heat, the bodies—I immediately tie my dirty-blonde locks into a low pony, grateful for my white halter dress that lets my arms and legs breathe.

Camila presses a cold beer bottle to her forehead behind the bar. "The air conditioning is broken!" she shouts at me. She's switched out her green "taken" necklace for a red crown. "We're on a break!" She must notice me staring.

"Sorry!" I yell back.

She shrugs and slides me my usual drink: a tequila sunrise. "You look like you need this."

I'd say it's my RBF, but I've had a shit week. On top of the Shay and Nikolai fight, a guy grabbed my ass after my aerial hoop act—about an hour ago. And training has been difficult. I struggle to do these challenging drops on aerial silk. No matter how hard I try, I just freeze up.

The mental block keeps me from progressing. Being graceful and lithe is out of the question if I can't perform the trick.

Self-doubt is a real killer.

"I did not sign up to drink in the pits of hell," John grumbles as he plops on the barstool next to me. He wipes his sweaty forehead with his arm and wafts his black shirt away from his chest.

I raise my brows at him.

"Don't give me that look."

"You're in a club called *The Red Death*. You don't think what you just said was a little ironic?"

"Everything I say has a level of unamusing irony. It's just the way it is. And unfortunately I have to live with myself longer than you do." He motions to Camila.

"No," Camila says, swatting his hand with a towel before she wipes the bar.

"At least quench my thirst while I'm *dying* here." He huffs and I tug at the collar of my dress. "I say we leave in five minutes if they don't fix the AC."

Camila gapes. "What about me?"

"What about you? You're being paid to suffocate. If I don't get free booze, there's no reason I should stay."

I lift my drink. "Comradery."

His eyes narrow at my tequila sunrise. "Is that free?" I see his eyes say: *You call that comradery?*

I suck the straw and bat my eyelashes innocently. "Bad day."

John swivels back to his cousin. And very seriously says, "I've had the most tragic Saturday—"

"You consider every day a tragic one," she cuts him off. "Nice try."

He extends his arms and then touches his chest. "My life is excessively shitty. I should be given *twenty* shots for that." He taps the bar aggressively.

Camila slaps his hand away again. "You cry wolf, there's a difference."

John rolls his eyes. "You're delirious from the heat, Camila. Cry wolf…" He snorts. "I don't cry wolf." If he had a beer, he'd chug it right now.

I check the clock behind the bar. Nikolai should be here soon if Amour ended about an hour ago. As the thought exits my brain, a *squish* noise triggers all around the club.

Sprinklers lower from the rafted ceiling and spray the dancers, drinkers, and bartenders with ice-cold water. Splitting cheers of excitement and glee crack through the pop music, and my muscles even relax in the chilly sheets.

Camila mutters curses, her purple mascara running down her cheeks already. "A warning would've been nice!" she shouts at the backroom and removes her makeup with a towel. I didn't put too much on tonight, so I think I'm safe on this front.

I turn to my left, to John. His dark brown hair dampens and sticks to his forehead. With his surly expression, you'd think a flock of birds just shit on his head.

I can't help it—I laugh. Really hard. It's honestly like a raincloud has sprung and decided to trickle on his head. Ironic, yes.

John latches his surly gaze on me and flashes an ill-humored smile. "What are you laughing about? I'm not the one wearing white."

My face falls, jaw drops. *No.* I'm not wearing a bra.

No.

I'm cool. It's not that wet…but even as I think it, my hair is soaked already. The sprinklers never dialing down. I slowly glance at my body…my nipples visible. The barbell piercing visible. My orange boy-short panties.

Visible.

What. Do I do?

John says, "I'd cheers to this shitty day, but oh—I can't. I'm just crying wolf."

Camila sighs and gives in to his incessant bickering, twisting the cap off a Bud Light. She slides it over to him. "Shut up."

He collects the beer. "Trust me, I would love nothing more than to stop hearing my voice, but I have vocal cords, so—blame God. I should've been mute."

"Truer words, old man." Timo fits in between our stools and rests his elbows on the wet bar. He's shirtless, in tight black jeans and when he pushes back his dark, drenched hair, I catch John giving him a *clear* once-over, swigging his beer. If Timo notices, he doesn't let on. "I need four shots of your best vodka." He places *two* hundred dollar bills on the bar, soaking in water, and catches me looking. "Won a grand this afternoon."

"Yeah, and you lost five grand yesterday," John retorts. I cringe. That much?

Timo chooses to ignore John. When Camila reaches for shot glasses, she slips on the wet floor, and just barely catches the counter before she goes down.

I give her the thumbs-up and then act like I'm rubbing the back of my neck, my arm successfully covering my nipples. I just…can't stand up. That's okay. It's all good. I'm living…life.

It feels hot in here again and it's still raining.

Hell.

John was right.

We're in hell. Where the reigning devil throws you in and says *step out of your box, Thora James.* My box consists of dark-colored clothes that can't possibly turn see-through. My box has back-up plans and emergency tampons. I can only leave it on two accounts: under the influence of tequila sunrises or under the charming persuasion of Nikolai Kotova.

The latter is missing.

Drink up.

I guzzle my cocktail.

"Whoa, slow down, Thora James!" Timo yells at me, his hand on my shoulder.

I raise a finger at him, still chugging.

Both John and Timo watch me until I finish the last drop.

"Bad day?" Timo asks me with furrowed brows, his lips near my ear so I can pick up his words.

"Sort of," I say, more softly, staring at the bottom of my cup. It's a sad cup now.

"Sort of?!" John shouts at me. "You got a free fucking drink for *sort of?*" He glares at Camila.

Camila points at his beer. "Ah, no complaining, cuz."

Timo laughs. "That's asking too much of him."

Camila finishes pouring Timo's shots, and I'm about to order another drink but she winks at me, already snatching the carton of orange juice. *Good friends,* I think with a smile.

John rotates to Timo fully. "At least I don't fuck middle-aged, potbelly bastards." This took a...weird turn. My eyes uneasily dart between them.

Timo stares straight ahead at the bar, wearing a pained smile, his abs constricting in his lean build. "Potbelly bastards..." He lets out a weak laugh. "Wow, that's a new one for you, John." Timo downs a shot.

"You can't be offended by what you sleep with," John retorts, his jaw locking.

Camila thankfully passes me the tequila sunrise and she unfortunately gestures to my boobs. *Nips*, she mouths.

I'm well aware. I'm a walking Saturday tragedy.

Or—technically I'm sitting. Fantastic.

Timo laughs weakly again. "Right." His palms are on the soaked bar, a chill wringing the air from the sprinklers.

While he swigs his beer, John stands, an inch taller than Timo, and smoothly slides behind him. I've never seen Timo tense before. But he does, especially as John rests his hands on the counter, on either side of Timo, essentially caging him in.

Damn.

It's hot.

It's even hotter when Timo turns his head, just slightly, to look at John. And John stares down like *you deserve better than middle-aged, pot-belly bastards.*

Camila has her fingers to her smile, watching them like me.

John's hand falls to Timo's waist, and he takes another step towards the bar, Timo's chest pressing against the counter's lip and John's pelvis up against Timo's ass. Okay, I've *never* seen Timo so flushed. John whispers in his ear, and there's no way I can make out the words from the pop song and spray of water.

"God of Russia! God of Russia!"

My shoulders lift at the new chant.

"Go get 'em," Camila tells me with another wink. She hands me my glass of liquid courage, and I spring off the barstool, forgetting for a moment that I'm in a see-through dress with a pierced nipple and bright orange panties.

I gulp the tequila sunrise, no longer feeling the burn of the alcohol. I leave my post at the bar to find Nikolai in the crowds. He hasn't stopped doing the Saturday night piercings and tattoos.

I told him not to.

I've noticed that out of every day of the week, he lets loose the most on this one. He allows himself one night to be uninhibited, to drink past his limit, to observe crowds, to read their body language and push them out of their comfort zone. It's a small glimpse of the kind of man he would've been—had he never raised three preteens and taken on more responsibility.

I would never take this fun from Nikolai.

But he's been kind enough not to choose body parts that are overtly sexual. No boobs, no asses, no thighs, definitely no nipples (his words). And he picks more guys now than girls, which is nice.

"God of Russia! God of Russia!"

I follow the chant towards the side entrance, where he usually enters as a "Masquerade employee"—John calls it bullshit since he can't even use that door. Me either.

"Hey, dance with me, baby!" a drunk preppy dude says behind me. He clasps my hips, both of us doused and the spray of water seems to be heavier here. I try to wiggle out and slip on the wet marble. He catches me before I face-plant, my heart rocketing to my throat.

I dropped my drink. On my strappy white heels.

No.

One fail after another.

Something pokes at my butt. He's grinding up against me without permission. This. This is what happens when you meet drunken fools in clubs. And you're not a drunken fool yet yourself.

"God of Russia! God of Russia!"

The chanting is closer. Louder. *Come here.* Light bulb moment. I do have a voice. "NIK!" I shout. Then I try to squirm out of the guy's grasp again. "Hey, no thanks." He cups my butt.

Honestly.

This is more than rude now.

I spin around on the green collared-shirt guy, pushing him physically in the chest, but he thinks I'm doing a creative dance move and clutches my wrists, tugging me closer. "No," I tell him.

He either can't hear me or he's too drunk to process the very important word. Ice cold sheets rain on us. His eyes are *right* on my hardened nipples. As though they're laser beams, shooting out rainbows.

And no—they're not even that magical.

"God of Russia! God of Russia!" That sounds right next to—

Nikolai hooks his arm around my waist, physically pulling me into his body and then shoving the other guy away with his hand. The groping guy squints at Nikolai, his lids droopy. "We were dancing—"

"No you weren't."

The guy seems to finally register Nikolai's size and territorial glare. And what's crazier, the energetic crowd that followed him spreads out into a circle, leaving us in the open center like Nikolai is about to breakdance. A burly Red Death employee even slides over a chair.

I guess this is where his stage will reside tonight.

Smack dab in the middle of the club.

You are in a see-through dress in the center of a circle, Thora.

Dear. God.

I spin into Nikolai's chest, and he rests a hand on the back of my neck, still watching the preppy guy closely. He motions to a bouncer near the door and they thread the masses to escort him away.

The power he has on Saturdays is not as foreign anymore.

But it still shrinks me.

I know I can never be like him, not to this extent. Some forms of confidence are natural, a gift that can't be learned. Like Timo. Nikolai once told me that he couldn't remember a time where Timo didn't know who he was. No questioning. No doubt. But he said it didn't make it easier.

Timo charged at life.

But life wasn't always ready for him.

I'm not as envious as I used to be. I'm more satisfied with who I am. Thora James: a series of fails but she'll stand up again.

I can most definitely live with that.

Nikolai tilts up my chin, and he studies my current clutch onto him. I study his wet hair, pushed out of his face. The water that rolls along his skin and drips off his lashes. It's not the most profound case study, but it warms my chilled blood.

"God of Russia!"

"They're calling for you," I say. *Step back, Thora.* I will. Baby steps.

"I hear that." And then he snaps off my glow necklace.

I flinch at the abrupt motion and notice his… "Nikolai…" He wears a green glow necklace. He's been *wearing* that this whole time. I shuffle back from him, forgetting about my see-through dress. I just have to see him, *it.*

Red strobe lights still comb over the club, but for the first time in months, he's declaring to *everyone* that he's taken.

I'm smiling.

He's not. Because his gaze rakes my body with conflicting expressions: arousal and concern. Maybe he's worried that I'm leaping out of my box tonight. Maybe he'd rather push me than unforeseeable circumstances do it for him.

I wrap my arm around my boobs.

"God of Russia!" Hands are now shooting into the air.

But Nikolai ignores them, his intensity all mine. He approaches the burly employee, and they switch glow necklaces. When Nik returns to me, he has a green one.

"Awwww," girls in the crowd *actually* make that noise, rooting for us.

His gaze never leaves me as he snaps the new necklace around my collar. "There's no confusion anymore, myshka."

I touch the necklace, wondering about his ex-girlfriend. I haven't ever asked about her, but the deeper we go, the more I know I'll have to.

I can't move past that gaze, the one that strips layers with rapid efficiency. It's even more intrusive than the first time we met. Because he knows for certain what lies beneath the sheet.

Then he kisses me soft, then harder, his tongue parting my lips. An ache tickles my throat, the drunken encouragements like a Greek chorus. Courage lifts my shoulders. It's not from booze. It's just from being near him.

His breath warms my ear. And he whispers, "I choose you."

My heart pounds.

He breaks away, fingers laced with mine, and his long once-over heats my core…and a lower place, clenching.

The cheers are even louder than before. I look up and *so many people* have gathered. The sprinklers don't shut off yet and everyone starts clapping to the beat of "Temperature" by Sean Paul, splashing water.

"They're excited—" he watches me absorb my surroundings "—because I've never done this with a girlfriend before."

Girlfriend. "I'm your girlfriend?" My smile is an uncontrollable one, where I can't for the life of me restrain or hide it.

He says something in Russian.

I don't have to wait for him to translate. He's said this phrase so many times.

You're cute.

I inhale strongly, *a handstand competition.* In a see-through dress. I can do this. I can. I know, for a fact, I can. However, I'm not sure if I'll beat him. That's the mystery.

Quickly I climb back over his earlier proclamation. He's never done this with another girlfriend. He's sharing this with me, his spectacle, his after-show—that's all him.

He's letting me experience his entire world.

"Can she even push you over!" someone shouts.

"Can you?" Nikolai asks me, his lips rising in an alluring smile.

I can try. I rest my palms on his chest, beads of water still rolling down. And I take a runner's stance and I try, with all my might, to shove him back.

He's a fortress.

A laughing fortress. "Try harder, myshka."

"I am," I retort, putting all my strength in my quads and biceps. My face reddens as I push, but I realize that he's positioned his legs in a way that deadens my force. I breathe heavily and crane my neck up to him.

He's way too entertained by this. "Little mouse," he says. "You can't knock me back, even if you tried."

"Oooh!" The crowds collectively make the noise. I hear the jest that I missed the first time against him, all lighthearted.

I catch my breath, my hands on my hips. "One day. I will. Even if it takes me years." *Years?* It sounds like I'm assuming we'll be together for that long. I open my mouth to clarify my slip, but he speaks first.

"Even if it takes you forever," he rephrases, his eyes bearing on my heart. "Are you ready?" He means for the handstand competition. But beneath his words there is so much more. Am I ready for a life with him?

"Yes." I nod, without hesitation. "I'm more than ready."

ACT THIRTY

I lost.

I can handle my liquor now. But I still can't beat him. My arms gave out, and I had to drop. I picked a piercing. He picked my other nipple.

Thankfully, though, he buttoned his black shirt on me before doing anything. I could tell it wasn't just for my benefit. He didn't want any of them to see my boobs as much as I didn't want them to be seen.

The Red Death shuts off the sprinklers about ten minutes before we head out, his hand on the small of my back, weaving through dancers.

"Are you sure you don't want to stay longer?" I ask him, my boob throbbing. He only did the bet with me. "I can wait at the bar—"

"I'm positive." He wraps his arm around my shoulders, as though to say *I just want to be with you.* I inhale a heady breath, his soaked button-down suctioning to parts of my body. I shiver, and we're not even out in the cold yet.

The red strobe lights stroke us, and as we near a staircase to the VIP area, I spot John. And Timo. I zero in on them, and my mouth instantly drops. John has Timo pressed against the wall, their lips touching, their tongues—it's a make-out session that brings the heat back to this club. No parting, eyes closed, like no one is watching. Timo clutches John's hair, their bodies welded together. And John drives the kiss deeper, more skilled than he lets on. They fit perfectly: their heights, their builds. On equal territory and footing.

Nikolai abruptly stops, causing me to stumble back into his chest. He places his hands on my shoulders, steadying me, and I follow his gaze back to his brother. Nikolai wavers uncertainly behind me.

If he could, he'd accompany his brother through every minor and major wreck of his life. But he can't. Timo will fall whether or not Nikolai is there. But he has so many people that'll help him stand back up if he struggles. That's what matters.

"He's okay," I tell Nik. If what John says is right—about Timo being promiscuous—then it's probably better that he's with John. And if Nikolai tries to split them apart right now, Timo will just run to someone else—someone not worthy of his attention.

Nikolai stays quiet, contemplating the situation. Whether or not he should intervene. "The hardest part is not knowing," he says lowly to me. I think I understand.

There are moments that do not belong to us.

Lives that we can only see fragments of, and as painful as it is to say goodbye to the whole picture, we're not supposed to have it anymore.

I imagine, for my parents, it was harder on them when I left for college. But it must've been so much worse when I moved across the country. It hurts them more than me. Just as this hurts Nikolai more than Timo.

"Can you imagine that wherever he is, he's happy?" I ask Nikolai.

He nods a few times. "I'm going to try. I *have* to try," he realizes. After another moment, he leads me away from them, through the club, towards the exit.

And he lets his brother go.

ACT THIRTY-ONE

"Who is she?" I ask aloud, surprising myself. I snap off the green necklace, my bare feet cold on the bathroom tiles. He runs the tub while I tremble from the sopping button-down and chilled air.

"Who are we talking about?" He unbuttons his slacks, distracting me as he steps out of them. Wearing only charcoal gray boxer-briefs.

I train my eyes on his tattoo, the inked lines along the inside of his bicep that create trees. It distracts me from his cock.

I open my mouth to say *your ex-girlfriend.* But the words stick. And I end up waving the green glow necklace in response.

He nears me and I back up into the sink counter, aware of my littleness to his largeness. It's not just the fact that he's taller than me. It's his broad build, his muscular frame. If he was Timo's size—lean, less muscle mass, a bit wiry—I would feel like we went together better.

But I'm very attracted to this, right here. In front of me. My speeding pulse, the tingles that prick along my arms, down my legs—it tells me so.

He begins to unbutton *his* shirt that's on *my* body. He's already examined my movements, reading me. "It's in the past," he says, realizing what I'm speaking of.

The gush of hot water, filling the tub, cuts through some of the silence. I press my palms flat on his hard chest. "But you know my past."

He consumes me with those grays eyes. "I'm older than you, myshka."

I believe it. I see it. But I don't want that to matter, on any account. "And…?"

"And I have five years of history on you. I'm not discounting your own experiences. I know for a fact that your first couple of times in bed left a mark on you." He lifts my chin, so that my eyes rise off the bathroom tiles. He is full of warmth. And light. "There's just more in my past."

"More," I whisper. *What more?* I ask through my soft eyes.

His chest rises and falls.

We're quiet for a moment, and I watch him unbutton the last of my shirt. He takes a couple steps back from me, my spine digging into the sink's lip.

Standing still, my black shirt is partially open, revealing the sides of my breasts and my wet orange panties. He has trouble focusing on my face and not my body, his concentration on more pleasurable things than this talk.

I have to know. I'm afraid I'll never grow the courage to ask again. "Why is she so complicated?"

He combs both hands through his hair, pushing the longer strands back. "Because…" He holds my gaze. "She was my partner."

"What?" My face falls.

"Tatyana Ulanova."

My mind rotates a million miles per hour, tilting, back-peddling, and out of all thoughts, the first I land on is so insignificant. "I thought it was Tatyana Ulanov, not Ulanova?" Maybe I begin with this because it's the easiest to touch.

"It's Ulanova. Whoever told you Ulanov was wrong." He rubs his jaw. "In Russian, surnames change according to whether you're male or female."

My face twists as I process this. "But Katya and you are both Kotova…wait, is that even your real last name?"

He tries hard not to smile.

"It's not funny," I say. "I don't even *know your name*."

"Yes you do, myshka. Tatyana is a Russian citizen, but I'm not. Those of us born in the United States had to take the same family name, by law. For whatever reason, they agreed on Kotova, not Kotov." He casually adds, "It's a sore subject with my father, considering he speaks very little English and holds Russian customs to a high standard. To the rest of us, it's just a name."

I bet Tatyana knew all of this about him. *Of course she did, Thora. She's Russian.* I'm at a disadvantage with a girl that I've never met. What'd he say about her? She's the best in her discipline. At aerial silk. She can communicate with him, in any language. And she probably fits better with him. Physically.

I tremble, cold sweeping my limbs, my wet shirt like ice.

"Thora…" He nears again, about to undress me. To warm me.

I press my palms on his chest again to stop him. "Just let me think…"

"She's out of the picture."

"She was injured," I remember. "She *got hurt*, Nikolai." I shield my wince with my hands and groan. "Is that why you broke up?"

Girl sustains a career-ending injury.

Girl no longer works with Guy.

Guy breaks up with Girl.

Girl leaves Vegas.

It seems callous on Nikolai's part, to desert a girl after something traumatic. Who am I really with?

He rubs his eyes like the memory is still raw. It shouldn't still be raw, right? That makes me the…

"Rebound," I whisper. "I'm your rebound."

Nikolai drops his hand and cocks his head like *you're so wrong*. "No. We broke up two months before she was injured. I was with her for three years romantically, longer professionally, but the feelings I have for her now are…" As he tries to find the right word, his face slowly contorts in a cringe, and he pinches the bridge of his nose. And then shakes his head.

"Your feelings seem to be strong," I breathe, crossing my arms for warmth. I shake some. *Stop shaking, Thora.*

"Not in the way you think." His voice is harder, more powerful. He shuts off the bath and then walks over to me, wanting so badly to take me out of the wet clothes. "You're freezing."

"I just need to process this with clothes on."

"I don't see what it matters if you're naked."

I exhale a tense breath. "Because I'll be distracted."

"By your own body?"

I scowl.

"You said it."

"By *you* staring at my naked body."

His lips curve upward, in a charming smile. "I'm not going to tell you that I'll look away because that'd be a lie." He tucks a piece of my hair behind my ear. "Can you hurry with your thoughts?"

My jumbled, tangled, helplessly confused thoughts. *Ask something important.* Everything feels important, so that really does not help my case. "Where is she now?" I manage to say. *Good one. You're doing good. Or well. Whatever.* I kind of want to shut off my brain now.

"Yekaterinburg. It's where she grew up."

So she's most likely with her family, at least those who aren't in the circus. "Is she coming back ever?" I ask.

"No. She wants to live in Russia." He watches my arms vibrate with the chill, concern narrowing his eyes. *Stay strong, Thora.* "I wouldn't be surprised if she has a boyfriend or a fiancé. Or even a husband by now." He doesn't pale or cringe or recoil by these facts.

"It doesn't bother you—"

"Why would it? I'm with you." Intensity still permanently latched to me, he removes his boxer-briefs, the last article of clothing. I breathe shallowly and seem to tremble more.

This is such a weird conversation to be undressing to. And I'm really to blame for that. *It needed to be said.* True. It's better with this knowledge.

He steps closer to me, until his body pins mine against the sink. "Anymore thoughts?"

With that one action, they've all escaped. I strain my neck just to see his hard, masculine face, flooded with desire. My arms are still crossed, pulling my shirt closed, despite being unbuttoned. He can't kiss me in this position. He'd need to back up so he can lean down, and it's frustrating on all accounts. I should've left my high heels on.

But he waits. For me. To say that I have no more thoughts.

"Why are you so patient with me?" I whisper.

"Because every part of me wants to take care of you." One of his hands drifts to the back of my neck, the other beneath my wet shirt, around my hip. "And to do that, I'd slow down to your speed."

"And what's your speed?" I ask.

"Much faster." He watches my reaction as he dips his hand beneath the band of my panties. My mouth opens in a heady breath. "Harder," he says lowly. His fingers brush the inside of my thigh before he pulls off the fabric. "Deeper." He peels the wet shirt off my arms, my lungs expanding in a strong breath.

The inhale lifts my chest, both barbells prominent, both pierced by him. It makes the throb in the hard bud feel more like pleasure than pain. He soaks in my body, every inch of skin with the most consuming gaze. After the sopping shirt hits the ground, we're both left bare against each other.

He makes the two guys that I was with seem like boys. Nothing as sexual, as arousing, as this. And all he did was undress me.

I tremble. This time, not from the cold.

Very swiftly, he lifts me around his waist, and his lips and tongue make skilled work on my neck, sucking the most sensitive part. I grind forward, my nerves lighting and dizzying me. I clutch him tightly, my arms not even close to wrapping around his frame. I bury my head into his muscular chest, protected, small.

"Just…no sex tonight," I whisper. *Not after that conversation.* I don't want to equate the first time to *her.*

He kisses my lips and then says, "Okay."

For a brief moment I wonder if he's really okay with it. Then he dominates every movement, doing whatever he pleases while I relax into the moment. And I realize, he's going to make it okay by doing so many other things.

His fingers slip inside of me. God. The fullness blinds me, and I cry into skin. We're in the middle of the bathroom. Not even against the wall. He easily holds me, driving his two fingers deeper, finding a spot that—

"Nik…" I gasp into another cry, spidering him with the hardest grip. It collapses his breath for a second. Then he lowers his head to suck my neck again, like I'm his play toy that he wants to pleasure. I throb. I pulse. I ache. Actually craving for his cock—actually wondering what he'd feel like.

While he screws me deep with his fingers, he carries me to the ledge of the marbled tub, setting me down. He remains standing, and using his free hand, he grips the shaft of his erection, which is much larger than anything I've seen up close.

Boys. You were with boys, Thora James.

"Open," he commands.

I am so wet. My back arches some, but I manage to part my lips. He fills my mouth, and I breathe through my nose, the erotic image like a trigger for my body. I nearly lose it, my toes curling and a raspy noise vibrates along his hardness. In my mouth. He places his hand on the back of my head, controlling how deeply I go. The movement. That mixed with his fingers in me.

I… almost fall backwards. Into the water.

He keeps me upright. And my hands slide onto his toned ass—Dear Lord. In heaven. It's the way he's looking at me too. His heavy breath, his arousal growing. He's getting off watching me get off.

I pop him out of my mouth, right as he hits a spot that sends me over. I cry, so loud that he instantly covers my lips with his large hand, drowning the noise. I haven't even caught my breath before he picks me up, as though I weigh nothing to him. And brings me into the tub.

My eyes are closed, but the hot water soothes my skin as soon as I'm lowered in it. He splays me against his chest. While he leans against the porcelain. His lips are on mine, but I can barely breathe still.

"You're going to come again, little mouse." His breath tickles my ear. "Until I decide to come with you." Fact: he loves watching me orgasm. I just can't imagine doing it again and again. And again.

"Not…possible," I pant.

He squeezes my ass, and then his fingers dive back between my legs, pressing against my swollen clit from a new angle. I tighten around him, pulsating. "Nik." I can't see straight. I can't even form another word. I am in his care, his possession. For the rest of the night.

"Anything is possible."

And I think, *only with my devil.*

ACT THIRTY-TWO

Four months at Phantom and I finally have a better routine for the aerial hoop. My training with Nikolai is thanks for that. My strength has improved, no more hoop burns. Top that with more sensual tricks, and I usually earn a warm applause at the end.

I even changed the music, no more emotional Broadway ballads. I go straight for mixes with sultry undertones. "My Song 5" by Haim blares through the amps and propels me forward. After weeks of Roger underpaying me for my "average performances" I caved—and it wasn't soul-crushing.

I'm still me.

Focusing on my routine, I do the splits, not just any though. I grasp the lower rung of the hoop, my legs outstretched, and then I channel my strength, lifting my body upside-down. I blow out breaths through my nose, making it look as effortless as possible.

Blood rushes to my head, but I keep my legs extended. This is the part where I have to ignore all the whistling and hollers.

Concentrate on the music, Thora. And I do.

I breathe out, and I point my legs straight, releasing a hand and supporting my weight with one single grip. As the music escalates, I lower onto the hoop, straddling the metal. I move more often than I hold shapes.

They enjoy watching me spin and twist and basically gyrate along the apparatus. *Gyrate.* Not my favorite word when I describe my profession.

No worries.

I exhale strongly.

January. I have to wait for January and then I'll be auditioning for Aerial Ethereal. *You can do this.* When my act finally ends, I receive that warm applause, and the hoop descends to the stage.

"Show us your tits next time!" Someone yells out.

My stomach lurches. That's a new one. My feet hit the stage, and I swallow the rising lump in my throat. They'll always want more, won't they? The fact is hard to digest.

On my way backstage, a man at a high-top table slaps my ass and then grabs it in a firm clutch. Fuck. The force is so hard that I wince, stinging, and the sound of the whack rings in my ears.

I spin around to shove him off. My heart races and pumps with adrenaline, but security already slips between me and him, separating his grip on my ass. *Let it go, Thora.*

My eyes burn.

Stop burning.

I lift my shoulders. *You're still you.* And I redirect my course. Away from the man, heading backstage. I avoid eye contact with everyone.

Safely in the employee's only area, I open my locker. Not far away, Roger is in a serious discussion with one of the veteran girls. She nods, her brown curls bobbing with her head. I step into sweat pants over my rouge lingerie and then tug on a baggy maroon shirt.

When I untie my hair from the loose braid, I notice faint bruises on my forearm from training with Nikolai. I'm not even sure how I acquired it—a mystery bruise. And not the first one. Nor the last. As long as I stick with it.

I close my locker and jump, my heart rocketing. Roger is *two feet* from me.

"Virgin Mary," he says. What? My face tightens. All week he's been calling me Thora. I even celebrated at The Red Death with an extra shot. "I need to talk to you."

I nod for him to continue.

"We're cutting your act."

"What?" My voice is a whisper. "Why?" I thought I've been doing better. I even did the splits. My rent, the bills, the food, clothes—I need this job. It's the only thing keeping me financially afloat.

"You're not great, but you've improved, sure. The cleavage helps." He gestures to my breasts, thankful they're covered in the shirt.

"There has to be something else…I can do, anything." *Anything.* It just came out, but I struggle to take it back. I am so, so desperate. I'm about to be a stray cat in the rain, wandering a freeway. And I have to bank on Roger, of all people.

"It's not about your routine," he says, grimacing like he hates pleading.

But I'd grovel, I think. I wonder if I'd shamefully drop to my knees. *No.* Yes. I don't know. My eyes burn again.

I'm about to lose my job.

He scratches at his thick red hair. "The owner wants to reduce the number of aerial acts in favor of go-go dancers." I open my mouth to offer, but he raises his hands, silencing me before I release a word. "You're not dancing for us. For starters, the other girls would look like giants next to you. And we're here to make them look fuckable, not like they popped out of Jack and the Beanstalk."

"So there's nothing else?" *I'd do anything.* That's what I'm telling him.

He scans me, from head to toe. Am I selling my soul right now? What the fuck are you doing, Thora? *Surviving. On my own.*

"There is something," he says. "We have these private shows for top clients. Just you and a low hanging hoop and a room. Maybe one or two men. No sex. Too many lawsuits there, but it has to be way sluttier than that shit you do up there." He checks his cell as my mind seesaws between my morals and my boyfriend and my independence. "That's all I have. You'll make twice what you make now."

"How much?"

"A grand."

"In a week?"

"A night."

A night. My heart stops. That's not just twice what I make now. That's so, so much more. Tempting—this part of Vegas is very tempting. *Say no.*

Say yes.

"I need to know by tomorrow. I have to start filling the calendar." He leaves me with my indecision. I can spend tonight and tomorrow searching for jobs, and if there's nothing—then I can proceed from there.

All I know is that I can't be broke.

If I'm broke, I go home.

I leave Vegas.

Return to a life that I have left behind. Start back at the beginning. Try to forget about the person who clutches my heart. Without money, I fail.

It's simple.

I'll figure it out. I have plans set for today and tomorrow. It'll be okay. Motivational boosts in check, I walk through the club, hoping to grab a drink from the bar on the way out.

I make it five feet, and I stop dead.

No.

Standing by the stage, right behind a bald bouncer that blocks drunken men from slipping into the dressing rooms—I see them.

My parents.

At Phantom.

ACT THIRTY-THREE

I bring my mom and dad to an Elvis-themed diner in The Masquerade, somewhere quieter where we can talk. They sit across from me in the red vinyl booth, music playing softly from a retro jukebox, frequently interjected by an "order-up" call from cooks.

The only thing they've told me is *why* they showed up at Phantom. A place I never told them I worked.

It was Shay.

He called them, out of worry for me, they said. And he confessed all of my sins, all the lies I've been telling for months. The betrayal sinks beneath an overpowering sentiment: guilt. Horrible, gut-wrenching guilt. A knife twists in my stomach, barely able to meet their eyes.

A phone call was too impersonal, my mom said.

They wanted to see for themselves. So they purchased plane tickets and saw my act tonight. They heard some guy scream at me to "show your tits" and watched another smack my ass.

I don't think this is what my parents hoped for me. It's not what anyone would want for their child.

When I raise my head, I see it in their eyes.

Disappointment in me. Hurt in them.

I drop my head again, my finger running over a sugar packet after we all order drinks.

"I don't even know where to begin," my mother says, her voice cracking. Her blonde hair splays on her thin shoulders, her makeup soft, with understated colors. Nothing like the bright red that stains my lips.

"This isn't how I wanted you to find out," I whisper. My eyes continue to burn, but I don't cry. Not in a semi-crowded diner, people sipping on milkshakes.

My dad remains silent, his fingers to his lips. His wispy hair has grayed almost completely. He's twelve years older than my mom, a fact that never seemed to be an issue for them. Not even when they accidentally became pregnant with Tanner—my dad already fifty-one at the time.

I know love when I see them.

Unfailingly together, their hands cupped beneath the table, as though prepared to confront this problem, *me*, with unity. I never even dreamed of finding love. It's been low on my list of pursuits. I thought I'd tackle that later. Maybe in ten years. I'd fall in love for the first time then.

I wish someone would've told me that you can't search for love. That one day, it will find you.

An unexpected thing.

"Where are you staying?" my dad asks. It's the first time he's spoken.

"I have an apartment." I let that hammer drop. My mom's eyes shift to the table. I add, "In a good location. Safe." These facts are important to them. Vital. Necessary things. And even as I say it, I know they won't believe me. They'll go back to their hotel room, Google search my address and research crime rates in the area, snoop on forums to see what real life people have to say.

"Why wouldn't you tell us, Thora?" My mom practically cries. No, she is crying. This opens the floodgates on my emotions, my heart palpitating as tears drip off her lashes. "If this is what you wanted… you know we would've supported you."

Don't cry, Thora. I'm trying not to. "Would you?" My voice quivers. "Because I didn't get the job, Mom. I wasn't good enough." A rock in my throat, I add, "I didn't have a place to stay. I didn't have a job at the time. You would've told me to get my ass home. Please don't say differently. I know you both too well."

"We would've helped." She dabs her eyes with a thin paper napkin. "You could have flown home and we would've started job hunting—"

"If I flew home, I would've stayed in Ohio." She would have broken down and cried, convincing me to stay. My father would've pointed at my mother and said *you're making her sick over this.* And the fear of leaving would've poached all my resilience that I mustered to come here in the first place.

"Stop it," my father cuts in, his voice like nails, full of angry disappointment. "Stop talking, Thora." His gaze shifts to the seat beside him, my mom burying her face in her hands, tears streaming full-force.

I look away.

And that's when I catch someone watching us. A girl at the bar. Long legs and arms and pale skin. Katya's round, globe eyes fix right on me. This is her favorite diner, so of course she's here.

Concern reflects in her gray irises, empathy for me.

Tears sting, clouding my vision. Once upon a time, I saw a broken girl sitting in a booth. That's how I met Katya. And now here she sees me. Fracturing in a booth, splitting apart. Life is a rollercoaster with no volunteers. We're all forced to take a seat and ride it out.

She mouths, *are you okay?*

Hot tears roll down my cheeks, but I nod. She shouldn't worry over my problems. Last month, I confessed to her that I'd been lying to my parents, after she asked what they thought of me being in Vegas. Wrong confession. To the wrong people. Always.

I turn my attention to my parents, both silent in thought. "I'm sorry," I say what I should've started with. I choke out the rest. "I didn't...I didn't know how to tell you."

"You lost your scholarship," my dad says, his face reddening in ire. "You had a *year* left of school. That's it. Was your college education not worth it to you?" For my father, this is a rhetorical question.

It has to be worth it to me. It's what'll pay my bills without headache, he believes.

I answer it anyway. "This was worth more."

I want them to see how much it took out of me to stay here. To be alone in a city with *no* familiar face. But their viewpoint is Shay's. To them, this is nothing more than foolish. A dumb move in the game of life. I went off the board, left the right path. And decided to take one that never existed in the first place.

When my father looks at me, it's as if he's laying eyes on a stranger. "So you're dancing at that club?" The disgust in his voice caves my chest. My mom still cries. Unable to produce words, she fists a crumpled tissue.

"I'm an aerialist at Phantom," I choke out, tears falling as I blink. I don't mention the turn of events after tonight. It's not the right time to bring it up—and I may...I may find a way out of it. Then I'll tell them. "And I'm...training with someone from Aerial Ethereal. I'm going to audition in January. I don't know if Shay told you about that."

"Your boyfriend is training you," my dad snaps. "That older Russian man." The way he says *man*, it sounds vile.

"He's twenty-six," I mutter, feeling sick all of a sudden. Nausea churning.

"That's okay, honey," my mom sniffs loudly. She shoots a look at my dad. She's defending me? I rub my watery eyes, my hand slick with tears. Why does her support hurt too? I don't understand…a larger pain just bears on my chest.

My dad shifts in his seat.

"We're not here to discuss your relationship," she says softly. "That's your business. You're old enough to make those choices. We just wished we were informed about the other part…" She sniffs harder, a croak in her voice. "After all we've…" Her lips vibrate now.

"I'm sorry," I cry out, reaching across the table for her hand. She lets me hold it. "I'm really sorry, Mom."

"I am too," she replies. "For making you feel like we would've swayed your decisions…" She shakes her head. "You're an adult, Thora. You can do whatever you want. We just want you to be safe and to help you choose right."

To help me choose right. But what happens if their choices don't align with mine? Moving against them is worse than moving against the grain. It's like trying to stop a wave from breaking.

My brick-walled father is not as eager to forgive and forget. "You're still working at this club?"

"I can't go home—"

"Yes you can," he says. "Stop this."

I shake my head.

"If you go back now, you'll only be a semester behind."

"No, I have auditions…" I trail off as his jaw hardens, his eyes shooting caustic bullets into me.

"Paul," my mom says in defense. "She's twenty-one—"

"She's still our daughter. This is so…" *stupid*, he's going to say. I'm being stupid. For being here. Taking this risk.

My gaze falls off them, agony coursing through again. This isn't going to have a good end. No bygones be bygones. The realization slashes my insides, cutting me to pieces. I look to the bar, but Katya isn't alone anymore.

Luka sits beside her, taking furtive glances in my direction. I check the Elvis clock hung beneath a neon sign. It's too early for Amour to be finished. Nikolai is still at work.

"Thora," my dad says, drawing my attention. "We'll compromise. You come back to Ohio with us, reenroll in college, and when auditions come around, we'll pay for your ticket to Vegas."

It's safe. Smart, even. "I…" I freeze.

He adds, "You shouldn't be working at that club either."

"It's…temporary." My swollen throat can barely release the words.

"And what were you planning on doing if the auditions didn't work in your favor?" he asks. "How temporary would it be then?"

He's slicing me at the knees.

My mom says, "We'll give you the night to think about it. Our flight leaves at noon tomorrow."

My dad can't just leave it there. He's silently fuming, fixated on what he saw tonight. He leans forward. "I don't care if your mom wants to talk to you, but as long as you have that job, I don't want to hear from you, Thora." He stands up like he banged a gavel on a podium, throwing an ultimatum at my face.

I can't move.

I can't even blink, haunted by his voice.

My mom pats my hand, my dad hurried to leave. He waits for her to scoot from the booth, and when they depart, everything slams into me. Doubts. Worries. So many fears.

I rest my elbows on the table, crying into my palms. How can this be worth it anymore? What if their offer is the right path and I'm being stupid by staying here? In Vegas.

A sob rips my chest open. And that's when I feel the seat undulate, someone scooting next to me. I lower one hand and see Katya, her cheeks splotched red like she's been crying.

I turn my head, and I see Luka across from me, his gaze just as bloodshot. But he smiles weakly, as though reminding me that I have people who care about me in this city—who are here for me. I struggle to return the smile, realizing I can't form one. An avalanche of tears forces me to shield my eyes again.

Katya hugs me around the waist. "You can't leave," she whispers, her voice so soft.

My second hand returns to my face, a mess of emotion. *You can't leave.* But I'm not sure if I should stay either. I try to set aside my feelings for Nikolai. I try so hard not to see him in the equation, and my achievements seem so small, so miniscule and pitiful.

My body shudders with each sob, the noise muffled in my palms. I never wanted this chapter in my life to be the biggest mistake, the biggest regret. I wanted it to mean something.

I wanted to be something more.

And yet, I sit here, pained, tired, sore, a wreck—and I just hear what everyone has been telling me all along. *You're not one in a million, Thora James.*

You will never amount to more than what you are.

Accept that.

I think I'm starting to.

For a long time, Katya and Luka remain quiet. Just here for me. Whether they know it or not—it conflicts me more. It makes it as hard to leave as it is to stay.

And then Luka tells me, "At least wait to talk to our brother before you make a decision. Please."

I nod once. It's the only confident choice I can make in this moment. Everything else is fragile and gray.

ACT THIRTY-FOUR

I curl up on the couch in Nikolai's suite while I wait for him, silent tears leaking onto a decorative pillow. Katya and Luka whisper quietly at the kitchen bar, her phone pinging each time she receives a new text. I'm mentally and emotionally spent, but these silent tears won't cease.

Minutes pass in a daze before I hear the door open. "Where is she?" Nikolai's worried voice fills me whole.

"Sleeping," Katya says. "I think she may leave, Nik." The sound of his feet dies midway.

Luka interjects in a whisper, "We don't know that, Kat."

"You saw her. She was thinking about it, and her parents looked upset. It's all because she's here. Normal parents don't want their kid in Vegas." She sniffs. "She can't leave, Nik."

He speaks in hurried, low Russian, pain—I hear pain in his voice.

"No," Katya suddenly cries. "Don't say that."

His tone carries so much weight. "It's not our choice to make, Kat."

"But you love her. And she loves you."

I shut my eyes, tears sliding down my slick cheeks. My whole chest heavy. My whole heart full. One has been crushing the other.

He whispers Russian that I can't understand. That I don't even pretend to.

"You have to fight for her," Katya cries. "Nik, you have to."

"Katya, listen to me," Nikolai says. "That's not what this is about."

She speaks Russian.

For the first time since I've known her—she speaks to him in clipped, pained Russian. A sob attached to her words.

He replies in the same language with finality. And Luka has to be the one to say, "It'll be okay, Kat."

Seconds later, strong arms slip underneath me, and Nik carries me to his bedroom. I keep my eyes closed, afraid to see Katya's expression. I never thought I'd make a mark on someone's life. I never thought people could love me that way. I'm average. Ordinary.

But I'm beginning to realize something…

We all traverse in and out of people's worlds, leaving footprints. Some larger, some smaller, but there is always a mark. We can't sweep it away.

In this moment, I think I'd like to sweep every mark. Every footprint. Every trace of me. No one will be hurt from my aspirations. From my pursuit of happiness.

It's best that way.

My back sinks into the soft, metallic comforter, his fingers stroking my cheek, a gentle breeze. I'm scared to open my eyes. To meet his. I'm supposed to stay in Vegas for my career, not for love. And I wonder if I'll forget this. If he'll flood me with sentiments too strong to let go.

I sense his knees on either side of my build. I sense his hands on either side of my head. "Open your eyes, Thora," he whispers.

Wake up.

I do. I am.

He hovers over me, his eyes directly in line with mine, matched, unwavering. Those gunmetal skies bearing down from up above. I can see, clearly, that he knows everything. His sister must have texted him the entire story that she overheard.

Tears slide from the creases of my eyes. "I'm a fool."

"No." He rubs my cheek with his thumb, drying the wet streaks. "You're brave."

I'm about to shake my head, but he clutches my face, keeping my gaze fixed on him. It hurts so badly. The truth. Every word my parents said. The ultimatum. My end. "It's over."

"It's only over if you want it to be," he refutes.

Instinct, I try to shake my head again. He clutches me tighter. "Nik..." My face twists as I cry. "You don't understand. I'm *not* good enough." I shield my face with my palms, and he brings both down, grasping my wrists.

His beautiful gray gaze is reddened but hard, determined, assured. Confident. Powerful. As though he has faith in me. As though his belief will carry me further than their doubt.

"You're better than you were," he says lowly. "I promise you that."

I remember what Shay said at the pool party. *He gives you false hope, so he can sleep with you.* "You're designed to say good things to me," I breathe, my eyes raw, my throat dry. "You're my boyfriend."

He inhales a strong breath and his jaw muscles tic. "You have to separate what I say as your trainer and as your boyfriend."

"It's hard," I whisper, "because both my trainer and my boyfriend are in agreement, aren't they?"

He stays quiet, not denying that he wants me here, in Vegas.

I ask the most painful question of the night, each word opening me whole. "How much of you wants me to stay because you love me...and how much because you know I will succeed?"

"Thora…" His gray eyes glass, distraught. He tries to rope me in, to lasso me one last time. Not even his intensity can lift me higher. He lowers his body closer to mine. And then he says, very slowly, "I don't love you."

My body collapses.

And his eyes begin to pool. "I don't love you, Thora." *Why does he have to repeat it?* He clutches my cheek as I try to turn away. He forces my tearful gaze to his watery one. "I will tell you this every single day if that's what you need to hear. Just to believe these truths. You're good enough, myshka. Because you work hard. Because you're willing to learn. And because you have talent. You wouldn't be able to pick up skills this quickly if you didn't. And if you go home now, you're giving up."

His words rush through my veins, a drug that tries to soothe the painful parts of me. "But if I stay, there is no guarantee that I'll land a contract." I hear my parents in my ear. I hear Shay. I hear everyone else but him.

"There was never a guarantee. And still, you flew out here. You still made a life here. All on your own." His hands warm my cheeks. "There are so many people in this world afraid to do what you've done. They'll wait around hoping that something will make it easier—a stable job, a friend in the city, any extra security. When it doesn't happen, they spend the rest of their lives without their passion, wondering what could have been. Don't latch onto their fear. Not now."

I hear him. I hear his words that come from a place of love for me. But nowhere in them does he convince me to stay for him. Not once.

My seesawing mind starts to lean towards him. "I think I know why people are so afraid to do this," I whisper, my face scrunching as I try to hold back another wave of tears. "It feels greater than me."

Nikolai pulls me into his chest, lying on his side, so that I'm cocooned against him. I bury my face in the warmth of his body, and he strokes my hair, one hand protectively on my neck. "I made one choice in my life that scared me," he says, "and it felt much bigger than I was at the time."

I think I know. When he was twenty. When he took on raising his brothers and sister. I lift my chin up to him.

He stares down. "They weren't little kids—Timo, Luka and Katya. They were at the parts of their lives that would affect them, shape who they were. I felt a responsibility to make sure they turned out okay. Every day was hard. Every day is hard. But the things we love—the people we love—give us reason to keep living. To keep trying." He wipes the last of my tears with his thumbs, my attention all his. "The things greater than us, Thora, they're not impossible. It's just fear talking, telling you that you *can't* when you can. I know you can."

I stare in awe of him, wondering how someone can fill me with so much more than I've ever been able to give myself. I was always my number one cheerleader. My number one fan. I think I've been replaced. "Where did you come from?" I ask what he asked me once.

He just gives me a small smile, tucking a strand of my hair, less distressed by my hesitance. Maybe he sees what I feel.

I can do this.

It's not over.

You'll be good enough. But I press my forehead to his chest, silently drifting into the fragile memory of tonight. My parent's offer and my father's ultimatum. If I reject both, I may damage my relationship with them. I'm not even sure if it'll be beyond repair—since I've never hurt them before.

"What is it?" he asks me, studying my complex state of mind.

"Is this worth hurting my parents?"

"They should be happy if you're happy, Thora."

It's not that simple. I wish appearances didn't matter—but they do. I don't want to shame them for having a daughter who works in Vegas, in a risqué club. Or for dropping out of college. And likewise, I don't want to feel ashamed for what I do with my life.

"This sucks." My voice cracks.

He hugs me closer. Tighter, small in his protective, strong arms. And his lips brush my ear. "Sleep on it," he breathes. "And I'll be here when you wake up."

This is an offer that I can say yes to, without falter.

ACT THIRTY-FIVE

"If you stay in Vegas, you have to support yourself," my mother tells me over the phone. I lie on my stomach, still on Nikolai's bed. Only six in the morning, still dark outside.

"I have been." I block out Phantom firing me and the second decision I have to make in a short period of time. This has to be resolved first.

She inhales sharply, like she may start crying. I exhale deeply, trying to combat my own emotions. Round two.

Nikolai rubs my back, leaning against the headboard. Here for support. It's a little easier.

My cellphone is cold to my ear.

"I thought your father and I taught you that college is more important than…" Her voice breaks. *Than a boy.* I hear the unsaid words.

"I'm staying because I have a better chance at landing a contract here, Mom. I can still train until January."

She's quiet for a moment, but a muffled voice leaks onto the line. It must be my dad. Then she asks, "Are you still going to work at that club?"

Had I not been fired, I would've said yes. I feel that answer in my bones. "I think so," I say what my gut tells me. "I need the money."

I imagine my father's gutted expression, the disappointment, the rage, frustration. It seeps into me, but I don't back down.

"Did this boy sway you?" my mom asks, her voice shaking with hurt. I already know she probably didn't sleep last night.

But neither did I. My thoughts were set to a noisy radio channel that I couldn't turn off.

Before I answer, my father's anger is apparent from the background, "He's not a boy, Dana. He's a *man*." As though Nikolai is old enough to take advantage of me, to brainwash me, to force me here.

Nikolai must've heard him through the speakers, even though it's pressed to my ear. His hand stops its rhythmic motion, placed on my lower back. And he removes it altogether. I watch him stand up and disappear into the walk-in closet, simultaneously giving me space and getting dressed for the day.

I tell my mom, "He just reminded me why I'm here." I don't need them to express their doubts, in any part of my life, so I quickly speak again. "This is the hardest choice I've had to make. But I'm not going back on it." I've gotten this far.

"We love you," my mom cries. "Our door is *always* open for you. When you're ready, you come home."

My chest tightens. "Thanks, Mom. I love you both too." After another reiteration of these sentiments—with no interjections of *good luck* or *love you* from my father—we hang up. And I stuff my face in the pillow, groaning. You'd think after that I'd feel weightless, a certain kind of relief.

But I'd prefer to sink into this bed and wallow for a good hour or two.

Nikolai emerges from the closet, already in workout shorts, shirtless: his abs chiseled, the V of his muscles prominent by his waistband. He ties a rolled red bandana behind his head, strands of his hair already hanging over the fabric. "You okay?" he asks me, concern in his voice.

"I've been better," I whisper. I've never cried for that long or been that emotional in my entire twenty-one years of living. My eyes and throat feel like sandpaper. "Are we training?"

He nods after he finishes tying the bandana. "Right now."

Right now?

I glance at the bedside digital clock. It's only six-thirty in the morning. My body is too heavy to move. I collapse back onto the pillow with another muffled groan, working my way up to rolling over. *Roll over. You can do this.*

My muscles don't budge.

"Get dressed," he orders, his tone already all business.

I've left some clothes here, in case he calls an impromptu training session like this one. It happens often, but rarely this early.

I mumble something that sounds like: *in a minute.* But with the pillow in my face, I doubt he hears me. The bed suddenly rocks, Nikolai kneeling on either side of my body.

Lips to my ear, he whispers, "I'm giving you ten seconds."

That's not long enough for my rusted joints to cooperate. Or maybe it's all in my mind. That's a definite possibility. "Thirty," I mumble.

"This isn't a negotiation. My rules."

Okay. Okay—I'll get up. I try propping my elbows, but I honestly end up hugging the pillow above my head. Mind and body, at war once again.

"Five seconds left," he warns me. Still on my stomach, I try to crane my neck over my shoulder.

He's practically straddling me. His pelvis in line with my ass. It's a position I've never been in with another guy—especially not one who stares at me with harsh, tireless gray eyes. He gives me an expression like *you're here to train, myshka, not collapse in self-pity.* Or have sex with him.

And he's right, of course.

Get up, Thora. I prop my elbows on the mattress this time, but I hesitate, a mental, emotional, physical block. I think my pity party needs one more hour.

Nikolai isn't having it. "Time's up." He pulls my baggy tee off, leaving me in my lacy red bra, part of my Phantom costume. He won't let me slack off, not for my emotions, not for him. Not for anything.

I think I love him more for it.

Love.

It's a strong word, but I'm not sure what else to call this. It's greater than just *like.* It's more powerful than friendship. If I'm not falling in love with him, then I'm missing the definition of the level right below it. Sort-of-love. Almost-love.

Maybe-one-day-love.

"You're a slug," he says, unclipping my bra. "A melancholic, defeated slug."

He's trying to put a fire under my ass by insulting me, since I'm rarely sluggish or defeated. My lips rise in the pillow. I definitely love him.

And then he yanks down my pants and lacy underwear, exposing my bare bottom. I feel him tense, and I look over my shoulder again. His severely stern gaze is locked on a new reddish bruise along my ass, which has begun to purple.

From when the drunken guy slapped and grabbed me at Phantom last night.

Out of instinct, I try to roll onto my back, to hide the shape of the mark, but his firm hand bears on my shoulders, keeping me in place.

His chest rises and falls in a heavier rhythm. "Someone slapped you," he deduces, his voice hollow, like the depths of a cave. My stomach overturns. I can't see as well as him, but there must be five dots like fingerprints.

"Hazards of the job," I say under my breath.

His unflinching, hot eyes burn holes right into me. And then he climbs off the bed, his muscles more flexed. I uneasily lift my pants back to my waist and clip my bra. "Nikolai…?"

He stops short by the bathroom door, his back facing me. "Just… give me a second." He's collecting his anger, his volatile emotions that burst and harden his broad shoulders. Since Coco Roma, the costume shopping, we rarely talk about Phantom, almost not at all.

I slide to the edge of the bed, waiting for him to turn around. "It rarely happens."

"Rarely?" He finally faces me, so much anguish contorting his features. "You think that'll make me feel better?" His cold voice stings more. "I don't want it to happen *at all*, Thora."

"I get bruises from training," I defend. "Can you pretend that I just fell?"

He looks at me like I stuck my fist in his chest. "No. I can't pretend, because you didn't just fall. A man *assaulted* you. I'm *never* going to be okay with that."

The weight of Roger's proposition still hangs over my head. I need this job, and it's become a whole hell of a lot risker than what it was. "I know you're angry at me, but—"

"I'm not angry at you. I'm *furious* at every piece of shit that walks into Phantom and believes they have the right to touch you."

I hang my head, the guilt pummeling me down. This probably wasn't the reaction he hoped for.

"What aren't you telling me?" he asks lowly, reading me too well.

I twist my small simple pinky ring, avoiding his gaze. "They cancelled my act last night, at Phantom." I swallow hard. "It was right before my parents showed up."

"And?" His voice sounds tight, knowing this doesn't end on a happy note. I wouldn't be this sullen if it did.

"They said the only way that I can still work there is if I perform my act in private shows." I pause, but he stays quiet. So I continue on, "I don't have many details to go on, but they said that I'd make a lot of money. And that I have to give them a decision today."

He rubs his face with his hands, as though he's trying to wake up. Then he meets my eyes. "You already said yes." It's not a question. And the pain in his voice hurts me more.

"I was going to…"

He shakes his head repeatedly. "Thora, you have *no* idea what you're getting into."

"It's probably not as bad as you think."

He stares at me like I'm out of my mind. "You're *completely* naïve if you believe there won't be a sexual favor involved. They'll make you strip, suck him off, give him—"

"Stop," I cringe.

"No, you *have* to hear this." He steps nearer, until he towers above me. "I won't let you take a job that you believe is something it's not."

I'm conflicted, all over again. But I remember my plan. "I'm going to try to find another job today. I'll call John. He got me the one at Phantom. And I'll ask around and look online, but if I can't find anything…" Tears well at the devastation in his eyes. "I need this job, Nik."

"Live with me," he says.

For so many reasons, this isn't possible. "You know I can't." The words hurt as much to hear as they are to say. And as horrible as it seems, I think it'd be different if he was just a friend. If I was crashing at his place for a couple nights like at the beginning. But to rely on him this way now—it feels like defeat, like I failed at my purpose for being here.

He kneels. At my feet. I don't have to strain my neck anymore. And he places his hands on my thighs. "I know you want to be independent, but it shouldn't cost what you say you're willing to pay."

"I wouldn't…" My voice cracks and I shake my head. "I wouldn't blow another guy. I wouldn't do anything like that, Nik."

"And what if they put you in that position?"

"I'll leave," I say, adamant about this.

"And what if they don't let you leave?" His jaw muscles tense.

"They will." I have to believe they will. Before he rebuts, I add, "I can't leech off you. Timo spends all of his money, and you support him and Katya and Luka. You can't afford to provide for me too."

He doesn't refute me—because it's true. He suddenly rises to his feet. "We're not training today."

My stomach drops. "Wait—"

"I have to make some calls," he clarifies. "If you only have today to find another job, then I want to use every hour."

My lips part in shock. "You're going to help me?" I'm not sure what I expected his reaction to be, maybe to throw an ultimatum at me. *Him or this job.* Like my dad did. But this outcome overwhelms me, in a bigger way.

He tilts his head, his eyes softening. And he speaks in hushed Russian. Not long after, he says in English, "I'd help you every day so that you could see a better tomorrow. I will never give you less than that."

My heart expands with each syllable.

And I wonder if his briefly spoken Russian was what those gray eyes convey now. The sentiments too strong to ignore.

I love you.

I see those words all over him.

I feel them.

But neither of us can say them aloud. Maybe we both refuse to wedge *I love you* between my purpose for being here, in Vegas.

Love—it has to come second.

ACT THIRTY-SIX

After non-stop job hunting, Nikolai and I came up short.

I agreed to the private shows about three days ago. Roger booked me one for tonight. And in those three extra days, available jobs seemed nonexistent. At least ones in my skillset. John said that most clubs are cutting back on aerialists, and I didn't have enough experience to be a bartender or a dealer.

The waitressing gigs also were out of my element. I tried a couple places and they said my height would be a problem or I wasn't the "right fit"—which John said was the subtle way of telling me that I wasn't "hot enough" for the men there.

But I strangely get it. A lot of the waitresses here are aspiring models. I'm just not the illusion this city wants to create. Nikolai wouldn't tell me who he talked to or who he called, but he still has no potential leads.

So here I am.

At Phantom, dressed in black lingerie beneath my sweats.

I wait for Roger by the employee lockers, rocking on the balls of my feet, my nerves escalating. I exhale a measured breath. "You can do this," I mutter. I probably look like the crazy girl, talking to herself.

My cliché pep talk is all I have right now. I can't welch.

When I see the mop of red hair, my spirits simultaneously lift and fall. My feet glue to the ground. *You can do this. Move forward.* My soles are still cemented.

Roger approaches me, making it easy. He scrolls through his phone and says, "Looks like you're off for the night. The client cancelled."

"Cancelled?" My shoulders drop in relief. *You can't be relieved, Thora. You needed this money.* My eyes begin to burn.

"Did I stutter?" he shoots back. "This happens sometimes." My resting bitch face must be going strong because he holds up a hand. "Look, I can try to get you another gig in a couple days."

A couple days…

This isn't a salary-paying job. I don't see a check unless I work.

His phone rings. "I have to take this. You're done for the night." He slides past me.

I check my phone. It's still early, and Nikolai has a show. But now I have more time to research. For a better job than this one.

I SIT AT A PENNY SLOT, BETTING ABOUT TWENTY cents every two minutes. I've taken gambling to a whole new slow level. My excuse is my cellphone in hand. I scroll through job openings in Vegas, not picky on the exact location since I've become used to public transportation.

Unfortunately, most are dealers and bartenders.

I click into the Masquerade's website and search for full-time jobs within the hotel. *Assistant chef, baker for the pastry shop, master sushi cook, sous chef.* In another life, I'm without a doubt becoming a chef.

I rub my temples the more I read. An elderly woman with a fanny pack scowls at me as she passes. I guess I'm not concentrating enough on the machine. Fine.

I hit the "bet" button. Lines start popping up on the screen, forming many zig-zags. Wait…

My heart lifts. I won something. Right? Fate is finally on my—

Fifty cents.

Fifty cents? I have to stare at the number for thirty full seconds to digest this. But there were so many damn lines. And that's all I won. This is rigged. I don't even know what the lines are pointing to or what they mean. I scan the machine for instructions.

Nothing.

Stupid machine.

I focus back on my phone and notice another job position. *Assistant housekeeper.* It's full-time. My shoulders rise with hope, only to be squashed with the words "one-year experience in housekeeping for large casino or hotel required."

Apparently people don't start their on-the-job training in places like The Masquerade.

When I accepted the private aerialist gig at Phantom, Roger told me that many girls want this job and even fewer are ever hired. So I should realize how lucky I am—that he'd even offer it to me. That he wouldn't have if I didn't work there before.

It puts things into perspective. Like how hard it may be to find something else.

My phone vibrates.

Call me when you can. I care about you, and I just thought they'd be able to help you. I'm really sorry. – Shay

I click out of the text, a pit in my stomach. He's been trying to call since my parents flew back to Ohio. I think he expected me to be on the plane with them. I haven't had the courage to respond to his voicemails or messages. Not yet at least.

I know what Shay did wasn't out of malice, but it doesn't change the fact that there's still a knife wedged between my shoulder blades.

My cell rumbles again.

Amour ended. Where are you? – Nikolai

At a penny machine near the black and gold bar.

We agreed to meet up after work, to discuss my first night at my "new" job. I try to rehearse what I'll say, but I'm blank for a good while. Just kind of wishing I won a jackpot right now.

You and everyone else, Thora James.

"Hey."

I spin on the leather stool. Nikolai stands a few feet away, in a pair of drawstring pants. His makeup is all washed off except for a thin purple streak by his hairline, like he rushed to be here.

"I won fifty cents." I motion to the machine.

"Thora." My name sounds raw off his tongue, and he studies my body language for signs that I've come out without a scar.

"It was cancelled," I say quickly, so he can stop worrying. "I have a couple more days until I work. So…it's pretty good, I think. Extra time."

He hardly relaxes, but he does nod in agreement. That's a good sign. Right? *Most definitely.* I exhale a tight breath.

I wait for him to speak, but he stares off, as though he's thinking about the inevitable. Me working a private show.

"Do you…maybe want to see my apartment?" I suddenly ask.

I catch him off guard. His head whips to me, surprise coating his face. In the months that we've been together, he's yet to even see my apartment complex.

"I mean, you don't *have* to. It's not much, or anything." Nerves swarm, especially as his gaze bores through me, heating my core. "It's, um, small. But I have a bed." *Of course you have a bed. Why wouldn't I have a bed?* I made this weird.

His lips curve upwards. "I'm glad you have a bed, myshka." His voice is sex. I swear it.

"Thank you…" Lame. So lame.

He laughs into a bigger smile. "You lead the way."

Something tells me that we're going to switch to his speed tonight.

ACT THIRTY-SEVEN

During the taxi ride to my apartment, Nikolai keeps his focus on the street, trying to determine where we're headed. He has no clue what part of town I live in, not until the taxi rolls to a stop at the building. And he seems to exhale for the first time.

After climbing out of the car, he places his hand on the small of my back, walking towards the stucco 5-story apartment complex, plenty of bikes locked and chained to a nearby rack.

"You live farther away than I thought." He finally speaks as we ascend the staircase.

"Safe area though, right?" I holster the urge to fill the pregnant pauses.

He digs in his pocket for his phone. "Relatively speaking." He hates me living here. I know it. I watch him text someone. "I'm making sure Katya knows she's alone tonight."

"She won't go out or anything…will she?" I remember the 2 a.m. hunt for Katya Kotova. If there's been another chase, I haven't been a part of it.

"No she's still at practice," he says. "She'll be too tired."

I almost smile, not at her being tired, but for her trying harder. She's been working on landing a full-in, full-out on the Russian bar for a while. Extra practice has been helping her a lot, Nikolai said.

He slips his phone back in his pocket. And I stop by my door, apartment 4E. He scans the outdoor hall: the fluorescent lights, bugs flocking it, and my neighbor's dingy welcome mat that says *Nice Underwear.*

There is a faint smell of dog crap in the air and stale pizza. But I'm still happy to have this place, something that's mine.

When I push open the door, I begin to hold my breath for his ultimate reaction. He follows me inside, and I scoot around him to lock it back. I take a little while longer to achieve this, my heart on turbo-speed.

"I can give you a tour…" I slide the deadbolt and spin on my heels. The blinds are shut, three of them broken, rays of moonlight casting shadows in the darkly lit room.

"Bedroom," he says, nodding to the mattress on the floor. The blankets are haphazardly thrown on it. *Why didn't you make your bed?* I really didn't think this invite through.

"Yeah…that's my bed." I nod. "It's also the couch. Like a bedroom-living-room situation. Cozy." Do people still use that word? *Cozy.* I exhale through my nose and focus on him instead of my furniture (or lack thereof).

He stands between the bathroom door and the edge of the mattress. Literally like five feet of space. His body seems larger here. Taller. The ceilings lower. The room smaller.

I brought a Ken doll into a Polly Pocket house. I'm a Polly Pocket playing with a Ken doll. This is…not right. *It'll be fine, I think.* My brain even sounds uncertain.

"There's the kitchen," I say, pointing to the cramped area with moveable counters and a hot plate. "And the bathroom is behind you. But you know what a bathroom looks like, so…" I clear my throat. I'm acting like we haven't been dating for months, but this is just new. Him here. The possibility of sex. It's nerve-inducing. The pressure is a little higher.

His eyes stop dancing around the room, and they land on me. He gestures me to walk over to him. I am lingering by the deadbolt. There isn't much room between the mattress and the bathroom door. *That's the point.*

Right.

I set my keys on a small wall hook (aka a nail), and I kick off my shoes and sidle to him. I immediately regret my lack of shoes as the top of my head reaches his shoulders.

He cups my face, his thumb caressing my cheek. "Your eyes are black, myshka."

Are they?

I'm just overly concerned about how large he looks in my tiny apartment. And how tiny I am compared to him. Tiny things don't fit with big ones. Those are the laws of physics. Or geometry. Whatever class I wasn't paying attention to in high school.

"It's dark in here," I note. I wish I was better with words. God, do I wish that right now. "But yeah, they still do that sometimes."

"When you're angry," he replies, stepping closer, my pulse racing. *Not always.* "When you're confused." *Sometimes.* His hand drifts to the back of my neck.

I ache between my legs, loving his touch there. Always that firm, protective grasp. Always in that place.

"And when you're aroused." *That…I wouldn't know.*

I dizzy as his thumb skims the soft flesh along my jaw.

"So right now, which is it?" His other hand descends to my thigh, and in one rapid, lithe movement, he has me at his waist, supporting me here with a single palm. I'm almost eye-level, my arms clinging to his shoulders, my legs around his torso. His mouth brushes just outside my lips. "Thora?"

I haven't answered him yet. My heart thumps. "You're too big."

He holds my face again, his strict gaze full of reassurance. "You have to trust me."

"I want to…but I'm scared." It's one of the most truthful things I've ever said, ever admitted aloud. I just can't stop thinking about the differences between us: our ages, our heights, our sizes, our—

He kisses me, so deeply, as though to show me how much we do fit together. My muscles flame in pleasurable heat, and while his tongue parts my lips, he walks backwards, towards the bathroom. Nikolai opens the door, but instead of slipping through, my spine hits the wooden frame. He pins me here.

When he breaks the kiss, his eyes bore into mine, pulling off my baggy tee. Then he removes his. He unbuttons his pants, steps out. Never detaching from me. Never leaving me. His attention, his intensity is mine. He takes off my bottoms, leaving me in black Phantom lingerie.

My heart can't slow. Even for a second.

"I'm going to fit inside of you," he says lowly, his voice masculine and deep, filling a silent, small room. "Since you've only had sex twice, it'll hurt at first, but it will feel better."

I nod, digesting his honesty.

His fingers slip into my hair. "You don't have to think about anything. Not how this'll work or what to do next. Just relax, and I'll take care of you."

It's this proclamation that calms my restless nerves the most. "Okay," I whisper, blood pumping. This time, when his lips drift to my nape, I let go, closing my eyes and just burning with the swelter of his strong movements. No more thinking about our differences. No more zoned in on the parts that make us a bad pairing.

As his hands roam, undressing me, undressing him, I forget everything except this pleasure. His lips meet mine, hungrily, achingly. He extends my legs more, stretching one up, the other still hooked around his waist. My back arches, his hardness close, and I already begin to pulsate, his fingers rubbing me.

I grow soaked by the second, and I can't close my mouth, breathless and warm all over. "Nik…" I clutch onto his biceps for support.

He says something in hot, sexy Russian that only stirs me more. His thumb flicks my barbell piercing, the sensitivity pricking my neck.

And then his body presses up against mine, to the point where I figure out what's about to happen next. My eyes open, and I wrap my arms tighter around his chest, bracing myself for the fullness that I simultaneously crave and fear.

It won't hurt. It won't hurt.

Even if he said it will.

Stop thinking.

That's when he slides his erection deep inside of me, not slow, but hard. He thrusts forward, the pinch is worse than the first couple times I had sex. Because he's bigger. My fingers dig into his back, stifling a wince, but he never hesitates, just rocking at a melodic, fast pace.

It builds up my arousal, and he dips his head to kiss my neck, sucking—devouring me. He lets out a deep noise, a grunt as he goes deeper. The pleasure flooding his face, and it sends me to a new plane of existence, one where pain is replaced by a high, floating. Near the broiling sun.

I turn my head, a fraction, in a dazed state. And I catch sight of ourselves in the bathroom mirror. Dear God…

That can't be me. The girl enveloped by this man. His cock disappearing between my legs. His hands on either side of the wall, cocooning me for a further, more intimate entry. Rocking forward. Into me.

My chest is on fire.

My heart set ablaze.

Seconds later, my toes curl, a cry rips through my throat, and my body curves, right into him. He never stops his rhythm, never slows his powerful stride, and I feel myself being wound all over again. The pain is gone to these other senses, like a drug numbing a wound.

I reach up to touch his jaw, my head dizzied, my eyelids drooping.

He takes his hand in mine before my fingers even skim his cheek, and he kisses my palm, staring straight into me as he thrusts. I've never felt closer to Nikolai than right now. And I trust him. With every single part of my life—I trust this man.

I'm in love with you.

I hope one day I can grow the courage to say the words out loud.

"HOW DO YOU FEEL?" NIKOLAI ASKS ME, THE morning light streaming through my broken blinds. I lie on my stomach, my firm mattress beneath me. His hand drifts along my bare back, my teal sheet just barely covering my bottom.

How do I feel? I never even dreamed of sex like that, full of strength and emotions. Beyond the physical parts, I think our love for each other made it more intense.

But I can't lie—it hurt when he pulled out. He knew it did. Afterwards he held me in his arms, caringly, until I fell asleep. And now… "Sore, mostly. I mean, not that much, but…" It's hard to stretch my legs in a split without feeling pain.

I press my cheek on my pillow, my eyes meeting his. He's on his side, his body propped by his arm.

"We're not training today," he tells me, "so you have time to rest." In part, I think he wants to use some of today to help me find a job. I try to read his features, but he seems content, more at peace.

"How…was it for you?" I ask tentatively.

His lips rise. "Extraordinary." He sits up and pulls me into his arms, kissing me now. "I'm waiting for you to catch your breath before we go again."

My eyes widen. *Again?* I expect him to add, *just kidding.* Any time now…

He features lighten in a more charismatic smile. "You look frightened."

"I'm not…I'm just…"

"Sore," he states. "But I'll take care of you, my demon." He's still wearing that charming smile.

I scowl. Though it makes me curious about a second time with him. And a third. Fourth, however many more there will be. *Infinity plus, Thora.* The nervous, excited flutters return. "What happened to resting?"

He tilts his head. "Training is more exhausting than sex."

For him, maybe. My endurance has depleted since last night. And he barely exerts any effort to achieve what I do. He's just built that way.

And I wonder… "Why do they call you the God of Russia?" Is it because of his skills in bed? I mean, they're pretty godly. But that's scary—that everyone would know that about him.

"It's easier to do a lot of circus tricks being shorter; your center of gravity is lower. But you know this."

I nod. Though, when paired, it's a bit easier to do lifts if the guy outsizes the girl. So for aerial silk, there's a small benefit to the size difference.

"In my extended family, only Dimitri comes close to my height. Most everyone is around Timofei's size. He's not short by any means, but it's still easier." He combs his fingers through my dirty-blonde hair, his eyes dancing over my features. "When I was young, they all thought I'd struggle with the harder tricks, the way that Dimitri did."

"But you didn't struggle," I realize.

He nods. "I always found my balance."

He's naturally, supremely talented. Gifted beyond immeasurable doubt. It makes more sense, the jealousy between Dimitri and Nikolai. The competitiveness that derived as children. Always being compared.

Nikolai always coming out on top. Strangely enough, I empathize more with his cousin on that account.

"My older brother, Sergei, jokingly called me the God of Russia. It catches on wherever I go because my cousins never stop using it. Mostly because they like how it infuriates Dimitri." His gaze narrows by a degree.

And I recognize something else. Nikolai has never referred to the nickname, never acknowledged it or fed into it. "You hate it," I say.

"I won't put my cousin down to make myself feel better," he says. "Dimitri is a lot of things that I dislike, but he's also a lot of things that I love. It's what makes him family."

I smile, never expecting this answer from Nikolai. His humbleness attracts me, melts me. I think it would've been easy to grow up with a sense of entitlement, being that talented. But maybe his cousin's struggles grounded him—made him appreciate what he has more.

"The way you look at me…" he breathes and shakes his head like there are no words to describe it.

"I'm not scowling, am I?"

His lips curve upward in another smile, and he draws me even closer. "No, myshka. The way you stare at me…it's like…" His gray eyes light up. "It's like you admire parts of me that no one else sees." He collects my hand and presses it to his chest, to his heart, and the beat drums against my palm. Fast, quick, as though I'm overwhelming him.

My pulse begins to accelerate, matching his. I think about how when this all started, I envied him. And somewhere, I took a turn, and I no longer wanted what he has. He's made me appreciate myself more, love myself more, and as a result, I've come to see him as more than just a great athlete, a charismatic performer.

Nikolai Kotova is the sum of his brothers and sister. And more.

He is selfless, loyal, dedicated and wholly determined—the most responsible twenty-six-year-old, the most mature man. He is power and strength. But most importantly, he is love. And family.

He kisses me again, his hand warming the back of my neck. "Whatever happens, just know that the parts of my life with you have been my favorite."

My smile slowly fades, wondering why that sounds like a goodbye. "What do you mean, whatever happens?"

He pulls back, his thumb stroking my cheek. And he's quiet for a moment, collecting the right words. "Come January," he says, "after auditions, you could land a contract in a traveling show."

My stomach sinks. "What?" I thought I had a good shot at Infini or Viva, *Vegas* shows. The traveling ones are all full.

"Last night, Helen told me that Aerial Ethereal is reviving Somnio. They'll need performers, so you have a much better chance…" he trails off, maybe at my contorted expression, but his seems to reflect mine. "Myshka…" His muscles constrict and his Adam's apple bobs.

Chills snake up my skin, at the thought of leaving him. For the circus. *That's the right thing.* Months ago, I would've been elated by this news. My reaction now—it frightens me.

He tucks my comforter around my shoulders and presses me closer, to warm me. Lips to my ear, he whispers, "You can't choose me over the circus."

I know.

My heart clenches, a fist squeezing the life out of it. I never thought it'd be this hard to choose between the two. "I don't want to think about it." It hasn't happened yet. I don't have to decide now. This is just all hypothetical. Right?

He holds me, as though remembering this moment. Like there's a countdown to a time where this all ends.

ACT THIRTY-EIGHT

I've never seen so many Kotovas in the gym before. They pile around the teeterboard/metal cube contraption, some of the guys messing around like they're at recess, shoving each other's arms, laughing and cracking jokes. But this is their work.

I remember Nikolai mentioning that they've all wanted to increase the difficulty of the teeterboard act, but the creative director has been telling them to stick to the regular choreography.

Apparently they're ignoring that suggestion.

I stretch my legs on the blue mats near the aerial silk, waiting for Nikolai to finish up. Usually I'm here at odd hours, when people are sparsely strewn on different structures, but Nikolai texted me to train now.

With a pop song blasting, sounding like Bruno Mars, Timo hops on one end of the teeterboard, the apparatus resembling a seesaw. Dimitri, much larger, jumps on the other side, catapulting Timo in the air. Instead of flailing about, he gracefully lands on a metal rung.

Timo sings to the song, clapping his hands to the beat and moving his body like he's in an episode of *Dancing with the Stars.* As the professional. Not the uncoordinated celebrity.

It's impossible to stop staring.

I glance around, wondering if anyone else is entranced—and surprisingly, this is not all in my head. The girls on trapeze, a couple on a trampoline, and the cluster of guys by the Russian swing pause for longer than a second.

All eyes on him.

He's dancing. For fun. Only he's spinning, shifting his hips, and tilting his head back while walking the bar like a tightrope.

I feel a smile grow on my face.

Timo's movements are effortless, and I see a bit of Nikolai in him. Even though he's more energetic, spirited, he compels everyone's attention the same way as his older brother.

His dangling cross earring whips back and forth with his head. His sweaty dark hair hangs in his eyes, the sides shorter though. He jumps onto another rung, and my heart nosedives. But he easily makes the gap, and claps his hands over his head before doing a backflip and spinning on the tips of his toes.

I'm surprised there's not a crotch-grab in his freestyle routine.

"Ready?"

I flinch at Nikolai's sudden appearance, too hypnotized by Timo. Nik towers above me, his hands on his waist as he breathes heavily from finishing his own workout. I scan the length of him, flashbacks of yesterday morning and afternoon playing on rewind and repeat. We had sex in my apartment. Again. And again. Apparently Nikolai's speed is not only fast but frequent.

Even the memories heat me another time around.

"Yeah." I rise to my feet, my pulse racing. I expect there to be weirdness between us, for him to silently acknowledge that we've had sex. Or maybe it's just all me.

Thinking about it. Obsessing over it. *Focus, Thora James.* Right. I'm here for training. I exhale. I inhale. Breathing *normally.*

Nikolai remains completely strict, the same as usual. He acts like the hardass coach, who in no way would sleep with his trainee. Because that would be unprofessional.

"Give me your hands." He studies my reaction and gives me a strange look.

"What?" I flip them over, not able to read his expression.

"You're glowing." He sprays resin on my palms.

I gape, my mouth slightly falling. "No, I'm not. I'm just…happy." I need to work on my excuses and my words. Always my words.

His lips barely tic upwards. All business. "You need to execute the modified straddle slide smoothly."

Smoothly?

I haven't been able to execute it higher than ten feet from the mat. Smoothly isn't on the menu if I can't even perform it at all.

Nikolai wants me to climb fifty feet and fall head-first to the ground, with my legs extended in a split. If wrapped correctly, the silk is supposed to catch me right before my face smashes into the mat. But if I screw up the intricate wrap, I could break more than just my nose.

"Can we call it what it is?" I ask him softly.

He hands me the silk. "It's a modified straddle slide." His no-nonsense voice tries to put my head in the game.

"It's a *death* drop," I emphasize.

I'm not being dramatic about this either. The longer title is a butterfly drop *into* a death drop with some alterations. Honestly, I've never even heard most of the tricks he's taught me so far. Some he flat-out created from scratch. And others, he's tweaked so they appear more dangerous.

Modified straddle slide really does not encompass the fear that I feel from this one.

"If I thought you'd die, I'd never let you try this above twenty feet." He steps back from me. "Climb."

I inhale a motivational breath and start my ascent. Since the beginning of my training, I doubt I'd be able to scale the silk this easily and this fluidly. Nikolai's instruction has been invaluable. When I begin wrapping my legs in the silk, I try to harness whatever grace I possess.

"You look angry!" Nikolai calls up from the bottom. "Relax your face."

He knows that's my "concentration face" and he says if I exhibit that expression during auditions, no one will want to hire me. I open and close my jaw. *Go away, bitch face.* I think it'd be more amusing if I didn't just refer to my own face as a bitch.

Now fully wrapped and facial muscles softened, I'm ready for the drop. I think.

Catch yourself, Thora. You can do this.

Nikolai is at the base, his arms crossed over his chest. With a fixed gaze, lines crease his forehead, his focus only on me.

Do it, Thora. My heart slams into my ribcage.

Wait.

"Am I wrapped right?" I ask Nik, just double-checking.

"You know you are." Though his eyes flit around my body, just to confirm it himself.

Do it.

I hesitate.

"Drop, Thora."

I pull my knees through loops in the silk, and legs spread, I shoot downwards without the support. I squeeze my eyes closed, scared. Rarely am I ever scared about heights in general. Then I feel my body jerk upwards, the silk tightening around my thighs and catching my fall.

I open one eye. And then two.

I'm upside-down. And still too high up. About seven feet, maybe a little less.

Nikolai approaches, straight-faced. When he stops, our lips are in perfect symmetry, but he stays still, a commander that refuses to kiss his soldier. A teacher unwilling to make a pass at his student.

At least not in the classroom.

"Your face should be an inch from the mat, not right in front of me." He grips the fabric above my foot.

"I realize this," I say softly.

"When you begin the wrap, you need to give yourself more slack, more than you think is necessary."

But the terrifying part is what happens if I give myself too much slack.

He reads me well. "Don't be afraid." His gaze flickers to my lips, like he may break his own rules this once.

My heart is on its own death drop.

"Nikolai…?" That's not me. The voice, with a string of Russian jargon, comes from a petite, willowy platinum-blonde a few feet behind him.

I recognize Elena from tryouts months ago, and I've had the good fortune of never running into her here. Nikolai spins around and listens to her talk. I roll out of my position, climbing down from the aerial silk. Elena jabs her finger in my direction, her cheeks flushed with what appears to be anger.

Nikolai runs his hands through his hair, pushing back the longer strands. He replies in gruffer Russian.

I uneasily shift my weight from one foot to the other, noticing how she steps near him. Noticing how her body language isn't closed off, despite being frustrated and incensed. She leans towards him. Like they're good friends.

I've blocked out his dynamic with Elena, the *passion* they're supposed to exude on stage. I just pretend that she doesn't exist.

The same way he pretends I don't work at Phantom.

My chest caves, and I realize that training is going to be cut short. By me. "I'm going to go," I tell Nikolai when there's a pause in his conversation.

He rubs his eyes, exhausted, by whatever she's telling him. "I wish you wouldn't."

Elena is throwing knives into my body, glowering like I've stolen her time with him. In this situation, maybe I have.

"You should practice with her." I let go of the silk. "I'll see you tomorrow."

"Tonight," he rephrases.

I shake my head. "I'm going to head home." It's weird that I consider my apartment my home now, when Ohio still exists. Waiting for me. I guess I'm not waiting for it anymore.

Nikolai looks more conflicted, but Elena distracts him with a barrage of Russian. I'm too used to not understanding three-quarters of conversations to be annoyed. I simply wave him goodbye and depart, planning on a hot shower and a night with my paranormal book.

I still have time to conquer the death drop, RBF, gracefulness, and passion before auditions. I hope. It feels like a lot.

Like more than me.

ACT THIRTY-NINE

Luka plops down in the auditorium seat with two buckets of popcorn, offering me one. I raise my brows at him, not exactly trusting how he acquired it. Our "Skittles" pact still exists—I won't rat him out.

He smiles, a contagious one that his brothers usually possess too. "I paid for them, I swear." He shakes the tub.

I accept one graciously. "That's sweet of you then."

He kicks his feet on the empty velveteen seat. "It still would've been sweet regardless if I paid for it or not."

"But this is better."

"Why?" He scoops popcorn, a smirk playing at his lips. He knows I suck at back-and-forth.

And now I'm open-mouthed, trying to find a suitable answer. "Because…" *it just is.* In another life, I hope to be a wordsmith. And a chef. A chef with great words.

"I like *because*." He lets me off the hook, seeing my struggle.

Thankfully.

I return my attention to the round stage, the surface cherry wood, sleek and more elegant than concrete.

Nikolai surprised me with a ticket to Amour tonight, rerouting my plans to fall asleep to a vampire and werewolf battle. I think this is his way of apologizing for Elena's appearance at practice. I couldn't turn him down. I'm not that prideful, and I've really, really wanted to see this show since I first arrived in Vegas. The tickets are so expensive that I haven't been able to watch Nikolai perform.

Artists don't even receive complimentary tickets for family and friends, so I know Nik paid for me to be here too. From middle-center seats, I drink in the atmosphere for the first time, trying to stare at everything at once.

The long icicle lights drip from seemingly nowhere, a city skyline painted as a backdrop. It's like Amour takes place in New York, during the holidays. While more people find their seats, music plays, a serene violin tune, romantic and subdued. Layers of fog already ooze across the stage in white puffs.

A flash of light goes off in my face.

I scowl at Luka who has his phone braced at me. He snaps another photo with a laugh.

"Is that necessary?" I shield my eyes, wondering if we're going to be in trouble. We're not supposed to take pictures in the auditorium.

"Oh yeah," he says. "I promised my brother I'd get your first reaction. And the pissed off one is an added bonus." He clicks into the photo and holds his cell to me so I can see myself.

I'm drooling at the sight of the stage: my eyes wide in awe and a fool-hearted smile spread across my cheeks. I look like a little kid about to witness a Christmas miracle. "I'd say delete it, but I know you won't."

He grins like I'm correct. "Nikolai will love it."

That fact swells my heart. I twiddle my fingers, nervous for the show to begin, for Nikolai. And he's done this so many times before.

Ten minutes later, the seats fill a little more than half up, which should be decent for a weeknight, but I know The Masquerade feels differently. The lights dim, shrouding the audience into blackness. The violins echo, beautiful and haunting music. And then red silk descends from the cavernous ceiling.

Soon Nikolai emerges, arms spread out, the silk wrapped around each wrist, head hanging. His sculpted, chiseled body is the sole object of everyone's gaze. He lifts his build, using the power in his biceps and broad shoulders. His legs straight, he strikes masculine poses that show off his strength and agility. Men like Nikolai were the muses of Renaissance sculptors—their strong figures carved in marble and stone.

My heart slows, waiting to stop all together.

He's… There are no perfect words for what I feel. For what I see. It's staring at a Michelangelo painting and being intimate with the subject beneath the brush strokes. It's falling to your knees and looking up at a god, who belongs to you.

Another flash goes off. This time, too apparent in the dark auditorium.

"Luka," I hiss, squinting my eyes. Nikolai is still descending towards the stage, a commanding, quiet intro.

"I had to capture love," he refutes.

Uh…

Security leans over our row, just one man in an Amour T-shirt, plastic badge tethered on a lanyard. "No pictures."

Luka whispers back, "Sorry, dude." He makes a gesture like he's putting his phone away, but when security disappears, he leaves it on his thigh with a bigger, satisfied smile. What a rebel.

I redirect my attention, just as Nikolai's soles hit the bottom of the stage, cloaked by fog. In the very center, he breathes deeply, like he's witnessing what *we* just saw. Like he's the one being overcome.

The hairs rise on my arms.

He scans the audience, pulling us all in individually. It's what he does at The Red Death—it's how he captivates and turns one head from the next.

His purple and silver paint across his eyes darken the romantic look of his red pants. It's here—as he steps forward, alone—that I begin to realize the importance of Nikolai Kotova to Amour. He's going to guide the audience through each act.

The storyteller.

The person that bridges every type of love together.

As his eyes flit around the audience, he says, "Do you know love?" The pain in his gaze palpitates my heart, and somehow, he finds me in the crowd.

He fixes his line of sight in my direction. Whether or not he can see me clearly, I can't know for certain. But this one look from him, while he's working, on stage—it solidifies me to the chair.

"I believe there are *many*, many kinds of love." His eyes seem to smile at me. Knowing I'm unraveling at this intimacy. "And I have seen them all."

I find myself touching my lips, feeling the force of his on mine, from memory.

And then he steps back, once and twice, the fog thinning around him. He wraps a single hand in the silk. "Tonight," he says lowly, "you will know love. Just as I do." And he rises in the air, the apparatus lifted by riggers, giving the illusion that he's cast away.

When he vanishes, acrobats suddenly scale rafters, *smooth* and nimble. Other dancers perform sensual choreography as a transition between the major acts. Everyone is dressed in modern attire: pants, shirts, and…lingerie. Not as risqué as Phantom, more like delicate babydoll tops with spandex shorts.

As the show continues, I replay Nikolai's intro in my head. Even when he appears on stage again, assisting trapeze, I still hear his deep voice. I still see him staring straight into me. With that soul-bearing gaze.

After many minutes pass, Luka leans into my shoulder. "This is where the aerial silk act goes." It's supposed to be the halfway-point, the highlight before intermission.

We've already seen trapeze (teasing) and hand-to-hand (gentle). I flip through the program, trying to see what's left if aerial silk (passion) is out. Next up: Chinese poles (destructive), teeterboard (obsessive), and the conclusion is the Russian swing (friendship).

As we move onto the poles, it feels like the swelter of the story is missing. But maybe that's just me, knowing this act should've been here.

When we reach Timo's act, I realize that he's the climax of Amour.

Obsessive love.

The metal cube structure encompasses the entire stage, teeterboard beneath. My nerves escalate again. The danger is all in this act.

I swear.

Artificial snow flutters from the ceiling, "Carol of the Bells" playing, crazed and fast-paced. A girl in a white nightgown sits idly on a bar, swinging her legs.

Then Timo takes a running start from the side stage, seemingly coming out of nowhere, and he uses a hidden trampoline to propel his body through the air.

Everyone gasps.

He lands right on the highest rung of the apparatus. His hair slicked back, in black leather pants. He's not the sprightly young kid.

He's dark. Sinister, black paint across his eyes. The girl startles, standing. And he proceeds to chase after her, through the cube, using rungs like monkey bars, accompanied with flips, tucks, somersaults, and things I've honestly never seen performed before.

The girl stops a few times, letting him catch up to her, and she's in a whole other class too. A pit wedges in my ribs. *You're not ready for this, Thora.* Not even close. She drapes her back along the rung, fluid like silk. And he cages her with his body. She rolls out of the position, dropping…into the arms of Dimitri.

More people flood the stage.

What happens next is the most intricate choreography I've ever witnessed, bodies moving swiftly, in unison through the bars. About five run in a *handstand* position, on the highest beam, chasing a new group of acrobats. Others concentrate on the teeterboard below, shooting straight up, landing straight back down. My eyes dart to so many places, wanting to see everything at once.

I want to do that, I think as I see a beautiful triple layout.

I can't do that, is my thought for three-fourths of this act. It's insane.

What I do notice: the looks every Kotova give each other, the slight head nod. The way they all spot Timo when he soars higher through the metal cube. Timo is clearly the best flyer, with a greater level of difficulty in each rotation.

And it shows.

The audience claps enthusiastically when he lands with ease.

My phone buzzes. I hesitate to answer, but it could be my parents… not that I'm dying to talk to them. I just keep hoping my dad will have a change of heart.

With my hand cupped over the screen, I open the text.

> We have a client wanting you, right now. Get your ass here in five minutes or we'll give the gig to Lana. – Roger

My stomach overturns. Another buzz.

> And slut up your costume. – Roger

I worry. About everything. As my bank account depletes, with no job alternatives in view, I wonder if this is my last shot. If I reject this,

Roger will never offer me anything else. Nausea barrels, sickness rising in my throat, and I can't tell if it's from having to choose between staying here and leaving or what I may be walking into.

Luka nudges my arm and whispers, "You okay?"

"I have to leave," my gut tells me to say. "Work stuff. I'm sorry."

"Are you sure?" Even in the dark, I spot his deep frown. Luka has no idea that my job description has changed at Phantom. If he did, I have a feeling he'd run after me. It's a red flag—what I'm about to do. *You can't lose this job, Thora.*

"I can't lose this job," I whisper to him.

He nods in understanding. I set the popcorn at my feet and stand in a crouch, careful not to block anyone as I slip out.

It's only dancing. I may be fooling myself. But this one thought is the only way I can proceed without falter.

And take this risk.

ACT FORTY

Roger ushers me along a dark corridor. Another girl in lingerie shuts a door and walks back up the hall. I cover my chest with my arms, hiding my mesh, push-up bra, the white sfabric see-through. Barbells and nipples unfortunately visible. I would've never chosen this outfit, but I had nothing else. I was lucky enough that they had an extra costume, Roger told me.

The bra is a half-size too small, and the cups squeeze my boobs uncomfortably together. I refuse to look down at the panties, also mesh, also white, and only covering half of my ass. If I do look, I may chicken out.

"Same deal as if you're on stage," Roger tells me quickly. "You'll have a purple light flash at the one minute mark, and then you descend, bow or whatever the fuck you do. Leave out the back, alright?"

I nod. The neon sign at the end of the hallway says: *yes yes ohh yes*

We stop by a closed door, and he puts a hand on my shoulder. "Hey, look fucking sexy, not like you're going to hurl on the clients."

I swallow more nausea. "Sorry."

He shakes his head at me like *come on, girl.* And then he grabs my wrists so that I'm no longer in a shell, my boobs exposed. "You're lucky that you even have a gig. Other girls would kill for this." Roger has expressed this sentiment about six times in the past five minutes.

You're lucky, Thora James. Be excited.

My body is anything but. I try to exhale my reservations. Maybe when I see the hoop, all the nerves will float away. It'll feel normal and natural again.

There you go.

You can do this.

"Don't hurl," Roger demands again. And then he turns the knob, letting me inside the mysterious room. With each step, I concentrate on all the pros to this decision and willfully ignore the cons. It buries more of my anxiety.

I see the low metal hoop and the black leather couch it faces. Two men, in suits. Waiting for me. I quickly look away, avoiding eye contact. As soon as I near the hoop, I realize I'm close enough to outstretch my arm and touch the men.

They're middle-aged, I guess. Businessmen, according to their clean-shaven faces, their well-groomed hair.

The music kicks on. *Thank you.* The sultry tune puts me in motion, and I begin to dance around the hoop, to the best of my ability. I'm nearly naked. *Don't fixate on it.* My body is stiffer than usual, even with these last-ditch encouragements.

It's so hard to be lithe and beautiful and graceful when my raucous pulse has decided to be even more erratic. Inside I'm tribal drums and metal bands. Outside, I'm hopefully classical portraits and poetry.

"Do you see her piercings?" I hear one of them whisper, his voice too eager.

"She's—" *Ignore.*

I'm sure it looks like I'm painting by numbers, my joints tense and needing oiled. I can't help it though. My mind and body are in another heated disagreement.

I make a quick decision and cut the dancing short. I jump to grab the bottom rung of the hoop. Unlike the main stage, this hoop is stationary and won't rise any higher than it is.

I swing my leg over the bottom rung and begin to spin, creating large circles before I hook my ankles and drop upside-down. And this—this is worse than dancing.

I stare right at them, so close that I distinguish their eye colors. Blue and hazel. Blue Eyes leans into his friend next to him, his gaze still pinned to me, sizing me up. Sweeping me over. Undressing the last of my clothes.

The sickness returns. *Swallow it.* I try. I always try.

But it's like he's marking every bit of me in his memory. Every freckle. Every eyelash. Like I belong to him tonight. *How is this different than Nikolai being on stage? He was the object of your gaze, moments ago, Thora.* My conscience is working hard to sway me. But it is different. For starters, Nikolai is far away from the audience. He's not physically this close.

And I'm not an awe-inspiring aerialist like him. People pay to watch his talent. I'm just a woman these two men bought for the night, to ogle and fantasize.

My nerves fire off, vibrating my concentration. And in one second, my grip loosens, and I fall. Hard, on my shoulder, my tendons shrieking in pain.

"Jesus, are you okay?" Hazel Eyes jumps to his feet, and he hovers over me.

"I'm fine," I say softly. "Sorry about…" I trail off as his hand rests on my elbow and my hip, helping me to a stance. His touch coils the rest of my muscles. In the small space between the hoop and the couch, my legs have knocked into his. I inhale, and the strong musk of his cologne churns my stomach.

I can't.

I can't.

"I'm sorry," I say, backing up abruptly, and my head collides with the metal hoop. Fuck. *That really hurt.* White spots dance in my vision.

"Careful," Hazel Eyes tells me, but I push away from him before he steadies me again. I press my hand to my forehead, shuffling back in my stiletto heels.

"I can't. I'm sorry." I recognize how much I don't want to do this. And the sad thing is that I wish I could suck it up and finish the act. I wish I could be that fearless, no-holds-barred girl. Who can separate work and emotions—who can bask in the paycheck afterwards.

But I found my personal limitation. I can't do whatever it takes to be here. I want to be okay with that, I do. I should be. *You tried, Thora.*

"What do you mean?" Blue Eyes asks.

I shake my pounding head in a daze. "I'm sorry." And I rush out of the room before anyone stops me. I beeline down the dark corridor, walking as fast as my heart hammers. Once in the dressing room, I catch sight of myself in a vanity mirror, my skin ashen and a stream of blood trickling down my forehead.

"Fantastic," I mutter, my throat swollen. I snatch a tissue and blot the skin that's split open. I pass a couple giggling dancers to reach my locker. Which is...empty.

What? I turn to one of the dancers in confusion.

"Lana was pissed you took her gig," the go-go dancer says.

I didn't even realize it was hers. "So she stole my clothes?"

"I think she threw them in the trash out back."

My eyes burn. Right. I inhale, pressure bearing on my chest.

"Virgin Mary."

My blood runs cold at Roger's voice. Maybe this is all karma. But if I didn't try tonight...I would've always questioned if I did everything

I could. I know I'm justifying a mistake so that I'll feel better, but it's easier than living with bigger regret.

The moment I feel it, I'll start crying. And I don't want to cry right now. I just want to go fall asleep and pretend that everything turned out in my favor. That I'm lucky, just like Roger said.

I shield my boobs with my arm and face him.

His anger flushes his skin. "What are you fucking doing?"

"I can't…" I feel blood trickle down my forehead sliding over my brow. I try to dab it up with the tissue.

Roger notices. "Because you bumped your head? Wipe it off and get your ass back there. You've committed tonight. They *paid* for you."

"I quit."

He's boiling. "Are you shitting me? You *just* started." He shakes his head repeatedly. "Okay, you have two options." He raises two fingers in my face. "You go and finish your act, or you pay for the time *you've* wasted the club."

I can't finish. I know I can't. I'll puke all over myself, for one. For another, I can't live with the memory of them watching me like that. I already want to scrub the partial one from my brain.

"I'll pay," I say.

"One grand."

I feel more color drain from my cheeks. "I…I don't have that kind of money."

"Then get your ass back in that room."

I made a costly mistake—one that was supposed to do the inverse of what's happening now. I can't even worry about paying for rent. That's gone. It's not even on the table anymore. Maybe I can max out credit cards and search for a solution later.

"I'll pay you."

He rolls his eyes like *make up your fucking mind.* I've made it. I made it the moment I walked out of the private room. I'm certain that I'm never walking back in.

In the next five minutes, I find a thin blue jacket, zipper broken. If I choose to pull it closed over my chest, the hem rises higher than my ass. I pick my losses and expose my bottom, in favor of not flashing everyone. Then, with Roger's assistance, I swipe credit cards and pay off a debt.

I'm out of Phantom for good.

Tonight of all nights.

Not long after, I teeter in my high heels along the uneven cobblestone, inside The Masquerade's lobby. Blood drips down my forehead, and I am one-hundred percent mooning people on the slots. I'm pale. Close to crying. And just really, really wanting to erase myself.

For just one moment.

Please.

"Thora!"

My heart lurches, and I rotate towards the voice.

Nikolai is running down the east wing, past a 24-hour café and gift shop, silver and purple paint streaked over his eyes. But it can't mask his raw concern.

I sway to a stop, queasy and despondent, too many feelings entering me at once. *Don't cry.* His distraught presence tries to puncture the dam I've built. I skim him quickly: shirtless, red slacks, hair slicked back—he's in his costume. I check the giant 1920s inspired clock that hangs in the center lobby. Amour is still playing, isn't it?

"Thora..." He reaches me, his phone in a fist. His other hand holds my face, scrutinizing the line of blood. His eyes flit rapidly over my features, studying my state of being.

"What happened?" I ask him.

He flies over my question. "A guy hit you with something," he states, brushing my hair back and examining the cut. His phone rings incessantly, adding to my confusion. He lets out an irritated growl at his cell, ignoring the call.

I hone in on that phone. "Did Amour end?" I think I know the answer. And it scares me.

"Thora—" His phone rings again. He curses under his breath, presses another button, and slips it in his pocket. He holds my face once more. "What the fuck happened?" The distress in his eyes nearly sweeps me backwards.

I open my mouth to gush forth the night's events, but those words aren't the ones that come. "Why are you here? I mean, *how* are you here?"

He breathes heavily, like I'm chasing him up a mountain with these questions. He's making me just as out of breath with uncertainty. He glances over my shoulder, and before I have time to capsize his previous assumptions, he storms towards Phantom, where I just left. Where I am *never* returning.

I sprint around him, almost face-planting with these stupid heels. But I manage to place my palms on his chest, in a runner's stance. "Stop." I try to push him backwards with all my might.

"We've already played this game before." He peels my hands off.

That's right. We did this in The Red Death. And I lost. But I foolishly never stop trying.

My failures are finally starting to catch up to me.

"What are you planning on doing?" I question with a frown.

"Do you even know what you look like right now?" His voice is gritty with anger. "You're pale. You're bleeding, and I have no idea—"

"I hurt myself," I tell him. "I smacked into the hoop. Okay?" I try to push him back again, but he's not budging. And he's still glaring at the direction of Phantom, as though my pain and all the answers lie there.

His phone rings again. "Goddammit," he curses and puts the cell to his ear. He shouts Russian, and my insides start to twist again.

He left Amour for you.

I shove him in the chest, pissed, tears welling. "Go back…right now, go back." He still has time. He can make the last act, right?

Except for the firm hand on my shoulder, Nikolai ignores me, focusing on his phone conversation. He can't be here right now. I grip his wrist and try to yank him towards The Masquerade's globe auditorium, marching ahead.

His foreign words accelerate, and then he shouts at me, "Thora!" Just my name, his arm hooking around my waist and drawing me back into him, so quickly. He spins me and opens my jacket, skimming the length of my body, noticing my wardrobe for the first time.

He must have seen my exposed bottom, when I tried to tug him in the other direction. I swat his hands off and point towards the auditorium. He shakes his head like *no.* But he only speaks Russian, to the phone line, trying to multitask between me and someone else. He touches his bare chest, as if ready to give me his nonexistent shirt.

His costume just reminds me where he should be.

"Go back," I say, my eyes stinging with tears. "You shouldn't…" I choke on my own words, guilt pummeling me. And I inhale. "You can't be here."

He gives me a harsh look like *how can you think I wouldn't?*

"You go back," I tell him strongly. "And I'm going to leave you now. Okay?"

He speaks rapidly in the phone as I begin to walk away, towards the revolving glass doors. "Thora!" He catches up to me, slipping his cell into his pocket. He draws me to his chest again, shielding my half-naked body from the old women at slots, the casino carpet semi-full of gamblers.

"Let me go, Nik," I say in a shaky tone.

His gray eyes puncture me. "There's no chance of that. So stop pushing me away right now."

I try to layer on a glare of my own, and I point at the east wing again. "You can still finish—"

"I can't." It's a knife in my gut. "Amour ended."

I relax a bit with this new hope. "So you left after it finished?"

He shakes his head once.

And my heart nosedives. "No," I wince. "Nik, you can't—"

"I did," he forces. "I chose you tonight, and you have to fucking accept that so I can take care of you." If our situations were reversed, he would've never let me pick him. He would've made me stay at the show. This isn't right.

"The circus is your love," I whisper. "You told me that, remember? You can't choose me over your passion."

He stares at me with this stern expression, like we're back at the gym. And then he lifts me in his arms, his hands underneath my bottom, covering my ass from onlookers. My legs instinctively wrap around his waist, even though I want to be on the ground.

I want him to reverse time and not chase after me. I never wanted my dreams to negatively impact him, and I'm beginning to realize they have. Right now, they're tearing through his life, and I don't need him to be assailed by the paths I take.

"Put me down," I say.

He ignores me, carrying me to the elevators. His phone starts ringing again, but he talks over the default tone. "Luka texted me during the show."

I curl my hands into shaky fists. I feel *horrible.* "You should've stayed until it ended. I was fine."

He jaw locks, and he glares down at me. "You're bleeding, barely clothed and shaking. That's not fine, Thora." He punches the light on the elevator, thankfully no one else waiting for one. It's not long before doors slide open.

Once inside, Nikolai sets me on my feet and he swipes his keycard, pressing the number of his floor.

As we begin to rise, I rest my body against the mirrored wall. "There's nothing you could've done. I had to try, to see if I could do this," I choke out the last words.

His nose flares as he restrains more emotion. And then he stares down at me like I've impaled him repeatedly tonight, but doesn't he understand…

"I took you away from your job," I nearly cry. On top of more awful outcomes tonight. "I feel *so* badly…"

"What do you want me to say?" His voice is so low. "Do you want me to apologize for caring about you?"

I shake my head. "No." I blink, and tears roll down.

He steps forward, to comfort me, but I raise a hand to stop him. "Myshka—"

"This only works if we don't choose each other first." He knows I'm talking about our relationship.

He tilts his head at me, with that no-nonsense look.

"I may leave soon," I remind him. "Are you going to run after me then?" His whole world is in Vegas. His life, his family, his career. I'm just a small blip that will fly in and out.

His eyes redden. "Do you want me to feel guilty for loving you?"

It's one of the most painful things—each word, each syllable. "I just—I want you to always choose the circus over me."

He shakes his head repeatedly, and I can't tell if he's rejecting this notion or if he's just hoping it'll never come to fruition. He will push me towards Somnio if I land the role, and I have a horrible feeling that he'll want to leave everything behind to join me.

"I'll stay here," I say. "I'll choose you if you choose me."

"No," he forces. And then his face hardens, understanding my initial proclamation. This only works if we don't pick each other.

"You once told me that there are things you can't leave behind. You meant your family." I point at the floor. "You meant Katya, and Luka, and Timo and all the people you *love*."

"You're a part of my family, whether you realize it or not."

It rocks me back. And he steps closer now. His eyes dance over my features. He uses the hem of my jacket to wipe my cut that still bleeds.

"We don't have to decide anything tonight," he says.

I nod. "I'm broke." I just come right out and say it. He doesn't look surprised, so I elaborate, "I owed Phantom a grand for bailing on the gig tonight. I was stupid, right?"

His face hardens. "You couldn't have known..." He shakes his head. "We don't have foresight. You take risks, some pay off, others don't. But we all have to take them."

The weight on my chest starts to lift some. "Can you...let me know when the hard choices end? I mean, there has to be a point for both of us, right...where there are only easy choices left to make?" My voice cracks. "Right?"

He cups my face, his thumb drying my tears. "Thora," he says my name like it comes from a place deep, deep within him. "Whatever you need, I'm going to give you."

"A place to stay?" I wipe my eyes with the back of my hand.

He kisses my lips, hot pressure beneath the touch, a silent *yes.*

"A shirt," I whisper.

Another kiss, this time, his body melding against mine, more urgent. I stand on the tips of my toes, to reach him.

Tears keep streaming, wetting his hands that hold my jaw. "Tissues?"

He smiles into the next kiss. A breath away, he says, "Yes, myshka."

I never thought that love could be this difficult. Once you have it—that should be it. No more hardships. No more confusion. But clarity hasn't struck me yet.

There's just more guilt. And my only hope is by January, we'll be free of it.

ACT FORTY-ONE

I learned that Nikolai's incessant phone calls were from cousins, who were chastising him for leaving Amour for a girl. I can most definitely empathize with those voices. I've heard them all before.

Some of the other calls were from his siblings, asking how I was.

I'm alright.

Well, more focused, in a way. I acquired a part-time job in the lobby's gift store, but since it doesn't help me train, I've spent all of my free time at the gym with and without Nikolai. Where I should be. I want to pool my energy into these auditions. Minimize some of my distractions. After watching Amour live, I've recognized how much work I still need.

I return from the gym now, riding up the elevator. My phone vibrates in my palm.

Send me pics of you beside any souvenir statutes, like the mini ones :) – Shay

I opened the lines of communication with him a few days ago. An olive branch. We've been cordial ever since, sliding back into our normal groove. I didn't want to end an eight-year friendship, not if his intentions were good. It seemed wrong and petty.

I text back: No way.

He's quick to respond.

I'm just trying to imagine you at work, the tourist becoming the...what's your job description? – Shay

Cashier :P

Lame – Shay

I roll my eyes but smile. My phone buzzes again, but it's not from Shay.

Where are you? – Nikolai

I check my watch. It's two in the morning, so he has reason to be concerned.

Just heading back from the gym.

I press send, having to wait for tipsy couples to enter the elevator on floor 15.

Another text. From another person.

Just transferred the money to your account. If you need anything else, honey, please call. There's always a room for you here. – Mom

My throat closes. I had a two-hour phone conversation with my parents that turned into a Skype session where we were all crying. My dad said, "I'm proud of you, Thora." He was happy I quit Phantom and took the thousand dollar penalty. And he helped me pay it off. Every penny. Because "I love you," he said.

I love them more than they probably realize too.

I didn't think they'd help me without stipulation, not after I chose to stay in Vegas. But I don't think family is something I can shake off easily. Neither of us wants to severe our relationship, even if my father believed he could, out of principle.

After the couples unload, the elevator finally reaches the floor where all the Aerial Ethereal performers live. It's a Tuesday night, quiet. Along the hotel's carpeted hallway, room service trays and dirtied plates sit outside of a few doors. Others have curled magazines that they haven't brought inside yet.

It's weird—rooming here and not being in the circus. But aspiring to be. Maybe it's why I enter the suite late every night.

One of the doors cracks open, a few down from Nikolai's. I slow my pace, recognizing the voices before I see their bodies.

"Did someone piss in your Cheerios as a kid?" Timo asks, a smile in his light tone. "Come on, old man, stretch your mind that far."

John backs into the hallway while Timo leans his shoulder on the door frame. "You're only slightly amusing, you know. Actually, that's giving you too much credit. You're like two-percent amusing," John says, surly as usual. "And half of what you say, I just start tuning out."

"You forgot your hearing aid again?"

John looks as unamused as he claims to be. I pause mid-step, more than curious about the development of their relationship. And then

John says, "You are by far the most annoying human in this hallway." Then he tilts Timo's chin and kisses him.

Timo reciprocates, his lips rising in a smile. Their bodies pull closer together, attracted more than their words let on. John breaks away first and then kisses Timo's forehead. "See you tomorrow."

"If you need directions back here," Timo says, "there's this thing called Google maps on this thing called the internet."

John flips him off.

Timo winks and then shuts the door.

The moment John spins around, he sees me and pauses like I caught him in a walk of shame. He is epically private about his sex life and diverts the topic when Camila and I bring it up. So I'm not surprised when he groans like I ruined his master stealth plan.

I immediately start laughing.

John shakes his head at me. "You—are just the bane of my existence."

I bite my gums to try to control myself. "You consider everyone the bane of your existence."

"Because everyone is horrible," he refutes. "I have many banes." He walks closer, and I can't hold this one fact inside anymore.

"Hey, John, remember when you told me *you fuck a Kotova and you go directly to hell?*" My eyes dart from him and Timo's closed door, the suggestion hopefully clear.

"I'm currently in hell." He glowers. "I realize that. Thanks for reminding me, *Thora.*" I swear the corner of his lips curve upward as he passes me, unable to suppress the burgeoning happiness.

"You love it in hell, John?" I laugh into a bigger smile.

He spins around, walking backwards to the elevators, and he says, "All my friends are here. So it beats everywhere else."

Friends. He admitted to having multiple friends. My cheeks hurt.

He turns around, back facing me, and waves. "Night, Thora. Keep making stupid decisions."

"Night, John." And he disappears around the corner.

I SCRUB THE RESIN OFF MY HANDS IN NIK'S bathroom sink. About to take a shower.

He enters, leaning a hip against the counter. "I missed you coming in."

"I didn't want to wake you." He was asleep on the couch, ESPN on mute in the background. When the channel isn't on reality television, Nikolai plays sports on cable, mostly football and MMA. My tastes—*The Vampire Diaries, Bitten, Witches of East End* and *True Blood* (RIP)—are outliers here. Still, I seem to fit in just fine.

Instead of talking, he stands behind me, his hands lowering to my waist. My heart double-skips, not immune to his advances, even living together now, even after we've run around the bases. He pulls my back into his chest, away from the sink.

My body heats. "I have…to…" My thoughts pop the moment he lowers his head to my neck, kissing me right *there*. A certain place throbs for more. *Shower. You need to shower, Thora.* "I smell." Why did I just say that?

I feel him smile into my neck. "You smell fine to me."

That's what every girl loves to hear. *Fine.* Not like vanilla or roses or a fuckable scent. Fine is *you'll do for now.* I rotate and put my hands on his chest. "I…would rather smell like soap."

He stares down at me, his gaze raking my frame. "I'd rather fuck you." And then he lifts me up, splitting my legs apart and setting me on the counter. I can't combat him, not when his lips meet mine and his tongue skillfully slips into my mouth. It's an eager, aggressive kiss that steals breath and puts me in his possession.

Yeah—that shower is not happening.

His movements are more rushed than usual, no slow build up. He practically tears off my shirt, my bra, shorts, panties, and he pulls off his shirt, steps out of his pants, all in between a make-out session that numbs my lips. I moan the minute his fingers graze the spot between my legs.

He covers my mouth with his palm—since we don't live in this suite alone. I've found it hard to restrain noises. My mind wants to shut it down, but my body loves the climax too much, always on its own agenda.

He kneads my breast, and then pushes into me without hesitation. I shut my eyes tightly, the fullness great, but the pain…not that much. It's less than it used to be, so I know in time, it'll all go away. It'll feel better.

He kisses me again, trying to distract me, trying to wrap me in more pleasure. I clutch his arms while he thrusts into me, harder than usual. I open my eyes, and he's absorbing my body with that intensity, in the way we fit together. His cock sliding right inside—I buck up, a cry stuck in my throat.

I reach out and accidentally splash the running water from the faucet that I never turned off. Still needing support, I cling back to him, now sufficiently wetting both of us. I don't care much. The pain is starting to dissipate as my climax nears.

I meet his penetrating grays, and it sends me over.

"Nik...I…" My toes curl, my body clenching around him.

He says something in Russian, as if I can translate. I swear he does this to torment me. He kisses my cheek and then presses me to his chest, lifting me from the counter. While his hardness still fills me, he carries me to his bedroom, setting my back…on the desk.

He pounds against me, not finished yet. A layer of sweat coats my skin and his. He keeps his hand over my mouth and uses the other hand to lift one of my legs higher.

My eyelids slowly close, drowning in the way he thumps against my body: the melodic, hard, *fast* rhythm. Each time he slams into me, it's like he's trying to expel his pent-up emotions. I realize I should've asked how his day was, instead of worrying about a shower.

He rocks harder, and my noise dies in his palm.

Then he pulls out—*ow*—still erect, and he carries me to his bed. He tosses me on the mattress, tiny and little enough to throw me around. Usually it's fun. But tonight, I think I need to ask, "How was your day?" I pant out the words.

He gives me a look like I asked about nuclear warfare in bed. And he crawls on top of me, kissing me deeply before he grips his shaft and slides right back in. *Owww.* I let out an audible cry, of pain, and he combs my hair affectionately, slowing his movement, only for a second.

This position is harder for me. Regular missionary—it's like our hips don't align right unless I have a pillow under my ass. And he's not putting one there. Normally, he'll turn on his side, making it more comfortable and easier.

My breath is shallow, and I close my eyes and just relax more. If he doesn't want to talk yet, then I'd rather this be pleasurable. After another minute or two, he hits a peak. He's gentler when he pulls out of me this time. So I think he'll finally exhale, slow down, and hold me.

But he steps off the bed and yanks me to the edge. My heart hammers. And he lowers his head between my legs, kissing the spot—*holy…shit.* I reach out and clench his hair. I turn my cheek into the metallic comforter, noticing that he strokes himself at the same time his tongue flicks—

I moan.

He stares at me with a smile in his eyes.

This is more. Than what I thought would happen. Right now. I can't even quantify how much time has passed. All I know is that he's harder and I'm wetter. He flips me over, lifting me on my knees and hands. This is not going to go well.

"Nik," I warn him, my heart thrashing. This is the worst position for us. He climbs onto the bed, kneeling behind me. He's too tall. I'm too short, and our pelvises do *not* line up.

"Stay still," he says.

Well no way am I going to move. He grasps my hips, lifting me higher so that I meet his cock, but now my knees are no longer on the bed. He slips in from behind. My arms quake, my fingers just barely touching the mattress.

I have very little support, but he has no trouble bracing my body weight. He leans forward, pushing even deeper, just to kiss the back of my neck. I shut my eyes and drift in the pulsing pleasure.

Maybe fifteen minutes later, he's successfully fucked his emotions out. And I'm too exhausted to move or even consider a shower.

He holds me to his chest, brushing his fingers through my hair. I listen to his heartbeat slow, and I mentally try to reroute my brain to him, to his day. I hate when I'm so consumed by my own that I forget to ask. And I just hope that whatever went down, it's not catastrophically bad.

It still feels likes he's inside of me, even though he's not. I cross my legs some, and then I ask, "What happened today?"

He exhales deeply and stares down at me.

I look up.

"Why do you think something happened?"

I'm not crazy. Am I? I didn't make this up. "You're just…more aggressive than usual."

His brows furrow and his eyes flit down my naked body. "I didn't hurt you…"

"No," I say. "I mean, no more than usual."

He glares. "I don't enjoy hurting you when I sleep with you, just so you know."

"It's better than before," I assure him.

He nods, relaxing a bit. "You're right."

"About…?"

He sighs heavily, another deep breath. "About something happening today." He licks his lips and stares off for a second. When his eyes meet mine, they're full of power, of what he always possesses, the unwavering contact. "I don't know how to say it."

My nerves escalate, and I sit up, not much. I just place an arm on his chest while he lies on his back. So that I'm the one staring down at him. So that he's looking up at me. "Let me guess."

His lips tic upwards. "Okay, myshka."

I read his body language. He's content now. Of course. But before, he was stressed. He's been at work all day, so… "It has to do with Amour."

He nods.

I take in the time. It's almost at that five-month mark. Which means— "Elena," I suddenly say. "It has to do with your partner."

Surprise coats his face. I guessed right. "I've taught you well," he murmurs.

He can't dodge this. "What happened?" Elena is supposed to be in her first show next week, the aerial silk act returning to Amour.

His fingers skim the bareness of my shoulder blades. "She was fired."

My face falls. "What?"

"She wasn't improving to Aerial Ethereal's standards, 'not ready to perform' they cited, and so management revoked her contract. They let her go this evening."

My mind spins, trying to determine his sentiments on the situation and my own. He's upset, I realize quickly. Really upset. The nonstop sex says enough. "I'm sorry," I tell him. "What does this mean for you?"

"They're putting the aerial silk act on hiatus, not retiring it but not actively seeking a replacement. I spent *five months* with Elena, training her, working with her. And it's all a waste." His gray eyes storm below me.

I touch his strong jaw and kiss his lips gently. "It'll be okay," I say. "Helen and the rest of the directors love you." But I can't forget how Elena looked at me—in the gym. And I wonder how much time I ate from her training. He's reading me right now. My lost expression.

"It's not your fault," he says.

Why didn't I question it though? "Did you train her more than you did me?"

He's quiet.

My stomach drops and I gape. "Nik."

"I wouldn't have practiced with her any more than I did, regardless if you were in Vegas or not."

I want to believe him. Otherwise, it hurts too much to think that I may be the reason his act is shelved for eternity. And the reason why Elena was sent home.

That's not how this is supposed to go. Not at all.

ACT FORTY-TWO

It's midnight, the gym empty and only half the lights turned on. The trapeze and Russian swing are shrouded in darkness. I've been here since noon and still no one has really filtered inside. It's Thanksgiving, and instead of sulking about not being with family, not having the money for a plane ticket, I just focus on training.

I breathe heavily, lying supine on the blue mats. I still can't land everything I saw in Amour, during that climatic group act. Not without being harnessed.

But I'm closer to nailing the aerial silk drop. When I fall, I'm now five feet from the floor, not seven. That has to count for something. Right?

The heavy double doors click open, and I prop my sore body on my elbows. The hall light streams into the darker area of the gym, until the door shuts. For a split second, I wonder if coming to the gym alone was such a good idea. But Nikolai had Thanksgiving festivities with his whole extended family, and I didn't need him to miss that for me.

"You look exhausted."

My shoulders sag at the familiar, deep voice. "It's been a long day."

Nikolai emerges into the light, his hands in his black slacks. He removes them as he sits in front of me, resting his forearms on his bent knees.

I notice a bit of…I motion to his hairline. "Pie?" I smile.

He brushes the pumpkin residue. "Dimitri."

"Did you get him back?" I ask, slightly sad I missed it. *You needed to train. That's why you're here, Thora.* I know.

"With a butter cream pie." His lips curve up in that charming smile, the one I see on Saturday nights. "I wish you were there."

"This is more important." I hate that each word hurts to say and to hear.

He nods, this tension stretching between us, from the uncertainty of our futures. It'd be easier if we knew where we'll stand. But we're riding towards a big gray cloud.

The double doors click open again, louder voices emanating. "He was *not* flirting with me," Katya refutes. Nikolai stiffens, but Katya is still in darkness, the door thudding closed.

"I fear for you, sister," Timo says. "Said boy tells you that you're pretty, that you have nice legs, and he touches your hair. Said girl thinks he's friendly. Next thing you know, you'll be in bed with him and think *oh wait, he* actually *likes me.*"

"He didn't compliment me like that," she refutes.

Timo whistles. "Someone's in denial. What do you think, Luka? Flirting or no flirting?"

"Honestly, I want to self-eject from this conversation."

Timo laughs, and all three siblings step into the light. Literally. "Thora James," Timo exclaims with a wide, dazzling grin. He carries a half-eaten apple pie and a bundle of forks. Luka has a pumpkin one in hand. Katya, a chocolate.

"Hey," I say, a smile growing. "How was the family feast?"

"Boring," Luka says, sitting next to Nikolai.

Timo plops next to me, slinging his arm around my shoulder. "Entertaining."

"Draining," Katya adds with a sigh. She chooses the spot between me and Nikolai. Which is really the only free place in the circle, since I face him.

Boring. Entertaining. Draining.

"In that order," Nikolai says to me, lightness in his eyes. I'm having a hard time not smiling right now, even sweaty, muscles achy and heart on a slow descent.

Timo passes me a fork. "Luka's pie is the worst."

Luka looks uncaring. "No one taught me how to cook."

"No one taught me how to cook, but mine still turned out edible."

Katya pushes the chocolate one towards me. "Mine is actually the best." When I first met her, I doubt she'd ever consider herself better than her brothers, in any arena.

I believe it. I try a small portion, the taste richer than I expected, making me smile. It's really good. I give her a thumbs-up, and her orb-like eyes brighten. After another bite, I ask, "So who's this boy?"

She groans. "You heard that?" Her eyes flicker nervously to Nikolai. What is he going to do? I think about all his rules with me and training. Yeah—I'm sure he has an equally long list for Katya and dating.

"How old is he?" Nikolai layers on the *no bullshit, no humor* expression to the millionth degree.

"He's no one," Katya refutes. "I met him in the hallway."

Nikolai almost chokes on a bite of pie.

"The hallway?" I say. I don't get it. Is that a meeting spot for people in the circus—like code for *under the bleachers*?

"He was just here for the weekend," she clarifies.

It clicks. "Like a bachelor party kind of thing?"

"Yeah." She nods.

Nikolai starts, "You didn't give him your number—"

"I know the rules. Okay? I wouldn't do that."

"And plus, she was oblivious." Timo points his fork at Katya. "You need to take my class: Timofei 101. I'll teach you the ways of men, little sister."

I don't see all three siblings together often, only because they spend more time together than they do with Nikolai. And I'm usually with him. So I eat silently, my eyes pinging between the Kotovas.

"She's *sixteen*," Nikolai says sternly.

Katya sighs like she's heard this all before.

Luka rips open a packet of Junior Mints, exiting the conversation and stepping away from the spotlight that his little brother adores.

Timo gives Nikolai a look, as though he's living in the wrong decade. "And I lost my virginity at fourteen."

Nikolai pinches his eyes. "I don't want to know this, Timo."

Timo redirects his attention to me. "Thora James." His grin seems to twinkle in his eyes, in a sprightly *evil* way. "When did you lose it?"

A piece of pie lodges halfway down.

Nikolai smacks the back of Timo's head and says something in Russian that I'm almost certain has to do with tact.

Timo touches his chest innocently. "I'm friends with her."

"That doesn't mean you can ask her that."

"Do you not know the answer?" Timo wonders with the tilt of his head.

I can't let this progress any further. I simply say, "I was eighteen. But in all honesty, I wish I waited for the right person."

"Nikolai?" Luka adds.

Nik is about to smack his head, but he sways out of his reach with a humored laugh. And with the extension of Nik's arm, I notice his tattoo again: long black lines, inked on the inside of his bicep, creating trees at the end. I've never asked what it meant to him. There are questions that always sit on the tip of my tongue, but I struggle to let them out. Not knowing the perfect time. Not knowing the perfect way to ask.

I'm not good with words.

At least I've known that for a while.

Timo catches me scrutinizing Nikolai's arm with confusion. He waves his fork at one of the shorter lines. "That's me."

My heart skips, and Nikolai meets my gaze with a nod, like *he's right.* He motions to the other series of lines that form trees, starting with the shortest. "Katya, Timo, Luka, Peter, Sergei, and…my parents."

His family.

The symbolism is sweeter than he realizes.

Katya asks softly, "What do you think they're doing today?"

"Eating pie," Luka states plainly.

"They don't celebrate Thanksgiving," Timo interjects, deconstructing any fantasy that Luka and Nikolai fog her in.

"You don't know that," Katya retorts with a frown.

"Ask Nikolai. It's an American tradition. Dad hates that shit, doesn't he?"

Nikolai has his eyes on me, more rigid. He sets down his fork. "Let's talk about something else."

"Does she not know?" Timo squeezes my shoulder. "He didn't tell you, Thora James?"

Chills snake up my spine. What am I missing? "Tell me what…?"

Nikolai runs a hand through his hair. "She knows, Timo. Let it go."

"Then why are you being so weird about it?" Timo asks, his features darkening. "You're keeping something from us then…?" They stare at each other for a long moment, both good at reading body language. Both superior at compelling one's attention. Both exceptionally talented. And yet, it's clear who'll leave with the upper-hand.

Timo shakes his head first, more confused than before. Same. I sit in a mystery with the rest of them.

"Talk about something else." Nikolai looks to Luka, to save him from this. His younger brother opens his mouth, but Timo springs to his feet, silencing Luka.

He gains a height advantage that he probably rarely has over Nikolai. "I hate when you do this," Timo proclaims. "I'm not a little kid anymore. I can handle whatever you're keeping from me. We all can." He gestures to Luka and Katya. "It's not fair to *us*."

"It makes no difference," Nikolai says to him. "Just sit down, Timo."

Timo shouts something in Russian, pained, and he points to his chest. His determined tone reminds me of when he had a long screaming match with Nikolai. Months ago, in The Masquerade's lobby. It didn't end well.

Katya leans into me. "I hate when they fight."

I hug her, an arm around her waist. She rests her head on my shoulder. I realize, right now, that I'm not an interloper anymore. I have a place in the Kotova circle, albeit not the loudest place, but there is only so much room for Timo's and Nikolai's. I think Katya knows that more than anyone.

I hear Nikolai reply to Timo in calmer, sterner Russian.

In the brief silence between them, Timo stares at the ceiling. Then his glassy gaze returns to his brother. "Don't lie," he says. "You resent us. Every day. Peter and Sergei got off free, and you were forced to look after him and her—" he jabs a finger at Luka and Katya "—and me."

Forced. I hone in on Timo's choice of words while he continues on.

"How many times a day do you wish you were with them? Be honest."

Nikolai's eyes flicker to me.

Forced.

Oh my God.

Nikolai lied to them. He never told his siblings that he had a choice to be here, in Vegas, and before that, New York—that he could've been with the brothers around his age, all this time. If he wanted.

Sounding wounded, Timo adds, "I think it has to be five times a day. Maybe six. What do you think, Luka?"

"Shut up," Luka mutters, staring right at me. He's beginning to figure it out, I think. Maybe I wear the answers on my face. The realization.

Katya whispers, "What's going on?"

I open my mouth, but my lips press together quickly. This isn't my truth to share.

Nikolai rubs his eyes wearily and then looks up to me. "Happy Thanksgiving."

I give him one of my patented encouraging smiles. *You can do this.*

And he nods like, *I know, I have to tell them.*

He stares up at Timo, who has yet to sit down. "You want honesty?" He pauses, gathering his thoughts. "My life would be drastically different if I lived with Sergei and Peter, if I never had to take care of you." He shrugs tensely. "Is this what you want to hear: you drove me crazy, you fucking *worried* me sick every day of your life, and I kept chasing after you, expecting you to slow down, just once, to make it easy on me. And you never did."

Timo is crying. "No, I didn't want to hear that, you asshole."

"It's fucking true." Nikolai's eyes are past reddened, restraining his own emotion.

I hear Katya sniff beside me, and my emotions begin to rise. Luka watches like someone is unveiling blinds to his world—intently, keenly, cautiously.

"*Every day* I wonder what my life would've been like had I stayed with them," Nikolai says. "And I know I wouldn't be the same person. I don't even know who'd I'd be, but it's not someone I ever want to meet. Not for a moment or a second. I love this life, with you three." He pauses. "So every day, Timo, I am *thankful* for you, for Katya, for Luka—for giving me more than I had."

Timo is motionless, tears streaming down his cheeks, while Luka stares faraway at the wall.

My chest swells. This is the most accurate portrayal of Nikolai that's ever been spoken. Most of his twenties has been devoted to them, and I can't imagine who he was before. It must feel like another lifetime.

"I had a choice six years ago," Nikolai explains the crux. "You didn't."

"What?" Luka chokes.

"Peter, Sergei and me—we were older than you. We could do what we wanted. I chose to be here, with the three of you. I don't regret that decision."

Katya lifts her head off my shoulder, her jaw unhinged. "But…why wouldn't you tell us that?"

"I didn't want you to think poorly of Peter and Sergei for their choices."

Timo drops to the mat and cries into his hands. I hug Katya as she tears up more from her brother's sadness.

Nik reaches out and puts a hand on his shoulder. "Timo—"

Timo looks up, his face splotched red and slick with tears. "You bastard…you made me hate you growing up!" His voice trembles with grief. "I thought you didn't want to be here. You could've at least *acted* like you gave a shit."

"You mean all those nights I drove around New York City, searching for you? Helping you with your homework assignments, making sure you had lunch, spotting you at the gym when I should've been training—is that not giving a shit?" He's still strict, severe. He has trouble softening for them completely, even when Timo is crying.

Timo buries his face in his hands again.

Luka crawls over to his little brother and he wraps his arm around his shoulder. Then he meets Nikolai's gaze. "Thanks." My heart fills. "For choosing us."

I engrain Nikolai's expression for life, a look measured in deep, familial love. As though the galaxy parted, just for one moment, to show another blindingly beautiful universe. He responds with a Russian sentiment, sounding tender.

Katya whispers, "I can't even imagine…"

Timo lifts his head. "I can," he says to Nikolai. "I couldn't…I needed you. Growing up, I needed you."

"And you had me," Nikolai says lowly.

Timo exhales deeply, his eyes traveling over the pies. And then he looks to me and back to Nikolai. "I need you to not worry about me anymore. I want you to live the life that you gave up for us. Can you do that?"

"I didn't give up my life," Nikolai explains. "You're a part of it, Timo. The good and the bad. You're not keeping me from living, brother."

Luka squeezes Timo's shoulder, and Timo nods a few times. He says something in Russian, that I'm certain means *I love you*, or a form of the endearment.

Nikolai replies with the same words.

Then Timo nudges the barely eaten pumpkin pie towards *me*. "You be the judge, Thora James."

This one gesture somehow unwinds the coiled air. Alone in a gym, surrounded by pies and four siblings who maddeningly, unequivocally love each other—it's a moment I won't forget.

Even if I have to leave their world, I promise myself that I'll always remember this. Because when I grow old and gray, I can only hope to have a family as passionate and faithful as theirs.

ACT FORTY-THREE

Living with a guy is strange.

It's not a sleepover, where you legitimately know you'll return home after a brief weekend, back to your own shower, your own sink, your own bed. It's been about a month, and I've just barely accepted that I share all of those with another person. A male person. A guy.

The causal nights—where I return from the gym, he returns from Amour—are the most interesting. There are no boozy 3 a.m. make-out sessions on these nights, no flirty drunk tendencies and my sloppy drunk movements.

It's just…normal.

On the bed, I flip through *One Last Kiss, Please* for possibility the thirtieth time, the spine falling apart. My head is on Nikolai's chest while he talks on the phone in Russian. Almost every night Sergei and Peter call, just to stay in touch with Nikolai, even if they can't see each other in person.

I dog-ear one of my favorite pages, lines already marked with yellow highlighter. And then the book is suddenly swiped from my hands.

"Hey," I say, watching Nikolai skim the page. His phone is shut off.

He's reading your book, Thora.

My heart spasms, and I spring to action, straddling him to try and retrieve the paperback. "That's mine…" I have no other defense besides this one. Lame.

He smiles that charming smile and tucks the book closer to his chest. "You intrigue me, myshka. Let me read."

I gape. "You're not a reader."

He tilts his head. "And how do you know that?" He thinks he's stumped me.

"Because…" *Maybe he has stumped you, Thora.*

His smile keeps growing, waiting for me to collect my words.

I scan the room and my evidence clicks. "Because there aren't any books in this room, besides maybe one…" I squint at the desk. "…*Sports Illustrated* magazine, which is not a book." His free time is usually spent in the company of family. Not with a trade paperback. I mean, I downloaded an iPhone game for him once as something to do, and his attention span lasted about thirty seconds. It was a good one too: Tiny Wings. But it ended with the phone thudding to the floor.

And me under Nikolai Kotova.

"You're breathing heavy."

I press my lips together. "No…I'm not."

His gray eyes penetrate me. That's not helping my cause. Then he returns to the vampire book, actually digesting the words. He stiffens some. "What is this?" he asks, looking genuinely curious as he turns another page.

"Okay, you've seen enough," I say, leaning forward on his body to snatch it. He easily blocks my arm with his.

And he reads aloud, "*Her flesh slapped my flesh in the heat of the night, the noises heightening our blood thirst and my…*" He pauses and breaks into an even bigger smile.

"It's not funny," I say. "It's a *good book*."

"I can't believe you've been reading this every night in bed." He's not judging, just surprised, I guess. Maybe he thought I was reading something more innocent. I'm really happy he doesn't remember that I loaned this one to his little sister. I doubt he would approve.

He flips the page and reads, "*Her wetness glistened in the candlelight. 'You taste so good, baby,' I groaned, licking the softness of her...*" His brows rise at me.

My eyes have popped out of my face.

He rolls me over so that I'm underneath him, the weight of his body adding a hot pressure. I instinctively split my legs open, around him. Is this really happening?

With the paperback still opened in his hand, he reads, "*I grip her face as her lips wrap around my member.*" He gives me a confused look at the word *member.*

"Cock," I say.

He tilts his head again, his intense gaze heating all of me. "I've never heard you say that word."

"Really?" *I think it all the time.* "I…definitely said the word cocktail before."

His lips keep rising, and he watches my ribcage jut in and out, just in a baggy shirt and fleece shorts while he's in gray, thin cotton pants.

Then he reads, "'*Right there, baby. Good girl.*' That turns you on, myshka."

"Not always…" I admit. I swallow, lust swimming in his grays. "I like what you do."

He leans down and kisses my neck, sucking. "And what do I do?" he whispers in my nape, before kissing again.

I let out a breathy noise at the sensitivity, my nerves sparking. I arch up into him. He has to clasp my waist to keep me still. "That," I breathe.

Before I can float away with these sensations, he sits up, skimming another page with a devilish grin. His eyes flicker to me as he reads. "*I sank my fangs into her nape and pounded my erection between her curvy thighs.*"

I can't control my staggered breathing. "I've never heard you say that word," I tell him now. *Erection.*

He runs a hand through his hair, pushing the longer strands back—I'm soaked. For sure. "Fangs?" His lips keep rising higher.

I shake my head. "Not that word…I mean, I actually…" *I've never heard you say that either.* I have no more oxygen to speak properly. He's chasing me around the room, even if reality says I'm lying beneath him. It doesn't feel that way.

"Thighs?" he says, more huskily, his hands running up the bareness of mine.

I tensely shake my head, my legs tightening around him, pulsing more intense.

"Erection." He eye-fucks me.

I buck up, and a tight, low noise catches in his throat. He grips my hip again, and he keeps me still beneath him. I shut my eyes, his gaze basically drilling into me.

"Open your eyes, myshka." I hear the smile in his voice.

"I'm going to come…and you're just speaking to me." My eyes staying closed so this will last longer.

"But I haven't even reached the best part." His thumb caresses my cheek, daring me to look at him, to take a quick peek of his features.

It's too tempting. And I'm too curious to stay in darkness. So I open one eye. And then two, half of his attention planted on the book, scanning a new part.

Nikolai meets my gaze. "*With her, and only with her, the dead in me is alive.*"

I highlighted that line. And underlined it. And starred it. Coming from his lips—it does more to me than all the others.

He says, "I love that quote."

"Why?" I have to ask.

It takes him a moment to collect his thoughts, staring off. I watch as his eyes seem to lighten with more and more clarity. And then he focuses back on me.

"I couldn't explain, for the longest time, why I wanted you near me," he says. "I knew I was attracted to you, but it was more than that. Your energy, your idealism and optimism—I missed those things, the places inside of me that made me feel more alive. And for years, I only sought them out on Saturday nights."

Performing. During his after-show. His one time to let go and be free.

"And I realized," he says lowly, "you are my Saturday nights. Being with you makes me come alive all over again."

My heart thrums and soars at his proclamation. Even if I could speak, I'm not even sure how to express my feelings. He's never said anything like this to me before.

Thankfully he leans closer, kissing me, not urging me to fill the silence with my voice. He sets the book aside, tugging me to his chest. As though we're cuddling. His actions are all smooth and fluid like skilled choreography.

Nikolai drapes my leg over his waist. Then he tugs down his boxer-briefs, pulling aside my panties and shorts. He slides his hardness far into me, filling my need.

After many experiences with him, there's no pain this time. Just pleasure.

I hold him tighter, my fingers gripping the longer hairs by his neck. He's slow and sweet, powerful and deep. The fullness lights me on fire, and I relax into his body, into the way he has me protectively in his arms.

As he thrusts, his gaze meets mine again, those hypnotic, gunmetal skies.

And I don't want to lose all these moments with him.

Not yet.

ACT FORTY-FOUR

Nikolai believes red and green stockings and a yule log on the television are enough to satisfy all Christmas requirements. He apparently hates dragging a real tree into the suite, but Katya begged for one, citing me as a source for it.

I'm without my family.

It's sad.

He caved, so now we're wandering along gravel paths, searching for the perfect evergreen. My hair whips in the wind, strands sticking to my lips. A cold-front moved into Nevada this weekend, chilling any exposed skin.

"I don't know how she does it," I say aloud, watching Katya skip off towards a punier looking spruce.

Nikolai clasps my gloved hand after I drop my arm. "Does what?"

"Spends the holidays without her parents." She hasn't been with her mom or dad since she was ten. It made me realize that I have no room for self-pity this Christmas.

"She's not happy about it," Nikolai replies. "This is actually the only year she hasn't complained. Though it's more because of you than suddenly not caring." Our breath smokes the air. "She's auditioning in January too."

I frown. "What?"

"For Noctis," he clarifies, stone-faced and brick-walled. "She landed the full-in, full-out last night, and she's been able to repeat it just as well."

"That's great," I say, trying to be happy for her. She's accomplishing her dreams. She worked hard for it, but…I know if she leaves on a traveling circus show, I won't ever see her again. *You won't see her if you leave too, Thora.*

Right.

My stay here may be temporary as well.

I strain my neck to look up at him. If I miss Katya, his feelings have to be stronger. "What are the odds she'll make it?" I ask him.

"High." He stops by a towering lopsided tree, to keep some distance between us and his sister while we talk. "She's wanted to be with them since the day she left, so this is good." He nods like he's trying to convince himself.

"And you'll still have Luka and Timo here."

His brows harden, and his darker gaze falls to me. "Luka has been working on a new discipline. There's a good chance they'll either put him in Somnio or Infini soon. He has better use there than as a porter."

I digest this. "So that leaves you with Timo—"

"Kat! I found a winner!" Timo rounds the corner, his fingers cupped to his mouth as he yells. His pink fingers are exposed from his cut-off gloves.

Katya spins on her heels. "Is it big?!"

Timo snorts. "Who do you think I am? It's the biggest one in this place."

Nikolai makes a noise that sounds close to a groan. I can tell he's picturing himself carrying the tree into the hotel. "You were saying about Timo?" he asks me.

I rub his back, trying not to smile too much. He loves his little brother, despite the irritations. "Sorry," I apologize with a grimace. "In my defense, I had no idea Timo would want the largest tree."

"He lives his life in excess," Nikolai reminds me. "He wants the biggest, grandest *everything*. And he'll take too much enjoyment watching me lug the fucking thing inside."

After Thanksgiving though, their relationship is much better. They haven't had a drag-out screaming match since then. Now when they poke jabs at each other, they're the friendly kind, not the ones with undercut, hurt feelings.

I look up at him again. Masculine, his hair disheveled in the wind. His jaw unshaven. His eyes piercingly gray. The moment he meets my ogling gaze, his lips curve up. "You're supposed to stare at me like I'm a devil, not a god."

Wittier words actually come to me, my face lighting before I say, "I think you've always been both."

Nikolai clasps me by the waist and draws me behind the crooked tree, large enough to conceal us from the gravel pathway. It's too hard to hide my smile or stop my heart from racing. I just travel with the feelings.

Nik lifts me up around his waist, so my lips align more with his, and he kisses me deeply, slowly, his hand warming the back of my neck.

And then my phone buzzes in my army-green cargo jacket. I break our lips apart. "…it could be my mom." Though if she could see me now, legs wrapped around a six-foot-five acrobat's waist, I wonder what she'd say.

"Tell her I said hi," Nikolai says. He needs to be liked by my parents if we ever want to make this long-term. He knows how much they mean to me.

"Sure..." I trail off as I check the caller ID: SHAY. "Or maybe not." I hesitate to answer, on account of Shay and Nikolai fighting that one time. I never mention Shay to him. Or vice versa.

Nikolai sees the screen and reads my body language. "Take it."

"You sure?" I frown.

He still has me in his arms, and his hold tightens like he doesn't want to set me down yet. "As much as I dislike him, I'm not going to ruin your friendship."

My shoulders rise, less anxiety. I mouth, *thank you*, right before I put the phone to my ear.

"I can't believe I'm not spending Christmas with you," are Shay's first words. "Who's going to build a stupid igloo with me?"

I'm not sure if Nikolai can hear Shay's voice on the line, but he gently places me on my feet.

It puts a pain in my chest, but I try to ignore it. "We've never built a whole igloo," I remind him. It always takes too long and it always gets too cold.

"Even if it doesn't have a roof, it's still an igloo."

"Are you sure about that? I think it'd be considered a wall."

He groans. "You're making me want to do a Google search and that just takes too much energy." He lets out a real yawn, actually tired. "But seriously, I called because I have some good news."

"What about?" I watch Nikolai take a few steps away from me, scanning the rest of the trees from afar. He keeps glancing back though, too interested in the conversation to leave altogether.

"You're going to see me soon."

I smile. "You're coming to visit?" I try to block out what happened last time he stopped by.

"Not exactly."

This is a puzzle that I can't solve. My face tightens in a scowl, just concentrating on what he could be referring to. But I draw a blank. "So how am I seeing you?"

Nikolai faces me, about five feet separating us. He crosses his arms over his chest, more on the defensive and Shay isn't even here yet.

"I'm auditioning for Aerial Ethereal's open positions."

So many mixed emotions assault me at once. I don't know what I feel. "Shay…"

Nikoli runs his hands through his hair, frustrated that he can't hear everything. Or maybe he can hear. I'm not sure of anything anymore.

"I know it's hypocritical of me," he says. "I've been bashing you about it all year, but I've been to *five* job interviews and I hate every single one of them." He takes a deep breath. "You know, I graduated two weeks ago, and I can't see myself doing anything but what I've been doing. It sucks." I hear the sound of a rubber bouncy ball, hitting the floor. "And then I thought about you and Aerial Ethereal. I don't know…it seems like a better life."

I imagine Shay with me, in the circus. My lips rise, but another pain forms inside my stomach. If we both land contracts for Somnio, I may be able to perform alongside Shay, but it means leaving Nikolai behind in Vegas. Bittersweet isn't even the right feeling.

It just hurts.

"Thora?" His voice leaks concern. "You know I'm sorry, about giving you a hard time. Hey, there's a good chance I may not even make it."

But he's more hopeful for himself than he ever was for me. Because he's more talented. "I hope you make it," I say, trying to stay positive.

"Yeah?"

Nikolai shifts, slightly turning his back to me. He rubs his unshaven jaw and glares at the tree trunk.

Blocking out my own involvement, I want my friend to be happy. I just wish there wasn't pain attached to that desire. "Definitely."

There's a short pause, the silence filled with thuds against the wall. I can tell there's more. "When I see you," he begins, "I promise to not start anything with your friend."

"Boyfriend," I correct.

Nikolai rotates slowly, facing me again. His features are still harsh, strict cuts that he usually wears for his siblings or in the gym.

I hear the squeak of bed springs as Shay plops down. "Whatever he is, I'm going to try to be nice to him for you."

That's better than nothing. "I hope so."

And then he says, "Be safe, okay?"

I smile, a weaker one than usual. "Be happy, alright?"

A moment passes. "I will be," he says softly. And we hang up at the same time.

I pocket the phone, and Nikolai exhales a deep, tense breath, his muscles flexed in his arms and shoulders. And I mutter, "He's auditioning in January."

Nikolai rolls his eyes and he shakes his head repeatedly like this has to be some big joke.

"He said he'd be nice—"

"I don't care what he is." He lets out a short laugh, his face going through those series of mixed emotions, reflecting what I felt. And then he turns around. With a lengthy, incensed stride, he heads towards Katya.

I run to catch up to him, clasping his wrist. "Nikolai—"

"Nik!" Katya shouts, sprinting up to us. "We found it!" She wipes her reddened nose with her gloved hand. She looks between us for a moment, and her smile begins to fade.

I drop Nikolai's wrist.

Nik tells her, "Let's see it then."

She brushes our expressions under the rug, the way we do, and takes both of our hands, pulling us in the direction of the Christmas tree.

NIKOLAI IS ON HIS FOURTH BEER WHILE I HELP Katya string bulbs around the large spruce. It *almost* knocks into the flat-screen television. Timo claimed it was a Christmas miracle that the tree even fit in the room. He was planning on laughing his ass off (and recording it) when it smashed into the ceiling.

Nikolai didn't look amused, but my phone call with Shay depleted most of his Christmas cheer.

We just need a moment to talk.

Between the tree limbs, I notice Nikolai hovering around the kitchen, not able to sit down and relax. I feel like I'm channeling his volatile emotions, my muscles never loosening. This is worse than a normal bout of holiday stress.

Nikolai motions to Luka who's opening a package of ornaments, Timo shuffling through holiday tunes on his iPod nearby. "Where did you get the lights?" he asks.

"I bought them." Luka raises his hands. "I promise."

"The receipt is in the bag," Katya calls out, crouched near my feet.

Nikolai fists his beer bottle, not checking.

Luka glares. "Please look, okay?"

"I don't need to. I believe you."

Luka groans. "I don't want you to believe me. I need you to *know* with actual proof." Nikolai doesn't budge. Maybe he's wary to encounter more bad news. "*Please.*" Luka says a few more words in Russian before Nikolai leaves his post beside the bar.

He picks out the receipt from the paper bag. And with an indecipherable expression, he puts it back.

"And?" Luka asks.

Nikolai doesn't blink. "And I said I believed you."

Luka sighs exasperatedly. "You could at least look proud of me."

"I am proud, Luk," he says, his words coarse. And I know it's not from his brother. He's still fixated on other things. Okay, this has to end. I quickly plug the lights into the outlet, only half blinking on.

"Oh crap," Katya says, her voice muffled as she crawls around the tree.

I squeeze out from behind it, being whacked by pine needles, and I hurry over to Nikolai.

Luka holds a couple blue ornaments, meeting my gaze. He gestures to his older brother. "Fix him, please."

Nikolai glares. "I'm fine." He growled those words.

Timo switches the song to "You're A Mean One, Mr. Grinch." He's too amused by this.

"Let's talk," I tell Nik, grabbing his hand. I just hope I find the right things to say.

He follows me towards his bedroom, and Timo calls out in a sing-song voice, "You've got garlic in your soul! I wouldn't touch you with a—"

I shut the door.

Nik sets the beer on the dresser. He waits for me to speak since I dragged him in here.

"I know you're upset, but nothing has happened yet…" I trail off as his gaze narrows and jaw muscles twitch.

Cold sweeps me, even with hot air blowing from the vents.

After a long moment, he finally says, "It's hard enough accepting the idea that I may lose you to your career, but now I may lose you to Shay and to the same fucking show that split apart my family."

The connection between the original Somnio and the revival next year puts a pit in my stomach. I tread lightly over that and say, "Shay and I aren't together."

His shoulders lock. "It doesn't matter, Thora. He'll be *with you*, close to you, able to see you *every single day.* Able to hold your hand and touch your face." He grimaces, hurt flashing at the image and puncturing me.

"I don't care if it's friendly…The thought of him even five feet near you while I'm an ocean away…" He has to drop his gaze from me. "I am just trying to process this."

A weight bears on my chest. "Whatever happens, just know…" And I can't say the words. They're stuck in my throat. They won't come out. *Say it, Thora.*

He stares down at me, waiting. I always pause. And he rarely fills the silence with his own voice. He just looks so deeply into me and gives me time to find the right thing…

"I'm in love with you," I whisper.

He tries to smile but his eyes flood instead. "Don't love me more than your dreams, myshka. Because I love you too much to let you give them up for me."

It feels like a snowplow has rolled over my body, fracturing every bone. "I'm going to choose the circus," I say in a shaky voice, "but it won't change my feelings for you."

"You'll always remember me then," he says softly with a weaker smile. "I'm happy to be a chapter in your life."

Tears fall when I blink. "Don't say that. You don't know what's going to happen."

"Try your best at the auditions. If you don't, you'd hate yourself for it. And I'd be disappointed in you."

"Nik—"

"It's okay," he says, convincing himself. He grabs his beer. "I'm okay. We follow our passions. That's what we're made to do."

I shift uneasily, having trouble responding.

He rakes a hand through his messy hair. "I'm going to take a shower."

I nod, watching him walk tensely across the room, finishing the last of his beer.

I never thought saying I love you, out loud, for the first time would hurt so much. And strangely, I don't want to take it back.

I know that I can still love him and choose the contract. But the reality is less sweet than it was before. Nikolai spelled it out. If I'm with him, I'm not in the circus. If I'm in the circus, I'm not with him.

Either way, I lose.

ACT FORTY-FIVE

"Thank you all for being here," Helen says, a clipboard perched beneath her arm. Her phone buzzes and she takes a moment to read a message.

There are about a hundred wannabe artists, sitting along the blue mats as we wait for instruction. First cuts were last week, and we're all that's left.

Shay leans into my arm and whispers, "We have to be working on the apparatuses today."

I nod. "You're probably right." We already danced—did improv acting—kind of like my first auditions for Amour. I'm happy to have at least passed that part again. I keep cracking my knuckles, a nervous habit.

I look up, half-hoping to see Nikolai sitting with the row of directors and choreographers. To give me that single nod like *you're doing well, myshka.*

He's not here. I see wrinkled foreheads as men and women try to pick the best cast for each show. So that it'll make the most money. I can't tell whether they look at me and see dollar signs.

I can only hope that I'm more than just background. After months of training, I know there's nothing more I can do.

Helen pockets her cell. "We have fourteen spots to fill for Somnio, two for Infini and one for Viva."

Infini and Viva mean that I stay in Vegas.

Somnio means I travel far, far away from Nikolai.

I inhale strongly, trying to push these thoughts out.

"We're going to test you on multiple disciplines. We're looking for stand-out performers," Helen explains. "Those who catch our eye will be awarded a one-year contract. At the end of the year, we'll either ask you to renew or to leave us." There's not much time to digest the rest of the facts. She adds, "We're splitting everyone up in groups of five. When I call your number, please come forward."

I press my hand to the number 29, stuck to my black leotard, just to ensure it's still there. That I'm still in the running.

Before Helen speaks again, I remember what Nikolai told me this morning. I was pulling my dirty-blonde hair into a tight pony while he sat on the edge of the bed.

He said, "All you need is luck. The rest, you'll do great at."

I smiled. "Is that my trainer speaking?"

"Yes," he said, "but you'd probably think it's a problem."

I hesitated, "Why's that?"

He stood up, towering above me with those intense grays. "Your trainer is in love with you."

I don't have a problem with it, not even a little bit. Nikolai is brutally honest, and he'd tell me if I sucked. He wouldn't watch me fall flat on my face and fail. I trust his words.

I just need some luck today.

"Twenty-nine," Helen calls.

With one last motivational breath, I rise to my feet.

ACT FORTY-SIX

"I didn't think you could ever do that," Shay tells me, taking a swig from his water bottle. I wipe my forehead with my towel. The directors have been in deliberation for the past thirty minutes, so we're all just waiting on the mats again.

"Was I okay?" I wonder, even though I know I did my personal best. They made me climb a Chinese pole, which I'd worked on with Nikolai, and I performed several drops and poses on aerial silk. I didn't think too hard about the movements. I tried to relax my face and just follow the music.

I felt stronger. Better. More graceful.

I'm just crossing my fingers that they thought so too.

"You were awesome." He sounds genuine. "Like I said, I never thought you could do that."

It makes me realize how far I've come since the start. "You nailed that full twisting layout," I mention. They harnessed everyone for the Russian swing, just for safety. But Shay started with some of the hardest tricks, and he landed almost all of them.

"Yeah, I got the feel of the swing pretty fast," he says. "But I tripped up on the double."

I give him a look. "You barely stumbled." He's too hard on himself. I stuff my towel in my gym bag.

"I hate when I'm a little off though. It's like leaving the bathroom with a piece of toilet paper hanging from my pants."

He's always been a perfectionist with gymnastics. I think the avoidable fumbles frustrate him the most.

He takes another swig of water. "So where are we going to celebrate after?"

"The Red Death is the best club…" My voice fades as Helen and the rest of the directors exit the office and enter the gym. Everyone quiets when they parade over to the long table.

Helen is the only one left standing, her clipboard outstretched with all the answers. She clears her throat. "Thank you again for coming out. We know we have a great crop of artists here. We don't want to keep you long, so if I call your number, please stay after to sign the necessary paperwork."

I watch her flip a page in her clipboard, a breath caged in my lungs. I take a peek at Shay's number on the band of his red Ohio State gym shorts: 88.

"For Viva, number thirty-three."

Heads turn as we all silently look for the person with the number. It's not hard to find the smiling, elated girl with a French braid.

Two more spots left for a show in Vegas.

Please call twenty-nine. I repeat the mantra over and over, hoping. Just hoping.

"For Infini, numbers seventy-four and sixty-two."

My heart sinks. *It's okay.*

It's okay.

I don't want to picture Nikolai right now, but all I see is me leaving him. He's altered the landscape of my aspirations, and it's not as sunny when he's not in it.

Shay hangs his arm around my shoulder, casually, like he's silently saying *hey, we're going to be in the same traveling show.* That's a positive I cling to.

"For Somnio," Helen continues, flipping another page. I inhale without the exhale. "We want numbers eighteen, five, six—" she traces the line with her finger "—forty-eight, twenty-eight."

My heart skips at that close number. *Please twenty-nine.*

"Thirty," Helen continues. "Ninety-two, eighty-eight."

Shay's shoulders lift at the sound of his number, and his smile explodes. I can't hug him yet, not when Helen reads quickly and my mind has already lost count of the spots left.

"Twelve, thirty-four, thirty six, thirty-nine…"

Shay begins to tense as much as me. *Please twenty-nine.*

"Nineteen and…"

Helen flips another page.

"Twenty-one."

I shut my eyes, a swift kick to my chest. This isn't how this was supposed to go. It's barely processing… *you didn't make the cut, Thora.*

Stop. I don't want to hear it yet. I can't…

"Congratulations to every number I called. To those I didn't, there may be spots open next year. So we encourage you to submit videos again. You were all great, but you're just not what we're looking for at this time."

These are the horrifying facts that keep berating me: I spent seven months in Vegas. Away from family. Pushing my body to its limitations. Stepping outside my comfort zone. Struggling to support myself. I tried. I tried *so hard.*

And then Shay flew here. One day. One time.

And he made it.

I can always try again. There's always next year. But it's exhausting. Mentally, emotionally, physically, financially—there are reasons why people give up after a while. Why they move on.

"Thora…" Shay squeezes my shoulder. "It's going to be okay."

I slowly rise to my feet, my eyes welling. And I collect my gym bag before I break down in front of him. "I'll see you later?" My voice is a whisper.

"Yeah," he says. "I'll text you, okay?"

I nod stiffly and dazedly exit. Now what do I do. I pause in the middle of the hallway and think *where do I go from here?*

I'm lost.

I let out a tight breath; my body is hot as nausea brims. I need air. I need a lot of things, but air is definitely the easiest to obtain. So I ride up the elevator, a few other dejected acrobats with me. And then I walk through The Masquerade's lobby, following the signs to the pool.

Don't cry.

Don't cry.

I'm crying.

"Thora!"

The voice comes as soon as I push through the doors, into the chilly forty-degree night, high-rises lit and dazzling. Cars honking. The city never sleeping. It's exactly the same as it was seven months ago. Those noises, those smells, those lights.

Nothing has changed besides the person behind me.

"It's fine…" I barely whisper, not able to look Nikolai face-to-face. He must've been waiting for me in the lobby. And I didn't see him.

I just set my bag on one of the white lounge chairs. The enormous pool is black in the darkness. I numbly head towards it.

"Thora!" Nikolai calls, his voice nearer.

Wake up, Thora James.

I need to wake up.

For once in my life. I don't want to be hurt anymore by failures. I just want to succeed. Please. I shut my eyes. And I walk straight into the water, the icy plunge enough to grip my chest.

I stay beneath for a second.

And I scream.

As loud as I can.

Emotions barreling into me. I just scream.

My voice is lost in the water, but everything pours out of me.

Then a figure splashes down beneath and scoops me in his arms. My head breaches the surface with Nikolai's and I gasp, the cold even worse up here. But I feel better.

Without a word, he pulls me out of the water. I wobbly stand, my teeth chattering. He towers above me with the most concerned look.

"I'm…okay. I just…I needed that," I try to explain, tears rising again. *No, don't cry.*

"You didn't make it," he assumes right.

I nod, watching water drip from his shaking body, the cold biting our skin. His gray shirt is plastered to his chest, his jeans soaked. I can tell he wants to lift me in his arms and carry me to warmth, but I'd rather stay outside. I feel less in a daze. So I walk to one of the outside cabanas with an overhang and pillows.

I rub my nose with the back of my hand.

Nikolai collects a few white pool towels from the *take one, please* stand. And when he returns, I already claim a seat on the soft cream cushion, hugging a navy-blue pillow to my wet body.

He pushes the long strands of his damp hair back, and climbs on, spreading his legs in front of me so I fit more between them. But he's still facing me. Which means he wants to talk. A serious talk.

"You don't…have to say anything," I tell him.

He wraps two of the towels around my shoulders. "I have to." He uses the other to dry his hair that keeps dripping. "This isn't over, Thora."

I laugh weakly, my voice cracking. "That's what I always say, you know? It's not over yet." I point at my chest. "*I can do this.*" My chin trembles and I shake my head a couple times. "But I can't do this anymore…I can't spend another year *trying* just to see the same outcome." I stare off, my eyes pooled with hot tears. "I've been defeated…okay?"

He cups my face with one hand, brushing away my tears. "No, myshka. I'm not okay with that."

Why can't he let me give up? "Let me give up," I say, pain fisting my lungs. "I don't want to fight for this anymore."

"Let's go down to the office."

My body shudders with a cry. "No." *I'm done.*

He pulls me closer. "Let's tell them the truth."

"Give up on me," I beg. "Please."

His bloodshot eyes bore into me. "Let's tell them how you should be in Amour. How you know the aerial silk routine."

My face contorts in confusion and hurt. "I don't…" *I don't know that routine.* "I don't know that routine."

"You've never seen it performed. So how would you know if you do or don't?" He wipes some of my tears while my brows knot, processing, but not understanding…

"Thora," he says lowly, "*I* taught you that routine. For months, I've been teaching it to you."

No…

"Every trick," he explains, "is one that you needed for Amour."

It hits me like a forty-foot wave. I sway back, and he holds my hips so I don't drift too far. I barely whisper, "The death drop."

"The modified straddle slide," he rephrases.

I digest our months of time together. I never saw the aerial silk routine. It was removed from the show before I even arrived in Vegas. And I never watched Elena and Nikolai practice together. I remember that Nikolai was incessant I drop closer to the ground for the straddle slide. He wouldn't let me leave it at seven feet.

He wanted it to be perfect, I realize. To the choreographer's standards.

"No…" My voice cracks again. "No, you didn't do that." I shake my head again and again and again.

"I did," he refutes, his emotions welling to the surface, his features as brutal as mine.

"Why would you…?" It doesn't make sense.

"Because I wanted you to be my partner."

"Elena—"

"Never had chemistry with me. And the entire piece is about *passion*." The way he says passion, it's with his entire soul. "And you—*we* had it. From the first audition, it was there."

I point at him accusingly, tear-streaked and still overwhelmed. *He taught you the entire routine, Thora. He wanted you to be his partner.* "You tricked me." I don't know why I land on this statement, of all statements. But it's what comes out.

"Because you wouldn't have wanted me to teach it to you," he explains. "You would've thought I was screwing over another girl."

My stomach drops. "Did you?" Elena was fired. She was let go because she couldn't "cut it"—was he resigned with her since he had a backup plan? He had me.

"No," he says. "I didn't screw her over."

"But she was fired—"

"For not showing enough emotion on stage," he clarifies. "There was a point, Thora, where I needed Elena. I thought you'd be going to Somnio."

I shut my eyes tightly as I recall the timeframe of all these events. Elena was fired after we learned that Somnio was being revived. So he was genuinely upset when she was let go. He truly thought his act would be retired. Because I wouldn't be in it.

"I was prepared to lose you," he suddenly says.

My chest rises in a sharp inhale. *He was prepared to let me go to Somnio.* "Why?"

Beads of water still roll down his temple. "You worked hard to land a contract on your own, and I wasn't going to take that from you."

We're closer. We've drawn together somehow. I'm clutching onto his arms. And he's holding me around the waist, his body warm.

"Even if it benefited you to have me stay?" I ask. If I left, then there was a greater chance they'd retire his act. After months of training me for that role—he'd give it all up.

His eyes dance over my features, reading me well. "I knew what I was losing. But you would've been more proud of earning a spot in Somnio than feeling like I pulled strings for you in Amour."

I wish he was wrong. But this isn't the purest avenue. It's cutting corners. I will cut corners if I go down to that office and tell them what I can do in Amour. *You know the routine.* God—how did I not realize? He had to have taught me it in fragments, trick by trick.

He adds, "If you landed a role in another show, I wouldn't have offered Amour as a choice." He's saying that I would've never known he taught me the routine.

My eyes sear, scald. Burn. "Why?"

"You know why."

I do. There's a stigma attached to this role: *you slept your way to the top. You're only in Amour because Nikolai is your boyfriend. You cheated.* "…so the only way I could ever be in the circus is by being with a guy," I say aloud. I feel ashamed by it. Every time I think of myself in this role, I will hear my conscience say *you didn't do this right. You don't deserve this. You're not good enough to be here.* I don't want to feel that. Not even a little bit.

I just want to be happy and proud. That I finally made it.

"You're wrong," he says, holding me tighter. He looks at me like he so desperately wishes I could see his view. Where it's better. And brighter. I wonder if that's usually where I stand.

"Don't you see it?" I breathe, tears dripping. "Had I not met you, I wouldn't be here."

"Had you not met me, you wouldn't have the skills to try out at all." He removes the pillow from my chest, so there are no more barriers between us. "If you think for a second that you haven't succeeded, you need to look at my little sister." His voice softens.

And I notice more redness in his eyes, from stifling tears.

"You inspired her. Not because you were with me, but because you tried. You never gave up on the things you wanted. So she tried harder, she became better, and she accomplished her goal."

"She made Noctis?" I'm happy. And proud. I'm proud of Katya.

He nods. "She made it."

"I'm glad," I whisper. "I'm happy."

He's too perceptive to take faith in my words. "You're in pain," he states.

"I'm trying not to be." I exhale, but my chest is still tight. *You can still be in the circus. It's not over.* I'm searching for my lost optimism.

"I know this still feels like failure to you, but there are two things you need to always remember."

I listen intently, letting him rope me into his gunmetal eyes. He lifts my chin, our lips close, aligned as much as we can be.

"Regardless of what anyone else thinks, you earned this spot. You trained seven months for it. If you couldn't land those tricks, they'd never even consider you."

I nod, letting this sink in. He's certain that it'll only take a run to the office to land the role. And maybe a small demonstration. If I know the routine—if Aerial Ethereal doesn't have to spend money to train someone else—I can see how it'd be easier to hire me.

"What's the second thing?" I ask.

"Every day you're on stage, prove them wrong."

I nod again, tears rolling. *Prove them wrong.*

"That you deserved to be here from the start. That they made a mistake, that *you* and only you, Thora James, my little mouse…my demon—were meant for this role."

He begins to fill me with things that I've lost.

Thank you, I want to say.

And he kisses my cheek, his lips scorching my flesh. "Your choice," he whispers.

My choice.

He wanted me to have this role. Maybe even before we started dating. Maybe when he propositioned training me. I wonder if we weren't in a relationship—if I would've had an easier time saying yes to this offer. I know I'd feel less judgment, but I don't regret that first date. Or all our times at The Red Death.

Love isn't a mistake.

Neither is courage.

And I want to be courageous enough to not care about what other people think. *My choice.*

In my heart of hearts, I know what it took to reach this place. I know how hard I worked. That's all that should matter. My heart, my love, my passion.

My choice.

What are you going to do, Thora James?

ACT FORTY-SEVEN

I'm in the circus.

I wonder when it'll stop feeling surreal. Maybe when I perform on stage in Amour for the first time next week—then it'll hit me. Right now, it's the third day of practice with Nikolai at The Masquerade's gym, and the directors greenlit the aerial silk act yesterday, when we went through the whole routine.

He had taught me all the tricks, with him as my partner, so it took one training session to put it all together, seamlessly.

"Don't trip when you walk over to me," he warns.

I gape. "I'm not going to trip." We're practicing in wardrobe for the first time, his red slacks on while he breathes heavily, hands on his waist and silk rigged above him. His bandana is tied around his forehead like usual, pieces of damp hair hanging along the fabric—not part of his costume. So technically he's cheating.

I pointed this out and he gave me a look like *and what are you going to do about it?*

It was a look that deserved a great response, but I was too tongue-tied and open-mouthed to say anything. I shrugged and walked away, feeling his grin on my back.

Now I'm about twenty feet from him, more in the middle of the gym, wearing a white draping costume. With so many thin, wispy pieces of fabric that it skims my legs and the floor. It's a hazard, I realize too. But it's not supposed to stay on my body for long.

His lips curve upward. "Then come to me," he says, huskily.

My heart bursts.

Just standing here.

Just seeing him.

Knowing that this is going to turn into a bigger reality next week. I almost can't accept it fully. I hesitate to bask in the joy and accomplishment. After so much disappointment, I guess I expect more to hit me soon, another stipulation, another setback.

I'm not the fool-hearted, idealistic girl anymore. I've been shaken enough to be wary. And it's a mark that'll stay with me. For better or for worse.

I inhale a deep, motivational breath.

And I sprint towards him, as fast as my feet will go. In a split-second, the fabric tangles with my foot. *You're going down.* I realize that too.

I thud to the mat like a sack of flour, catching myself on my elbows. I mean, it's not the most terrible place to land. My face would've been worse.

I hear clapping. Not from Nikolai. Turning my head, the Kotovas on the metal cube apparatus give me applause and whistles for my fall.

"Looking good, Thora James!" Timo calls, sitting on the highest rung like he's just chilling.

A smile stretches my face, and I pick myself up and kneel. Nikolai walks over with lightness sweeping his strong, masculine features.

For the first time, I'm not the outsider looking in. I'm a part of this grand, magical thing called the circus. Where every person on stage is family.

"What were you saying about not tripping?" he asks, a few feet away.

I open my mouth to reply, but someone in my peripheral catches my attention. Shay adjusts his duffel bag on his shoulder. It's not a gym bag but his luggage. *He's leaving.* I quickly stand as he approaches.

"I came to say goodbye." His eyes cautiously flicker to Nikolai behind me. A lot of us went to Club Zero a couple days ago for happy hour, including Nikolai and Shay, and the uncomfortable tension between them never dissolved. It is what it is, I guess. I can't make two people like each other.

Nikolai's hand brushes my hip before he gives us space, returning to the red silk.

"When's your flight?" I ask.

"At four," he tells me. "They're sending all of us to Montreal for training first, and then they'll start staging the show."

It sounds like the start of an adventure. I smile, recognizing that I've been on one for a long while. "Are you excited?"

"Yeah," he nods. "It's something new."

"No more same-old-same-old."

He laughs and stares up at the ceiling, as though a higher power changed his life path. Maybe fate, luck—or him. His choice. He took the risk. That's all Shay.

I hug him, standing on my toes to wrap my arms fully around his shoulders.

He hugs me tighter with one arm. And he whispers, "Be happy, okay?"

My heart clenches, and I look up.

"I know you'll be safe." He nods, accepting this. "So be happy for me."

I smile. "I already am."

He kisses my cheek, and we let each other go. I watch him head out the exit where he came from. I know we'll see each other again. Sometime. In the faraway future.

This is the bittersweet portion of my life, but I'm happy. For each of us choosing the better life, even if it was a harder road to take.

Nikolai squeezes my shoulders. "He'll be okay."

"I know," I say, spinning around to face him. "Which part were we at?"

"The part where I take your clothes off." He's being serious, and he's also right. My pulse races as his eyes tear through me.

I think he's already mentally ripped part of my costume off.

A girl shrieks. Our head whips towards the trapeze, the group of artists excitedly jump up and down with a magazine in their hand. I squint at the title from afar. *Celebrity Crush*, a tabloid.

"Who's pregnant?!" Timo calls.

The girl gleefully bounces. "They're coming here!"

"What?" I say aloud.

Every girl speaks at once and I barely uncover the names in their enthusiasm: *Ryke Meadows* and *Daisy Calloway*. The reality stars of *Princesses of Philly*. A famous family. Famous couple. They're seeing Amour next week.

My nerves shoot up. "Dear God…" I whisper aloud, on accident.

"What happened to them being in Costa Rica?!" Timo shouts, interested in the family like his little sister.

"They're on route there afterwards," is the reply from about three girls.

I fixate on the simple fact that famous people will be watching the premiere of the show. Add in my parents and the directors of Amour—the pressure keeps mounting.

Nikolai's thumb skims my neck. "You can't distinguish faces in the audience," he reminds me. "You'll be fine."

The Calloways are infamous. This show will be all over the news… in a good way. Amour needs the publicity, but what if the magazines are littered with bad reviews? "This is worse than having the cast of *The Vampire Diaries* here," I realize.

"They were here last week," Nikolai tells me.

I gape. "What?" I missed them? What was I doing? *God, what if you were washing your hair. How lame.* I look up and Nikolai is close to laughing.

"Joking," he says. "I don't even know what *The Vampire Diaries* is."

I scowl. "It's a show, a *great* show."

With a more charming smile, he pulls me closer. My arms swoop around his waist, the heat of his skin warming me.

"When you're on stage, stay in the moment," he says, more encouraging. "Nothing else matters."

Loud, coarse Russian infiltrates our conversation, the voice familiar by now. Dimitri stands close with a water bottle in hand, passing our apparatus to reach the teeterboard. He speaks straight to Nikolai, but he's gesturing to me.

After hanging around the Kotovas nearly every single day, I can pick apart certain words. "What's not a good idea?" I ask Dimitri.

He glances over his shoulder, as though to make sure no one listens in, and then he nears us. My eyes widen as I crane my neck to look up between them, inadvertently being sandwiched between two of the tallest Russian men here.

"Tell Thora," Dimitri says.

Nikolai marbleizes. "We promised her that we wouldn't tell anyone." For some reason, I know that the "her" is not referring to me.

Dimitri rests a hand on my head and speaks in Russian. Um…

Nikolai smacks his hand away and replies, "It's not the same."

"No one wants the show to suffer again because of a break up." *Suffer again.* He's referring to Nikolai's last partner. His last girlfriend. Tatyana. His *it's complicated.* I'm beginning to think Dimitri is afraid of history repeating itself.

I didn't even think of that. "We won't…" I can't finish the words. Both guys are *glaring* at each other, seemingly speaking through their eyes.

And Dimitri is the first to crack. "Go ahead and tell her what happened with Tatyana."

Nikolai's jaw muscles clench. "I wish she hadn't told you anything."

"We're friends. The way we're friends." He motions to his chest to Nikolai's, back and forth.

"Bullshit," Nikolai says. "You loved her. She didn't love you."

He snorts. "What are you talking about love? I just wanted to fuck her."

I cringe at the crudeness of Dimitri Kotova. I will never become used to it. Maybe that's a good thing. "Nikolai," I cut in while he throws daggers into Dimitri. "What's going on?"

He won't meet my gaze. He's still fixated on his friend. "I broke up with Tatyana a couple months before her injury."

He's telling you the whole story, Thora.

I inhale strongly, waiting for him to release the truth.

Nikolai continues, "I just didn't love her the way that she loved me, and it wasn't fair to her—to be in a one-sided relationship. She deserved more than me."

Dimitri points at himself.

Nikolai retorts, "Definitely not you."

Dimitri extends his arms. "I'm a great motherfucking catch. Right, Thora?" He winks at me.

My insides curdle. "Uh…"

Dimitri cocks his head. "You'll come around."

Not in that way. I hear the humor in his voice, the joke that I might've not been able to pick up on first meeting. I hone in on Nikolai's proclamation: *I just didn't love her the way that she loved me.* My face tightens as I wonder: how do I know that our love is equal?

How does anyone know?

Nikolai sweeps my features. "The thought of Tatyana ever leaving—it made me feel free. That's when I knew."

I recall all the moments he thought I'd leave Vegas. I saw despair.

"With you," he says, "it's the inverse."

"Get to the important part," Dimitri interjects, waving him on.

Nikolai rubs his eyes and shakes his head at his cousin. "You think it's easy for me to say this?" *It's complicated.*

"It's okay…" I tell him. "Whatever it is…" I have no idea what it could be. Not even a little hint or suspicion.

"I can rip it off," Dimitri declares, about to explain the rest.

"No." Nikolai stares past me, past his cousin, as though bringing the memory to the front of his mind. "No, I can tell her." He looks haunted, tormented by this moment in his life. One he's buried. "I broke up with Tatyana, but we were still in Amour together. And…you know the routine. It's intense."

I nod, trying not to picture them together on the aerial silk act. Each trick is strung with emotions. With lust in touching, in kissing, in flying

It's something that would be complicated with an ex-boyfriend.

"I could act my way through it," he continues. "And every night, I knew it tore her down, believing that I loved her when I didn't…I'd come off the stage and I was cold. I didn't want to confuse her, but I kept hurting her…and there's nothing I could do. It was the worst two months I've ever experienced."

Dimitri is quiet and more respectful than I thought he'd be. Maybe those months were hard for him too, if he was close to Tatyana.

I can't even imagine what it must be like—to not love someone when they love you. To love someone when they don't love you. To have to hurt each other, with no way to end it… "Wait," I whisper, my eyes growing again, the gears clicking.

"She couldn't get out of her contract." Nikolai lowers his voice so no one else can hear but the three of us.

My mouth falls. *No.*

"Her injury wasn't an accident. She wanted an out, and at practice for the Russian swing, without telling anyone, she added an extra rotation in a triple sault. And she knew that she didn't have enough room to land it." He pauses, his eyes reddening. "Tatyana made it seem like an accident. Not very many people knew we weren't doing well. We were always professional in the gym, but…I knew her. I knew that I had emotionally pushed her to that place."

It's complicated. It seems like an understatement now. This is… there are no words. I reach out and hold his hand, a small gesture, not knowing what else to do.

I ask softly, "Did she…admit to it?"

"To me," he nods. "I confronted her about it in the hospital."

"And to me," Dimitri adds.

That's it. She told two people the truth, and I guess she made them promise to keep it a secret. "Do I even want to know her injury?"

Nikolai shakes his head at the same time Dimitri says, "She broke her tibia and fibula, right leg."

I cringe into a worse wince. "God…"

Nikolai shoots Dimitri a glare. "Thanks."

"She might as well know everything," he says, "because if this happens again—"

"It won't," I cut him off. "It won't." I can't imagine reaching a place that low, and if I did—I don't think I'd be able to hurt myself like that. I just—I can't…even fathom it. I feel so horrible for her, if she felt like this was the only avenue to end her pain.

Dimitri nods. "We're on the same page then." He pats my head and then he swigs his water, heading to the teeterboard.

Nikolai is staring at the mats, at my feet. It's a rare sight, one that pulls at my heart.

"Hey," I whisper. "It's okay…"

He lifts his gaze. "I used to wonder, every day, if I made the right decision to break up with her. I could've saved her the pain, but why cage her in a lie? I didn't want Tatyana to waste her love on me."

He wanted her to be free too.

"You're a good person, Nikolai."

"You're a better person than me," he refutes. "I've just lived longer."

"And made more right choices?"

"No," he says, staring through me. "Just choices. Right or wrong, I don't know."

I nod and step forward, until I'm close enough to hug him around the waist. His hand finds the back of my neck, both of us still in costume. Still needing to practice the rest of the routine.

And he murmurs, "Where did we leave off?"

"At the beginning."

The beginning, all over again.

ACT FORTY-EIGHT

"I keep waiting for someone to say *gotcha, Thora James, you're really not supposed to be here*," I admit to Nikolai while we ride down the elevator, the strap of my gym bag slung on his shoulder. Tonight is my first time in Amour. Tonight is when it all becomes real.

"You're going to be waiting for a long time, myshka."

Because no one is going to pull a fast-one on me. Hopefully.

The elevator doors slide open, and we head to the lobby. "They're going to meet you here?" he asks, checking his watch. We still have plenty of time.

"Yeah, my mom just texted that she's waiting for my dad and Tanner in the hotel room." In my family, the men take longer to corral than the women.

We stop on the cobblestone, next to a map kiosk of The Masquerade, the 1920s clock hanging above us. I catch sight of a few familiar faces along the west wing, headed this way.

Timo, Luka, and Katya are talking in a huddle as they walk, gesturing to the fountain wall that the Dionysus statue sits in.

They're up to no good.

Nikolai is zeroed in on them, his face all strict lines. "Don't do it," he says under his breath.

And then the three siblings break apart. Maybe we're both paranoid. "They're probably just talking—" I cut myself off as the three of them *sprint* towards the wall.

"Shit," he curses.

Heads all across the lobby follow the three teenagers. In unison, they run up the tiled wall and flip backwards, trying to land on the fountain ledge. Timo sticks it at first, but then he staggers on the lip of the marble and splashes into the water. Luka tries to help him up, but he loses his balance and follows his brother, drenched from the waist-down.

Leaving Katya the lone victor, only her feet wet, still standing.

People start clapping. I join in. Damn—that was cool.

I look to my left, and Nikolai is applauding too. Katya meets our gaze with the biggest grin. It lifts my spirits, my nerves about tonight beginning to wane.

Then I remember that she'll be gone in a week, and my brief smile fades. Nikolai was on the phone with Sergei all last night, talking about Katya. And when he hung up, he threw the cell at the wall. Apparently his parents aren't that excited about her joining Noctis.

They'd rather she stayed here. Because it's "more stable"—Nikolai used air quotes when he told me. As though it was all a joke. He wants them to love Katya the way that he does, to be as thrilled to see their daughter as she is to see them.

But it's not likely that'll happen.

He's handing Katya off to people with less love to give, less care to offer, and it's killing him inside.

"Hey!" security calls, aiming towards Nikolai's siblings.

"Run," Luka says, grabbing Timo and lifting him to a stance. They race away, down the east wing, slipping on the cobblestone and laughing.

Katya shakes her head at them and steps off the fountain ledge. Security just watches her, and she points to us. "I'm with them."

Nikolai raises his brows. "You're going to have to find a new scapegoat when you're in Noctis."

Her shoes squish and leave wet footprints as she approaches. "No, I'm not."

I frown in confusion.

She rocks on the balls of her feet, her long brown hair parted in the center. Her big, round eyes seem to sparkle like her brothers' now. "Because…" She smiles, tears filling her eyes. "I'm staying here."

Nikolai's face falls in shock. "What?" He looks to me, as if I planned this.

I hold up my hands. "I didn't know anything."

"It was my decision." Katya fiddles with her fingers. "I've thought about it since Thanksgiving…" She takes a deep breath. "…I only wanted to go to Noctis because Mom and Dad were there. And it took me some time but I realized something important." She rubs her eyes with her hand, cheeks already splotchy.

"And what's that?" Nikolai asks.

She laughs into a tearful, happy smile. "I realized," she says, "that *you're* more of a parent to me than they ever were." She laughs again and points at him. "You're my favorite brother, Nik. You know that?"

He has his hand over his mouth, his eyes flooding. When he drops his arm, he says, "And you're my favorite sister."

"I'm your only sister," she reminds him.

He hugs her, and I hear him whisper in Russian that sounds close to *thank you.* He wanted her to stay.

I wanted her to stay. I blow out a breath, relief loosening my muscles. She chose him over her parents.

This good news comes on the heels of Luka's. He accepted a role in Infini yesterday, after learning a new discipline. They've added the Wheel of Death back into the show, the apparatus that Timo was previously known for. The one that Luka didn't think he had the patience or skill to learn.

I realize exactly what this means for the future.

Katya will be in Vegas.

With Luka. Timo.

Nikolai.

And me.

I smile. So much. It's a better ending than the one we'd all been imagining.

When they break apart, Katya looks to me, wiping her eyes again. "Can I keep *Darkest Warmest Night* until I finish?" she asks me.

I nod and Nikolai gives me a look. "What kind of book is that?"

I clear my throat, a tickle where my lie sits. "It's not romantic."

"It's about a werewolf family," Katya says. "It's a good book."

I really can't stop smiling. "Exactly."

He wraps his arm around my waist, pulling me closer. And that's when I see my mom, dad, and little brother emerge from the elevators. My pulse picks up speed.

"Good luck tonight," Katya tells me, noticing my family. "I'll be in the nosebleeds with Luka, but we'll be there." She waves goodbye and heads down the east wing.

The nerves return.

"Act normal," I say to Nikolai. *This'll be fine. Don't sweat it.* The closest I've come to this moment was introducing my homecoming date to my parents. I was sixteen. Not living with him, of course. This is a different caliber.

Nikolai stares down at me. "As opposed to all the times I act abnormal."

Right. No, wait, not *right.* "You pierced my…"

"Thora!" My mom exclaims, throwing her hands in the air to hug me. That was a close call. She squeezes me tightly, my dad nearby with a proud smile.

"Pierced what?" Tanner asks. *Or not.*

My thirteen-year-old brother is taller than me. It's not right. He has his hands in his jeans, sizing up Nikolai.

"I pierced her friend's ear," Nikolai lies easily.

Tanner looks impressed. "Really?"

"It's easy if you have a piercing needle."

"Huh," he says.

I'm in a death-grip with my mom, frozen at the string of lies. *No one thinks they're lies but you.* Right. I release my mom so she can breathe and then gently hug my dad.

"I'm proud of you, Thora," he says again. He tells me that almost every day now. Even though I achieved this position with my boyfriend's help—they see it as a true success. I didn't think they would, but their joy—it's everything to me.

Don't cry.

I've been doing well so far. "Thank you. And thanks for coming." I hug Tanner next.

And he whispers, "Your boyfriend is a fucking beast." He has an f-bomb problem.

"He's not that tall."

Tanner steps back from me and gives me a weird look. "Did Vegas make you stupid?"

"Hey," my dad cuts in.

"Just saying," Tanner says, raising his hands. "I'd still live here… even if it rots a couple brain cells." He nods his head, fixated on a *much* older cocktail waitress at the casino bar.

"I'm sure," I say. Now for the hard part. "Mom, Dad…this is Nikolai." I gesture between the three of them. My two worlds are colliding again. This time, it's a much smoother fusion.

Nikolai shakes my father's hand, both amicable.

"Thanks for looking after my daughter," my dad says.

"She did well on her own." He looks down at me, his lips rising.

My mom is full-blown smiling. "How long have you two been together?"

"Almost seven months," he answers.

Seven months. It went by quickly but in the same breath, I feel like I've spent years with him. Maybe because we shared every day together training.

"Seven months?" She smiles more, if that's even possible. "Wow."

I say, "It's been wow." I end up grimacing. What even was that? *It's been wow.* That's not how you describe a relationship. "I mean…you know what I mean." *Stop while you're ahead, Thora.*

"Well, you have a show to get to," my dad begins. "We just wanted to wish you good luck. And we'll see you after?"

"But we won't keep you too long," my mom interjects. "We know you'll want to celebrate with your friends."

I start crying. I don't know why. Maybe having them here. My two worlds meeting. Their pride. Their love for me. My mom hugs me again, tears welling in her eyes.

"We're so very proud of you, Thora," she whispers again.

No matter how many times they say it, it will always overwhelm me. I think it's the part of me that wants to please them the most—the piece of my heart that craves their satisfaction—that soars with that phrase.

I'm flying today. In all ways.

ACT FORTY-NINE

Behind stage, I wait for my cue.

My heart races, not matching the slow-burning tempo of the music to our act. Nikolai is already in front of the audience. I exhale a few trained breaths, my costume's white wispy fabric away from my feet. Icicle lights are strung, the background a romantic, cloudy night sky.

And I focus on the melodic sounds of a violin.

Another exhale.

Relax, relax.

My mind traverses a million miles an hour, but I land on Nikolai's advice, from a long time ago. His deep voice resonates in my mind like a whisper.

Whatever passion you've ever encountered in your life, you use it now, Thora.

It's not hard to search for it, existing right at the surface, unlike before. I peek out, where the audience can't see me. Nikolai descends from the aerial silk, eyes masked in purple and silver paint, his chest rising and falling in a powerful rhythm.

This is our act.

Our passion.

He looks my way.

Someone taps my shoulder, my cue. I'm ready. Without second-guessing, without falter, I sprint onto stage. I run towards him without slowing.

Nikolai stands tall, beckoning me, and I leap with all my strength. He bends only slightly, my left leg catching above his shoulder as I latch onto him. The gasp from the audience is the last thing I hear, blocking out the rest.

I clutch his hair, and he grips my back, our inhales in sync. Our exhales timed. My heart explodes.

In a billion pieces at the way he stares at me. At how he holds my face, caringly, like the love of his life just ran into his arms. He whispers something in Russian that I know means: *I love you.*

It builds something in me.

And his desire fuels mine.

Slowly, he kisses me, an ache in my throat, and he grasps me like it pains him to be away. I lean backwards, breathless, and flip onto the cold stage. Smooth, agile. He grasps the hem of my costume, tearing off the extra fabric with my momentum. Leaving me in a thinner, shorter white slip.

My nerves are gone. I think he knows it, a smile in his eyes. Almost like *you're doing well, myshka.* I contort my body, languidly flipping onto my feet. He circles me, stands behind me, and I only watch him, looking up.

Over my shoulder.

He lowers his head, lips touching mine again, the silk wrapped around each of his hands. And I spin to face him and hook my arms around his neck, like I'd rather slow dance.

In the air.

The riggers pull the fabric higher, so he's lifted off the ground, and we stay in the same position, Nikolai's strength keeping us airborne, afloat. And soon slicing through eighty-feet of nothingness. Of uncharted, untouched space.

I trust this man.

With my life.

My heart. My soul.

WE'VE DRESSED INTO REGULAR CLOTHES AND washed the makeup off our faces, Amour ending about twenty minutes ago. I realize that I don't mind what people thought. I felt alive. Happy. For one of the first times, I know I belong in this world. It can be mine too.

After I zip my gym bag backstage, Nikolai leans against the vanity, smiling. "You were beautiful."

I try not to smile too much. My cheeks hurt during the standing ovation for the entire cast. It was a lot to take in. Overwhelming. "Thanks for not dropping me…" That's what I choose to say? *Recover.* I clear my throat. "I was worried during that last half." I think I made it worse.

He wears that no-nonsense, all business look for a long moment. And then he bursts into a charismatic smile. It sends me dizzily backward, into the bottles of hairspray and trays of makeup.

He clasps me around the waist. "I never drop my partner, myshka."

"That's…good to know." My lungs have catapulted out of my body.

When his humor fades, what remains is longing. In deep Russian, he whispers a phrase that I've only heard once before. The day of The Masquerade's pool party.

"What does that mean?" I ask, my pulse beginning to race again as I catch certain words.

"Here is my heart." His thumb skims my neck. "It is full of love."

"You said that to me before..."*All the way back then.* I mean, that alone is reason to start flipping through a Russian dictionary. I'm getting better at the language. I'm trying.

"I did," he admits. "I also have something else to tell you."

My face tightens at his serious tone. "If this is about The Red Death, I promised Camila we would be there at midnight. I don't think I can change that..." I trail off at the look in his eyes. It's not about our plans tonight.

He says another Russian phrase, his lips curving.

I translate it as: *you're cute.*

And then he motions with his head towards the stage. "Follow me." Before I oil my joints, he clasps my hand and leads me out into the middle.

"Stop right here." He stands behind me, placing his firm palms on my shoulders.

I stare out at all the rows and rows of empty seats. It's quiet here, only the mutterings of voices backstage. Katya said it was a full house tonight. Not because of me or the aerial silk act. The two famous faces did it, but it's nice to know that Amour can sell out.

"What am I looking at?" I ask him.

"Your dream."

I smile. *My dream.* I'm living my dream. "You know," I say softly, staring out at the seats. "I used to wake up and wonder...is this it?" I pause. "Is there more out there? To finally reach the *more* part of my life..." I laugh into my tears and shake my head. "How do you describe the love of your life?"

"If you could see yourself, you'd realize you just did."

"I'm not scowling?"

He turns me around and brushes his fingers beneath my eyes. "No. You're not scowling."

"That's...good."

He laughs and it's his turn to shake his head, as he stares straight into me. "You once asked me if it was impossible to love two things equally. At the time…it seemed like it to me. I never loved someone as much as I loved this, here, tonight." He looks up at the ceiling, at the dangling lights, fake snow still fluttering off the rafters, onto us.

"The circus," I realize. His family.

"But I've found the truest form of love," he tells me. "It's two loves that can live in harmony." He looks down at me.

I stare up at him. My heart on an ascent.

"The circus and you," he whispers, "amour amour."

Two loves. Two passions. At perfect balance.

I finally feel it too.

ACT FIFTY

"Are you single?!" the new hostess asks us. Erin, the aspiring model, quit last week. She decided to fly out to New York for job opportunities, Camila said.

Nikolai has his arm around my waist, but in the dark corridor of The Red Death, it's hard to see anything but the stack of red, blue, and green glow sticks.

"She's with me," Nikolai says lowly, collecting the green glow necklaces from the box himself and snapping one behind my neck before he clasps his own. He holds the black curtain open for me, the club in full swing, red strobe lights sweeping the grinding bodies.

I'm just happy the air conditioning works.

"Will they swarm you?!" I ask Nik over the music when we descend into the club. Usually people flock him and start shouting his name, but this is my first time entering by his side since I'm in Amour now (I'll never be used to that phrase). I'm not sure how much time he has before the mad rush of spectators.

"Not yet," he tells me. I barely catch his words through the pop music. "We didn't enter through the back."

Good. I have time to see Camila before he begins his after-show. I sidle to the bar, Nikolai's hand on the small of my back.

"Thora!" Camila calls, waving little toothpick flags in celebration. "You were amazing!"

"Hey!" I shout back, squeezing between two stools. "You saw the show?" I thought she had to work. She said that all the girls at The Red Death asked for the night off, wanting to spot Ryke Meadows, the celebrity, so he could sign their boobs. The way Camila reiterated the story—interjecting *I am insanely attracted to him, he speaks Spanish, he's my soul mate*—I knew she would've joined their mission.

She leans forward in a low whisper. "Okay, don't tell, but I told John to film like a five-second clip." She raises her hands with the flags. "I know it's illegal, *but* it's so short and you mostly see John's finger and him muttering, *this is such a fucking bad idea.*"

Her impersonation is spot on. "You sound just like him."

She claps her hands. "Shots!"

I notice that she no longer has a red glow necklace. She wears a blue one like a crown. "What happened?" I ask her, gesturing to the necklace.

"I broke up with Craig," she says while she pours tequila into six shot glasses. "I can do better." I'm happy that she's come to realize it too.

Nikolai leans against the bar, searching the crowds from afar. I bet he's looking for his little brother.

"So did they give you a suite yet?" Camila asks.

"Yeah," I say. "They gave me a key yesterday." I now officially have my own place at The Masquerade, a floor above Nikolai's. "It's..."

surreal. I wish I had something better to say, but this seems like the most accurate word, for however redundant.

"You better be here for the full year!" Camila shouts over a new song, scrounging for the lime.

"I will be!" I tell her. My contract ends in one year. It'll only be renewed if the directors like me enough, and even then, The Masquerade can shut down Amour at any time. I try not to think too hard about the logistics. It's the storm that hasn't passed yet, and I'm choosing to bask beneath the sun.

Camila starts sliding shots. "This is the *you deserve a thousand standing ovations* shot." She pushes it to me, and my chest swells. "The *oh my God, look at that handsome fellow next to you* shot." She passes it to Nikolai. He gives her a look. Camila is the best bartender, an immediate friend. "The *thanks for being the best roomie I've ever had* shot." Another for me.

"The *you're certifiably insane and could have cracked your fucking head open* shot." That is John. He steals that shot and drinks it before Camila even slides it over.

His cousin is not amused. "You just drank a celebratory shot. That was not for you." She swats his wrist.

"I'm celebrating the fact that Thora is alive right now. And it's a fucking miracle if you ask me."

"Thanks, John," I say with a smile, and he toasts to that with another shot.

Camila growls in frustration. "You just downed the *John Ruiz is a gloomy, pessimistic—*"

"Old man," Timo finishes with a blinding smile. He slings his arm around John's shoulders. Camila's lips immediately rise with mine. It's hard not to smile at the sight of them, both wearing green glow necklaces.

Taken. It's official.

John acknowledges Timo with the roll of his eyes. "All true except the old man, *kid.*" He stands up straighter and kisses Timo in hello.

And then Timo nods to me. "Killed it, Thora James!" He squeezes my shoulder and then give his brother a thumbs-up.

Nikolai is having a hard time not smiling too. This may be the first time where we're all happy together, a good day all around.

I'm about to say thanks to Timo when the chanting suddenly begins. "God of Russia! God of Russia!"

The circle is starting to form right *here.* At the bar. The people create a semi-open space where Timo, John, me, and Nikolai reside.

John groans. "This is my stool." He points at the one he *always* sits at. "This stupidity can't happen at *my* fucking stool."

"You love it, John," Camila retorts. "And technically this is happening at my bar. And I say, *proceed.*" She waves Nikolai on, who's watching me, waiting for me. He takes a couple steps into the middle of the semi-circle, and he begins to unbutton his black shirt.

People holler, excited that his after-show is finally beginning.

I prepared for this tonight, even going as far to wear spandex shorts underneath my aquamarine dress. Maybe he realizes this. *Don't back down now.*

I won't.

I don't want to.

I grip the bar behind me, my back digging into it, and then I raise my hand, our eyes never drifting apart. I say, "Choose me."

His lips rise, and the girls let out a series of *awwwws.* He removes his shirt fully, his body chiseled, sculpted—familiar.

He reaches me, lifting me onto the bar so that our lips are parallel. My heart hammers, my pulse throbbing.

A breath away, he whispers, "Every day."

The hot kiss burns my skin, and I accidentally knock over one of the celebratory shots.

Every day, he chooses me. It rings in my ears.

When he parts, he turns to the crowd and tells them exactly what we'll be doing. A one-handed handstand competition. I watch him climb onto the bar, standing, towering above us all. And extends his arm, for me to take his hand.

I do, and he pulls me swiftly to my feet.

His gaze flies across my features. "Your eyes are black."

"They're always like that…" I lose my thoughts at the devilish smile he wears, the red strobe lights bathing us in the hue.

"You're ready," he states, reading me well.

I nod.

And we split apart. We're doing this *on* the bar. For the entire club to see. The crowd—it's larger than ever before, pushing up to the lip of the bar, and John still has his stool, Timo next to him.

You can do this, Thora James.

"On the count of three," Nikolai calls out.

"One!" the club yells.

"Two!"

I inhale.

"Three!"

And I place my hand on the sticky bar, my legs broken apart at first, but when I find my balance, I put them together. Straight, like a board. I glance over, and notice Nikolai in the same position.

Don't fall.

There's nothing that says I can't beat him. The cheers from the crowd jumble together, but I hear my name, from multiple, indistinguishable voices.

"Thora! Thora!"

What?

My eyes flicker to Nik again. And even upside-down, his curved lips are unmistakable.

Very rarely does anyone root against the God of Russia. And he's happy. Really happy that they are.

"Thora! Thora!"

I shut my eyes, concentrating, smiling, unable to stop my pulse from speeding. My muscles ache, pull and stretch, but I ignore the pain. Mentally sound, I stay at peace, motionless and still.

Thirty minutes pass and my eyes snap open at the gasps and "Ohhhhhs!"

I turn my head.

Nikolai dropped.

No way.

He sits on the bar, his forehead beaded with sweat. Looking shocked, he shakes his head over and over. I bet he'd already picked out a place to pierce me. When he sees me as I sit next to him, he lets out a short, humored laugh. "You're beaming!" The crowds are so noisy that I barely distinguish the words.

"I can't believe you lost!"

"You won!" he rephrases.

I won. My heart somersaults. Which means… "Tattoo or piercing?!"

He runs a hand through his hair, still in disbelief. Nikolai is not the kind of man who'd lose on purpose, even for his girlfriend. This is a true win, one that everyone in the club sees. It's insane. The whole night.

"Tattoo," he says.

My smile fades. I have no idea how to ink a tattoo on someone. I could permanently mark him with a messy blob.

He leans into me. "I'll guide you." And then he motions for the tattoo gun from someone, and he asks them for another thing—his words lost behind me.

I scan his body, and it takes me a quick second to figure out what I want to draw. Where I want to draw it. *At least you're sober.*

Yeah—I'm not sure my sloppy self would tattoo something pretty.

Nikolai passes me…a magic marker. "Draw it first."

I nod, relaxing at this idea. Without hesitation, I straddle him. On the bar. Whistling—everyone is whistling. Including Camila, who even winks at me and I read her lips: *get 'em, Thora.*

Timo is tossing dollar bills at us, and John is muttering things—that I can only assume are variations of *this is so stupid and crazy and is that tattoo gun sterile?*

Nikolai turns my chin, so that I focus on him, his eyes descending into mine. "What's it going to be?"

I open my mouth to tell him my plan.

"Show me," he says.

"You don't want to know first?" I question.

He shakes his head. "I trust you."

I am full of life today. Uncapping the marker, I place one hand on his chest, his heart pounding in a drumbeat that matches mine. Deep. Slow. With the other hand, I pinch the marker between two fingers and lean close to his ribcage. In my neatest cursive, I write three small words.

circus is family

His hands rise up my thighs, up to my hips and when he sees what I drew, his face floods with too many emotions to pick apart. Our gazes lock, and the noises around us seem to drown into silence.

"Where did you come from?" he asks again, shaking his head more. In a daze.

I have a better response this time. "Cincinnati, Ohio."

He breaks into a laugh, and he kisses me, my skin tingling, on fire. His hand warms the back of my neck. And I feel his smile against my lips.

I'm average. I've been average most of my life, but there are moments where I feel extraordinary. Invincible. Able to conquer any fear and step outside any box. There is no illusion, no fantasy. I can climb a forty-foot pole. I can fly eighty-feet in the air. I can be taller than tall.

It's a dream that I'm living.

Every day. With him.

EPILOGUE

ONE YEAR LATER

I shift on an office chair, the wheels squeaking beneath me.

"Sign here." The shaggy-haired businessman pushes a stack of white papers, flipping it open to a highlighted line. "And all the pages with marks."

I've already spent fifteen minutes reading the papers, so I click my pen and scrawl *Thora James* in each and every free space. I smile when I reach the last one.

"Is that it?" I ask.

"You're all done," he verifies, standing up with me. And then he extends his arm, for me to shake his hand. "We're ecstatic to have you, Thora." He's reiterated this sentiment a few times since I entered the office, praising me with more and more compliments.

I almost wonder if they thought I wouldn't sign. "Two more years," I say with a bigger smile. Two more years in Amour. It's the longest-term contract they could offer me.

"Twelve more years," he rephrases, shaking my hand like *we did it.*

It's the first time I've ever met him: the creator of Aerial Ethereal. I absorb his words *twelve more years.* Meaning—he plans to keep me around, in this same act, for maybe that long. It's more than I expected coming in here today. I was just happy that The Masquerade bought Amour for another twelve years, their contract signed and sealed last week.

"Thank you," I say, my smile stretching. My eyes burn. *Don't cry.*

"Take care of yourself now," he tells me as I head outside of the office, not into the gym but into the carpeted hotel hallway.

Nikolai leans against the wall, in workout clothes, his bandana rolled over his forehead. I decide to play a trick on him, knowing he'll try to read my features before he asks me what happened.

I wear a morose expression, my lips downturned and shoulders curved.

He straightens the moment he sees me. "They gave you a year," he assumes.

I shake my head, layering on the distress. His features darken, thinking I've been denied a contract.

And then he strides past me, to *storm* into the office. I expected him to use his words on *me* before using them on the creator of Aerial Ethereal.

"Whoa…Nik." I grab his wrist and yank him backwards, strong enough that he stumbles some.

"This is—"

"Two years," I cut him off, my heart pounding, a large smile replacing my frown. "I have two more years."

The realization hits him. "That wasn't funny."

"It kind of was for me."

His lips begin to rise, letting this good news sink in. He signed his two-year contract this morning. And then he lifts me, suddenly, up around his waist, kissing me. This still feels new. "Two more years," he says lowly. He walks with me like this, kissing me down the hallway.

"Maybe more…" I cling to him, clutching his arms. "Like twelve."

"Or forever," he breathes, parting my lips with his tongue. I inhale into the kiss, our bodies melded together. And then he stops walking. Standing in front of the Amour show poster.

"No, keep moving," I say.

Unfortunately, he sets me on my feet and then spins me around to the framed poster.

My face.

Technically, the side of my face, my profile, stares back at me. My lips are parted, my eyes shut like I'm dreaming, my hair pulled tight. *Amour* is in purple and pink colors across my cheek with the tagline: *love is a circus.*

And Camila said my eyebrow has never been so fierce.

I'm on most of the promotional material for Amour. All because of a quote from Daisy Calloway. One person, one famous person changed another portion of my life with just a sentence: *The aerial silk act stole the show for me, dangerous and beautiful.*

Luck.

This is more luck than I ever needed, and I'll never stop being grateful for it—this dream. My dream. It's surreal. Every day is surreal. *Hold it tight, Thora James. Don't let go.*

Nikolai tilts my chin, and I stare up at those gunmetal skies, ones that I meet twice a day on stage. And afterwards, when the lights fade. In our passion.

His lips lift in a burgeoning, heartfelt smile. And he says, "Well done, myshka."

ACKNOWLEDGEMENTS

Thank you all. For believing in us. For being champions of our work. For choosing to read this book when there are so many others out there. Whether you realize it or not—you've helped us live our passion, our dream. And there will never be enough *thank yous* to encompass the sentiments we feel and how grateful we are.

But like Thora, we'll *try* (it's the best we can do) and begin here:

To our mom and dad—hello there. Your pride for us, well, there are very few things greater in our eyes and in our hearts. And we've felt it tenfold this past year. Thank you for being a constant support, for never telling us we "couldn't" and always telling us we "could" and for making us believe that we could do anything and be anything. We're 23-year-old dreamers, in large, because of you.

To our brother—thank you for being our cheerleader. We love you for every encouragement with each new book. We couldn't ask for a better older brother.

To Niki—our courageous cousin. We admire you so, so much, for taking that plunge into the unknown after college, for being independent, for traveling around the world, for your free spirit and "where the wind takes me" bravery. No family. No familiar faces. You changed your landscape on your own. And bits and pieces of your spirit are in this book. We love you, our favorite couch-surfer, our big sister. We hope to see you sometime soon.

And lastly, to the Fizzle Force, with love—that phrase, you know, is written in stone. With love. From us to you. So it goes with every book. Our friends, our readers, our fans: thank you. For everything.

Until next time. Be happy, okay?

CIRCUS IS FAMILY SERIES

CONTINUES WITH

THE SECRET EX-BOYFRIEND

Continue reading for a sneak peek of the prologue and first chapter

Date: January 1st

Subject: Happy New Year AE Artists

From: Marc Duval, Creative Director of Aerial Ethereal

Bcc: Luka Kotova, *and other undisclosed recipients*

Aerial Ethereal Artists,

A new year means big changes. Please keep this in mind as we begin the process of hiring new & veteran artists. As a reminder, the current Aerial Ethereal show roster is as follows.

Touring Shows: Somnio, Noctis, Seraphine

Resident Show in Montreal (The Palace Blitz): Nova Vega

Resident Show in New York (The Opal Hotel): Celeste

Resident Shows in Las Vegas (The Masquerade Hotel & Casino): Viva, Amour, Infini

I'd also like to remind every artist (i.e., acrobatic performers, clowns, instrumentalists, dancers, singers, etc.) of the Wellness Policy that you're **required to follow** while under contract with Aerial Ethereal.

On behalf of the company, I wish the cast of Viva all the best with their performance tonight.

Marc Duval
Creative Director of Aerial Ethereal
marcduval@aerialethereal.com

I cup my phone and read the email. Everyone in the Masquerade's backstage dressing room pauses to check their cells. I hate mass company emails—almost as much as I hate *personal* company emails.

One of my cousins grumbles, "Damn Wellness Policy," and simultaneously reads the email while jumping into a spandex costume: forest-green, silver splashes of glitter on the neckline and sleeves.

I set my phone aside and return to the mirror.

Bulbous lights outline the frame and illuminate my features: tousled brown hair, captivating gray eyes (just not as much as my brothers'), and sculpted but lean arms and torso.

(I have to lift one of my cousins on my shoulders, for fuck's sake. And he's a two-hundred pound *dude*.)

I touch my carved jaw, my face a contradiction of hard and soft angles—and depending on the day, I suppose my personality is just like that too.

My cheeks are half-painted. Vibrant green swirls form leaves, but I have to add more yellow detail. I work on my eyes, blending green shadow into gold.

If someone out there wants to grant me some luck, tonight will be the *last* time I do the Viva makeup.

"Twenty minutes until opening!" someone shouts into the room.

Swiftly, I swipe out of my email and into my music. Earbuds in and makeup brush in hand, I nod my head to the rhythm and prepare for my job.

Date: January 16th
Subject: Welcome to Infini
From: Antoine Perrot, Director of Infini
To: Luka Kotova

Luka Kotova:

I'd like to formally welcome you back to Infini. This season, we're hiring a brand new choreographer who'll oversee every act in the show.

Including your discipline: Wheel of Death.

We want you to take these new changes with stride, and as a veteran artist, I need you to set an example at work. I hope we can count on you.

Antoine Perrot
Director of Infini
antoineperrot@aerialethereal.com

I dance. Half-intoxicated by the liquor in my veins. Half-intoxicated by the bass thumping the Vegas club called *Verona*. Raising my phone up, I squint at the bright screen and try to read the work email. I retain about a quarter.

It goes something like: *welcome back blah blah blah new choreographer blah changes blah blah.* Then I shove my phone in my jeans.

I just *dance.*

Date: January 17th
Subject: Congratulations
From: Marc Duval, Creative Director of Aerial Ethereal
Bcc: Luka Kotova, *and other undisclosed recipients*

Aerial Ethereal Artists,

On behalf of the company, congratulations to all the new artists who have signed on for the upcoming year(s). We'd also like to give the warmest welcome to the new female aerialist Thora James, who'll be a lead in Amour's aerial silk act.

As most of you may already know, AE has had to make serious changes with our veteran shows. Infini alone has recast 90% of its roles. We appreciate all the support **and compliance** moving forward. We expect to make more changes in the coming months.

We're a company striving to improve in all avenues: creative and financial.

Marc Duval
Creative Director of Aerial Ethereal
marcduval@aerialethereal.com

Shoving a piece of pizza in my mouth, I jog towards the performance gym inside the Masquerade Hotel & Casino. I'll probably puke. (Nothing new.)

In my other hand, I grasp my phone, trying to read and walk.

Multitasking like a motherfucker.

Date: January 19th
Subject: Infini News
From: Geoffrey Lesage, Choreographer
Bcc: Luka Kotova, *and other undisclosed recipients*

Infini Artists:

Firstly, I am not here to be your friend. I'm here to make Infini the best damn show on Aerial Ethereal's roster. Most of you choreographed your own routines in the past.

Not happening this year. All acts will be created and approved by **me**.

Here's the sad truth: **Infini is stale.** It's why more than half of your co-workers were fired (or shifted to other shows). If the audience is bored to tears, do you think they'll return for a second and third viewing? No. They'll just go gamble at the casino instead.

No whining. No complaining. If I see any empty chairs in the audience this season, I'll push you all harder. Don't kid yourself, **Marc Duval will axe Infini if it underperforms this year.** You. Must. Sell. Tickets.

No excuses.

No exceptions.

While we wait for new artists to fly in and get accommodated at the Masquerade, remember to condition. **Do not waste my time.** First meeting/practice is February 15th.

For those asking for cast sheets, Antoine Perrot and the rest of the creative team are keeping Infini's shakeups quiet from the press. You'll meet all the artists in person on the 15th.

Geoffrey Lesage
Infini Choreographer
geoffreylesage@mailme.com

My older cousin's brash and crude voice blares through my phone, complaining about the email from Geoffrey.

While he curses, I toss the cell on my mattress and empty my pockets. Three packs of Junior Mints. Five bottles of tiny hotel shampoos. A Masquerade souvenir keychain. A half-opened bag of Skittles. My gym card.

Date: January 20th
Subject: you there?
From: sergeikotova@aerialethereal.com
To: Luka Kotova

Nik says you blocked my number and that's why you haven't responded to my texts. Unblock me. We need to talk.

- Sergei

I slam the washing machine closed with more force than I intend. It's old anyway.

The hotel hasn't updated the 42nd and 43rd floor communal washers and dryers since I moved to Vegas three years ago. And they were already archaic back then. I glance back at my phone.

I hesitate.

And then I swipe right to delete.

Date: January 21st
Subject: Reminder
From: Marc Duval, Creative Director of Aerial Ethereal
Bcc: Luka Kotova, *and other undisclosed recipients*

Aerial Ethereal Artists,

The Wellness Policy is not optional. All artists need to maintain in good standing in order to perform. We will not hesitate to suspend you from a show.

Marc Duval
Creative Director of Aerial Ethereal
marcduval@aerialethereal.com

Cigarette hanging loosely between my fingers, I blow smoke in the frigid air. The gray plume is visible in the night. Flashy, multicolored lights stretch along the never-ending Vegas strip, radiating.

So fucking bright.

Date: January 21st
Subject: you there????
From: sergeikotova@aerialethereal.com
To: Luka Kotova

I'm your brother. Unblock me so I can at least text you. That is if you're even getting these fucking emails.

- Sergei

I hesitate again, for longer than a split-second. I pass my phone from one hand to the other.

And then I delete the email.

ACT ONE
LUKA KOTOVA

Date: January 22nd
Subject: Masquerade Room Changes
From: Marc Duval, Creative Director of Aerial Ethereal
Bcc: Luka Kotova, *and other undisclosed recipients*

Aerial Ethereal Artists,

In the past week, each of you should've received a letter from Human Resources detailing your new room assignment. I should not even have to send out this email. Nor should any of you be contacting me or AE's creative with trivial complaints. No one in the company, and I mean no one, will accommodate any room changes. They are set for a reason.

New seasons mean new changes. You know this.

In an effort to reduce costs, we had to reduce artist housing from two floors in the Masquerade to one floor. As a result, there are 4 occupants per room instead of 2.

Need I remind you that each artist still has free room & board at the Masquerade's luxury suites. This huge bonus should not be overlooked. If you're unhappy with your room assignment, you have the option to pay for apartments or housing in the Las Vegas area.

Any further complaints about room assignments will not be tolerated.

Marc Duval
Creative Director of Aerial Ethereal
marcduval@aerialethereal.com

I recheck the email—surprised it wasn't directly addressed to me. A few days ago, I learned my new room assignment and sent Marc a short but pointed email.

Something like: *I've roomed with my little brother for 19 years. His whole life. Nearly all of mine. Can you please change my assignment? It's kind of bullshit. (Sent from phone)*

It was an emotional response. One that I regretted the moment I pressed *send.* I didn't even sign my name at the bottom. Just figured he'd recognize me by my work email.

I've been Corporate's Least Favorite Kotova since I was fifteen. And with an extended family that fills one-third of all Aerial Ethereal shows, being the *worst* or *best* Kotova takes actual effort.

Circus is family.

For most of us, we mean it literally.

My email to Marc probably sealed my *least favorite* title. And I'm twenty-years-old now.

Look, I understand the whole corporate hierarchy better than anyone. Marc is the founder of the entire Aerial Ethereal troupe and rarely has contact with the artists unless it's through company emails. The only time he does one-on-ones is for terrific news (a long-term contract) or fucking horrific (you're harming the company's standards).

I've met him twice.

Obviously for *horrific* reasons.

An artist's fate lies in many corporate hands, but Marc Duval's hand encases all of the higher-ups. Emailing him directly is like whining to God. He could've easily fired me on the spot.

Shit, if Nik even knew I sent it…

I rake my fingers through my dark brown hair, panicked that I've now started the season on the *worst* footing. I don't actively shoot for "good"—just somewhere between "okay" and "mediocre" but not *worst.*

(What can I say? My name is Luka Kotova. I'm an irresponsible fuck-up. Thanks for your time. Now let me be.)

I ride the Masquerade's elevator to the suites. Alone. Numbers tick higher and higher, and then the elevator glides to a stop.

42nd floor. The doors open to mayhem.

Overflowing boxes, clear plastic tubs, lamps, rugs, and other household belongings fill the hotel hallway. Voices emanate from ajar doors. People rush in and out. Carrying as much shit in their arms as they can since no luggage cart can fit through this disaster.

I step over a drum set and what looks like an empty aquarium. Ducking beneath a coat rack, I spot my suite towards the end of the hallway.

Cardboard boxes are stacked outside the door, the name *Timo* scribbled on the flaps.

Reality hits me all of a sudden.

We have to move.

If the email hadn't already cemented our future, the apocalyptic hallway and my little brother's boxes just did.

Aerial Ethereal has always given artists the 42nd and 43rd floors of the Masquerade. Taking away an entire floor is another swift kick in the gut and the ass. AE has so much control over our lives.

At last notice, they can change *anything*.

All we have are our contracts, but even those usually only last one year. Then they're rewritten all over again. Our lives are in constant flux, and as much as I love the circus—this one aspect never stops eating at me.

With a heavy breath, I slip through the cracked door.

"Shit," I mutter at the barren state.

It's a typical two-bedroom, modern hotel suite: sleek black and white furniture, floor-length windows that, from this side, overlook the ginormous Vegas pool. After being here for three years, the living room had real character.

An old New York Knicks blanket and throw-rug are gone, and walls that once housed *West Side Story* and *Les Misérables* posters are stark white.

Timo removed the cactus-shaped thumbtacks that said *don't be a prick*, my glass bowl of jelly beans, and his own ceramic Warhol coasters.

I turn left and right. Mixed emotions bearing on me. My jaw and lip twitches, and my throat bobs as I swallow hard.

I'm grateful that Timo packed up so I don't have to, but mostly, the disappearance of all my shit makes me uneasy. It's not like I haven't moved before.

I have.

Plenty of times growing up.

But for a while there, I felt rooted to something.

It's one fucking floor, I remind myself and comb my hands through my hair again. *One floor*. It's not a big deal. My family sees me as the "go with the flow" Kotova, and in a lot of ways, I am.

I'll go with the flow with this. With everything.

It doesn't mean it won't knot my stomach. Doesn't mean that I'm unfeeling, like some of my cousins believe. It just means I'm not going to whine or throw a tantrum.

Faster, I pass the kitchenette, sponged-clean, and head to my bedroom. When I push inside, I immediately spot my sixteen-year-old sister.

Katya peers beneath the wooden frame of my stripped bed. I shut the door, and her head pops up. Long, straight brown hair sticks to her overdone pink-glossed lips.

I frown at my little sister. When did she start wearing makeup on regular weekdays?

Her saucer eyes widen even bigger on me. "Oh crap," she says, clutching a...*really?*

I sigh. She grips a black heavy-duty trash bag, partially filled.

"It was Timo's idea." Katya picks herself off the floor, skinny and long-limbed like a ballerina but with prominent, ethereal features: orb-like eyes, pronounced ears, and big lips. "He said that you wouldn't mind if we packed up for you."

I don't mind.

What bothers me is that he enlisted Katya's help to *throw away* my things. Here's the deal: I'm really close to Timo and Kat—as close as most siblings come—but they still have no clue what I can't get rid of.

(The cactus paraphernalia better not be trashed.)

"Can you say something?" she asks. "You just look...sad."

"I'm not sad," I say coolly. "Just please don't trash my shit unless you ask, Kat."

She drops the garbage bag like it's suddenly toxic waste. "I won't again. I promise." Guilt sweeps her youthful face.

My features soften almost instantly, and I nod. Kat, more than anyone, respects my privacy. Whenever our older brother Nikolai tries to pry through my things, she's the most vocal: *just trust Luka, Nik. Why are you searching through his gym bag?*

I ask, "Where's Timo?"

She points to the walk-in closet.

I shuffle around an open box, stuffed with my wardrobe: a lot of gym clothes, plain T-shirts, some jeans, and baseball caps. Nothing flashy or brazen.

At the closet, I stretch the door further open. I distinguish the back of my brother's head that bounces to the beat of music. He's wearing earbuds, the song inaudible.

Timo is also lost in a mound of shoeboxes and towering stacks of snow globes, and to be completely honest, a lot of shitty Vegas paraphernalia that has no place or name.

It's junk.

I can admit that any day, any time.

Timo rifles through a shoebox, not noticing me, and after careful examination, he chucks the box into his trash bag.

"Timo," I call out, loud enough that he spins around.

Items clatter beside his lean, athletic frame, but he manages to crawl out. Sweating, he shoves the longer strands of his dark, disheveled hair out of his charismatic face. He's only a year and a half younger than me, but I'm an inch taller.

His gray eyes glimmer like a thousand-watt bulb, and he smiles an incredibly contagious smile. To the point where I *almost* forget that I'm supposed to be irritated.

Timo pops an earbud out, an upbeat song blaring through the tiny speaker. "Hey, Luk." Then he unplugs the cord, music booming through his phone. Timo swings his head heavier to the rhythm and shifts his body with the harmony, goading me to join his dance.

My body craves soulful rhythms like an animal craves an endless field to sprint. To run.

For me, it's unnatural not to dance. I don't know how, and it takes effort to force my body still and not move to the beat.

Timo must see that something's off with me, so he lowers the volume of his music. His black cross earring sways, and he pockets his phone in his cut-off shorts. Wearing a leather jacket, no shirt beneath—Timo is the kind of guy you wish you knew. Intriguing. *Captivating.*

I'm the shadow to his ceaseless light.

(Don't pity me.) I'm grateful to be anything next to Timo. Even a shadow. That's how much I love him.

I nod to the garbage. "Dude, what the hell is that?"

Timo eyes me weirdly. "Trash…?" His mouth falls. "Are you glaring at me?" He rocks backwards, surprised.

"You can't just throw away my shit without asking." My knuckles whiten as I grip the door frame harder.

Timo touches his chest. "I'm doing both of us a favor. Didn't you read AE's email—no, scratch that, you probably skimmed it. Which is why you're not panicked." He tosses the garbage bag past me. Glass clinks, the trash thudding by my bed.

"What do you mean?" I don't scroll through my emails for proof. I trust Timo to tell me the news.

He raises his brows. "We have to move by *five p.m.* or else they'll fine us a grand."

"Fuck," I groan.

"We're way past *fuck*, brother. Aerial Ethereal isn't playing games with this one." He strolls past me and effortlessly hoists himself on my dresser.

I spin around, unable to detach from the closet door. On the floor, Katya refolds my clothes and places them more gently in the boxes.

Our salaries aren't that great, but none of us perform for the money. We do it for the art and to be close to our family.

And because I literally don't know how to do anything else. I was *raised* for this. Only this.

Timo catches my gaze. "You could give me a hundred bucks and I'll turn it into a grand downstairs. Buy us extra time."

"No," I decline fast. He could easily spend all day at the casino tables and slots, and while he does win a lot, he loses too. I haven't given him cash to gamble in about a year.

"Kat?" Timo asks, pouting his bottom lip.

"I can't afford to share my money anymore," she says, her words sounding rehearsed.

Timo and I exchange a confused look.

I prod first. "Why not?"

"I'm saving up." She avoids our intrusive gazes by refolding my shirt. "It's private, so don't ask *what for*."

"Ouch." Timo wears mock hurt, but more than a fraction of that is actually real.

I thought we were closer than that, I want to say, but I'm harboring a secret bigger than either of them have ever imagined or considered.

It involves a girl.

I nearly shut my eyes and yell at myself, *don't think about her. Don't fucking think about her.*

So I stay quiet in terms of Katya's declaration. She fills the tense silence. "I'm sixteen," she tells us like we've forgotten. "I'm a woman."

"No shit," Timo says.

I'm not catching on either.

Katya sighs. "You wouldn't understand."

"Okay," I say, really baffled.

In our profession and our family, the ratio of men to women is severely off balance. I'm not great at math, but it's pretty much all male around here. Sometimes I really don't understand my little sister's female needs.

I unfasten myself from the closet and snatch my Knicks hat from a box, fitting it on backwards. My younger siblings watch me take a seat on my bare mattress.

"What's left to pack?" I ask Timo.

"Your closet, mostly." He holds my gaze, a thousand uncomfortable words passing silently between us. I hate each one because they're all about the shit stuffed in my closet. "You know—"

"Don't say it," I cut him off.

He tilts his head. "I was just going to tell you that I rolled all of your Broadway posters into tubes."

(So I love watching sports, preferably pro-basketball, and Broadway. If anyone wants to laugh or call me a pussy, the exit is stage left.)

Timo adds, "I even took better care of them than my film posters."

"Yeah right," I say casually. Where I thumbtacked my posters, Timo framed his favorite foreign language and classic films. *La Belle et la Bête* and *The Red Shoes* were preserved behind glass.

Timo gapes. "I glued the torn corner of *Chicago* for you—and you know how much I dislike that one."

Katya starts singing "All That Jazz" off-key. She takes my side over his, and Timo clutches his heart firmer and drops off the dresser. Gasping for air.

"You've killed me, sister," he chokes, pretending to die better than most people ever could or would.

My lips quirk.

It's difficult being upset at them. For anything. He settles down when I push the trash bag with my sneaker. I feel the heat of their gazes.

Timo rolls onto his side. Propping his head up with his hand, he grabs a Santa Claus snow globe from the bag, the price sticker stuck to the bottom.

"Technically," he begins—*don't say it.* "These aren't really your things." He shakes the globe hard, and fake flurries swarm the glass.

My muscles cramp, and I just stare off. Most stores leave on price stickers, even if you buy the item. But I didn't buy that.

I didn't buy *any* of it.

Timo sits up and leans against the dresser, the globe limp in his hand. My brother and sister know that my room is full of useless, stolen shit.

I seize my brother's knowing gaze again, and I speak through my own eyes: *like you don't have your own issues.*

His reply: *this isn't about me.*

Katya swings her head back and forth, realizing one of us is about to explode.

Look, over anyone else, we'll usually vent to each other about a bad day's work, grievances, personal bullshit. Because we're certain that we won't fucking blab.

We're in a workplace where everyone knows everyone. Each Aerial Ethereal show employs around 50 to 100 performers tops, and rumors and gossip reach every single ear.

Katya couldn't even keep her first period a secret. Our cousins (all male) sent her boxes of tampons and pads by the *hour*.

On top of that, I never attended a typical high school. Aerial Ethereal hires tutors for all minors in between practices and performances, but I bet the gossip here is about as bad as a locker-lined hallway or college campus.

Kat examines us one last time before standing. "I'll go pack the last of your fridge."

Our biggest fights start when two of us gang up on the other one, so Kat willingly pulls herself out of the confrontation.

I don't like when she's in the crossfires of anything.

Remember how I said there's a shit ton of Kotovas? Well in our generation, Kat is the *only* Kotova girl by blood—which means she's been protected and bubble-wrapped a thousand times over by all of us.

"What about your suite?" I ask as she reaches the door. Kat lives with our older brother, Nikolai, and since she's still a minor, he's her legal guardian.

He used to be all of ours, too.

"Already boxed and moved hours ago," she says.

(Of course.)

Nik wouldn't wait until the last minute for any Aerial Ethereal deadline, and Timo has probably been working just as long to clean up our place.

My little brother is one of the most professional artists here. Always on-time for rehearsals, stagings, and meetings. Goes above and beyond at practice, and would *never* send Marc Duval an email that called his decision bullshit.

As soon as Katya shuts the door on her way out, Timo says, "You said you wouldn't start hoarding."

"Dude." I sigh heavily. "I'm *not* hoarding. I have no attachment to most of this stuff. You can throw out a ton of it."

(Just not anything that reminds me of her—it's all I have left.)

I ache to say it, to plead, to tell him all that's weighed on me for years.

But I do what I have to do.

I push her aside. I try to forget.

Yet, I'm still clinging.

Timo balances the snow globe on his bent knee. In smooth Russian, he tells me, "*I'm just worried.*"

In the same language, I say, "*You shouldn't be.*"

He rolls the Christmas globe into the trash bag. "Luka…"

"It's just my shit to deal with, okay?" I'm upset because I don't want them to see how much I've been stealing recently. I wish I threw out all that stuff ages ago, but I just put things off. Shove them aside and try not to look back.

That's my life.

I cram my figurative drawers full of shit and more shit and pretend it's all nonexistent. That it's not bearing on my chest like a fifty-ton elephant.

Timo rests the back of his head against my dresser. "I like focusing on your Robin Hood tactics. It helps take my mind off our new room situation *and* the fact that my life is completely fucked."

I kick the trash bag out of our way. "Your life isn't completely fucked."

Timo laughs once. "*You*, Luk, are the best roommate in the world. You don't hound me when I stumble in late or blare music. You don't care when I bring my boyfriend over and fuck loudly. Really, it takes extreme work to piss you off." He pauses, as though saying, *seeing you pissed today scares me.*

I rotate my baseball cap, brim in front.

Lately, I just feel like I'm losing all of my control with Corporate. Not that I had much to begin with, but I was artfully fooling myself for a while there.

"Henceforth," Timo continues, "my new roommate will never be as great as you." (Likewise, Timo.)

I give him a look. "*Henceforth?*"

"It annoys John when I say it." He smiles wide, a magnetic grin that could make grown men and women bow in adoration.

I shake my head. *Henceforth.* "I don't think you're using that word right." Maybe he is. I don't really know.

"That's the beauty of it," Timo says easily. "Henceforth, I will say it however I want."

I smile, my chest lighter just talking to him. He has that effect on most people.

As the quiet falls, we skim the emptied room and the trash bags. Half of my life is filled with garbage. The other half with necessities. The problem is trying to sort out which is which.

Nineteen years of living with Timo. *Gone.*

In one fucking email.

"Who are you rooming with anyway?" I ask him.

He scratches his temple, his face a little pained. "I'll tell you later."

Timo has no enemies. Where I'm the Least Favorite Kotova, he's without a doubt the Most Beloved. Last year, Marc Duval said he was "life and youth personified"—and he's never slept with anyone in Aerial Ethereal, so he's pretty drama-free too.

"Okay," I say, not pressuring my brother. I know he'll open up in his own time.

Timo nods to me. "What about you?"

I dig in my pants pocket and pull out the crumpled letter from HR with my room assignment. I hand the paper to Timo. I've read it a hundred times already.

Artists Assigned to Room 4303

L. Kotova

D. Kotova

Z. Li

B. Wright

That last name—B. Wright—skids my heart to a complete stop every single time. It's not a good feeling. No matter how much I wish it could be.

Her name so close to my name is just bad.

CPSIA information can be obtained
at www.ICGtesting.com
Printed in the USA
LVHW030340070821
694695LV00002B/353

9 781950 165292